MW01127285

Printed by CreateSpace
an Amazon.com Company
CreateSpace, Charleston, South Carolina

Cover illustration by Rachiel Cox

Edited by Christine Thompson
Student edit by Lindsay Dominguez

Available from Amazon.com and other bookstores.
Available on Kindle and other devices.

SWEET HOME ALLE BAMMA

Every time someone close to us dies, a part of us dies with them and we are never quite the same, never quite whole again. Certainly that is how we felt with the death of Lunnie – dear sweet Lunnie – who could never be serious, always taunting someone with a wise crack or joke. Yet, when the time came for someone to put their life on the line for the sake of others, Lunnie accepted the challenge. I had known her only a very short time – just a few weeks really. It was Lunnie who made me realize how much I loved her sister, Kala, and it was Lunnie's impish nature that brought Kala and me together.

Then there was Captain Maxette, the first person I talked to after leaving Earth. True, it was over a vid screen; but still, his commanding and reassuring voice was a welcome relief from the silence and the unknowns of deep space. I looked up to Maxette. He was more than a friend; and though we didn't spend a lot of time together, there seemed to be a real connection with the man. I trusted him. He had lived up to that trust and more; and now he, too, was gone.

I wasn't familiar with the death rites practiced in the Federation. Kala said that ceremonies varied from planet to planet; but for military people who died in the line of duty there were two accepted ceremonial methods. One was cremation, similar to traditional Earth cremation practices; and the other was, I suppose, also cremation in a way, or perhaps like a combination of cremation and burial at sea, as the remains were ejected from a ship into the nearest star.

Because of the significance of the heroic deaths that occurred in the battle for control of the galaxy's entire supply of solbidyum, the Federation decided that the cremations for the fallen would take place on the capital planet of Megelleon.   Over 6,000 civilians, dignitaries and military troops died in battle and as a result of the tidal wave created in the Western Ocean when the subsea rebel base was destroyed.   Private services had already been held for the civilians; but those that wore the uniforms of the Federation military forces were to be cremated in a large public ceremony at a site just outside the capital city.

The service took place in a large valley basin surrounded on three sides by rolling hills. On the slopes of these hills gathered countless citizens, who had walked over a kilometer to the ceremony site from the arrival area. Thousands of funeral pyres were configured across the valley floor, each fueled by intense gas flames from individual burners. Nearly every crematory unit on the planet was required for this single service.   The bodies were laid out in concentric circular arrangements separated by avenues stretching out like the spokes of a wheel away from a central hub, where the crematories of Captain Maxette and Corporal Luinella were situated. Once lit, each pyre would produce a bright, almost white flame, except for the pyres of Lunnie and Captain Maxette, which would burn an intense blue-white from a special chemical mixed into the fuel. I asked Kala to explain the symbolism of the blue flame, but she couldn't speak through the tears and emotions to tell me; so I never did learn the significance. It suffices to say that it showed special honor to Lunnie and Maxette for sacrificing their lives to save the planet, the Federation and the solbidyum. The Federation had commissioned two statues in their honor and posthumously named them

First Citizens, the highest honor that can be bestowed on any individual in the Federation.

As a recognized dignitary, I had planned to wear a black suit of the dignitary cut, similar to Earth's Nehru jackets of the late 1960s era; but Kala informed me that I should wear the formal white military cut instead. I had been made an honorary vice admiral by the Federation Space Force; and though I had no authority in the military sense, I was to be shown all the respect and honors reserved for one of the rank of vice admiral. Inasmuch as this was a military function to honor fallen soldiers, Kala said it would be inappropriate for me to dress in anything other than the uniform that identified this rank and stature.

Unlike the bugle or bagpipe music played at Earth services that are held in honor of fallen military and public servants, the Federation ceremonies instead used a squad of Federation drummers who performed throughout the service in a complex interplay of rhythms on large base drums. When preparing me for the ceremony, Kala showed me vids that demonstrated the role of the drummers. I had once seen a unique group of Japanese drummers perform on Earth and I found this drumming vaguely reminiscent of that occasion.

Kala said that the ceremony of a single individual normally included a detail of five to eight drummers. At this ceremony I watched a squad of at least 200 assemble at attention in a ringed formation amid the concentric circles of pyres. I asked Kala about the origins of the drumming tradition, but she said that no one was certain anymore. Drums had been part of funeral rituals for thousands of years, but no one knew why. I would imagine the same could be said for the bagpipes found in a multitude of cultures on Earth, though I had heard once that the bagpipe tradition had something to do with the belief in keeping banshees away from the dead.

Funeral services in the Federation had no speeches; those had been made during earlier memorial gatherings. People arrived in solemn and respectful silence, speaking only when necessary and in the lowest of voices. As the ceremony began with the deep rumble of drums, Admiral Regeny and I made our way to the central area with a small entourage of Federation military officers and Leader Rieam, one of the three ruling leaders of the Federation. At my side were Lieutenant Commander Kalana, Lieutenant Marranalis, Captain Stonbersa and Kerabac – all members of my crew and personal staff who had played significant roles in the victory over the rebel faction called the BROTHERHOOD OF LIGHT.

We stood together in formation before the funeral pyre of Lunnie and Captain Maxette. At a specific drum cadence we came to attention and placed our right hands on our left shoulders in the traditional Federation salute. The drums rolled into a low crescendo as the fires of the central pyres were lit into twin pillars of blue-white flame. The immediate emotional impact of the percussion and the fires caught me off guard and I could feel my chest well with grief. After a few moments we turned to face away from the center and slowly walk outward through a central passage, repeating the salute when we arrived at each successive ring of funeral pyres, which then ignited into enormous halos of white flame behind us as we passed.

As we progressed toward the drummers, their formation retreated outward, never pausing in their rhythms. I could feel the intense heat at my back from the growing number of burning pyres and I began to perspire. At the same time, the hollow reverberation of the drums sent an intense chill through my body, as one group of drummers would strike up a particular rhythm, which was then echoed by another group, followed by another, on and on around the wheel. The effect of this relentless and powerful dialogue of rhythms was deeply and painfully moving, but also cathartic and healing, evoking feelings of strength, power, and pride in those who had fallen. The percussion resonated inside all of us, unifying us in one understanding – that the sacrifices made by these men and women had indeed not been in vain and that every glory and honor was due to them for all eternity.

Finally, as we reached the last ring of pyres, we turned back to face the valley. The intensity of the bright white flames was nearly blinding and the heat was overwhelming. I almost expected to see our clothing scorched and smoldering.

The drummers then took up a steady beat in unison. The rhythm grew into a powerful crescendo that consumed my body and mind until I lost all sense of time and I could think of nothing – not the pain from my injuries, not the people that stood with me to honor the dead, not even my grief. I stood there with my companions for I don't know how long, looking into the rings of fire as the echoing rhythms filled every recess of my being. Finally, the drumming culminated in a single, thunderous boom that echoed off the surrounding hills and released me from its transfixing grasp on my soul. Then, in one voice made up of thousands, the masses of people on the surrounding hills shouted *"Hoye' Aah!"* which means *"Forever Peace!"*

Silently but rapidly everyone then crossed over the hilltops, escaping the nearly unbearable heat to return to their transports in the parking area. As we came to the crest of the hill, Kala took my hand and we paused to look back at the sea of white fire that formed mesmerizing circles around two bright blue flames. The rising glow of smoke carried the blue beams aloft, and our eyes followed upward toward the stars where they pointed. There we saw the bright light of the *DUSTEN* in high orbit, the ship where most of the honored had served and died.

For the next two days Kala and I did very little. We held each other and listened to music; we took leisurely swims, not racing in the competitive way that we sometimes did. We spoke little; and when we did, it was not about Lunnie or the battle. On the fourth day the estate medic stopped by and asked to inspect the knife wounds I had received at the hands of the traitor, Lexmal. The wounds had been sealed with some kind of liquid that formed a skin-like bandage. After a quick examination he announced that everything was looking good and he gave me a bottle of liquid that I was to use in about three days to remove all the residue of the bandages. Thereafter, it was expected that my wounds would be healed.

When he left our suite of rooms, Kala put her arms around me. "Tib, I don't know what I would have done if I had lost you, too. You're all I have left in this universe."

I kissed her and then leaned back to look at her. "Now that you mention it, you're all I have in this universe too. I think that means we really need to stick together." For the first time since Lunnie's death Kala laughed. She kissed me over and over again, all over my face, laughing softly between kisses. Of course I kissed her back and ultimately it ended with the two of us in bed, making love for the first time since the battle to recover the *DUSTEN*.

Later, I woke from our nap to see Kala lying on her side, gazing at me thoughtfully. She asked, "Tibby, before you regained consciousness in the infirmary on the *DUSTEN*, you were mumbling, '*Wait Lunnie... come back Lunnie*,' as though you could see her. Do you remember anything about it?"

"I did see her, Kala," I said. "I think I was dead – or almost dead anyway. I found myself standing in an open meadow with knee-high grass. To the right and left of me were hills covered in huge, old trees. A breeze blew through the grasses; and ahead I could see Lunnie walking away from me. I tried to call out to her, but my voice wouldn't work. As she reached the crest of a small hill she turned to look back at me. She smiled and said, '*Go back, Tibby, it's not yet your time. You still have more to do. Go back to Kala. Take care of her, Tibby, she loves you.*' Then I felt myself being pulled back; and when I opened my eyes, you were there."

"Tib, you *were* dead!" Kala said, "You were dead for two full minutes. You had no pulse, no brain waves, nothing! The defibrillator administered electrical shocks several times in attempts to restart you heart. The medics were about to give up when your heart started beating again after the last attempt. Tell me, what did Lunnie look like when you saw her?"

"Well," I began, "she looked like Lunnie, but she didn't have any wounds or scars. Oh, and she was naked, now that I think about it. I believe I was too. She looked happy and at peace, like there wasn't a care in the world for her. I think it's the first time that she didn't make some sort of wise crack. She seemed serious, yet happy at the same time."

Kala was about to say something else when a call came in from her assistant. Using her wrist com Kala asked, "This is Kalana, what do you need?"

"Cantolla, Dakko and Rivez have been calling for two days now, wondering what they're supposed to do. They completed the project you asked of them and now they would like to be paid and transported home. Cantolla in particular wants to speak to Tibby before she leaves; but Dakko and Rivez just want to receive their pay and go."

Kala turned to me, raising an eyebrow in a questioning manner.

I interjected, "Pay them all, plus triple the bonus I promised them. They earned it. As for Cantolla.... Where are they, anyway, on the ship or here at the estate?"

"They're here. They came down with us on the shuttle, don't you remember?"   Kala said with a concerned look.

"Oh yeah, right," I said. "I guess with all the activity and the pain from the wounds and all, I kind of blocked out our return to the surface. Well, tell her to meet us for dinner this evening out on that pretty garden terrace we like so much. Hmmm, make it at sunset... and have the chef fix up something especially nice."

Kala relayed the message to her assistant and looked at me strangely. "What are you up to, Tib? I thought you were trying to keep Cantolla away from me?"

I laughed, as I played with Kala's disheveled hair. "She may be a lesbian with the hots for you, Kala, but I also think she is an ethical person. I don't think she's going to put the moves on you, especially this evening. Quite the opposite – I think she's going to ask me for a job."

"Oh?" Kala replied with a look of surprise, "and what makes you think that?"

"Cantolla is a very bright woman. She likes challenges and likes to prove herself." I playfully pulled a length of Kala's hair under her nose to fashion a mustache as I continued. "And, while funding at the university allows her to demonstrate her capabilities, she is restricted by budgets and other red tape. Working for me would allow her to broaden her research with a virtually unlimited budget. She would be able to accomplish far more in a few years of working for me than she could ever hope to accomplish at the university in a lifetime. Plus I think she likes the adventure."

When the time came for dinner, I rifled through the wardrobe, looking for something new to wear. I was getting tired of always being dressed in official diplomatic attire. Now, because of my new title as vice admiral, I had even more uniforms and formalwear filling my closet. I was longing for something more casual.

While we had been away from the estate, fighting to overcome the Brotherhood and recover the *DUSTEN*, Piesew, who served as the majordomo on my space yacht, the *NEW ORLEANS*, had recommended an associate of his to serve as majordomo at the estate. His name was Piebar Nokaran, apparently a cousin to Piesew. I called Piebar to my suite and explained to him that I wanted a shirt, basically like a polo shirt (which I had to describe). Piebar scratched his head a moment, then went to the vid screen and began giving it verbal commands. Apparently, the main issue was one of collars. It seemed that shirt collars, as I knew them on Earth, seemed to be either out of fashion in the Federation or never existed at all. Eventually, I settled on a short-sleeved crew neck type shirt that was far more casual than the suits and uniforms – and comfortable as well. Piebar had a dozen made up for me in differing colors. I chose a beige color and a pair of dark pants to wear for the evening meal. While I fussed over my clothing, Kala was away giving instructions to her staff. When she returned, she stood with her hands on her hips, eying me up and down. She said with a smile, "I like it. It looks good. You might just start a new dress fad."

"I hope so," I replied, "because frankly, I am getting tired of being dressed up like a –," I wanted to say monkey, but she wouldn't have understood that. I wasn't able to find a word in Federation language that would work, so I simply said, "diplomat."

It's funny how some words translate readily into the Federation language, while others have no equal. *Fish* translates easily because there are fish or fish-like creatures on many of the Federation planets; but *monkey* really has no equivalent, though there are some non-human simian-like creatures on many of the planets. The words *husband* and *wife* likewise do not translate well in to Federation language, but the phrase *bond mate* comes close to having the same meaning.

Kala donned an emerald green dress that had a distinctively Asian-like Earth style. She looked absolutely stunning. I almost feared that Cantolla might be tempted to make another pass at Kala, like she had on her first visit to the estate.

We were standing at railing on the terrace, where we looked out over a garden waterfall and stream, when we heard Cantolla arrive. We turned to see her walk across the patio toward us. She wore a most unusual dress. There was nothing necessarily unique about the cut of the dress; it was similar to many formal cut gowns that one might see on Earth. What was unusual was that the fabric kept changing colors. Waves of shifting hues moved across the fabric in a never-ending flow. I remarked to Kala that I had never seen anything like it before. Kala hadn't either. I was beginning to feel terribly underdressed in my crew neck shirt and slacks. But then, it was my place and I was paying the bills; so if the ladies didn't like it they could, as we would say on Earth, '*lump it.*'

"Good evening, Vice Admiral and Lieutenant Commander," Cantolla began. "Or do I call you First Citizen Tibby and First Citizen Kalana? I'm not sure. What *is* proper protocol on that matter?"

"Just Tibby, if you please," I said, "unless we're in a formal setting where protocol dictates one of the titles."

"The same goes for me," Kala said. "When here on the estate or when on the *NEW ORLEANS*, we would prefer that you call us Tibby and Kalana."

"Thank you," Cantolla answered. "You both honor me."

"Please be seated." I indicated a chair at the table that Piebar had arranged with a white linen table cloth – or something like linen anyway. A small lamp of some sort sat in the middle of the table, casting light from a single flickering flame.

"Would either of you care for something to drink?" I asked.

"Yes, I believe I would like a glass of Morrev wine, if you have any," replied Cantolla. I saw Piebar glance at a small portable vid screen and then nod to me.

"How about you, Kala?" I asked.

"I think I'll have a Maldarian Moon Glow," she answered. I looked at Piebar to see his fingers rapidly flying over his vid screen for a moment before he looked up and again nodded.

Personally I wanted a beer; however, since leaving Earth, I'd not found anything like beer in a Federation beverage dispenser. Of course, that thing could produce thousands of drinks and I had tried only about a dozen or so. I called Piebar to the table.

"Piebar, on Earth we had a drink that was very popular. It was an alcoholic beverage made from brewed grains and yeast. The mixture was allowed to ferment into a golden colored liquid that had a slightly bitter taste. Do you know of anything like that here?"

Piebar, Cantolla and Kala all gave me the same incredulous look. "Surely you don't mean *afex*," Kala exclaimed.

"I don't know if that's what I mean or not, given that I have never tasted it."

"Afex is a very common drink on all the Federation planets," Kala explained, "except on those that ban alcoholic beverages. It's considered to be the drink of the working class, although everyone does drink it. People of higher standing in the Federation never do so in public and definitely not at special events."

"So then, since I am in my own home, and this is not a public or social event," I stated, slightly red-faced, "I can drink it if I want to?"

I could see Cantolla smirking as Kala answered, "Uh, yes, I guess, if that's what you want."

"I really won't know until I try it. Piebar, one ice-cold glass of afex, if you please!" Behind Piebar I could see one of the house staff members grinning; and I thought Cantolla was going to break out laughing, but she resisted. Piebar, looking somewhat distressed, turned and nodded to the waiter, who promptly headed off for our drinks.

"This really is quite lovely here," Cantolla said as she looked around at the surroundings. "I really didn't have much time before now to actually look over the estate."

"I apologize for that," I said, "but as you now realize, the urgency of the situation demanded it. What you accomplished in the short time that you had available is impressive. Without your efforts the Brotherhood would have won and the people of Megelleon would now be at their mercy. I hope that you're satisfied with the compensation you've received."

"Oh, definitely. Your generosity has given me more than I would have earned in a lifetime at the university. I feel like I have accomplished in a week what would have taken me years there, which brings me to my reason for meeting with you this evening."

Kala cast a glance at me over a sip of Maldarian Moon Glow, knowing that I had already anticipated what Cantolla was about to say.

"Tibby, I would like to work for you... or, at the very least, I would like you to fund my projects. You would have all rights to anything I develop or discover, of course, if I can have the credit of the discovery or invention. I see you as an individual of vision and I think you, like Galetils, have both the ideas and the money to bring them to fruition. I've always felt that, given the opportunity, I could accomplish a great deal; but I never really had the chance until you put me in charge of developing the learning device. Now that I've had a taste of what I can do, I want more.

Both Cantolla and Kala stared at me. Cantolla was waiting with anticipation to hear what I would say. Kala knew that I had already thought this through, but she didn't exactly know what I was going to say in reply.

"Before I answer, let me ask you a few questions. How extensive is your scientific knowledge? Are you restricted to the learning headband technology or are you versed in other areas as well?"

"I was at the top of my class in all the sciences, but didn't really know which field to pursue. Basically, the choice was made for me when I was contacted by an old instructor of mine who had begun teaching at University on Essen She asked me to come there as an assistant and to work on improvements to the learning headband technology. Recently my instructor died and I was asked to take over the program. I still have not given them my answer. Right now I'm holding off, because I think my opportunities will be better with you."

While Cantolla spoke, the servant had returned with my afex in a crystal glass. The color and frothy head on the drink certainly reminded me of beer. When I took my first sip, I was pleasantly surprised to find it was indeed beer – and very good beer at that.

"I actually do need someone to head up several projects that I have in mind," I began. "If I hire you, I don't expect you to do all the work yourself. You will, however, be expected to hire teams of experts that will advance the projects under your guidance and input. The level to which you personally get involved with each project will be up to you. From time to time, I may dictate the priority of a particular project based on my needs. When I do, I will expect your full compliance and attention to that project until it is completed successfully. Can you work under those conditions?"

Cantolla's eyes glistened as she sat forward in her chair. "That's exactly what I want, and yes, I can live with that."

"Okay then. If you're willing to work for ten times what the university paid you and receive bonuses for jobs well done, and if you're willing to travel – because there will be many times I will want you working on projects as we travel on the *NEW ORLEANS* – you're hired." I looked at Kala to see her grinning. By this point she was used to seeing me negotiate with job candidates and had come to enjoy seeing their jaws drop at the offers I made.

Cantolla's green eyes sparkled as she flipped away a strand of long chestnut-colored hair that drifted across her face. "Tibby, that's exactly the kind of job I want."

I turned to the ever-present Piebar. "Piebar, please get with Cantolla after dinner and allow her to select a suite suitable for her tastes from the available accommodations here."

Just as we concluded this order of business, our meal was served.

When Kala and I first met Cantolla, her behavior and gestures toward Kala were of a rather obvious flirtatious nature. Later Kala informed me that Cantolla taught at a university on the planet Essen, which was strictly for lesbians. Since that time, however, Cantolla had not made any overtures toward Kala – at least not to my knowledge.

"I don't suppose there are any other offices on the estate with a large fish aquarium wall similar to yours, Tibby?" asked Cantolla.

"To be honest, I have no idea. This place is so vast that I will most likely never see all of it myself. Why do you ask?"

"I really liked that office and thought I would like something similar for myself, if there is one available."

"Well, if there isn't we can certainly have one made for you. Piebar, would you check into that for us?" Piebar assured me he would do so immediately, as he entered a request on his vid pad.

As we dined, Cantolla surprised me with a very candid admission. "Kalana and Tibby, I want to apologize to you both. When I was first introduced to you, I was a bit brazen in my flirtation with Kalana. At the time I was not aware of the relationship between the two of you and, well frankly, I found Kala highly attractive. Likewise, I had no idea of the nature of the offer you were about to make us and I didn't anticipate being around here very long. Had I known what I know now, I never would have behaved as I did; so please accept my apology. It won't happen again, I promise you that. I have only the highest respect for the two of you; and I feel somewhat embarrassed about my foolish behavior of that day."

I had to grin as Kala's cheeks redden just a bit. "You needn't worry. I probably would have been insulted if you had *not* found Kala attractive; but it's nice to know that you won't be pursuing her in the future."

"Oh, well for that matter, Tibby, if I were inclined to pursue a man, you would be at the very top of my list. I'm attracted to intelligent, fast thinkers; and you're no slouch physically either. But, in the end, I admire and respect what you and Kalana have together and I would never do anything to jeopardize that."

"Now I'm starting to wonder whether I need to worry about you and Tib," Kala said teasingly.

I have to confess that sitting with these two highly attractive women really was giving me a bit of a buzz – either that or the afex was a bit stronger than the beer back on Earth. Whatever it was, I was feeling very good at that moment.

"Cantolla, I do have a project I want you to get started on right away. The Federation planets that will be receiving solbidyum will also need reactors. My understanding is that, over the past 500 years, the original plan for those reactors was lost and only the existing reactor units are installed in the *TRITYTE* and the *NEW ORLEANS*. The one in the *NEW ORLEANS* was developed by Lunnie from old plans she found in the computer archives on the *TRITYTE*. I need you to recover those plans and see what you can do to improve upon them for use with planetary power distribution systems. I'm not certain how much work it will require; perhaps you'll conclude that the original design or Lunnie's design will be sufficient as is. I need you to make this a priority and I suggest that you go up to the *NEW ORLEANS* to look into it as soon as possible. The *TRITYTE* has been moved back into the hangar on the *NEW ORLEANS*. It's basically without power, unless the fusion battery Lunnie installed is still connected. Do what you must to get the information from the *TRITYTE*'s computer. In fact, I would like you to create two complete backups of the *TRITYTE's* databases and operating systems and then have the computer completely replaced with an installation of only the standard operating programs. Who knows what other information may be in there; and with the *TRITYTE* about to become a traveling museum, I don't want any information falling into the wrong hands. While you're up there, get Piesew to assist you in finding a permanent suite and a space you can develop into a laboratory. Notify Captain Stonbersa of any required modifications. He will approve and direct any structural changes and sign off orders for special materials as needed.

In fact, before you talk to Piesew, seek out the captain and let him know that I suggested Piesew might help you. I may own the ship, but Stonbersa is the captain; and on the ship his word is law. I don't want to appear to be bypassing him." Kala smiled and nodded in agreement at this comment. "Kala, can you think of anything more?"

"Yes. I have a few questions, too, Cantolla. Since you're going to be part of this big happy family, I'd like to know a little more about you."

"What specifically would you like to know?" Cantolla reclined comfortably against the back of her chair.

"Oh the usual things, like where you're from, your family background, your interests and hobbies, and anything else you might like us to know."

"I was born on Puryces, where both my father and mother were scientists. Dad was a physicist and mother was a botanist. I had two brothers, both older; and I grew up thinking for the longest time that I was a boy, I guess. At least, I had no interest in feminine things until I hit my teens; and then I saw girls not as sisterly companions, but as romantic attractions. When I was young, I could always be found tinkering about with dad in his laboratory or helping mother cultivate something in her greenhouse; so science has always been a huge part of my life. My eldest brother lives on Nigarreah. My younger brother was killed by the solar flare on Astamagota."

"Astamagota?" I interjected. "Where Galetils founded and operated his industries?"

"Yes. My brother was working for him at the time of the solar flare. Kind of ironic, isn't it, that here I am living and working at the estate and on the ship built by Galetils?"

"Maybe," I said, "and then just maybe you're meant to finish something your brother started."

"Like what?" Cantolla asked curiously.

"Only time will answer that question," I said.

Cantolla went on to talk about the awards she had won in school while participating in projects as a member of various research teams. She also told us of the death of her mother. Her father was injured during an accidental exposure to radiation; and the resulting damage his brain left him in a vegetative state until he eventually died from other complications.

We remained on the patio until the chill of the evening became uncomfortable, and then we said our goodnights.

As Kala and I walked arm in arm back to our suite, she said to me, "Well, it looks like you were right. So tell me what's going to happen next?"

"We'll be getting a visit from Admiral Regeny, I suspect – most likely tomorrow."

"Oh, and what makes you think so?" Kala asked.

"Because we still have the solbidyum on the *NEW ORLEANS*, for one thing. Beyond that, there is most certainly a leak in the Federation Office of Investigation; and if he and the rest of the High Command can't trust the FOI, they have no reliable way to identify Brotherhood infiltrators that are known to still be present throughout the Federation military. Also, since the main headquarters and offices were destroyed in the attempt to kill the High Command, their operations are momentarily displaced. The admiral is going to want our help. I have no doubt."

Kala looked at me and laughed. "Are you sure you didn't come here from the future? You seem to know an awful lot about things that are going to happen."

The next morning we were awakened by a message from Kala's assistant, who told us that Admiral Regeny was requesting to meet with me on the *NEW ORLEANS* later in the day.

I wasn't surprised that the admiral asked specifically to meet on the *NEW ORLEANS*. It was without a doubt the safest and most secure location in the galaxy, if not the entire universe. First, my crew had been thoroughly tested and every one of them was known to be completely loyal to the Federation, unadulterated by the Brotherhood or any other subversive group. The recent coup attempt on the capital planet of Megelleon revealed that the BROTHERHOOD OF LIGHT had been operating quietly within nearly every level of Federation military authority for an unknown period of time – at least for decades. During the assault on Federation High Command headquarters, the rebels also took control of the space frigate *TASSAGORA* and the star ship *DUSTEN*, along with several hundred patrol ships. Fortunately, the High Command had already left the premises at my suggestion and were all harbored safely with me on the *NEW ORLEANS* at the time of the revolt. Since then, the *DUSTEN* had been recovered and the remaining stolen ships of the rebel fleet destroyed. The Brotherhood had been defeated, but certainly not eliminated.

The second reason the admiral wanted to meet there was that the *NEW ORLEANS* was the only ship in the galaxy equipped with a working Reverse Magnetic Force Field (RMFF) as well as a unique cloaking device. The RMFF made the ship safe from attack and the cloaking made it impossible to locate. There were too many opportunities for someone to spy on a classified meeting held anywhere on the planet – or on any other ship, for that matter. The admiral couldn't take the risk of speaking in any environment that potentially allowed Brotherhood operatives to infiltrate or bug the meeting. Only on the *NEW* ORLEANS could meetings take place without the fear of information leaks or threats of attack.

It was shortly before noon when Cantolla, Lieutenant Marranalis (my security chief), Lieutenant Commander Kalana and I took the shuttle from our estate to the orbiting *NEW ORLEANS*. The early departure allowed us a bit of time to get settled in and eat before the admiral and his staff were scheduled to arrive.

The *NEW ORLEANS* was a huge space yacht, large enough to house over 1,000 people in luxury accommodations. There were multiple dining halls, meeting rooms, gyms and pools onboard, not to mention shops and entertainment centers. The yacht had been built for a rich industrialist named Galetils, who apparently committed suicide when his industrial complex and his home planet were destroyed by a giant solar flare. At the time of his death, the yacht was still under construction at the shipyard located on the moon of the planet Nibaria. After my accidental journey from Earth brought me to the Federation territories, I was able to purchase Galetils' nearly completed yacht and his estate on Megelleon near the capital city using the vast wealth I had been given as reward for finding and returning the *TRITYTE* and its solbidyum cargo.

Before we left the estate, I contacted Piesew on the *NEW ORLEANS* and advised him that we would require a meal to be served in my personal dining room. There we met with Captain Stonbersa and Kerabac to briefly discuss everything of importance that had taken place in the past few days. Captain Stonbersa was informed that Cantolla was now a permanent staff member and that she would require accommodations and space for a laboratory. Neither of these were a problem, because this enormous ship was filled with available accommodations and workspaces. It wasn't exactly clear what Galetils' intentions were when he had the yacht built; but from the number of luxury guest accommodations, dining rooms, ball rooms and associated support facilities included in the design, he clearly intended to do some very high-class entertaining. In addition to these areas were numerous offices and conference rooms, as well as smaller, but still luxurious, personal quarters for crew and staff.

Perhaps the most amazing aspects of the ship were its armaments, as the yacht was fully armed with the latest defense technologies and weapons, like a military warship. It was also equipped with the only functioning RMFF system, which also supported a cloaking device, as we learned somewhat by accident.

These last two items were not functioning when I acquired the *NEW ORLEANS*, as the amount of energy required to power the RMFF was greater than the capacity of the fusion reactor that powered the yacht. It was the solbidyum reactor of the *TRITYTE* that offered the answer to rendering the RMFF system functional. Lunnie had managed to construct a small working reactor for the *NEW ORLEANS* in a hidden location and disguised it to look like a common pump, so the actual source of power for the RMFF system would remain a mystery.   Only a few of my closest and trusted associated knew of its existence.

It was while we were attempting to resolve a communication system problem associated with the RMFF that Kerabac accidently discovered how to also utilize the field to support a cloaking system.   Other secrets of the RMFF system had been discovered as well, but these were not yet fully understood.   Among these were the amplification of energy and speed of weapon fire directed out and away from the ship from inside the boundaries of the RMFF.

We were just finishing our meal when word came from the bridge for Captain Stonbersa that the shuttle carrying Admiral Regeny was departing the planet and that he would be docking in about 30 minutes.

"Please excuse me," said Stonbersa as he rose from the table.   "I must see to the arrival of the admiral and his staff."

"Certainly, Captain.   Kala and I will meet you in the hangar bay shortly."   I looked at Kala and said, "Please tell me that I don't have to put on my vice admiral uniform."

Kala laughed, "I'm afraid you do, Tibby... protocol, you know.   It's the price you pay for your fame and fortune."

I growled as I got up from the table and excused myself from the gathering.   Since Kala was still active military, she wore her military uniform most of the time.   However, since she was permanently assigned as my attaché, there were some occasional liberties from this requirement. Today was not one of those days. Kala went with me, most likely to make sure that I didn't put on wrong uniform. Except for formal events, captains and admirals wore Kelly green uniforms. However, since I was only an honorary vice admiral, my own uniform differed by gold threat piping, indicating that I had no direct authority in military matters. Unfortunately, this honorary position meant that I had to receive and give a lot of salutes, which I always detested; but, as Kala always reminded me, it was the price I had to pay for all the wealth and fame bestowed upon me.

Kala and I arrived at the hangar bay just as the admiral's shuttle arrived. Though I should have been used to it by now, I was nevertheless surprised to see that the shuttle had been escorted by a dozen patrol ships, two of which preceded the shuttle into the hangar bay and the remainder of which maintained stations outside and around the *NEW ORLEANS*.

Unlike Earth, where a person was expected to request permission of the commanding officer of that vessel before boarding, the Federation had no such formal procedure. While such requests were obviously made routinely out of respect and professional courtesy, they were not performed in the formal manner of Earth; so when the admiral walked off the ship and into the hangar bay, Captain Stonbersa simply said, "Welcome aboard the *NEW ORLEANS*, Admiral. It's nice to have you with us again."

"It's nice to be here again, Captain. I must say I envy you. While this is not the largest ship in the galaxy, it certainly is the finest and safest."

The admiral then turned to me. "Vice Admiral Tibby, so good to see you again. It warms my heart to see you in that uniform; and in truth, I think your title should be more than just honorary. But then, as it is, I think you have greater flexibility and power than if you were a full vice admiral in the Federation."

"It's good to see you again, Admiral; but I'm assuming you and your staff haven't come all this way for a social visit. Shall we move to the conference room used by you and your staff when you were here last? Captain Stonbersa, would you please see that the bridge activates the RMFF while the admiral is aboard?"

"Certainly, sir," replied Stonbersa, as the admiral and his party began to follow Kala and me out of the hangar area.

By the time we arrived at the conference room used by Admiral Regeny and the High Command during the confrontation with the BROTHERHOOD OF LIGHT when the *DUSTEN* and *TASSAGORA* were seized, Piesew had already seen to the placement of refreshments at each person's seat. Having served in the Federation Space Force aboard the *DUSTEN* as a majordomo for many years, he already knew the beverage preferences of each attendee and where they would be seated.

During the time of the siege of the *DUSTEN*, the Federation emblem had been mounted on the wall behind a raised dais at one end of the conference room, allowing the High Command to make vid announcements to the Federation populace in a fashion that showed them to be safe and in control of the alliance's military defenses. The guise had worked to preserve the morale of the inhabitants of Megelleon. I didn't expect to see the Federation emblem still displayed there and I thought that perhaps by some oversight on the part of my staff it had not been returned to the *NIGHTBRIDGE*, the Federation corvette from which it had been borrowed.

I was about to say something about it when the admiral remarked, "Ah, I see that you've displayed a Federation emblem in here. Is that just for us?"

Before I could reply to say that I had no idea, Kala spoke up. "After your last visit here Piesew felt there may be a future need for us to have the Federation emblem handy, so he had one made up to be available for such a situation."

"Good old Piesew, he always served me well when I was aboard the *DUSTEN*. I hated to see him leave the Federation forces. It seems, though, that his transition here to you is not our loss but everyone's gain.

"Shall we begin?" he said as we all took our seats.

"Tibby, I'll get right to the point," he continued, "though I suspect you've already surmised most of what I'm about to say. While everyone on Megelleon is celebrating our victory over the Brotherhood, you and I both know that the rest of the Federation territories have yet to hear any of the news about what transpired in recent weeks. Hell, most of them still haven't even gotten word about the recovery of the solbidyum. With light years between Megelleon and many of the aligned planets, news from the capital arrives only when a message pod comes within broadcast range or when an incoming ship carries news. We have to believe, based on recent events, that the Brotherhood has a strong following throughout the galaxy and that every Federation ship and outpost base includes Brotherhood members in its ranks. We just discovered that the most significant weak link in our intelligence is within the Federation Office of Investigation. We never anticipated that the FOI would be infiltrated as well. Much of our current situation is a result of the false and distorted information they've been providing to the military – probably for decades or more. Now we can't rely on *anything* reported by that agency until their staff is all retested for loyalty and the organization is completely sanitized of infiltrators, which will take years.

"In addition to this complication, we have to resolve the problem of secure distribution of the solbidyum. So far two different groups have made concentrated efforts to seize the solbidyum – the Bunemnites and the BROTHERHOOD OF LIGHT. I don't think we need to worry about the Bunemnites, as they are now petitioning to rejoin the Federation; and since they never officially acted against the Federation and they're claiming ignorance of the pirating of the *TRITYTE* by Lieutenant Lexmal and the rogue crew on the freighter, I think the Federation will ultimately grant their admission in the interest of peace.

"The Brotherhood, however, is a much larger matter. It would appear that their overall objective is much greater than just acquiring the solbidyum, as they have clearly demonstrated they want to dominate the galaxy.

"Also, as we move distribution toward the outer reaches of the Federation territories, there will be many other non-aligned planetary communities like the Bunem System who will likely try to obtain the solbidyum by similar means. We can most certainly also expect to encounter a number of privateers, pirates and mercenaries throughout the galaxy. While the Federation has several million ships at its command, we don't even know where half of them are at any given time; and recalling enough of them to assemble an armada for protection and distribution of the solbidyum would take years. In that amount of time the planetary governments, no doubt fired by Brotherhood rebels, would begin to believe that the solbidyum is being hoarded, just as they did 500 years ago when it was first lost. Under those conditions, the Great Wars of that era will be repeated and entire planets could again be decimated. At the moment, other than a handful of people on this ship and Commander Wanoll on the *DUSTEN*, no one knows that the solbidyum is stashed here on the *NEW ORLEANS*.

"Tibby, I'm going to be very direct. We need your help, first and foremost to deliver the solbidyum – not all of it – but enough to promote positive image to other Federation planets that distribution is underway and to establish a level of confidence with the Federation peoples as to our intentions and sincerity of efforts. We simply cannot wait for a fleet to assemble here to begin transport. Even if we could move forward with the assurance of screened and loyal crews, we would still not be as safe and secure in delivering the solbidyum as would the *NEW ORLEANS*.

"Secondly, some of my staff and I need to make personal appearances at many of our bases to personally see to the implementation of the new, more stringent procedures for filtering out infiltrators and establishing secure ships, bases and squadrons that can see to the sanitization of subsequent facilities and crews. This must be done as quickly as possible, before word spreads of the recent events here at the capital and before the

Brotherhood decides to take action at other locations. Right now we have only two ships staffed with loyal crews that we know of – the *DUSTEN* and the *NIGHTBRIDGE* – and we need to keep both of them here for the defense of the capital.

"Tibby, I know we've asked a lot of you since you arrived here and I know that it has cost both you and Kalana dearly; but I want you to think of this – if the Brotherhood isn't cleared out of the Federation forces quickly, before they know what's happening, we will probably fail in more ways than one and the deaths of Lunnie and Captain Maxette and the thousands of others will have been in vain.

"We need the *NEW ORLEANS* to transport the solbidyum and the High Command, at least until we can establish enough ships and loyal crews to defend the Federation. We also need *you*, Tibby. It's been hundreds of years since the Federation military has had any real need for any expertise in warfare, since we haven't seen war for generations. Essentially we've been performing roles related only to police actions in contained civil disputes – and in those situations we've achieved resolution by brute force and numbers, not by advanced military strategy. And, unlike your planet Earth, the Federation didn't bother to preserve detailed war histories and strategic plans. You simply know more about leveraging our military strengths than we do and we're going to need every possible strategic advantage we can get when dealing with the Brotherhood."

"Admiral, I think it would be an educational experience for me to see more of the Federation planets. I'll be happy to share with you what I know about Earth's battles and strategies, but I'm not a military expert. What I do know I learned mostly from stories and TV documentaries similar to vid presentations. I got the idea for using the solbidyum container to get our men aboard the *DUSTEN* from the Trojan War, one of the most famous wars on Earth.

"I *can* suggest a few immediate courses of action based on things that have been done on Earth. One thing that I would recommend right now is that you establish another government intelligence agency – a secret one, at least for now, that consists of spies and operatives who infiltrate and collect intelligence not only from groups like the Brotherhood but from agencies within the Federation itself, like the FOI. You can call this new investigative body something like the *Federation Security Organization*. In order to be most effective, the organization would have to employ a rather diverse group of agents that are able to infiltrate key agencies of governments within and apart from the Federation authority as a means of providing you with a warning when trouble is brewing elsewhere. I'm not sure how your funding is set up or by what means you get approval for funding, but the fewer people within your own government that know about the activities or existence of the FSO, the more effectively it will be to operate and gather data. The biggest drawback to setting up such an agency is ensuring that impingement of the rights of individual citizens is prevented, which becomes very tricky.

"Another thing I recommend is the development of Special Operations units within your military – teams trained specifically for covert operations and hostage situations like the one that occurred on the *DUSTEN*. You won't always need thousands of troops to address a conflict, if you have task forces in place that are specially trained with the proper skills. I think I can provide some assistance in that area; and now that we've successfully modified the learning headbands to pass on martial arts skills, we may be able to expedite training. I know that, at the moment, all the loyal troops you have here at Megelleon have received the martial arts training and are practicing the skills daily to enhance their performance. I think we can expand on that to include other areas of training as well; and as you clear military people from other ships and bases during our travels, you can also pass on these skills almost instantly, which will make every one of your troopers equal to four or five of the Brotherhood rebels. If this program is implemented properly, the training of loyal forces can occur so quickly that, if the Brotherhood does not become aware of what you're doing, you can have them – and any other factions – filtered out very quickly and replaced by new recruits that can be trained for duty and deployed in combat-ready teams within weeks instead of months.

"I do have some other ideas, but I'm not ready to discuss them at the moment. I'm still contemplating some of the details.

"I take it, Admiral, that you intend to personally go on this mission so you can provide the authority for the testing and the replacement, dismissal or incarceration of Brotherhood sympathizers, in case the highest ranking officer at a facility or ship happens to be a Brotherhood member. Am I correct?"

"Yes, you're correct. I don't see how it will work otherwise."

"Okay. I'm also assuming that you want the bulk of your higher ranking staff members to remain here so you maintain a strong presence at the capital. I also suspect that, once we get the crews of several ships cleared, you'll send one or two more back here to Megelleon to defend against potential subsequent attempts at occupation or destruction. I would suggest you take along ten squads of twelve per squad. That's 120 troopers. We can train them en route.

"As for the FSO, I would suggest that the immediate plan calls for fifty agents. Again, we will have to train them en route. I would suggest you pick men and women of various planetary origins who possess a variety of skills; for example, explosives experts (bomb-making and disposal), marksmen, communication officers and, if you can find them, police detectives – really good ones. Maybe also a chemist or two and a couple of electricians. We'll need all of them to download their skills and knowledge bases into the learning devices. Ultimately, your FSO agents will need to be the most highly cross-trained team in the Federation. The *NEW ORLEANS* has sufficient room for all of these personnel, so we won't be over-crowded. The arrangement will be good for my staff, too. They'll have something substantial to do for a change.

"How long will it take you to assemble these people and be ready to start out?"

"Five days – seven at the most," the admiral said.

"Make it six" I replied. "I'll inform Captain Stonbersa that we will be departing in six days and to have accommodations ready for your staff by then. You'll also need to bring a number of patrol ships. The hangar bays of the *NEW ORLEANS* can hold about a dozen of yours – plus two shuttles."

Admiral Regeny stared at me with a somewhat stunned look on his face as he absorbed my suggestions. "Did you just come up with that all just now or did you anticipate my concerns beforehand and have this planned out?"

"A bit of both, sir," I replied.

"That's incredible.   In just minutes you put together a complete strategy to deal with this situation. It would have taken us weeks and we would not have come up with anything nearly this elaborate or efficient. I get the impression from the way you approach these situations that yours is a planet plagued with frequent wars and that strategic planning is a way of life there."

"To be honest, Admiral, I never really stopped to think about it; but, in retrospect, I don't know of a period during my lifetime – or any period, really – when there *wasn't* a war or two going on someplace on Earth.   In many Earth cultures even the games children play, especially on computers, are based on war and combat. Warfare has played a huge part in Earth history, so many of Earth's citizens (scholarly historians and hobbyists alike) continue to study wars and battles. There are even annual staged events where battles of some of the more famous wars are reenacted. Nonetheless, the majority of Earth's people live in peace."

"So you're a war history hobbyist?"

"Me? No, not by any means. What I know was learned in school and from what you would call vid documentaries that are watched for education and entertainment."

"People watch war stories for entertainment on your planet? Incredible," said Admiral Regeny with a look of astonishment. "What's even more incredible is that you claim your knowledge is limited; yet you seem so well prepared to handle these situations."

"I don't know what to tell you, sir, other than the last thing that I want to see is the devastation of war. While I was completing my military training, the Navy wanted to transfer me to the War College, but I wasn't interested and managed to avoid that assignment."

"War College?" Admiral Regeny exclaimed in astonishment. "They have a school for war?"

"Ah, well sort of. Each branch of the military has a school where they train their future leaders and strategists in problem solving, decision making, and effective definition and execution of objectives. For instance, the US Naval War College is described by its founder as "a place of original research on all questions relating to war and to statesmanship connected with war or the prevention of war." Hence, they study past wars as documented by all parties in the conflict. More specifically, these scholars study military strategies applied to past battles to analyze those that succeeded and those that went wrong. They also set up and rehearse various hypothetical scenarios to examine possible outcomes."

"This is done without there actually being a real threat?"

"Well, sometimes the scenarios are based on existing threats where engagement in conflict is considered a real possibility. Under those conditions they analyze as many scenarios as they can to identify the best courses of action. Other times they make up fictitious situations just to practice and hone their skills."

"I can see where there could be a value in such a program. I think it's something the Federation military may find beneficial; but in the meantime, I'm afraid we'll need to draw on your knowledge to help us."

For the next few hours we discussed how to go about setting up the FSO and defining its parameters of power and capability. The Federation had never seen a need for anything like this before and the admiral wasn't sure how funding could be obtained from the Senate without making all of the FSO's actions transparent. Considering the vast number of senators and the probability that the Brotherhood had agents within the Senate itself, establishing the FSO in a way that would allow it function covertly was not going to be an easy matter. In the end, I volunteered to foot the bill, at least for the short term, until such time that the FSO could prove its worth to the Federation and support the need for secrecy within the FSO structure. Both the admiral and I felt that our best chance was to get the Senate to agree to leave the supervision and decision making about the budgeting of the FSO strictly to the Federation's three Leaders and the High Command. But there was a question of the legality of such action.

The Federation's government includes an entity parallel to what on Earth was called the United States Supreme Court, a membership of justices within one of the planet's governments that rules on matters of legality based on the country's supreme law or "Constitution." In the Federation this body is called the *Federation Legal Review Board* or FLRB. Unlike Earth's Supreme Court, FLRB members are not required to be judges, nor are they appointed by a Leader or president; rather, they are a constituency of members who have been selected according to their demonstrated knowledge of the law as defined in the Federation Constitution. Every university within the Federation territories submits their brightest and best law instructors and graduates to a pool of candidates who are subjected to a comprehensive exam. The exam is derived from millions of test questions compiled by all the universities. Randomly assembled questions appear in the test, which is given to all of the candidates. The highest scorers are tested again using a new set of questions. The top scoring candidates are then tested yet a third time, resulting in a final constituency of five members. The entire membership of the FLRB consists of fifty members, each serving on the FLRB for staggered terms of ten years, at which time they step down to be replaced by five new members. The rotation replaces five board members each year, resulting in a completely new constituency in any given 10-year period. If a member dies or is not able to serve their full term, that individual's chair remains empty until their term would have ended. No member can ever serve another term.

A two-thirds majority is required for a ruling to be made on a legal matter. If the panel is unable to reach a two-third majority within three votes, the matter is held until five new members began their terms, at which time the voting process is repeated. In the history of the Federation this situation had occurred only once.

The FSO was a matter that would have to face the legal challenge of the FLRB, not only for its formation but for its continuation and funding. For the time being, however, the admiral agreed that there was a need to go ahead with the establishment of the FSO under the legal caveat of Federation maritime defense actions; and he would fight the battle with the FLRB later.

It was close approaching the dinner hour and I asked the admiral if he and his staff would be staying. He declined, saying there were too many issues that needed his personal attention on the planet's surface. Captain Stonbersa, Kala and I saw them off at the hangar.

After they were gone Kala turned to me and said, "You look tense. I think we both could use a few laps in the pool."

One of the features of the *NEW ORLEANS* that I found most attractive when I purchased this space yacht was that it has not just one pool, but several pools – and gyms as well. My own personal suite was even designed with its own private gym and pool. I was still recovering from the stab wounds Lexmal had inflicted on me during the reclaiming of the *DUSTEN*, but the synthetic skin-like bandages had promoted effective healing of the wounds while also allowing me to bathe and swim. I knew that the regular exercise would continue to help heal and strengthen my injured muscles, so I accepted Kala's suggestion.

Taboos that are common on Earth are nonexistent throughout most of the Federation, especially taboos related to nudity. Consequently, the concept of bathing suits was foreign to its citizens and deemed silly by Federation standards. When I first met Kala, I was shocked when she joined me in a shower to "freshen up" before going to meet Captain Maxette on the *DUSTEN*. She was somewhat taken aback at the time when I described the customs and thinking of most of the cultures on Earth regarding nudity and sex. She was completely amazed that it was considered OK for a man to be topless at a beach, but not a woman, especially since, as she put it, "Both have nipples don't they?"

Kala had made me rethink many of the preconceptions, taboos and customs of Earth. For instance, why were certain foods reserved for certain meals? In the Federation there was no specific food that one ate only for breakfast or lunch or dinner; eating roast beef for breakfast and scrambled eggs and pancakes for dinner would not be looked on as out of the norm in the Federation. Also, marriage, as understood and practiced on Earth, didn't exist in the Federation. Instead, there was a loosely practiced system referred to as *bonding*, which simply involved two people living together in a more or less exclusive relationship. Family units with children generally included bonded mates for parents, though single-parent families also existed. Ultimately, the legality of marriage simply didn't exist on most of the planets.

When we reached the pool, Kala wasted no time in shedding her uniform and diving in. I was a bit slower, as certain motions still caused me some pain. Lexmal had driven his knife into the muscles of my arms and legs and twisted the blade, leaving me with significant damage to the muscle tissues. Until I was fully recovered my movements would remain guarded and stiff. Nevertheless, I was soon undressed and slipping into the water to join Kala. In the past Kala and I swam laps together, equally matched in strength and speed; but now Kala clearly outperformed me while I swam at a firm, steady pace to work the aches and stiffness out of my muscles.

As I swam, I reflected on all that had happened in just a few months. This all began when I found the *TRITYTE* buried in the swamp back on Earth and, in the course of investigating the craft, I accidently activated the homing device that brought it here to the Federation's capital of Megelleon. I thought of all that had transpired since then, the friends I had made and, sadly, the friends I had lost. My journey since leaving Earth had been one unbelievable event after another and it didn't look like it was going to end. I found myself wondering if all of this was some sort of crazy dream.

When I reached the end of the pool, Kala was waiting and watching me finish my last lap. When I looked at her, I was even more doubtful that the experiences of these last few months were real. Kala was not only one of the loveliest women I had ever seen, but she was also the most incredible woman I had ever met. The fact that she was in love with me was almost too much to believe. Even though she was with me pretty much constantly, I regretted that we had so little time to share privately.

As I pulled myself up out of the pool, I could see her examining my body. Gently she reached out to trace her fingers over the bright red scars of my recently healed wounds. "You're going to have permanent scars unless you have the scars removed medically."

"I really don't care. It doesn't bother me to see them; but if they bother you I can," I said.

"No, I don't think they will bother me. I was just thinking... Lexmal stabbed you with the same knife that he used to kill Lunnie." A brief sob escaped with Kala's breath as she thought out loud, "Some of Lunnie's blood was still on that knife. It was mixed with your own; and now, in a sense, Lunnie is a part of you."

"Even without being stabbed with the same knife Lunnie is a part of me," I said. "Her memory will always be a part of me."

"What do you think about what Lunnie said in her message to me – I mean, about us having a daughter and naming her Luinella after her? Do you want to stay with me? Do you want us to have children? I understand your ideas about relationships and I personally agree with and like your traditional Earth values; but do you want us to stay together?"

My eyes filled with tears as she asked me these questions. "Kala there is no one I could want to be with more or to have children with more than you; and if – no, make that *when* we have a daughter, not only do I think we should name her Luinella, I *insist* she be named Luinella."

Kala threw her arms around my neck and kissed me. We stayed like that for several minutes, knowing that the other was not only reveling in the shared love, but also revisiting the grief of losing Lunnie. Then, to my surprise and amusement, Kala said, "I'm hungry let's get something to eat."

The next few days were bustling with activity, as all sorts of supplies and laboratory equipment were brought aboard for Cantolla's laboratory needs. A number of assistants hired by Cantolla also began to appear and each was tested by Kala to ensure that their loyalties did not lie with the Brotherhood or any other subversive group. Marranalis also had new recruits coming aboard to serve as my personal security force. Kala tested them as well, while Marranalis addressed provisions for their quarters and gear and set up the required training schedules. Then there was the admiral's staff; 120 troopers to be trained for Special Operations units and 50 more to be trained as undercover operatives in the newly formed FSO. Even with the addition of these people to the existing personnel on the ship, there still were many accommodations and other spaces on the *NEW ORLEANS* that were not in regular use – too many spaces left basically unseen. For security purposes I felt that there needed to be someone on the ship that was aware of all of them. While still preparing for our departure, I assigned Captain Stonbersa and Kerabac the task of visiting every space on the ship. However, by the time we were ready to embark on this long journey with the admiral and his officers, they reported that they had been able to survey and visit only about 80% of the ship. They both assured me, though, that once the ship was underway, there would be ample time for them to finish investigating the remaining unexplored areas.

Our first stop was to be Nibaria, the planet where the *NEW ORLEANS* had been designed and constructed. Nibaria was the closest inhabited Federation planet in the vicinity of Megelleon. By the time we arrived at the planet the reactor was ready. Cantolla had been able to resurrect the plans for the solbidyum reactor from the *TRITYTE*, just as Lunnie had done; and with minor adjustments she was able make a reactor design suitable for a planetary power production system. The only problem was that the Nibarians didn't know we were coming.

During my previous trip to Nibaria to purchase the *NEW ORLEANS*, I had met with Senator Tonclin, who represented the people of Nibaria within the Federation governmental and legislative body; so it was logical that he would be the first individual we would contact upon our arrival. Without revealing the purpose for our visit we contacted the senator and said that we had a matter of interest to Nibaria that we wished to discuss and asked whether it would be possible for him to join us for dinner on the *NEW ORELANS*. We received a reply almost immediately that Senator Tonclin would be most pleased to dine with us that evening, if it was convenient for us. As it turned out this was perfect timing.

Since we had arrived in orbit over Nibaria's capital city early in the morning, we had an opportunity to deal with other matters before the scheduled dinner. I requested a meeting with Admiral Regeny, which he accepted immediately. Instead of meeting in the large conference room with his staff, I elected to meet with him privately in my study, which was an exact duplicate of the study in my estate house on Megelleon. I was staring into the large aquarium behind my desk, marveling at how many varieties of fish resembled the fish of Earth, when Piesew announced the arrival of the admiral.

"Admiral, thank you for responding so quickly to my invitation. I know how busy you must be as you get settled in and organized," I said.

"Actually, Tibby, I'm at a loss for something to do at the moment, as my staff is still making all the necessary arrangements; so I have a bit of free time. Besides, it would be rude not to respond to your request after all you've done and are doing for the Federation. By the way, I must say this is an incredible office you have here. Absolutely amazing! I love the aquarium wall; and the dark wood paneling gives this space a real air of class and power. But I'm guessing you didn't invite me here to see your office, now, did you?"

I chuckled, "No, sir, I didn't. Please have a seat." I indicated two large, comfortable chairs arranged around a small table. "Would you care for something to drink?"

"Perhaps a cup of foccee," said the admiral. Piesew immediately went to a panel in the wall that opened to reveal a drink dispenser, from which he retrieved two cups of foccee, one for the admiral and one for me. Then, once his duties were performed, he departed the room in accordance with Federation protocol.

"What I want to discuss with you is a means of expediting the delivery of the solbidyum and reactors to some of the planets in the Federation. It will involve some risk, but if we can work out a few security issues, I think we can speed things up tremendously."

"You have my interest, let's hear your plan."

"The solbidyum reactors are quite small, considering the incredible power they produce, and the solbidyum itself is but a grain of sand. I was thinking, if you have people you know and trust on the receiving end, we could modify gravity wave message pods to deliver both the solbidyum and the reactors to planets where there is little likelihood of them falling into the wrong hands. We obviously would not be able to do it for very long, because word would quickly leak out to the Brotherhood and other nefarious parties, who would then be looking specifically to intercept the pods. If we could send out several hundred at the same time, before the Brotherhood or anyone else learns what we we're doing, you could quickly head off the political ploy that the Brotherhood will try to create by claiming that the solbidyum is being hoarded. The big problem is that we can't provide any preliminary warning that the delivery is coming. It's an uncertain option in more ways than one; but the biggest risk is that the party receiving the delivery is potentially not loyal to the Federation."

I could see the admiral mulling over the idea and weighing the risk against the benefits. Finally he said, "I must admit it, this course of action would prevent a lot of problems; I just don't know how we can assure that the people receiving it at the other end will see to it that it is employed properly. All it would take is for one delivery to go wrong to create dissention among a number of planets. However, that having been said, I would suggest that you stock up on GW message pods while we're here near the Nibarian suppliers."

Although the Federation had been able to overcome the restriction of light speed by using gravity waves for propulsion, they had not been able to come up with a method of instant communication over spans of light years. Even so, the Federation was able to communicate using gravity wave pods (GWPs) that could carry messages at faster than light speeds; however, communication beyond a solar system could take weeks or even months and two way communications was extremely limited. Because of these constraints, even GWP communication could take several months to arrive with news at the more remote planets of the Federation. The mutiny and coup of the Brotherhood and the news of their defeat still had not reached most of the planets in the Federation. In fact, nearly half the planets in the Federation still had not gotten word that the *TRITYTE* and the solbidyum had been found. It was still uncertain how large the Brotherhood was or the extent of their reach across the Federation; and it was entirely possible that, when news reached various branches of the Brotherhood in other parts of the Federation, their ranks might stage mutinies and revolts before hearing of the ultimate defeat of the Brotherhood at Megelleon. To compound matters, as word reached planets throughout the Federation of the discovery of *TRITYTE*, many other unscrupulous individuals and groups would be also be scheming intercept a shipment either for their own use, for black market sale or even for ransom.

"Tibby," Admiral Regeny said, "I've been thinking about what you said about your planet having vids – or what did you call it? *TV*, I believe – and documentaries of battles and wars on your planet. If we were to position satellite receivers 20 light years out from your planet to pick up broadcasts of these programs from the more distant past, we could glean a good amount of Earth's military history from these transmissions."

"Hm, you're right. I hadn't thought about that. If you placed twenty of them one light year apart you could basically get twenty years' worth of transmissions in one year."

"Exactly. I'll leave orders before we head out of the system. It will take several months to deploy and position all of the receivers; but once they're in place, we can immediately begin gathering data. Within a year we should have a good foundation of information as to how your planet wages war and implements battle strategies. It could make a huge difference in our dealings with the Brotherhood or other entities that may decide to engage the Federation in conflict over the solbidyum or any other matter. In the meantime, we can draw upon your knowledge to help us develop the proper approach to various encounters. I just wish we had a fleet of ships with RMFF and cloaking capabilities like the *NEW ORLEANS*, but the Federation has made it clear that using solbidyum to power our military airships is forbidden; and without solbidyum we can't produce enough power make an RMFF work."

"Sooner or later we will, Admiral. Perhaps I can get Cantolla working on that. Galetils had been working on it and was supposed to be in the final stages of developing a fusion reactor that could generate enough power for the RMFF, but the solar flare at Astamagota destroyed it. The factory, plans, and pretty much everything that might have given us a clue as to how far they had advanced the design are gone. I'm not sure how well it would work for some of your smaller ships; Galetils' design may only be suitable for something the size of the *DUSTEN*, as I know how large a space he had allotted for the fusion reactor here on the *NEW ORLEANS* – and it was a *very* large space. That reactor wouldn't fit in the *NIGHTBRIDGE*, of that I'm sure."

"Equipping only the star ships would still grant us a huge advantage. We would then have invulnerable bases of operation in any star system and a safe haven for our patrol ships and corvettes while in hostile territory – and, of course, the greatly enhanced firepower."

I briefly discussed this matter already with Cantolla when I hired her. Once she has her lab and staff functioning, she and her team are to make this project a priority and concentrate on trying to figure out what Galetils was doing. But even if she comes up with the answer, it will take quite a bit of time to modify a ship to include the fusion reactor as well as the RMFF equipment. Both are going to eat up some space. Fortunately your star ships are not lacking in space; but with all the diplomats and civilians you carry, I think you're going to require some layout modifications so there is a more rigorous isolation of military areas from non-military personnel."

"Yes, I agree, but it's not going to be an easy thing to accomplish. Many of our dignitaries and senators are going to be very sensitive on this matter. They feel they should have access to everything. Also, while I'm here, how soon do you think you can start training our FSO agents?"

"How about tomorrow, mid-morning?" I responded. "I would like to hold the first day of training in the conference room that we've been using for your meetings and Federation broadcasts. It's large enough to hold everyone and I think it's important to maintain the feeling of Federation discipline and jurisdiction in their training environment. We want super patriots for this type of work."

"What about our Special Operations troopers? We need to get started with their training as well."

"Initial training is scheduled to begin tomorrow morning in the sports arena on the upper level under the direction of Lieutenant Marranalis. The arena provides sufficient space for the first drills they will undergo. I'm going to be observing their abilities over the next few days to see who among them should be leaders. This may be a sensitive issue with you and some of them, but as of tomorrow they all have equal rank; and new ranks will be applied according to their demonstrated abilities. One other thing, I don't know how you selected these recruits; were they given a chance to volunteer or were they simply drafted?"

"All the candidates for the Special Ops units are volunteers. We made no secret of the formation of that unit. I'm not so sure about the equal ranks or how that will go over. I go along with it for the moment, but I think we need to readdress it after their training is complete. FSO candidates were drafted; only those with the highest skills and loyalty ratings were selected," explained the admiral, "but they were given the right to refuse the assignment if they wished."

"Normally, Admiral, I would say that only the top 30% would make it through the program. However, this organization is new and the Brotherhood is completely unaware of its formation, so they won't really be looking for them. Under these conditions we will probably retain every recruit, though some may strictly be clerical and desk operatives. We're going to have to go with what we have. Moving quickly will be the key to success with the fewest possible casualties."

"Again, I have to agree with you. I don't think most people have a clue what a nightmare we have in front of us between rooting out the Brotherhood and trying to safely distribute the solbidyum. One misstep and the entire Federation could go up like a super nova. I don't think I've had a good night's sleep since you showed up at Megelleon with the solbidyum – that's no reflection on you, Tibby." The admiral was about to continue, when a message came in over his personal communication link requesting his presence for a meeting with the High Command. "I'm afraid we will have to cut this short, Tibby, no doubt one of my staff has forgotten which shoe goes on which foot. Were there any other critical issues we needed to discuss at this time?"

"No, sir," I replied, "I think we've covered the major points for now. We'll be seeing you this evening, of course, for the reception dinner with Senator Tonclin?"

"Yes, definitely, it would hardly be proper if I didn't attend. I think I'll also enjoy seeing the surprise on his face when we tell him why we're here." The admiral chuckled at the thought. So did I.

After the admiral left I tracked down Kala and found her busy with her staff. As I approached, I heard her giving them instructions and helping them deal with problems that they were afraid to handle on their own.

She smiled when she saw me coming and said, "My hero comes to rescue me from a fate worse than death!" Then she turned to her staff and said, "You will have to handle these problems yourselves. That's what I hired you for. Right now I have more important business to attend to." With that she walked over to me, kissed me on the cheek, and laced her arm in mine while she led me away from her gaping staff.

"Where are we going?" I asked Kala, after we cleared the doorway of the administration area.

"You tell me; you're the one who rescued me," she said with a grin.

"I gather things are not going well with your staff?"

"Actually, things are going very well. They're all very competent and highly motivated, but they're also terrified of making decisions, given everything that's been going on. I don't think anyone in the Federation has had to work as hard and as fast as they have; I think it's just a bit overwhelming for them. Once they get used to making decisions and seeing them carried through successfully, they will all do fine. At this point I want them to stop relying on me to make decisions. They know what to do; and as soon as they start exercising some autonomy, they'll gain more confidence and understand their level of authority."

"Good thinking," I said. "Do you have any idea where Cantolla has set up operations here on the ship?"

"Actually, it just so happens that I do. Is that where we're going?"

"It is if you're willing to guide me there," I said. Kala poked me on the arm, then grinned and tugged me in a direction that took us to the aft end of the ship.

When we arrived I was astonished at what I saw. Cantolla had wasted no time in obtaining a staff and getting things organized and running. It was as though she had things set up in advance of my offering her the job. Cantolla looked up as we entered and came across the room to greet us. "Tibby and Kala, this is a surprise. To what do I owe this visit?"

"Wow, Cantolla, this is quite the setup. How were you able to accomplish so much so quickly?" I said.

"Well, to be honest Tibby, most of these people are here under contract on a trial basis. Those that work out I will keep and the others will be replaced as we journey on. I can't afford to spend years putting together a team before I get to work, now, can I?"

"No, I guess you can't; but I'm surprised you were able to find so many so fast."

"Actually, I had three times this many apply for positions, but a third of them didn't pass the psych/loyalty test and another third didn't meet my expectations. Is that what you wanted to talk to me about? The people?"

"No, actually I wanted to talk to you about another urgent project that requires your attention. I also need you to research any records you can find on a fusion reactor design that was under development by Galetils Industries before the solar flare destroyed Astamagota. Galetils had been working on a plan to build a fusion reactor ten times more powerful than anything operating in the Federation today, one that would be robust enough to power a fully functional RMFF system. We know the approximate physical size of it, because he had planned to install it on the *NEW ORLEANS*. I can show you the compartment where it would have been installed. Unfortunately, Astamagota was destroyed before the prototype was completed and, as far as we know, the plans and all the people who knew anything about the reactor were also annihilated in the event. The Federation has a pressing need for those reactors so they can install RMFF shielding systems on their star ships. For a number of reasons, it's also critical that the size of the reactor be kept minimal. I'm hoping that, since you seem to have a sizeable staff at your disposal, you would be able to make some rapid progress on this project. You should have no problem obtaining any special supplies you might need from the Nibarian merchants or, if necessary, from other sources on Megelleon. Have everything shipped here within the next 60 hours. Tell them to place a rush on the order if you must. Everything must be here by then and cost is of no consequence."

Cantolla laughed. "Tibby, if anyone else but you made that request, I would not take it seriously; but with you I have every reason to believe that you won't rest until you see it done. I will give it my very best effort; but what you ask is nearly impossible, as I understand it.   Of course, there is first time for everything. We'll give it our best shot."

"Tibby," Kala began, "I think the best place for Cantolla's team to build the reactor is in the originally planned compartment, where it was supposed to have been located to begin with.   Besides that, the compartment is adjacent to the hangar bay; so once it's completed, it can be easily transferred out of the *NEW ORLEANS* to whatever star ship is designated."

"Very good point, Kala. Why don't you show Cantolla the reactor compartment? I need to meet with Marranalis to discuss some training that begins tomorrow and I'm running out of time. Can you greet Senator Tonclin when he arrives? I'll try to be there before he docks; but if I don't make it, please extend my apology for my absence."

"Right.   But do try and be there, it really is important."

"Okay.   Oh, what outfit should I wear – dignitary or military?"

"Based on recent events, I think your vice admiral uniform would be the most appropriate. Plus, I personally get turned on when I see you in it," Kala said with a grin.

"Me too!" said Cantolla, with a glint in her eye and enough enthusiasm that, had I not known her sexual preferences, I might have taken her comment seriously.

As Kala and I left the lab to finish the day's business, we encountered Marranalis in the corridor. "Ah, Marranalis, I was just about to come looking for you. We're scheduled to begin training tomorrow morning for the Special Operations personnel that the admiral has sent us. Everything is ready, I trust?"

Marranalis is a big man, a good 120 cm taller than me and a lot heavier build. His brown skin, dark wavy black hair and brown eyes reminded me very much of a race on Earth we call Polynesian. I relied on him heavily. I found him to be a good natured individual who bore no grudges, followed orders, and eagerly performed his best at all times. He had a fair sense of humor, but tended to be on the quiet side. He rarely mentioned or discussed anything of a personal nature, so all that I really knew of him came from my personal experiences.

"Just about ready," Marranalis replied, "but we need to talk about ground training. Right now we can do a lot of fundamental training and certain types of exercises here on the ship, as there are still large expanses of unoccupied space where we can simulate shipboard actions; but we're going to need training facilities on a planet before we can teach other outdoor combat scenarios, clearing of buildings and so forth. And we definitely don't want to be working with live explosives here on the ship."

"Yes, I'm aware of our current constraints. Perhaps we can conduct training on some of the planets we encounter. I'm sure there are Federation bases on all of them; and I know the admiral will provide us the authorization to use whatever facilities we need. After all, these are his troops we're training. We will want to train for all environments – wet, dry, hot, cold, deep space and, of course, underwater and combatant swimmer training, since the Brotherhood operated out of a secret suboceanic base. These troops will become the

Federation's elite squadrons and I want them prepared for anything. I want them to be able to perform in combat as individuals and teams in ways no one has ever seen before. They need to be ready to do the unexpected and do it effectively."

While I was talking, a rather attractive blonde-haired woman in a trooper uniform that displayed the rank of major walked up to Marranalis and said, "Lieutenant, I need to talk to you."

"I'll be with you in a moment, ma'am," said Marranalis before returning his attention to me.

"Perhaps you didn't hear me, Lieutenant. I said I need to talk to you. You will come to attention and salute me and give proper greeting or I will have you written up. Is that understood, Lieutenant?"

"And I SAID I will be with you in a minute, Major; and on *this* ship you salute me; is THAT understood?" replied Marranalis with some irritation in his voice.

It was obvious that this officer had not been fully informed as to the modified protocols on the *NEW ORLEANS* or the status of my staff. Either that or she had not been paying attention when she was briefed. Either way, things were about to get interesting.

"Very well, Lieutenant, I'm going to have you brought up on charges of insubordination," the major fumed. "Lieutenant Commander Kalana, you witnessed his insubordination."

Kala looked at me with a smirk on her face.

"Actually, Major," I began, "if you will note the two gold stars on the lieutenant's collar, you will realize that he is part of the crew assigned by the High Command to my personal staff and, as such, on this ship or when taking part in any training program here or on the surface that is conducted by me or my staff, you answer to him, regardless of your rank with the Federation. Also, for the record, when you approached and interrupted our conversation, you failed to recognize both Lieutenant Commander Kalana and me with the salute and recognition due to us; so the insubordination is yours, not Lieutenant Marranalis'." I could see the major's face redden as I spoke.

"Begging your pardon, Vice Admiral," the Major began with some ice in her voice, "but you're not in uniform and your rank is only honorary; you have no real authority in this matter."

"That will be *enough*, Major," Kala said with fire in her voice. "You will never speak to Vice Admiral Renwalt like that again, and you will always salute and show him proper respect, *regardless* of what he is wearing, is that UNDERSTOOD, MAJOR?!" The major stood in shock for a moment and then replied, "Yes ma'am; but you should know that I intend to file a full complaint on this matter."

"Please do, Major, and be sure to file that complaint with Admiral Regeny personally. In fact, I am making it an order that you do so – to the admiral personally. Is that understood?"

"Yes, ma'am," replied the major while standing at attention.

"What's your name, Major? I intend to follow up to make sure that you do as you're ordered regarding this issue."

"Sokaia, ma'am," the major stammered. It was now becoming clear to her that she had bitten into something she shouldn't have and that her butt was hanging over the fire.

"Very well, Major Sokaia, I suggest you get on with filing your complaint. *Dismissed*!" said Kala with a tone of genuine anger in her voice.

"Yes, ma'am!" said the Major while retreating.

Marranalis smiled and said to Kala, "Do you think my chances of getting a date with her will be ruined by this minor confrontation?" Both Kala and I laughed.

One of the things that I found difficult to understand about the Federation military was that it was not organized into branches like the military on Earth. There was simply the Federation Space Force made up of troopers. There was no division of armed forces into equivalents of the Army, Navy, Air Force, Marines or Coast Guard. Rank was also confusing, as the Federation military seemed to be a mixture of all branches of service on Earth. There were no ensigns; however there were privates, corporals, sergeants, lieutenants and other ranks that were combined to reflect a somewhat different chain of authority. Also, unlike Earth's military, where more stripes on a uniform means a higher rank, the Federation's system was the converse – the more stripes, the lower the rank. Metals, ribbons and other such trappings were also nonexistent in the Federation.

Kala excused herself to prepare for the arrival of Senator Tonclin as I went over some of the details for the Special Ops unit the next day with Marranalis. When I finished, I went to my suite to prepare for Senator Tonclin's arrival. Fortunately, Piesew anticipated my arrival and had laid out my uniform for me. I dressed and arrived at the hangar just as the senator's shuttle arrived. Captain Stonbersa, Admiral Regeny and Kala were already there. Several troopers had taken up stations on both sides of the walkway leading away from the shuttle.

Senator Tonclin exited the shuttle accompanied by another Nibarian of similar stature and appearance, though the second Nibarian's skin texture seemed somewhat smoother. Nibarians are one of the few non-human races residing within in the Federation territories. One of the things I was surprised to discover as I learned about the peoples inhabiting the millions of Federation planets was that most were humans – or humanoid – and that they shared similar and even compatible DNA. But there were also planets that had environments not suitable for humans where sentient life had also evolved; and these people could be quite different in nature from humans. Nibaria was one of those planets. Nibarians are not exactly dependent on the nitrogen-rich atmosphere that defines their planet's environment, as they can breathe more human-friendly atmospheres without significant discomfort. Their skin is thick and looks much like gnarled tree bark. On average, they are shorter and more stoutly built than humans, yet they have amazingly high-pitched voices that are completely incongruent with their physical appearance. My personal experience with Nibarians, while limited at this point in my life among the Federation peoples, had shown them to be friendly, highly skilled, hardworking, and most certainly honest individuals; and I was happy to see Senator Tonclin once again.

As protocol directed, Captain Stonbersa greeted the senator first, welcoming him aboard the *NEW ORLEANS* as the captain and official host. Then, as First Citizens in the Federation, it was considered proper that Kala and I should exchange greetings next. As the senator moved toward us, I stepped forward. "It's good to see you again, Senator Tonclin, and it's a pleasure to have you join us on the *NEW ORLEANS*."

"Ah, First Citizen Tibby and First Citizen Kalana, it is my delight as well. May I present my daughter, Chanina. I trust it is acceptable that I brought her along this evening. When she heard that I would be meeting with you again, she declared fiercely how she wanted to meet you both and lamented endlessly about not being able to. I fear I am an overindulgent parent, even more so since the death of her mother."

"I assure you, we are very delighted to meet Chanina and she is indeed most welcome. Chanina, welcome aboard the *NEW ORLEANS*," I said warmly. Unlike the convention practiced on Earth, shaking hands as a gesture during greetings or when reaching an agreement didn't exist, nor was there anything to takes its place. One simply greeted or promised and that was it. My greeting to Chanina prompted her to let loose with a high-pitched sound that I later learned was the equivalent of a giggle in humans, which she then retracted with what appeared to be a mild embarrassment.

"It's my pleasure also," said Kala. "I hope you enjoy your visit here with us."

"Chanina!" Senator Tonclin said sternly. "What do you say?"

"Tha-thank you, First Citizens, it is a great hon-honor me-meeting you both," stammered Chanina with a tone of nervous awkwardness.

"Chanina is hoping that later she might be able to have a vid pic made with the two of you," said Senator Tonclin. "I do hope that will be alright."

"Certainly, Senator," I said while smiling at Chanina, who now was sweating brown droplets like drops of dark tea – something that is apparently normal for Nibarians when they're nervous, but which I had not previously observed.

After our greeting, the senator and his daughter moved on to Admiral Regeny and two of his senior officers, and lastly to Piesew Mecarta, the ships majordomo, who would oversee all of the guest services during their stay. After the greetings were completed, Piesew showed the senator and his daughter to their suite; and though none of us were aware in advance that Senator Tonclin was bringing his daughter, by the time Piesew showed them to their accommodations, a room within was already prepared specifically for Chanina. On hearing of her arrival, Piesew immediately communicated to his staff to make the additional arrangements. As the guests passed through the door to enter the ship from the hangar, a scanner would recorded their measurements and feed the information into the closet replicator so that an appropriate clothing selections would be available in their closets when they arrived.

It was approximately two hours later that we all met again in one of the dining rooms on the upper level. Even though the ship belonged to me, it was so large that I had not seen even half of it by this time. With each day I found myself more impressed with Galetils as a sophisticate and a visionary. Even though my own wealth was many times beyond what his was, his fine taste and his eye for detail in every design were admirable.

The room where we chose to dine was truly exquisite. One waist-high wall framed the circular room that measured approximately 18 meters in diameter. On top of this wall sat a convex bubble dome window of approximately eight meters at its highest point. At both ends of the room, lining up with the length of the ship were gently sloping ramps that descended back down into the lower decks of the ship. Giant fern-like potted palms that emitted a fragrance similar to Earth's balsam and pine were arranged around the perimeter of the room and along the rampways. Several easy chairs were arranged in intimate groupings around the room and turned to face outward so onlookers could peer through the domed window into space. The room itself was lit with down-lighting from fixtures located in coped recesses around the low wall of the room. In the middle of the room was the long oval dining table arranged with six chairs. A narrow, decorative pole extended upward about three meters from the center of the table, which then fountained outward into six gently curving arms, each of which held on its end a beautifully crafted directional light that illuminated each table setting beneath it with a subtle glow.

Piesew was present when everyone arrived. He greeted each guest individually and escorted them to the table. I was seated on one end of the oval and Kala on the other end. Next to me on my right was Admiral Regeny and on my Left Senator Tonclin. Next to the admiral was Captain Stonbersa and beside the senator sat Chanina, who was now wearing a gown of a dignitary cut. I found it hard to keep from staring at her, because the elegant but simple dress was so incongruous with her textured skin. Captain Stonbersa had given instructions to Kerabac to slowly rotate the ship so that the Nibarian planet below would slowly appear to move around the edge of the dome in such a manner that everyone would be able to see it periodically during the meal. Chanina was in total awe and could not stop staring at the view, tugging frequently on her father's arm so she could point out some feature on the planet that she recognized.

While enjoying the first plate, an exquisite dish of small marinated creatures from one of the aquatic worlds in the Federation, Admiral Regeny broached the topic of our visit with the senator.

"Senator Tonclin, our reason for inviting you to dinner this evening is to discuss the matter of delivery of Nibaria's solbidyum and its reactor. We need you to make secure arrangements for the transfer of these items with as few people knowing about it as possible. You will also need to arrange very tight security at the facility where you locate the reactor, as there will be those who will try to steal it from Nibaria."

Senator Tonclin had stopped eating when the admiral mentioned the phrase, *Nibaria's solbidyum.* "How soon would this delivery take place?" he asked with a tone of alarm in his voice.

"It could take place at any time, Senator. If you have a facility and ample security in place, we could deliver it tomorrow. We can give you two weeks to prepare, if you require; however, we would prefer that the transfer take place as quickly as possible for security reasons. No one knows that this shipment is about to take place or that Nibaria and Megelleon will be the first two planets to receive delivery. My own staff is seeing to arrangements for security on Megelleon and a location has already been prepared for the installation."

"Nibaria has a site that was prepared for the reactor over 500 years ago; however, when it appeared that the solbidyum was lost and would not be recovered, the space was used to store sensitive archived material. The area is very secure and well-guarded, but provisions must be made for the archives to be moved into another secure facility. This could take a week, provided there is a quick resolution to the relocation of the archives. But if I may ask, Admiral, do you have enough ships here to guard the delivery of the solbidyum? Please excuse my ignorance, as I do not wish to question the High Command's judgment; however I must look to the safety of my Nibarian people. I would have thought you would need an armada of ships to protect the cargo."

"Senator," the admiral chuckled, "I can assure you that we have all the security and protection we need to make the delivery to you securely here at Nibaria. Right now our enemies aren't expecting us to be able to deliver the solbidyum at all, which is one of the reasons we wish to do so – and as quickly and quietly as possible."

"Secrecy won't be a problem on Nibaria, sir. As you know, very few people from other Federation planets ever visit our surface, because our atmosphere is poisonous to humans. Likewise, few of us ever venture to other worlds. Although we have no problems breathing your air, things do not taste or smell right in your atmospheres, which is disturbing and uncomfortable to us; so we seldom venture beyond our own moon. We have run tests on our citizens and have not found one person on our planet to be a member of the Brotherhood, probably because none of us have ever been in contact with anyone from that organization long enough to be recruited. Our communications off world are generally restricted to commerce and trade, so the risk of information leaking out from Nibaria is negligible."

"That's good to hear, Senator. I was not aware that you had tested your people. It's interesting that none of your citizens were indoctrinated by the Brotherhood. I wonder if that holds true of the other non-human worlds. It would certainly make things simpler for the Federation if it were."

By now we had finished our meal and I noticed that Chanina was getting fidgety and perhaps a little bored.

"Senator, would your daughter like to see the ship?" Kala asked, also having noticed Chanina's restlessness. "I think we can arrange a tour while we discuss some of the details related to the transfer of the solbidyum."

The senator looked at his daughter and she nodded her head with excitement. Tonclin chuckled, which in his case was actually better described as a high-pitched screech. "I believe a tour of the ship would be the second most exciting experience in her entire youth – after meeting you and First Citizen Tibby, of course."

"Let me see if one of the staff is available," said Kala, addressing herself this time to Chanina. It was only a few minutes later that one of Kala's staff arrived and took the rather excited youngster on tour.

With Chanina now out of earshot for the remainder of our sensitive discussions, I decided to take Senator Tonclin into my – or our – confidence. "Admiral, since you have assigned me the task of training the Special Operations squads and developing the new intelligence division, I'm taking the liberty of briefing Senator Tonclin on our current activities. We're going to need support in the Senate sooner or later; and the earlier we bring trusted Senate people into awareness of what's taking place the better."

"Tibby, it's your show. I have complete confidence in your decisions on this issue. I've known the senator a long time and have always found him to be trustworthy."

"So I am to understand then," the senator began, "that there is more afoot then just the solbidyum deliveries?"

"Indeed there is Senator," I said. "As you are no doubt aware, the FOI not only failed to uncover the threat of the Brotherhood; but upon investigation within the organization, it was discovered that the FOI itself has been heavily penetrated with Brotherhood members. While the FOI is actively being purged of the Brotherhood members as we speak, the size of the organization and its distribution of agents over many light years demand that the agency undergo several years of vigorous testing and scrutiny before the subversive presence is eradicated and the agency can again be considered effective and reliable as an investigative organization. In the meantime, the need for an immediately effective investigative body is necessary –

one that consists of known reliable agents who are specially trained to secretly insert themselves into various organizations for the purpose of gathering and filtering data to ascertain dangers and provide intelligence to the Federation military.

"To this extent we recognize the immediate need to form a new organization tentatively called the Federation Security Organization which will serve as a covert investigative and intelligence agency. The FSO will not only be tasked with infiltrating organizations and governments that might harbor aggressive intentions toward the Federation, but also placing themselves in key positions within branches of our own government, such as the FOI, to find and ferret out enemy agents.

Now, having said this – and I am sure you know this better than anyone, Senator Tonclin – putting this before the Senate for approval of funding will take years. Meanwhile, all of our enemies – meaning the Brotherhood and any others yet to be identified – will most certainly receive information about the nature of this project and proposed agency, as it is guaranteed to be the subject of Senate debate for some time before any decisions are made. This means every subversive presence will have time to take countermeasures and secure additional levels of secrecy, which will make our task that much more difficult. To expedite the current efforts I'm personally funding the program until such time that the issue is brought before the Senate and the Federation Legal Review Board. While we have every intention of ensuring that the formation and functions of the FSO are above board and in accordance with the Federation constitution, we also recognize that questions will arise about its legality. Once it's discovered what we've done in creating the FSO, the Senate and FLRB will demand that a full accounting be made for the organization's activities. It is our hope that, by the time the Senate becomes aware of the existence of the FSO, we will have already infiltrated and uncovered Brotherhood cells operating across many branches of the government, including the military. It is also hoped that the FSO will be able to uncover hostile intentions from non-aligned planets that might be planning to intercept the ongoing shipments of solbidyum; and of course, we have every reason to believe such attempts will be made. If we are able to demonstrate a track record of successful reconnaissance that can be used by the Senate when vetting the FSO, the organization will more likely be able to continue their mission without interruption and ultimately facilitate safe delivery of solbidyum shipments to every Federation planet."

"I see," said Senator Tonclin thoughtfully. He sat back in his chair to contemplate the implications of an organization like the FSO that is operating at such a broad scale without initial sanction by the Federation's governing body. "And what is it exactly that you expect from me?"

"First and foremost, we ask that you feign ignorance of what we are doing; secondly, that you assist by providing a minimum of ten loyal natives of Nibaria to be trained as operatives and agents of the FSO and that you keep secret your knowledge of the agents you provide us. Lastly – and this will surely be the most difficult request we make of you – that you provide us with any information you may glean from your duties that indicates any Senate member's awareness of the FSO and its activities."

Senator Tonclin's growing concern was becoming apparent. "Please allow me to paraphrase your request for my own clarification. What you are requesting of me is that I act as an undercover agent within the Senate – the Senate of which I am a sworn member and within which I have avowed to uphold the Federation constitution?"

"In a word, yes, Senator Tonclin, but not in any way that violates your pledge or any Federation law. We don't expect you to lie, but we would ask that you not volunteer information or do anything that would alert the Senate to the existence or actions of the FSO or to your participation in our operations. We fully intend to operate within the laws and regulations of the constitution."

Senator Tonclin made a humming sound and stared at the table for some moments before replying. The admiral and I fully understood the magnitude of our request to the senator and we waited silently while he deliberated the situation. At last he said, "I can certainly see the need for what you say, and in all honesty I can see how taking rapid preemptive action against the Brotherhood and our enemies can thwart their advancement before they have a chance to execute their malevolent plans. However, I do have concerns for the legal rights of our citizens and their private lives."

"Senator, I fully understand and appreciate your apprehensions. On my home planet, Earth, a parallel situation resulted when similar organizations were formed to combat a growing problem with some very dangerous bands of insurgents and, frankly, we were not able to find a clear and easy solution to the controversy. The legality of many methods used by the investigative body created in my homeland have required the scrutiny of the Supreme Court, the equivalent of the FLRB. In order for such an organization to be effective, the FSO will have to walk on the edge of legality at times; but I assure you that we will make every effort to stay within the rules of the Federation's constitution, in spite of the fact that the organization is by nature not able to exercise the transparency expected of other agencies. Ultimately, the plan of action for the FSO consists of direct and conscionable efforts to preserve the freedom and prosperity of all good and moral citizens within the Federation."

The senator sat quietly again before voicing his decision. "Honored First Citizen, if anyone else presented me with this request, I would not hesitate to decline immediately." The usual melodic timbre in Senator Tonclin's voice had been replaced by a more monotone quality that left me unsure of his position on the matter. "However, I know the virtue of what you have done for the Federation thus far and the extent of your sacrifice for the good of the alliance of our peoples; and I understand the urgency and need for this sort of action and the gravity the overall situation. Hence...," Senator Tonclin paused, knowing that his next words carried a commitment that could not be undone, "I will agree."

Beside me I heard a deep exhale come from the admiral. He had been anxiously holding his breath in hopes of the senator's assent.

"I will see what I can do about providing you with ten individuals that would be willing to join your FSO and that I believe will be loyal to and suitable for your needs," the senator added.

It was at this point that Kala's assistant, who was supposed to be conducting the tour with Chanina, burst into the dining room and directed herself immediately to Kala. The absence of Chanina was blatantly obvious.

"Lieutenant Commander," the assistant began nervously. "I fear that Chanina is lost someplace on the ship. I was showing her the waterfall in the starboard atrium and when I turned around she was gone. I have alerted the crew. They are combing the ship and scanning all vid com screens to locate her. I am so sorry," she said, looking back and forth from Kala to the senator as she wrung her hands."

"Can you tell me what you were looking at just before you went into the atrium?" I asked.

"I had just shown her the entertainment lounge in that section."

"By any chance do you happen to have a version of a vid game called *Drizen Ride* among the available diversions in this lounge?" Senator Tonclin asked.

"Why, yes sir, we do. Chanina was most excited when she saw it."

"I fear that she probably ran back there to play that silly game. The child is totally addicted to it. In fact, that was one of my reasons for bringing her on this trip – to get her away from that game for a day or two. Please do not worry; her disappearance is not your fault," the senator said looking at Kala's aide. "If you return to the entertainment lounge, you will probably find her sitting at the game, oblivious to how long she has been there."

Just as the senator finished speaking, one the crew came into the dining room with an obviously embarrassed Chanina in tow.

"Where did you find her?" asked Senator Tonclin calmly, as he cast Chanina a scolding glance.

"Actually, Senator, she showed up at the bridge and advised that she had gotten lost. How she found her way there from the aft entertainment room I will never know. It's a rather complicated path."

The senator stared at his daughter as she replied, "I didn't find my way, father. The little man showed me the way."

"Little man?" asked Captain Stonbersa in a puzzled and concerned tone, "What little man? What did he look like?"

"Well he was shorter than me… and he walked kind of funny, like he was rocking when he walked… and he had a funny back, like he had a pillow under his shirt."

"Chanina! What have you been told about speaking of people's physical appearance?" the senator said in a chastising voice.

"Well he *did* father, and the captain asked what he looked like!" Chanina fumed.

"We have no one on the ship that looks like that – not to my knowledge anyway. Everyone on the ship should be taller than you are, Chanina," said the captain.

"Well, he was shorter than me," Chanina insisted. "I was crying when I couldn't find my way back. Suddenly he was there and asked me what was wrong… and I said I was lost… and he said he would help… and he took me to the bridge."

Captain Stonbersa turned to the crewman who brought Chanina to the dining room and said, "Did you see this individual?"

"No, sir. We were all occupied at our stations when she just sort of appeared on the bridge. None of us saw her arrive and when we *did* notice her, she was alone."

"See if you can find out who this person is!" ordered the captain and then he turned to me.

"This is most strange, Tibby. Just last week one of the crew was checking some circuits in the vacant quarters area on the aft end of the ship and he swore that he saw a little man of a similar description in one of the unused crew mess areas. The crewman reported that this individual simply disappeared and he was unable to find him anywhere in the area. At first we thought he might have seen another crew member and that from his vantage point the person just appeared to be short and deformed; but now we have this corroborating report. I must say, it sounds like we have a stowaway onboard."

The evidence certainly supported the idea of a stowaway. The *NEW ORLEANS* crew was placed on security alert and every crew and service staff member joined Marranalis and the security team to search for this elusive individual, but the search was fruitless. No one was seen in the vacant areas of the ship that shouldn't have been there. At the same time, no one that was questioned admitted to having helped Chanina find her way to the bridge either. Captain Stonbersa was most perplexed by this mystery and ordered all monitors in the ship activated. Many of the security monitors in the unused areas of the ship had been deactivated until this strange turn of events. Even after a diligent review, no one that was not part of the ship's known complement showed on any of these monitors.

The senator and his daughter spent the night on the ship and departed early the next morning. Shortly after, Cantolla announced that she was able to implement some small improvements to the solbidyum reactor unit after reviewing the plans that Lunnie had left behind and the original designs found in the *TRITYTE* archives. The new unit configuration was better suited for planetary power distribution and would allow the tremendous energy created in the reactors to be managed with complete efficiency, which meant power would be generated without leakage or dissipation and without the risk of overload on any element of the existing power grid. She and her team had already constructed two units, which were ready to be put into service.

I never ceased to marvel at the speed with which it was possible to manufacture items in the Federation territories. The Federation technology had produced robotic equipment and machinery capable of manufacturing raw goods into finished products within minutes or hours, where on Earth the same processes would have taken much longer. The solbidyum reactors, for instance, would have taken two weeks or more to manufacture on Earth; whereas the technologically advanced equipment of the Federation required only that the design was uploaded into the computer while the raw materials were supplied to the mechanized factory. After these initial provisions were made, the computer calculated the most efficient way to use the materials and complete the assembly. As one part of the factory cut and formed materials according to a template, another area assembled and installed electronic components. Observing these wondrous machines as they manufactured the solbidyum reactors was almost like watching time-lapse photography.

While the installation of the solbidyum reactor was taking place, I met with the new recruits for the FSO. When dining with Admiral Regeny, Captain Stonbersa and Kala earlier that morning, I was approached by Major Sokaia, who had confronted Marranalis the day before. "Vice Admiral Renwalt," she said snapping to attention before me, "I wish to make an apology for my comments and actions of yesterday. I was totally out of line." Admiral Regeny was seated across the small table from me with his back to the major, and I noted a smirk on his face as the major made her apology.

"I see. Tell me, Major," I began, "were you ordered to give this apology or did you come to this decision on your own?"

I could see the major redden and clearly become distressed by my question as Admiral Regeny raised an eyebrow and looked at me in surprise.

"Ah, actually, both sir," the major stammered. "Admiral Regeny did order me to apologize to both you and Lieutenant Marranalis. I had been off planet when the uprising took place and was unaware of the recent events that culminated in the honorary titles you received. After Admiral Regeny related to me all that had transpired and the valor you demonstrated on behalf of the Federation, I genuinely regretted my comments and actions. I assure you, sir, that I have the highest respect for you and your staff for what you've done and I will not make this mistake again, sir."

"Have you made your apology to Lieutenant Marranalis already?"

"No, sir. I plan to do so as soon as I leave here."

"Well, when you do apologize to Marranalis, tell him I said he is to make you his assistant. This means you will need to receive extra training from him; and though it will be more work for you, I think it will pay off in the long run."

"Yes, sir. Will that be all, sir?"

"Yes, Major. You're dismissed." The major turned briskly and departed, still showing bright crimson on her cheeks.

"Tibby, I'm glad you weren't my senior officer when I was in the ranks," the admiral chuckled. "Major Sokaia is actually one of our best troopers – a real go-getter and a dedicated officer. I like the way you handled her. I think her abilities and aptitude will surprise you as she moves through the training."

"I'm counting on it, Admiral. I just hope that I will be equally surprised with the trainees for the FSO. Speaking of the FSO, I need to get to the conference room to meet with them and begin their first training session, if you will excuse me."

To say that the Federation was clueless when it came to spying would be a lie; but for all their advanced technology they were not very sophisticated about their operations. Their methods were crude and awkward at best; and anyone with an ounce of paranoia would be quick to spot a Federation agent investigating or spying on them. The group that had been selected for the first candidates as FSO officers consisted of mostly humans and only about a dozen non-human species. One of the non-human recruits in particular caught my attention; he was a chameleon, of sorts, who could mimic the textures, patterns and colors of his surroundings on his skin in much the same way that some of Earth's aquatic cephalopods did. I could see where this individual might be an immense benefit on spy missions. Another non-human species was nocturnal and had to wear dark goggles during his training, as light levels for humans were painfully bright for him. Once again, I could see strong potential for him as an agent.

Nearly 40% of the group was female. I recognized my own surprise at this high ratio as a byproduct of the male chauvinism my culture on Earth, an attitude that I thought myself to be above. While I have always believed in equality among men and women, believing that anyone who can perform to requirements (regardless of gender) should be allowed to do so for equal compensation, I was nevertheless surprised to find so many qualified females among the recruits. I hadn't given it any thought with the Special Ops training group, as I knew that over a third of the Federation troopers were females; but for some reason it never dawned on me that they would also be included in the FSO recruits.

After explaining what would be expected of them as agents, I gave the recruits an assignment to establish their individual aptitudes for creativity and to demonstrate how they would need to think as spies. They were assigned to bug the conversations in any one of three areas of the ship and, in doing so, garner some piece of confidential or secret information. These areas included the bridge, the offices of the High Command and the officer's dining room. They were told that sweeps would be made of these spaces to locate bugging devices; anyone whose bug was located would be considered a failure and any information they retrieved would be deemed invalid. They were given permission to work in teams of no larger than five or they could work alone. They had two days to accomplish their task.

The troopers that were being trained for the Special Ops units required a somewhat different approach; these troopers required skills focused more on tactical stealth and intense physical engagement. With the enhancement of the learning headbands that was achieved by Cantolla and her team, martial arts knowledge and physical training was being given to all troops found to be loyal to the Federation. Since the enhancements included a version of the loyalty and truth tests, unsuitable candidates could be filtered out before imparting the martial arts skills. Troopers had no idea that they were being examined for loyalty via the headband device and the covert assessment proved to be especially effective in identifying those who had loyalty to and membership in the Brotherhood. These troopers were declared unfit and were relieved from duty in the Federation military, as long as it was found that they had not played a part in the recent rebellion. If the tests revealed that the troopers *had* been involved in the rebellion, they were brought up on charges of treason and mutiny.

The learning headband training had a double-edged effect in strengthening the Federation forces. Those who had not participated in the rebellion, but who had been a part of the Brotherhood, would be watched for future activities within the organization and, in the case of some individuals, their past membership in the Brotherhood also presented an opportunity for infiltration as spies. As the interrogations of these Brotherhood members progressed, it became clear that not all of them had known or realized exactly what the Brotherhood organization was really about; and once they found out, they had deserted its ranks. If they could be recruited into the FSO, these individuals could be trained as operatives. Once trained, they could solicit the Brotherhood to restore their membership, stating as a cover story that they had been dismissed from the military because they had failed the loyalty test.

Since all of the troopers in FSO training had already completed the loyalty tests and martial arts instruction via the learning device, I was not surprised when I entered the training area to see them engaged in fast paced martial arts combat under the direction of Marranalis. I noted that both Marranalis and Major Sokaia were actively supervising and advising the combats. Many of the sessions lasted only a few minutes before one opponent triumphed over the other. A few of the more closely matched adversaries sparred longer before one triumphed. When they finished, the losers were told that they would have extra duties for the evening. Marranalis was about to dismiss them for the day when I stepped forward. "Has Major Sokaia sparred with anyone today?" I inquired loudly enough for all the troopers in the group to hear.

"Ah… no, sir," replied Marranalis. "I made her my assistant, per your orders. She has been assisting me with instruction of the others."

"I see. And what about you, have you engaged in any combat practice today?"

"I demonstrated some techniques," Marranalis said tentatively.

"Not good enough. I expect you and the major to both engage in combat as well. So if you please, I wish to see the two of you engage in combat now."

I could see that Marranalis didn't like the idea. Conversely, the major was enthusiastic for the opportunity to demonstrate her superiority over Marranalis.

I finished my orders with, "Oh yes, and the loser joins with the rest of the defeated adversaries in extra duty."

Marranalis gave me a look that said, "Why are you doing this to me?" as he squared off with Sokaia.

Sokaia didn't waste any time. She attacked quickly and nearly caught Marranalis off guard; but all the practice and additional training that he had received over the past months gave him an edge in speed and reaction. Instead of having to plan or think about the techniques, his responses came instinctively. Sokaia attacked repeatedly and, before long, Marranalis realized that he had a distinct advantage over the major. He quickly relaxed into a more automatic defensive mode and was soon throwing Sokaia effortlessly, blocking her moves and using her attack movements to his advantage.

After toying with her a few moments, it became obvious to all that Sokaia was no match for Marranalis. Finally, he threw Sokaia and landed her in a position where he was poised to deliver what would have been a fatal blow; and the contest was over. Sokaia finished in a breathless sweat, but Marranalis showed no signs of stress.

As Marranalis helped Sokaia back to her feet, I said to the recruits, "I wanted you all to see that, while the learning bands can give you the intellectual understanding and knowledge of martial arts, you still need to practice to make these moves a natural action for you. Even at this basic level the knowledge will benefit you greatly over one who knows nothing of these techniques. However, the more you practice and spar, the more natural these moves will become and the more efficient you'll be able to execute your skills in real combat. You want these moves to become so automatic that they're as natural as walking or breathing – like a reflex. To insure that you are better, faster and stronger at these moves than any possible opponent, you will have to train harder and longer than standard troopers. You must advance further, endure more and never *ever* give up."

My lecture was interrupted by a communication from Captain Stonbersa via my wrist com. When I answered, the captain announced, "Tibby, we've had another incident with our mysterious passenger. This time we managed to capture him on the vid."

"I'll be right there, Captain," I replied, while motioning to Marranalis to come with me. "Major Sokaia, you're in charge of dismissing the troops until tomorrow."

When Marranalis and I arrived at the bridge, the captain had the vid images displayed on the screen. "He's exactly as they described him – short, hump on his back, and a sort of wobble in his walk. Look... you can see him activating the food dispenser in the aft quarters area. We set up a hidden surveillance camera and got a clip of him. I sent crew members to capture him; but when they arrived, he had again disappeared without a trace."

At one point the elusive figure turned to face the camera. The captain froze the image so we could get a closer look at him. My first thought was that I was looking at a hunchbacked munchkin from the Wizard of OZ, one of Earth's classic fictional vid stories that featured a race of tiny people who lived under the threat of a... well, an evil person. There were some differences between the figure on the screen and the munchkins in the story. His eyes were larger and closer together and his irises were yellow. His skin appeared to have a slight yellowish tint, as well. His face was more triangular and his nose more pointed; and he had long black hair that was tied back in a ponytail. While that image sounds somewhat sinister, it actually wasn't at all. In fact, he looked curiously friendly. He also had rather large ears that pivoted in different directions to catch sounds.

"Anyone know who or what he is?" asked Captain Stonbersa.

"I haven't a clue," Marranalis said. "I've seen lots of life forms during my time in the military, but none like that."

While we talked, Stonbersa activated the motion on the image again. We noticed that he had very small hands. Also, he chewed his food rapidly in small bites that reminded me of Earth creatures called squirrels and chipmunks.

Kerabac said, "I've tried running his image against all the species in the computer database; nothing matches. I have no idea where he's from."

Suddenly, the image on the screen froze its ears attentively in one direction and then quickly fled from the camera and around a corner just as crew members came into view. Kerabac continued, "The oddest part is that he disappeared into a long corridor that's basically a dead end. There is one outlet that loops back to tie into the central corridor; but we have another camera there that didn't show him coming out, so he's got to be back there somewhere."

"So far there is no evidence of him doing any harm to anything or anyone on the ship," added the captain. "If he's up to something, he hasn't showed any signs of attempting anything destructive. Repeated attempts by the crew to locate and capture him have been unsuccessful."

I turned to Marranalis. "You're in charge of my security operations, Marranalis. Locate and catch him, but I don't want him hurt. No one is to take any forceful actions against him, unless it's in self-defense, understood?"

"Understood," he repeated. "I'll get right on it."

Right after Senator Tonclin and his daughter left the ship Captain Stonbersa gave orders for the *NEW ORLEANS* to return to Megelleon to deliver the reactor and solbidyum. Up until this point we had not opened the real solbidyum container. It remained hidden within a compartment behind a wall on the *NEW ORLEANS*, while a fake container constructed by Lunnie had been turned over to the rebels on the *DUSTEN* during the recent conflict. Instead of holding the solbidyum, the fake container hid seven troopers and me inside so that we could get aboard the *DUSTEN* to reclaim the ship and free the hostages. Now that we were ready to commence delivery of the solbidyum and the reactors we needed to gain access to the real solbidyum container once more.

Only the admiral and a few highly placed individuals in the Federation had access to code that opened the container without activating the lethal booby traps that protected its contents. For the first time since I met the admiral I actually saw him sweat. His hands trembled slightly as he punched the codes into the keypad on the container. I don't think any of us had a clue what to expect, since it had been over 500 years since the container was sealed. I suppose we all anticipated the unlocked container to open at the top like a jar, leaving us to stare into a large container full of something that resembled sand. Instead, we heard a slight hum and a click before a small door opened about waist high below the key pad. The container apparently worked like a dispenser. In this small space was a capsule about the size and shape of a typical medicine pill used on Earth.

The capsule was clear and inside was a single sparkling grain of quartz-like sand. An astronomical number on the small digital display screen by the key pad decreased by one and below it in a new row appeared a value of one.

The admiral sighed in relief and picked up the small capsule between his two fingers, peering into it at the tiny crystal. "It looks like it dispenses just one grain of solbidyum at a time. That certainly simplifies things."

He nodded to one of his staff who stepped forward with a small metal case lined with foam padding. The admiral carefully placed the capsule in the center of the case and closed the lid. He then entered a code into the keypad on the box after which the aide and four armed troopers left the area with the case and boarded the shuttle that was to take them to the reactor location on Megelleon. Since no one outside a handful of people aboard the *NEW ORLEANS* knew anything about the delivery of the solbidyum and since we were certain of the loyalty of the personnel involved in the transport, we felt relatively secure in the delivery.

Our precautions and efforts were rewarded a few hours later when a coded message arrived for the admiral saying that the reactor had been installed and commissioned and that the system was now successfully distributing power to the planet. A cheer erupted in the High Command conference room when the admiral made the announcement.

It had been decided that public statements and press releases would be withheld until the system was also operational on Nibaria, in order to demonstrate to citizens on other planets that the solbidyum was not being hoarded and that deliveries were underway. By the time word reached most planets, subsequent deliveries would already be complete, resulting in a chain of reports that additional power plants were also online. There were bound to be planets that felt they should have received their shipment as a priority; but by the time they would be prepared to issue a formal complaint, their deliveries should arrive – at least that was our theory.

Megelleon's reactor site was actually located under the middle of the capital city in an area which had once been part of a planned underground transit system that was abandoned after a fault zone discovered in the path of the system brought an end to the project. The area where the reactor was located was solid and remote from the actual fault zone by many miles, so it was deemed safe and structurally sound. The site was surrounded by solid rock and accessible by only one tunnel. Sensors were installed in the surrounding rock that would detect any attempts to excavate other passageways long before reaching the reactor chamber.

The reactor itself was hauled on an open flatbed transport in a common crate marked as *Ventilation Fans* and the grain of solbidyum was concealed in a small container made to look like a standard bolt, which was carried inside a worker's toolbox. By the middle of the second day the reactor was installed and operating.

Our second day in orbit around Megelleon was the day that the FSO trainees were due to turn in their spying results for evaluation. Nearly all the individuals and teams were disqualified when their spy bugs were detected. Three teams and two individuals managed to avoid detection; but of those three only two actually obtained any information. I was a bit surprised that our chameleon candidate had failed; in fact, he was one of the first to be detected. Of the two remaining candidates the first managed to glean some information from the admiral's staff headquarters on the ship that certainly would have been useful if it had been information gained from reconnaissance of a hostile source. Even so, it was nothing in comparison to what the remaining candidate collected. What he revealed was the entire conversation that the admiral and I had with Senator Tonclin over dinner regarding the delivery of the solbidyum, as well every other conversation that took place in the dining area that evening. A complete sweep had been made of the dining room before, during, and after the meeting while the senator was present and nothing was found; so we all were quite eager to know how he had achieved this feat.

The trainee's name was Geston. He was a rather ordinary looking individual, the kind of ordinary that was perfect for spying.

"So, Geston, how did you manage to get this information without being detected?" I asked.

"Well, sir, I knew that any sweeps would reveal electronic devices in the room, so I decided to use an optical system instead.   I placed a fiber optic lead through a wall and aimed it at a light fixture on the far side of the room.   All sounds trigger minute changes in the surrounding light patterns as the sound waves pass through the room.   That light fluctuation is then measured and delivered via the fiber optics to a computer that converts those modulations back into sound and records them.

"An electronic sensor will not pick up a fiber optic lead," he said with a smile, "and the computer is too far removed from the room for the sensors to detect it."

"Very ingenious," I replied. I recalled seeing a demonstration years ago where a classmate achieved something similar by way of a flashlight and a photocell connected to a device he had built for a science project. "This is precisely the sort of ingenuity you will all need to have when you are on assignments.   Stealth is of the utmost importance.   Once a spying device is uncovered, your targets will be on guard and looking for you.   As long as they're unaware that they're under surveillance, achieving your objective safely will be a hundred times easier.   I want all of you to get with Geston and learn exactly what he did to successfully install and collect this information; and I expect each of you to build a working model of this device within the next two weeks.   In the meantime, we will be going to the surface for some survival training in the forest on my estate.   Are there any questions?"

"Yes, sir, I have a question," replied one of the recruits.   "What sort of supplies and gear shall we take with us?"

I grinned and replied, "Nothing. *Not one damn thing.* You will all be dropped off – naked – in different locations about the estate. You will take nothing with you. Your assignment is to get to the lodge at the far end of the estate within three days without detection. You'll obtain food and shelter from your natural surroundings by your own resourcefulness. You are not – I repeat – you are *not* permitted to team up with others and are to avoid all such contact. Anyone who doesn't make it to the lodge in three days and has to be retrieved in the wilderness will be washed out of the program. When you're released at the drop-off point, you'll be given information as to your location on the estate. In the meantime, it's up to you to obtain details regarding the layout of the estate, including locations of all relevant landmarks, structures and environmental factors that will influence your movements. Be at the hangar area in two hours for deployment to the surface. If there are no other questions, you're dismissed."

The look of shock on the faces of these recruits would have been amusing, had it not been for the seriousness of the jobs they were expected to perform in the future. I wondered how many of them would opt out by deliberately not showing up at the lodge on time.

After I left FSO training, I sought out Marranalis to check on his progress regarding our stowaway. I called him on my wrist com and he gave me his position within the vacant accommodations area. When I arrived, I found him staring dumbly at the wall, completely unaware of my presence.

"Is this some new investigative method?" I inquired.

"Oh… sorry, Tibby. I'm just puzzled, that's all.
I figured that, if our stowaway was using the food
dispenser in this section of the ship, he might likewise be
using one of the clothing replicators and cleaning units.
I did a computer search of the units installed in this area
of the ship. Since it's supposed to be unoccupied, none
of them should be in use; but the computer identified one
unit that is being used almost daily back here…meaning
right here," he said emphatically while gesturing around
him in the featureless end of a corridor. "I just can't find
it. Not only that, but there is supposed to be a food
dispenser near it. The ship's computer shows it as being
inoperative due to some malfunction, which is no doubt
why our stowaway is using the one at the other end of
the corridor. The thing is… I can't find either of the
dispensers. According to the floor plans and every
monitoring system for this accommodations section they
should be right here," he said as he stared again at the
blank wall.

"Interesting," I said. "Does the computer tell
you when and how long a dispenser has been in use and
the frequency of use?" I asked.

"Ah, yeah I think so. Let me look," he said,
lifting his vid tablet to input some commands.
"According to the records, they've both been in use for
nearly five months. The food dispenser has been out of
commission only for the past two weeks though."

"If that's true, it may mean our guest was
residing on this ship before I bought it and that he's been
hiding all this time. He would have been onboard here
when Galetils was still alive. I wonder if Galetils knew
about this person's presence on the ship."

"It's possible, I suppose; but why would he be hiding, unless he's a criminal or a fugitive of some sort? Maybe Galetils was trying to help him elude capture for some reason."

"I don't think so. If he were a fugitive, the computer would have recognized his image. But as it is, the computer can't even identify his race. So I don't think he's a criminal – at least not one wanted by the Federation."

"Well I'm open to suggestions," said Marranalis.

"Put your Special Ops unit on it. Make it an assignment for them to locate and capture him. Just remember – he is not to be harmed in any way."

"Right! Say, while you're here, I heard you're sending the FSO bunch to the estate on a survival exercise. Do you mind if I do that with my recruits? They also need that kind of training."

"I agree, but it's going to have to wait. We're headed back to Nibaria as soon as the FSO recruits are dropped off so we can complete the solbidyum and reactor delivery. I'm hoping that Tonclin will have some recruits ready from his planet by the time we arrive. Once we're done at Nibaria, we'll return here only briefly before heading out to deliver the next reactor; so your wilderness training will be delayed a bit, I'm afraid. If we had a competent instructor to leave with them, I would agree; but I need you with me and you're the only one I trust to conduct their training at the moment.

"By the way, find the bomb and explosive experts in your bunch and have them start training every one of your recruits. They'll all need to have those skill sets, given the Brotherhood has already demonstrated a

propensity for favoring explosive devices. Also, I want
them to be able to swim the entire length of the main
pool underwater in both directions without surfacing.
It's not going to be easy and it may take a long time
before they can do it, but I want it done. Push them on
it. Oh, and adjust the climbing wall, it's too easy."

Marranalis looked at me with a crooked grin and
shook his head, "Tibby, one thing is certain – when
you're done we'll have the toughest bunch of troopers in
the Federation. Either that or they'll all be dead."

I felt like I hadn't seen Kala in days, though in
truth it was just the previous night that we had been
together. It seemed that time crawled when our duties
kept us apart. Most of the time we worked together; but
on days like this one she needed to concentrate on
instructing her staff and sitting through updates and
briefings on events, while I attended to my obligations
related to training and other Federation matters.

I contacted Kala to see if she was available for
lunch and was glad when she said yes. We met a few
minutes later in an intimate corner of one of the atriums
by a pool and waterfall. A small table had been set up
near the water in advance and Piesew was present to see
to our dining needs.

Food in the Federation was, for the most part,
quite delicious, though in my experience thus far it often
lacked the variety of textures that I was accustomed to
experiencing in foods on Earth. Food replicators did a
superior job of creating the flavors of many dishes, but it
didn't seem to be able to duplicate the textures of things
like fresh vegetables and certain grains and meats. On
this particular day I was craving a good old-fashioned
bacon, lettuce and tomato sandwich on toast. I was

afraid of what I was actually going to get if I asked, but I thought I would give it a try anyway. I did my very best to describe bacon to Piesew. The tomato was not any easier and, while I could describe lettuce as a leafy vegetable, I couldn't define the taste. Describing the textures was even more challenging and, in Piesew's defense, he showed remarkable patience with my request. Kala made a few suggestions and comments to Piesew and he nodded his head. Describing mayonnaise was even more interesting. Fortunately, my grandmother made her own when I was a kid, so I knew the recipe; but the eggs that might be used in the process here was the wildcard.

What Piesew brought me was close – I have to admit that much – but whatever the synthesizer spit out as a tomato looked quite artificial and was not at all moist like a tomato. The bacon came very close to tasting like real bacon, but it lacked the greasy quality that makes bacon so appealing. The lettuce, the one item I couldn't figure out how to describe, was spot on. Piesew told me it was some plant he'd picked from the foliage in the atrium. The mayonnaise was perfect. The toast tasted more like rye bread than wheat, which was okay by me. I know all these terms mean very little to anyone who lacks my point of reference; it suffices to say that, while it wasn't the best BLT I'd ever had, it did satisfy my hunger for one.

I was pleasantly surprised when Piesew brought me a cold glass of afex, as I had not requested it; but it was the right choice. It was obvious that he had talked to Piebar. When she saw the afex, Kala smiled and said to Piesew, "You know, Piesew, I think I would like an afex also." Piesew nodded and retreated, returning almost immediately with a cold glass for Kala.

"You're quite the topic of discussion with the troopers in this sector of the Federation at the moment," Kala began. "Many of those who went out chasing after that dummy transmitter you launched as a decoy signature for the *TRITYTE* are now starting to trickle back to base. They're being briefed on the events that transpired in their absence. Most of them are pretty good-natured about it. They're laughing at how you tricked the Bunemnites and they're in awe of the tactics you employed to recapture the *DUSTEN*.

"There are also a few who are not so happy with you, as they were sure they were going to achieve great wealth and fortune when they found the *TRITYTE*. It's estimated that there are nearly a hundred ships from both the Federation and the Bunem System still out there searching that have yet to learn it was a decoy."

I had to chuckle. "I would hope at some point they give up. Captain Maxette told me that he hadn't targeted any specific end destination for the decoy; so it will likely just keep going right out of the galaxy all together. How long before you think the last pursuers give up?"

"When Roiax stole the *TRITYE* and everyone was out looking for him, there were people who spent their entire lives searching. It's possible that some of the searchers now *won't* give up and may never come back," Kala said.

I was a bit saddened by the thought that my idea to use a decoy could send some people on a wild hunt that would never end because there was nothing there to begin with. Still, it was a good plan that prevented a war between the Bunemnites and the Federation.

"Kala, do you regret me coming here with the *TRITYTE?*"

"What?!" said Kala with surprise.

"I mean, before I showed up, your life was stable and you had a less demanding routine. Since I arrived, you've been thrown from one action scene into another – each becoming more stressful." I had difficulty voicing the rest of my thoughts without choking back some tears. "If I hadn't shown up, Lunnie and Captain Maxette would still be alive, as would thousands of others." Kala reached across the table and took my hand.

"Tibby, you coming here has been the greatest experience of my life. Before you came, I lived a monotonous and repetitive life. I was bored and frustrated and I believed that my life and career were for nothing. Since you came along, I feel – no, I *know* – that I am a part of something important, something meaningful that will become part of history. Yes, I do regret losing Lunnie and Captain Maxette; but those losses were not your fault. *With great success and rewards come great sacrifices*, my mother used to say. But by far the best thing of all was meeting you and having you in my life. Lunnie saw that; and I know that if she were here, she would tell me it was worth the price. I never knew what real love was like until you came into my life; so no, I don't regret that you found your way to the Federation by accident or by any other means." Kala's eyes glistened with tears and her chin began to quiver. "Do you miss Earth? Do you want to go back?"

"I can't say that I miss Earth exactly. I really had no family or relatives left there; and by the time I got out of the Navy, most of my friends from school had all drifted off and gotten married or had new lives elsewhere. I had a few friends in the Navy during my tour of duty, but I wasn't really that close to them. I guess what I miss are some of the things from Earth, like my favorite foods. On Earth we didn't have food simulators and dispensers like you do here. Flavors and textures were more diverse and exotic. I miss the foods that were grown organically and harvested. I miss some of the entertainment of Earth as well. And I haven't had any real time to spend on a planet yet. I mean, I haven't been able to get out and have a real feel for any place. The most significant outdoor experience I've had to date was the walk to the valley where we held the cremation of the *DUSTEN* crew and Lunnie and Maxette, and that wasn't really what I'd call an outing."

"Hmm, I hadn't really thought about that, but you're right. We need to remedy that situation. Perhaps we can sneak down to the surface of one of the next planets we visit so you can experience some of these new worlds. As for food, you can still get organic foods, there are many people on the planets that eat nothing but organic foods and many grow their own in greenhouses, much like the ones you saw on Megelleon. Meats and fish are more culturally driven, so some planets are almost entirely carnivorous while others adhere to strictly vegetarian diets or synthetic foods. Ships generally rely on synthesizers, because they don't need to have as much space for food storage and preparation and because everything gets recycled. But if you want, you can instruct Piesew to stock up on organic foods and meats. I don't know if there is an organic chef onboard as part of the current service crew, but I'd almost bet Piesew has seen to it that we have at least one − or probably a half dozen. Why don't you get with him and describe the types of foods you like? You might be surprised what he comes up with."

Just as Kala finished, Piesew returned with some sort of dessert dish reminiscent of an Earth dish called *strawberry shortcake and whipped cream*. He called it *Norgein Delight*; and whatever was, it turned out to be delicious. "Piesew, Kala was telling me that it is possible for you to obtain organic foods and have them stored on the ship and that we can have a chef prepare them for us at times. She indicated that you may already have an organic chef on staff. Is that correct?"

"Indeed, First Citizen Renwalt." Piesew insisted on formality at all times, saying it would be inappropriate for a house majordomo to address anyone with familiarity. "In fact, one of the best chefs on the ship is a member of your personal staff."

"What? Who?" I asked trying to imagine who of the handful of my staff it might be.

"Kerabac," said Piesew. "He has even set up his own personal garden in the atrium attached to his quarters, which he maintains himself. When we returned to Megelleon from Nibaria, he ordered a small personal stock of meats and other organics, as well."

"Well I'll be...! I never would have guessed Kerabac to be a gourmet'" I exclaimed.

"Kerabac is quite accomplished in many areas," Piesew continued. "He is an excellent musician as well. He plays several instruments and has a wonderful singing voice."

"How do you know this?" I asked curiously.

"Why, he performs regularly for us in the crew entertainment lounge," Piesew said with a bit of surprise.

"We have an entertainment lounge?" I asked dumbfounded.

"Why, of course, sir. You were not aware of it? You must visit the lounge, sir. It's great fun for everyone onboard. There is music and dancing every night; and many of your crew demonstrate their talents in performances of songs and acts. It is really quite engaging."

I looked at Kala in amazement. She said, "I never thought to mention it to you; I assumed you knew. We've both been so busy that neither of us has really had time for entertainment."

"Well, we will tonight," I said. "I'll be damned if you and I are going to spend all our time working."

Kala grinned, "I look forward to it. Maybe you can teach me a few more Earth dance steps."

When we delivered the *TRITYTE* to Megelleon from the *DUSTEN*, Lunnie enticed Kala and me to dance together. I count those few minutes among my favorite memories still today. When I was growing up, my mother was a part time dance instructor. She taught me all the popular dances of the day; and ever since then dancing has been one of my favorite diversions. Kala and I danced only that one time; we hadn't really had an opportunity to dance again since then, mostly because my injuries took time to heal and the pace of work hadn't relented. So I, too, was looking forward to the opportunity to dance with Kala again.

"My dear, it will be my pleasure." I answered, just as my wrist communicator started to buzz. It was Lieutenant Commander Wabussie, an aide to the admiral, asking me if I could meet with the admiral for a brief discussion.

I arrived at the admiral's office a few minutes later. This was my first visit to the admiral's office. I don't know when he had the furnishings brought aboard or when the offices were decorated, but they were lavish to say the least. A dark green carpet covered the floor and behind his desk was a full wall vid screen displaying a super high-definition 3D view of one of the more spectacular nebulas in the system. The remaining walls of his office were paneled with rich wood and decorated with various portraits of figures in military uniforms that were either heroes, relatives, or prominent figures in Federation history – I have no idea which. On the front of his desk was a plate-sized emblem of the Federation. Two leather easy chairs faced the desk. When I entered his office he was standing with his hands behind his back facing the vid screen. He heard Lieutenant Commander Wabussie and I enter the room and he turned around to greet us.

"Ah, Tibby, I didn't expect you so quickly. Please sit down." He indicated a chair in front of his desk.

"Tibby, we received some bad news just a few minutes ago. When news of the mutiny on the *DUSTEN* reached Aburn, members of the Brotherhood in the crew of the *PURFIRE* attempted a rebellion there as well. Fortunately they were not successful. In the same message pod we managed to communicate to the captain details of developments here. He had already begun testing his crew for loyalty to the Federation, starting with the bridge crew. By the time the mutineers organized their attempt to take the ship, the captain had already sealed the bridge and defended its perimeter with a handful of loyal troopers. Two days later, when the second message pod arrived with news of the recovery of the *DUSTEN* and the fall of the mutineers, including all the news vids, he broadcast the newscasts over all the ships vid screens. The mutineers surrendered immediately thereafter. Fortunately, there were only a small number of casualties; but I fear this is just the beginning. We're going to see more of this as word spreads out from the capital. More ships will experience mutinies and some may actually fall to the Brotherhood. There's no telling how many people may die."

"That is *not* good news," I said. "We really need to find some way to implement a faster and more direct means of communication than GW message pods. Once you get beyond the range of a solar system, the time lag for standard transmission is way too long; and the GW pods are only a little better. It's just not good enough."

"I agree, Tibby. Our scientists have been working on it for years, but to no avail."

"I remember seeing a vid documentary on Earth about a branch of science called *quantum mechanics*. The earth scientists discovered something unique about particle behavior – and I don't know enough to speak intelligently about it – but it had to do with something called sympathetic particles. If one particle is induced to vibrate or oscillate, its sympathetic partner would duplicate the behavior at that exact same instance, no matter where it was in the universe. I wonder if such technology could be adapted to create an instantaneous communication system."

"I'm no scientist, Tibby. Those things are way beyond me and I don't know if our scientists have knowledge of this quality mechanics theory."

"Um, that's *quantum* mechanics, sir," I interjected.

"Ah, yeah right, *quantum* mechanics… or whatever," the admiral stammered. "But you may want to bring it up with someone more in tune with things like that. Maybe that Cantolla woman you have on your staff that did such a great job with the learning devices could investigate."

"I'll discuss it with her," I said. "I've assigned two projects to her and her team so far. We'll see what we can discover."

"Tibby, I hate to keep dumping things on you, but we also need some new ships – something about the size of the *NIGHTBRIDGE*; but we need the design to include more firepower and a working RMFF; and they need to be super fast. If we had a small fleet of those with, say, about 300 onboard, mostly your Special Operations troopers – Damn there I go again, wanting you to pull new technology out of your pocket like magic to solve my problems!" the admiral exclaimed.

"By the way," he continued, "I've been mulling over your idea about using the GW pods to deliver solbidyum and reactors to some of the planets where we are relatively sure of secure delivery. I think we will try to implement that idea. My staff is working on the profiling and selection of individuals we believe loyal to the Federation to serve as targets for the message pods. If we can get a few more planetary reactors in service and make an announcement to that effect, I think our progress will reduce the Brotherhood membership and gain us some time. But as to the real reason I brought you here, the recent attempt at mutiny on the *PURFIRE* has prompted me to want our next delivery target to be

Aburn. It's about a ten day trip from here. The delivery and installation period will give me an opportunity to meet with Captain Crafter and the *PURFIRE* crew. I think my personal appearance will help to solidify confidence in the Federation's perseverance; and I believe it will send a message to other ships where Brotherhood members may be thinking of planning a mutiny."

"Aburn it is, then, Admiral. As soon as we have successfully transferred the solbidyum reactor to the surface of Nibaria and received their candidates for the FSO, we can get underway to Aburn. I'll advise Captain Stonbersa. With any luck we can be underway sometime tomorrow."

After leaving Admiral Regeny's office I made my way to my personal gym. My recovery from the knife wounds I received at the hands of Lexmal had healed over, but I needed to exercise to regain my former strength and agility. I started out with a leisurely swim, gradually building speed until I was racing from one end of the pool to the other. After that I went through a martial arts routine and finished with some strength training on various pieces of equipment in the gym. By the time I was done my entire body tingled with fatigue. Kala was already at our quarters when I arrived. I asked her what she thought I should wear for our evening at the entertainment lounge.

"Why don't you wear one of those shirts that you had Piebar make up for you?" she offered. "You look rather handsome in that style; and I think when others see it, they will want some for themselves."

After showering I looked through my closet and picked a gray shirt made of a fabric that felt like a cross between silk and velvet and a pair of slightly darker gray slacks. I've never been one for light or bright colors and I prefer rather plain fabrics without patterns or elaborate weaves. Before long I was dressed and ready to go to the lounge.

Kala had decided not to wear her usual military uniform, opting instead for a lovely form-fitting, knee-length dress in a deep tangerine color. She looked absolutely stunning; and my pulse quickened when she walked into the room.

When we reached the lounge, I was surprised at the enormity of the room. I expected a small cozy area that maybe housed 120 people at most; but this room was five times that size. There were many similar features to some of the night clubs of Earth. A raised stage was positioned in the center of one wall. Tables surrounded an already busy dance floor. Opposite the stage was a bar with an honest-to-goodness bartender who, oddly enough, retrieved the drinks from a dispenser instead of mixing them by hand. Glowing bands of colored lights alternated in the walls and thousands of needle-thin beams of light shot around the room from the ceiling, but the lights never seemed to hit anyone on the face. I mentioned this to Kala and she explained that the computer used to control the lights was programmed with a sort of facial recognition so the lights would not be directed toward anyone's eyes, as the beams were intense enough to cause temporary blindness.

Although some of the people in the lounge were still in uniform, the vast majority wore civilian clothing. Since my arrival in the Federation, I hadn't had the opportunity to meet or see may people outside of the military or government; so I was a bit surprised to see some of the fashions. Actually, *fashion* is probably not the right word, as that would imply prevailing styles. These were more like costumes.

"Is this a costume party?" I asked Kala.

"A what?" she asked.

"Costume party… you know, where people dress according to a theme that represents a particular period, certain historical figures, story characters or something similar," I said as I gaped around the room.

"I've never heard of such a thing," said Kala as she looked at me in amazement. "None of these people are in costumes. This is their normal civilian clothing." As she spoke, a man in a purple velvety suit with a fluffy lace collar passed in front of us. His garb reminded me of a popular singer back on Earth that dressed in purple velvet outfits. With him was a woman wearing a dress that fully exposed her left breast. My momentary shock was followed by the realization that I was still not totally over my taboos of Earth. Nudity was a part of life the Federation. The citizens simply accepted it without any thought; and this same attitude extended into the clothing they wore.

In reality the taboos associated with nudity had not always existed on Earth either. In several historical periods and cultures attitudes and fashions similar to what I was seeing in the lounge had been common. The Minoans, Romans and Egyptians all achieved quite advanced cultures and technologies for their times; and nudity or partial nudity was a quite common feature of clothing styles in all levels of society. In a country called Japan multiple families gathered at community bath houses to bathe nude; and in Europe women wore dresses during one period that left their breasts exposed.

There were also what most of Earth's society like to think of as 'primitive' tribes that survived into present times. These people wore little or no clothing; and outside of ceremonial garb or items worn by royalty or shamans of the tribe, wearing clothing was considered superfluous and pointless. Regardless of the truths or realities of the issue, nudity was a non-issue throughout most of the Federation planets. Kala did tell me once in the past that there were a few worlds within the alliance that held strong to their own cultural perspectives or religions that included bans on nudity in varying degrees, but they tended to be few and far between.

The first time I heard Federation music was on the *TRITYTE*, when Kala and I found Lunnie and Reidecor dancing to music reminiscent of Earth's disco music. At the time I more or less assumed that it was the music of the day; however, as we entered the lounge on the *NEW ORLEANS*, the music I heard was more like tango and milonga rhythms. Without realizing it I had begun to move to the music.

"Ah, so you have dance steps for this music, as well," Kala said to me. "Want to teach me a few?"

When teaching both martial arts and dancing to Kala in recent months, I discovered that she needed to be shown a step or movement only once before it became a permanent and easily recalled skill. In just a few minutes we were doing a tango as finely and smoothly as I had ever danced with any partner. We kept our eyes glued on each other as the rhythm carried us; and when the music came to an abrupt end, we were shocked to hear cheering and applause all around the dance floor. Everyone had stopped dancing to watch us. Within seconds we were surrounded by people wanting to learn this "new" dance. Unfortunately, few of them were as fast as Kala at learning the steps.

After a few more tangos the music stopped. The lounge's presiding host announced that we would be entertained by Kerabac while we caught a breath and refreshed ourselves with some beverages. It was obvious that Kerabac was quite popular, as I could barely hear the remainder of the introduction over the huge applause and roar from the audience. A device stood in the middle of the stage that looked a little like a semi-circular table top mounted on a pedestal with a mushroomed base. Kerabac emerged in a spotlight and walked to center stage as the applause grew even louder. He wore an ivory short-sleeved shirt with a Nehru-like collar that contrasted sharply with his very dark skin. He took a seat at the small stool and placed his hands on the semi-circle and it immediately became clear that this was some kind of keyboard that could mimic almost any sound.

The audience immediately hushed and stared in awe as he played a long and most moving piece that was classical in nature. He finished to loud applause and cheering and he turned his head with a smile and a nod to the audience. From every recess of the lounge people began calling out song titles and other music requests. He glanced at Kala and me with a slight smile as he began to play a prelude for a melody; and then, in a voice that sounded astoundingly like a famous performer of Earth named Nat King Cole, he began to sing.

For a moment I was struck still and became filled with melancholy. Nat King Cole had been one of my mother's favorite singers. I was flooded with memories of learning my first dances with her to Nat's songs. I noted that no one was dancing, but that didn't matter to me. I took Kala by the hand and said, "Come on. I have some more dance steps to teach you."

"But, Tibby," Kala whispered, "no one dances to this type of music."

"Humph... my ship, my rules. If we want to dance to it, we can dance to it." Reluctantly, Kala got to her feet and followed me to the dance floor. I pulled her close to me and began to lead her through a few of the basic steps. In no time at all we were dancing gracefully about the dance floor as Kerabac sang one of the most beautiful ballads I had ever heard. Slowly, a few couples entered the dance floor to copy the steps by watching Kala and me. As we turned across the dance floor I looked toward the stage to see Kerabac gazing back at us with a broad smile of approval. I looked again at Kala, whose delight could barely be contained as she let the dance and the music fill her. For the first time since my grandparents died I felt like I was part of a family again.

When the song ended, applause and cheers once again filled the room. This time I think I was cheering and applauding the loudest of all. Kerabac beamed. Once again voices called out with requests and he picked another ballad. This time the floor was crowded, as everyone wanted to try out the new dance steps. I glanced around the room to see if I could recognize anyone. I saw Cantolla dancing with an attractive woman; and I was quite surprised to see Marranalis dancing with Major Sokaia. All of them seemed to be having a good time. I held Kala close and she laid her head on my shoulder, as we danced slowly past the front of the stage; and I felt like I *did indeed* own the universe.

The next morning a shuttle arrived from the surface of Nibaria. Senator Tonclin wasn't aboard, but there were ten Nibarians with instructions to seek me out for training as FSO agents. Trooper guards accompanied the admiral and me to the solbidyum container where, once again, the admiral punched in the code that released a capsule containing a single grain of solbidyum. The capsule was placed in a small metal case and sealed by the admiral, after which several Federation trooper guards and an equal contingent of Nibarian guards boarded the shuttle and returned to the surface with the solbidyum and reactor. Once on the surface, the Federation troopers would return to the *NEW ORLEANS* in the shuttle and the Nibarians guards would be responsible for completing the delivery, as humans could not breathe the atmosphere without wearing cumbersome gear. The entire round trip would take a little over three hours, after which we would be on our way back to Megelleon to pick up the FSO trainees we had left on the surface.

In the meantime, I had the day to get the Nibarian FSO trainees indoctrinated and settled into quarters. I hoped that Piesew would have enough time during this brief visit to bring some organic foods aboard and store them in stasis lockers. Once everything was loaded and the additional recruits were aboard, we would begin our journey to the Aburn System to deliver their solbidyum and reactor and to meet up with the *PURFIRE*.

Indoctrination of the Nibarians didn't go quite as easily as expected. I had difficulty explaining to them why spying on their friends, allies, and their own government is as much in everyone's best interest as spying on their enemies. I think the greater part of what made it so difficult was that I personally don't like it either; so trying to define the boundaries for others, as to how far one can and should go in their efforts to ascertain and intercept subversive elements in one's own government, was especially challenging. In the end, they all agreed to go through the training, taking an oath to serve and protect the Federation in their special duties and to execute all spying activities to that end alone. Some of their training would be different from that of the human recruits; physical constraints unique to the Nibarians would preclude them from serving on some planets, just as humans could not serve effectively on Nibaria. Just as humans had no real understanding of the unique culture that defined the peoples of Nibaria, there would likewise be practices and traditions on some worlds that would be too far outside the abilities of Nibarians to manage as agents.

As the session with the Nibarians came to an end, I asked if there were any questions. One Nibarian named Wonnuk asked, "Vice Admiral Renwalt, is it possible to have the nitrogen level raised in our quarters? While we can breathe your atmosphere without difficulty, foods do not taste right nor do things smell right; and it can be most distracting. The modified levels need not include the nitrogen compounds fatal to humans, of course."

"I think that can be arranged. However it may be valuable for you to breathe the atmosphere of humans for at least part of your training. Likewise, we may place the humans in a more nitrogen rich atmosphere for the same reason, minus the compounds fatal to them, of course. You must understand that we are establishing something new that has not been done before within the Federation, at least not in the remembered or recorded history of the Federation. There are no charts or lesson plans for us to follow; so we will be creating this program as we go along. For that reason, I encourage all of you to provide feedback so that we can continue to improve the parameters of your training and instruction."

After the night of dancing at the lounge I noted a distinct difference in the crew's attitude and behavior toward me. They had always been polite and pleasant, but somewhat more reserved and formal than was comfortable for me. Now they were more open, greeting me with warm smiles when they saw me approach. A few would even stop me on occasion to ask for a comment or two on what they were doing right or wrong with their dance steps. I suppose that some people may not like that degree of familiarity with their employees; but it gave me a real feeling of kinship with them. They were no longer just a crew that reported to me as their boss; we were becoming a family and the ship was our home. It was a feeling I really liked.

Early the next morning, shortly before sunrise passed over the capital city, the *NEW ORLEANS* took up an orbit above my estate on Megelleon. I rode down in one of four patrol ships that we were going to use to pick up the FSO trainees from their wilderness survival exercise. By the time I arrived, the last of them had made it into the resort. Some had fared relatively well and appeared no worse for the experience; but several were heavily compromised as a result of near starvation, exposure, or illness from drinking tainted water. These individuals were loaded onto a patrol ship equipped as a medical evacuation unit and treated en route to the *NEW ORLEANS*. Most suffered primarily from severe dehydration. One sustained a broken arm from a fall that occurred while trying to scale a rock face; and one had a rather bad infection that was contracted when he scratched his leg on the spine of a barb-a-sar, a plant that secretes a toxic sap known to break down the immune factors in humans and some animals. Fortunately, this very serious condition could be fixed with transfusions and a program that involved ultraviolet light exposure and treatment of the original wound with a salve that the Federation used to accelerate healing. It was strange to see the reactions of the recruits, which were easily differentiated into three distinct groups. The first and, by far, the happiest group was made up of those who had practically thrived in the wilderness. Finding shelter and food as they navigated to the pick-up point had been almost a delight for them. The second group consisted of those who had not fared as well, but were able to figure out how to stay alive. Some of these individuals managed to find a few food sources mostly by trial and error. The last group, of course, encompassed those who had not fared well at all. They huddled together in relative silence, looking dejected and ready to quit after their harrowing experience. If they performed well during the remainder of the program, these were the individuals who would most likely become office staff and technicians, processing the data that the other two groups brought in from the field and providing the much needed support behind the scenes that would sustain and integrate all of the FSO operations. Every one of them was needed. However, I ultimately understood that not all would offer the same strengths or fill the same types of positions. I soon realized that I was going to have to find someone in the admiral's staff to take charge of the FSO, as I had no intention of spending my life running this operation and the admiral had thus far not communicated a plan to appoint someone for the task. I had the perfect candidate in mind for the job.

When we got back to the ship I gave the recruits the three days off from physical training, but I reminded them they were still required to duplicate Geston's feat with his spy device. Then I went to see Admiral Regeny.

Though I hadn't made an appointment, I was immediately ushered into the admiral's office.

"Tibby, to what do I owe this visit? How did the exercise with the FSO recruits go? We didn't lose any, I hope."

"No, Admiral, they're all still with us. Some are a bit worse for wear, but everyone will recover. I think this exercise has shown us who will serve most effectively as field operatives and who will show greater strengths as support technicians and office staff. Some of them are simply not cut out for field work."

"Good thinking.   Defining each recruit's strengths early will allow us to focus training on their individual disciplines."

"Yes… and that brings me to the reason for my visit. I agreed to train them, but I didn't agree to run the FSO. You need one of your people to do that. Have you given it any thought?"

"Uh, err… to be honest, I was hoping you would sort of volunteer to head them up."

"No such luck, Admiral. Besides the fact that I don't want the job, you and I both know that the Senate and the Federation Legal Review Board would have both our asses if I headed the group. I do, however, have someone in mind."

"Good," chuckled the admiral. "For a minute I was afraid you were going to leave me hanging with that one to figure out for myself. Who do you recommend?"

"Lieutenant Commander Wabussie."

"Wabussie? Why, he's my right hand man. I can't – well, damn. You're right, of course. He's the best choice. I know that I need a position like that to be filled by one of my own people, someone whose leadership I trust and who will report all reconnaissance activity and information fully and regularly. Wabussie is the perfect candidate. I'll have to promote him to a full commander, though. But it's time for that anyway, I suppose. I'm going to hate losing him as my personal assistant. How soon do you need him?"

"The sooner the better. The quicker he's in the loop, the better he'll be able to run the agency."

"Okay, okay, let me call him in here and do this before I change my mind," Regeny said as he activated the communicator on his wrist. "Wabussie get in here!" he said into his communicator. He was barely done speaking when the door to his office opened and Lieutenant Commander Wabussie walked in.

"Congratulations, Lieutenant Commander, you are hereby advanced to the rank of commander. Oh, and your new assignment is to head up the FSO. Report to Vice Admiral Tibby tomorrow morning so he can bring you up to speed on training activities. I expect you to learn as much about the operation as possible and as quickly as possible so he can turn over the program to you."

Wabussie looked back and forth between the admiral and me as though he were expecting one or both of us to start laughing and tell him it was a joke; but when neither of us cracked a smile, he saluted both of us and said, "Yes, sir. I'll do my best, sir."

"Good," said the admiral. "I expect nothing less. Oh, and Commander, I expect you to keep me fully informed as to training status and activities within the FSO at all times. Is that understood?"

"Yes, sir."

"One more thing, see to getting someone to replace you out there on the desk. I still need an assistant."

Shortly after lunch I met with Marranalis. "What do you have to report on our stowaway?" I asked.

"I wish I had something to tell you," replied Marranalis with disappointment. "We've placed the Nibarian FSO contingency in the aft quarters, in the hopes that the modified atmosphere will either smoke out the stowaway or that the recruits will see and capture him. So far there has been no sign of him. He's most certainly still onboard and using the cleaning machine. And according to the main computer, his food dispenser is working once again, though we still can't locate it physically. It's the strangest thing I've ever seen."

"Okay, Marranalis. Keep me informed as to even the most minor changes. I'm headed to my office if you need me."

I truly loved my office, though I was able to spend very little time there. As I sat gazing into the huge aquarium behind my desk, I suddenly got the strangest feeling that I wasn't alone. I slowly turned my chair around to find myself staring at our little stowaway, who was seated in one of the wing-backed chairs in front of my desk. There was no doubt that it was the same figure I had observed in the vid screen with Captain Stonbersa. No one else on the ship even remotely resembled this short, hunchbacked figure, whose pointy chin and nose and tinted yellow skin seem exaggerated by the coal-black hair that was tied into a high ponytail. I gazed in silence at my visitor's remarkable yellow irises, waiting for him to introduce himself.

"Greetings, First Citizen Tibby," he said in a rich and mellow voice that reminded me of the typical radio and television announcers on Earth. "I felt it was time we met in person, before you have me captured and tossed off the ship."

Under normal circumstances I would have reacted with more surprise and anxiety over someone appearing mysteriously as he had; but there was something so casual and reassuring in his voice and manner that it was impossible for me to feel threatened in any way.

"My name is A'Lappe. I am sure you're wondering what I'm doing on your ship. First, let me assure you I wish no harm to you, your ship or the Federation. I am not a member of the Brotherhood, nor am I a criminal; though there are individuals who wish to find and kill me for reasons I will not discuss. This is part of the reason I have secreted myself within your ship. How I came to be here is a long tale; so I will give you the short of it. Galetils was a good friend of mine. I served him as an advisor in many areas as he built this yacht you now call the *NEW ORLEANS*. I should clarify; I was not on his payroll, as I do not need money. I worked for him in exchange for protection and secrecy and I am here to make the same offer to you. This entire ship was designed by me to Galetils' specifications with certain additions and modification that I suggested and he accepted, including your RMFF system. I know every millimeter of this ship intimately; though, as part of the deal I had with Galetils, none of the laborers who built the ship were ever made aware that I was living onboard in a hidden suite specifically designed for my needs. I also served as his chief architect and engineer for development of the 10X fusion reactor.

"Then, shortly after life on Astamagota was destroyed in the solar flare and Galetils' empire crumbled, I found myself without a patron and protector," he said with a tone of sadness in his voice. "I remained hidden here while I deliberated what to do next. Then you came along, bringing with you the *TRITYTE* and the solbidyum. Your presence introduced an entirely new set of variables and possibilities where my future was concerned. I was able to monitor newscasts of your accomplishments and deeds; and when you bought the ship from the Nibarians, I knew that I must figure out a way to introduce myself to you in such a way that you would want me to stay onboard to provide service to you in the same manner that I had for Galetils.

"I can help you – you *and* the Federation. I know that you and the Federation seek to have RMFF capabilities on all the Federation ships; and for that you need the 10X fusion reactors. I know that Cantolla is working on that project, but she and her team are a long way off from finding the solution and it could take them years to do so without my input. I can provide you with the plans for a reactor that will work – the original design, in fact, which I designed and Galetils was having built. However, in its current design, I fear it is only suitable for use on the larger Federation ships, such as the star ships and frigates. The size of the reactor is much too large to fit into anything smaller than that. Still, that would be a huge boon to the Federation.

"In addition, I can help you in your struggles with the Brotherhood. They are an enemy of mine, as well; and for far longer than the Federation has been aware of them. I know a great number of details about their operations, such as areas where they are strongly concentrated and even the names of some of the organization's highest ranking leadership. All I seek in return is to be allowed to continue my sanctuary on this ship. I have my own accommodations and the synthesizers provide the food and materials that I need."

He paused and waited patiently for my reply.

"Well A'Lappe, it's nice to finally meet the elusive individual that has had my ship in turmoil for the past few days. Your offer is intriguing; but how do I know I can trust you? How can I be certain that all you have told me is the truth?" I asked frankly.

A'Lappe shrugged his shoulders and threw up his small hands in a comical gesture. "You can always have me tested with one of your headbands", he said. "I will not object. But I must warn you, I will not provide you with any information as to my origins or my past history prior to working with Galetils. This stipulation is crucial; my life depends on it."

"Does harboring you here endanger my ship or crew in any way?" I asked.

"No, I don't believe so. Even if my enemies were to discover that I am aboard this ship, they would only attempt to apprehend me if they were certain that their actions would not endanger or threaten anyone else; of that I am sure. Of course, it is always possible that my enemies may try to bribe a crew member to kill me or turn me over to them."

I thought quietly for a moment. "You present a unique offer, but also a troubling one, A'Lappe. Not only are *you* unknown to the Federation, but your race is not known either. Why is that?"

"That question I will not answer. Again, my personal safety depends on it; but I can assure you I pose no threat to the Federation."

A'Lappe had a curious and almost mesmerizing way of blinking his eyes that made part of me feel reassured that he was a benign individual whose presence on the ship could be beneficial. As he spoke, I found myself simultaneously believing him and questioning my belief. I wondered if I was perhaps struggling with some sort of hypnotic manipulation. Just in case this was the situation, I decided to take a cautious approach.

"What if I say no to your proposal?"

A'Lappe shrugged his shoulders and pursed his lips. "Then I will go back in hiding and stay hidden until I am captured and removed from the ship," he said.

"So you believe you could get out of this room right now before I could capture you?" I asked somewhat incredulously.

"I don't *believe* it, I *know* it," A'Lappe said with a grin. Then, just like in a classic magician's stage act, he was shrouded in a sudden puff of smoke; and when the smoke cleared, the chair was empty and he was gone. I was startled for a moment, as I stared at the vacant chair and then looked about the room to see if I could locate him; but there wasn't a trace of him anywhere.

Then out of nowhere I heard his voice. "Think about my offer. I'll be in touch with you later for your decision."

After A'Lappe was gone I met with Kala, Admiral Regeny, Marranalis and Captain Stonbersa to discuss the event. Kala was in favor of giving A'Lappe a chance to prove himself. The admiral was in favor of capturing him and interrogating him until we had every possible bit of information squeezed out of him. Captain Stonbersa leaned a bit toward the admiral's point of view, only with far less force, and basically just wanted A'Lappe off the ship. Marranalis was surprisingly undecided on the matter and stated he was more inclined to see what A'Lappe's next move was before making a decision.

"I just don't like it," said the admiral. "We have nothing but his word that he's here to help us. If we agree to his offer, we pretty much have to take him into our confidence and tell him what we know and what we are planning."

"I don't think that's and issue, Admiral," I said. "I think he already knows our plans and what's going on. In fact, I think he knows more about what we are facing than we do. I suspect he has this room bugged in ways we can't imagine and is monitoring this discussion as we speak."

The admiral lifted his foccee cup and examined it as thought it might contain a bugging device. "How do we know we can trust him?"

"Kala can test him for honesty and loyalty in the same way that we test the troopers, crew members and recruits," I said.

"I just don't like that he stowed away on this ship," Stonbersa said in disgust.

"Well he didn't exactly stow away," I said. "He was a guest or, rather, an employee of Galetils. He just didn't leave after Galetils' death."

"Humph! But he didn't come forward and present himself either, did he?" Stonbersa retorted.

"No, and I don't think we are going to find out exactly why either. But he does make a good case for accepting his offer. If he really can deliver the 10X fusion reactor in a design suitable for installation on all your star ships and frigates, think of how much stronger the Federation forces will be. And, Captain, if A'Lappe really did design this ship, think of how valuable his knowledge would be to you directly."

"Mmmm," Stonbersa hummed. "You have a point there. There's a great deal to know about this ship and much of it is as much a mystery to me as it is to everyone else."

Everyone mulled over the circumstances quietly for a moment before the admiral spoke up. "Obviously, Tibby, the choice is yours, but I think we need to be prepared to take action against him at the first sign that he is trying to manipulate or mislead us. I have no aversion to dumping him into space if he proves to be ingenuine."

Everyone sort of laughed at the admiral's comment, but the admiral affirmed, "I'm serious. We have a huge and dangerous undertaking and we cannot afford any variables that put our mission at risk."

"Well, taking into account everyone's viewpoint, I think I'm going to accept his offer – with reservations of course – and he'll have to undergo immediate testing with Kala *and* Cantolla. I'm not going to trust just one evaluation. There is something about him that is almost hypnotic at times and I will feel more confident when I see results from two evaluations conducted by two different computers. For additional security in this regard I want both tests observed by three witnesses. If he passes under those conditions, I'm going to accept his offer."

"Wonderful, First Citizen Renwalt," said a deep melodious voice from the far end of the table. We all turned with surprise to see A'Lappe smiling widely from his chair. "I agree with your terms."

"How did you get in here?!" exclaimed Admiral Regeny.

"I was looking right at that chair... and he just suddenly appeared!" added Captain Stonbersa.

"How long have you been here and how much did you hear?" demanded a red-faced Regeny in an increasingly belligerent tone.

"Now, now, gentlemen... and lady," said A'Lappe, nodding in Kala's direction. "I was here long enough to hear that First Citizen Tibby agrees to the bargain I presented him, with reservations that require me to submit to stringent examination, which I accept. As to what I heard before that is a moot point. I would think, Admiral, that you would be happy, since you should be able to start outfitting your ships with 10X fusion reactors and RMFF shields within a few months. And you should be pleased as well, Captain Stonbersa, as I will be able to provide you with a thorough knowledge of functional capabilities and details about this ship that you cannot begin to imagine. But before any of this happens, I need to take Tibby on a tour of his ship as few have seen it. May I first, however, point out some problems with your execution of some aspects of your plans?

Without pausing for a response to that question, A'Lappe continued. "At the moment you are trying to deliver the solbidyum and reactor units using this ship. Oh, yes, you *plan* to use GW message pods to make some of those deliveries – good idea by the way – but even with your best efforts and fastest delivery times using both this ship and the GW pods, you would have to live several lifetimes to deliver all the solbidyum. It's physically impossible for you to make deliveries to one million planets; and if you think about it a moment, you will realize that this is true."

The admiral interrupted, "How do you know about our plans? Who have you passed the information on to?" He was not yet ready to relent on his confrontational posture.

A'Lappe continued, unruffled by the admiral's hostility, "Calm down, Admiral. I assure you, I have not told anyone your plans and your Federation secrets are safe with me. But that doesn't alter the fact that you are on a course that won't get you very far. Your idea that you need to demonstrate that the solbidyum is being delivered as promised is sound; however, it won't be long before planets start getting impatient for deliveries and, as fantastic as Tibby has been thus far, he can't deliver all your solbidyum fast enough to prevent war. Furthermore, I recognize your problem with the infiltration of the Brotherhood into the Federation military forces; but using your current plan for finding and removing them from your ranks will take decades."

"I suppose you have a better plan?" the admiral huffed.

"I think I do," A'Lappe said, blinking his huge yellow eyes in that hypnotic manner that I had observed in my office. "Take a course to Plosaxen. If I am not mistaken, that's your fleet headquarters in the central sector of the Federation territories. While en route, contact every available outlying star ship that can reach Plosaxen at about the same timeframe that you do, ordering them to rendezvous there with you immediately upon their arrival. If my calculations are correct you may be able to gather up to half a dozen outlying star ships, in addition to the three already stationed there with the 20 frigates and, I believe, 18 corvettes. You have nearly a million troopers stationed there, since it's also a training base; so, once you arrive, you can quickly set up and test nearly two million Federation troopers, staff all of the gathered ships with loyal crews and divide the solbidyum shipments for delivery to other sector headquarters. They can depart with protocols and orders issued by you, Admiral, which will make it possible for these well-armed and trained troopers to likewise test and establish loyal crews on other ships and distribute portions of solbidyum cargo to these ships for delivery to even more distant sector headquarters, once each of those sectors has also been cleared of Brotherhood members, of course. As the security of each star ship and sector is confirmed, the distribution of solbidyum and reactors can commence to individual planets within those systems using similar protocols to confirm the loyalty of the recipients at each planet. Using this exponential method of distribution, you can – by my calculations – deliver the entire cargo of solbidyum in eight to twelve years."

"Why eight to twelve years? Why not simply eight years?" Admiral Regeny badgered.

"Because I'm factoring in a contingency for problems and delays. You cannot reasonably believe you'll be able to distribute all the solbidyum without some attempts at theft by non-aligned worlds or mercenaries and pirates; and you cannot believe that there will not be more ships commandeered as the *DUSTEN* was, before successfully clearing their crews of Brotherhood infiltrators. You may even have entire planets fall to the Brotherhood before you can get this all accomplished. It's a fact – one you cannot avoid."

"Dammit," the admiral fumed, reluctantly recognizing the value of A'Lappe's perspective. "That's not what I want to hear, but it's undeniable. As much as I hate to face these facts, you are right."

"That's where Tibby's plan to train your select group of troopers to deal with these types of situations is going to come into play; and the sooner he gets this bunch trained so they can train others, the better off you will be. The FSO is also a step in the right direction, but I fear you will not be able to train and deploy them fast enough to provide you with the information you need now. I think I can also help you in that regard, as I have sources of information that may prove useful."

"Oh you do, do you? And would you mind sharing these sources with us?" the admiral asked.

"Yes, I do mind, and no, I won't tell you my sources. You will simply have to trust me on that account."

"I don't see a reason to trust you on *any* account," the admiral snorted.

"You will, Admiral, you will. I can provide you with a list of Brotherhood headquarters in many of the sectors in the galaxy for a start. I will provide Tibby with the plans for the 10X fusion reactor and the RMFF system. It will take several weeks to assemble one reactor; but once you have one completed and installed with the RMFF on one of your star ships, I think you will be more than willing to trust me."

"We'll see," Regeny said, "but I warn you; if you betray us in any way, I swear I will personally tear you limb from limb and eject your carcass into space."

A'Lappe smiled. "I assure you, Admiral, that will not be necessary. Now, Tibby, if you're ready, I would like to take you on a tour to show you things that no one else on your ship has seen to date."

"First things first," I said. "There is still a matter of Kala testing you for deception, truth and loyalty, which will take but a few minutes. Then I will be most happy to follow you about the ship."

A'Lappe grinned. "Ah, yes, those were the terms of our agreement. Very well. Let's have the test."

No time was wasted. Kala summoned one of her assistants to bring her vid pad and equipment. She performed the test on him in the conference room with all of us present as witnesses, so there could be no doubt in any of our minds about the administration or results of the procedure. Then she contacted Cantolla, who arrived shortly thereafter with her own equipment, including the headband. Both tests indicated that A'Lappe had been truthful in all he had told us and that he was no threat to the Federation. Having satisfied his agreement to the satisfaction of all parties, including a somewhat reluctant Admiral Regeny, A'Lappe reaffirmed that he was sincere and that he would keep his word not to reveal the secrets of the ship or the plans of the Federation. Then I let him take me on the tour that he promised would be so enlightening.

I rose from my chair and turned toward the exit, as I expected to leave through the door; so I was surprised when A'Lappe winked at me as he reached into his pocket and retrieved a small tool that used to insert into a small, almost indiscernible slot in the floor. He lifted a panel that revealed a set of stairs that descended into a tunnel below.

"Well I'll be damned," exclaimed both the captain and the admiral in unison.

A'Lappe led me down the stairs and into a narrow tunnel that had a low ceiling. At several places I had to duck to avoid hitting my head on a pipe or duct. As far as I could see in either direction were horizontal rows of cables bracketed to the tunnel walls. Periodically the cables terminated at switch panels that seemed to distribute more cables vertically in both directions. As we navigated through the corridor, we occasionally passed intersecting tunnels that led to other portions of the ship.

"So this is how you moved about undetected," I said.

"Some of the time. But I have other means as well," said A'Lappe with a bit of mischief in his voice. "There are things down here you need to see."

We progressed a bit farther through the tunnel before descending another section of stairs that brought us into what seemed to be a small hangar area that stowed a very unique spaceship. The craft was smaller and sleeker than a patrol ship and the design appeared to be adapted to both in- and out-of-atmosphere flight.

"Is this yours? I said with admiration.

A'Lappe laughed. "No, Tibby, it's yours. It comes with the ship. It was Galetils' personal shuttle. If you need, the craft can behave more like a patrol ship, though its smaller design allows for a crew of only two to three people. It's faster than the Federation patrol ships, but armed just as well as the larger version. You will also find that its speed is complemented with superb maneuverability. I've been working on an RMFF design for it, but I haven't developed a power source strong enough and small enough to fit in the ship."

"Maybe you can get with Cantolla and figure it out between the two of you. She's pretty sharp," I suggested.

"Yes, so I've heard. I knew her brother. He worked with me on the design of the 10X fusion reactor. He spoke of her often, bragging that she was the real brains in the family. It will be a pleasure to work with her, I'm sure. But come; let me show you the inside of this ship."

Unlike the patrol ships, which were sort of amorphous in design, this ship had very definite and sleek lines. The inside was compact but luxurious, as were all of Galetils' interior spaces, marked by rich wood paneling and plush leather-like upholstery. The bed appeared to be designed to accommodate two; and while I was able to stand upright in the walking space of the sleeping quarters, the foot of the bed was partially recessed under the curvature of the hull. The toilet and bath facilities were also compact and the shower allowed enough space for only one person. The galley consisted of a table large enough to seat two and smaller versions of the typical beverage and food dispensers. The control room included three seats and consoles arranged in a tight configuration. Since this room was situated against the forward hull, the ceiling was tapered and required a person to stoop over when entering – at least this was the case for me – A'Lappe had no problem standing anywhere in the ship. Part of the reason this craft was so compact was that it did not have a large cargo hold. Instead there was a small space large enough for a parcel of about one and a half meters by three meters. There was no engine room to speak of; engine access was from the exterior of the ship via a removable panel. There was also a small bunk-like sleeping space for a third person, not much bigger than a closet, which was attached to a very compact combination toilet/shower facility.

As we exited, A'Lappe explained that the sensors on this ship had nearly twice the range of the Federation ships, making it easier to avoid contact with hostile forces. Near this ship was a smaller craft, which looked remarkably like a child's toy. I was about to make a comment to this effect, when it occurred to me that this might be A'Lappe's craft.

"And what about this ship," I asked. "Is this yours?"

"Yes, it is indeed; though I regret that I will not be able to offer you a ride in it. It holds only one passenger and then only one of my stature. But come, I have other things to show you."

A'Lappe led me away from the small hangar down another tunnel until we came to a door. "Watch your head when you enter. I fear this place was not constructed with one of your size in mind."

When I entered, I indeed had to cock my head to the side to avoid bumping it on the ceiling. Beyond the door were several rooms, including a rather nicely arranged living area, a small but efficient dining area, and bath and sleeping areas. There was also a workspace consisting of a large vid screen and arrangement of computer consoles. A'Lappe showed me how he could monitor any portion of the ship, with the exception of a few cabins and rooms. He said Galetils had this well-hidden suite built specifically to meet his needs. The maintenance tunnels were accessed only by the ship's engineers and they were to have been sworn to secrecy, as far as A'Lappe's presence on the ship. Unfortunately the engineers never showed up, as Astamagota was destroyed before the yacht became fully operational. A'Lappe had taken up residence only a week before the solar flare with the intent of completing the necessary preparations for installation of the 10X fusion reactor, once its fabrication was complete.

"So now, Tibby, you have seen the inside of the beast and its children, so to speak. Tell me, what do you think?"

"Well, I would like to know where all these service tunnels go and where they come out, and also the locations where you have placed bugs on this ship. Oh, and one more thing... how does your personal cloaking device work?"

A'Lappe laughed. "So you figured out I have a personal cloaking device. Very good. How did you figure that out?"

"When you disappeared from my office, I heard a distinct swishing sound of your clothing as you moved across the room. I wasn't all together sure of it, until I heard the exact same sound as your clothing rubbed together while you led me down the tunnels earlier."

"Hmm, maybe I need to work on a sound dampening feature. Here, this is the device." He handed me a small box-shaped mechanism that he removed from his belt. On the box was a button. "Push the toggle button and you are cloaked; push it again and you are visible. It only works for a maximum of approximately twenty minutes before it runs out of power. I'm still working out the glitches. I hope to improve its functionality to sustain cloaking for an hour."

"Do you have any idea how great this will be for the Federation? It would be useful for not only for the FSO, but the Special Operations units as well."

"Yes, I'm aware of its potential; but I planned to withhold the technology until I had it perfected." I held out the small box to return it to A'Lappe, but he said, "No, you keep it. You may need it at some point. Besides, I'm working on a more advanced model; and at this point I no longer need to hide, now, do I?" He smiled and blinked one of his hypnotic blinks.

"Let me ask you one question, A'Lappe. When you blink in that way, is it intended to have a mesmerizing and calming effect or is it just a natural phenomenon?"

A'Lappe grinned and blinked, "That, my friend, is something you will have to figure out for yourself. Now come, let me show you more of the service tunnels and where they lead."

As I followed A'Lappe, I noted that he had a strange but not unpleasant smell, which somewhat reminded me of a tree we had on Earth called a cedar. The scent was not as strong as that of a cedar, but it was faintly reminiscent. It was an aroma that I was to identify with A'Lappe from then on, though I would never learn whether it was a natural smell, something he wore as a fragrance, or something in his diet that produced the smell. Whatever the source, it was not offensive; but then nothing about A'Lappe was offensive. I found myself wondering why anyone would be trying to kill him.

"A'Lappe, why did Galetils have his ship down here in this secret area instead of up in the main hangar bay with the other ships?"

"He wanted this craft to be relatively unknown so he could use it as an emergency craft in the event that he needed to get away. From the exterior of the yacht this hangar is undetectable unless it's open. Anyone trying to trap him on this ship from outside would be watching for an escape through the main hangar. This area cannot be seen from any position around the yacht where the main hangar can be observed. He would have been allowed to slip out and accelerate out of range before an aggressor had an opportunity to target him."

"I noted that the ship is built to accommodate three, but there are only two sleeping areas."

"Yes. Galetils and his companion planned to share the main cabin."

"Companion?   I wasn't aware he had a companion."

"Yes. She died on Astamagota when the flare hit. Galetils was devastated by her death."

"Is that why he committed suicide?" I asked.

"Suicide?! Is that what they told you – that he committed suicide?" A'Lappe exclaimed.

"Why, yes," I said. "Isn't that how he died?"

"I think it was meant to *look* like a suicide; but I think he died trying to protect me. Though, to be honest, I don't know for sure. He may have committed suicide; but knowing the man the way I did, that scenario seems most unlikely to me. I am more inclined to believe he was murdered."

"Murdered?! But why? Who? What motive would they have?" I asked.

"Ha, motives are abundant," A'Lappe said with a tone of gravity in his voice that I had not heard before now. "Word had leaked out about his intent to develop the 10X fusion reactor and, of course, in the absence of solbidyum, his reactor would have been the next best power source. The Bunemnites and several non-aligned planets had approached Galetils with some rather aggressive undertones, trying to pressure him into selling the reactors to them exclusively. When I say *pressure*, I mean that he was presented with numerous graphic threats as to what the consequences would be if he chose to not cooperate with them – not that it scared him any.

He intended to have the first reactor installed on this yacht, along with a fully functional RMFF. As far as he knew, no one else knew about the RMFF we had installed here. But that doesn't mean the other systems are not aware of RMFF technology or that they had not thought about using the 10X for their own ships in conjunction with RMFF defenses. RMFF technology has been understood for years, but no one has had the power to operate one – until now."

"So you're saying Galetils was killed by someone who was trying to steal the 10X plans?"

"I'm saying I don't buy the suicide explanation," A'Lappe said with a blink, "but as to what actually happened, I can't say."

"The third seat and smaller sleeping compartment on the shuttle," I said, "those were meant for you?"

A'Lappe paused a moment in our journey and turned toward me. "Yes," he said, "they were."

"Galetils intended to take you with him if he ever had to escape. He must have believed that the rest of the crew would be safe and that only the three of you were in potential danger. Am I right?"

"He didn't know for sure. Personally, I don't believe I would have been in danger, but he wasn't sure."

"He must have thought very highly of you to go to this measure," I said.

A'Lappe seemed to be holding his breath, finally giving into his grief as he covered his eyes with his hands and sobbed openly. "He was my closest and dearest friend. There is nothing he would not have done for me. His death is a more tragic loss than you can imagine. I do not believe my friend committed suicide, but I cannot prove that he didn't."

A'Lappe took a deep breath and tried to regain his composure. "Galetils had enemies. His enemies are the same as those faced by the Federation – the aggressors of non-aligned worlds, pirates and mercenaries and, of course, the Brotherhood. Just days before he was – before he died, he met with the FOI to warn them that the Brotherhood was trying to coerce him into turning over the 10X fusion reactor design and that the Brotherhood had offered him a senior position in their ranks, if he would agree to join them and hand over the plans. He told the FOI that his response to the Brotherhood was that he needed time to think about the offer – time he used to approach the FOI to divulge what he knew. Three days later he was dead."

"Does Regeny know this?" I asked.

"I don't believe so. As far as I know, no one outside the FOI ever learned of Galetils' visit to their office. But, as you and the admiral now know, the FOI was – and is – corrupt, or at least heavily compromised with the infiltration of Brotherhood agents; and I think that's why he is dead."

"I see. Thank you for telling me, A'Lappe. This certainly justifies my belief in the need for the FSO. I only hope we can get it operating soon enough to be effective."

"I may be able to give you some help there. There is an agent in the FOI that Galetils believed he could trust. Unfortunately, this person is not who he met with on Megelleon. This trusted agent is on Plosaxen; Galetils never got a chance to meet with him."

"Why did Galetils believe he could trust him?"

"Because he is Galetils' brother," replied A'Lappe.

When I returned to the main deck, confirming that Galetils' brother was an active FOI agent was not a problem. Though there was no trans-solar-system internet, there was a rather effective system of updateable data cubes. Anyone could acquire a data cube and system interface for a small cost. By inserting the cube into an interface receptacle, the cube would be updated with the latest out-system data for the local solar system. In the case of the military, security codes allowed the interface to update the cube with the latest classified and non-classified government and military data that had reached that particular solar system. In this case, no special updating steps were required, as Admiral Regeny's cube automatically received new postings on a daily basis; so when his staff conducted a data search, they quickly found that Galetils' brother was indeed an FOI agent on Plosaxen.

"This could work to our advantage," I suggested to Admiral Regeny. "If we can speak with Galetils' brother and get him to spy within the FOI for us, it could put us ahead of the game – especially if he is able to direct us to other key individuals that he knows to be loyal to the Federation. Most likely he can, which will allow us to more quickly establish a network and method to weed out the rogue agents sooner than we originally planned."

"I hope so, but we will have to tread carefully," cautioned the admiral. "While I do have some say as to what goes on in the FOI, my power is limited. The FOI is headed by Garfreed Aliquatee; and he answers directly to the Senate and first leaders. Within the Federation itself his position is about equal to my own; and while I can make requests for service from the FOI and expect results, I cannot appear to circumvent Garfreed in any way."

"What do you know of Garfreed's loyalties?" I asked.

"Honestly, I don't know. I've met him and dealt with him on a professional level, but never more than that. He's always presented himself very professionally and has never given me any difficulty or appeared to be anything but cooperative; but there haven't been any interagency issues to date that have dealt with the Brotherhood; and I have never questioned or had a reason to verify the information he has provided me. For all I know, he could be a highly placed Brotherhood operative himself. I can't order him to have a loyalty test – only the Senate could do that; but it would take years to get them to agree to it."

"What about the first leaders... could a consensus from two of them order it?"

"Yes, if we can demonstrate a legitimate and desperate need for it; but right now, without more proof of threats than we currently have, I don't see them issuing such an order."

After meeting with the admiral I met with Commander Wabussie. We had a long discussion about the FSO and the scope of his role in the leadership of the group's training and clandestine activities. A matrix had been prepared that listed the recruits by name along with their particular skill sets and their scored performance in each skill area. Those who had fared poorly on the survival test but had demonstrated stronger proficiency and aptitude in other areas were placed in administrative or technical support functions. Of the 150 Federation recruits provided by the admiral and the ten Nibarians we had acquired with the help of Senator Tonclin we were able to identify 103 that qualified as potential field operatives – a number slightly higher than I originally anticipated. Those that would be moving forward with additional preparations for specific field assignments were sent to Marranalis for more physical training along with the Special Ops troopers, while Wabussie and I worked on placement and organization of specialized training for administrative and technical support functions that applied to the remaining recruits.

When I finished with Wabussie, I decided to seek out Kerabac. I knew that he was off duty and I had a special personal project I was hoping he would accept. Using my wrist com I was able to locate him in his suite and he invited me to join him there.

Kerabac's accommodations were tastefully decorated in what I can only describe as a style reminiscent of the Art Deco style that existed on Earth. Scone lighting was abundant and provided the bulk of the lighting. Elegant arrangements of statuaries and potted ferns and palm-type plants accented the decor. The floor looked like polished black marble, while the walls were a very light shade of green. There was a sunken living room, a lavish dining room and a fantastic kitchen that supported Piesew's comments about Kerabac's talents as a chef.

"Tibby, I'm honored that you've come to visit me. Please come in and have a seat. Would you care for something to eat or drink? I have some delicious Magarian shellfish marinated in Ivevashe brandy, if you would care to try them."

"I was going to say no; but come to think of it, I haven't eaten so far today and I always enjoy trying new foods... so I'll accept your offer."

"What would you like to drink?" he asked. "I've heard that you enjoy afex. Would you care for one?"

"Oh, gosh," I said, "I'm afraid this is becoming an embarrassment to Kala. As I understand it, afex is not something I should be favoring in my – well – my *role* in the Federation."

Kerabac laughed. "Tibby, I think you are exempt from all the rules. Whether you know it or not, you are already having an impact on the Federation culture and many consider it vogue to emulate your fashions and tastes. Your casual shirts are already being copied by many of the crew when off duty, and since you have made your preference for afex known, more people are ordering and drinking it publically than ever before. And your dances have become all the rage in the entertainment lounge, I might add.

"Excuse me one moment, I'll be right back." Kerabac retreated to the kitchen and returned shortly with a glass of afex and a plate of something that resembled an Earth dish called *escargot*. There was a small cup of dipping sauce in the middle and a small silver pick used to extract the creatures from their shells. He retreated again to the kitchen and returned a moment later with a plate and a glass of afex for himself.

"So, Tibby, to what do I owe the honor of this visit?" he asked with his usual warm grin.

"I have a very special request of you... and I hope you will accept the challenge."

"I will certainly try."

"On Earth there was a very famous and beloved singer named Nat King Cole, who lived a few generations before my time. Your voice is remarkably like his. He was my mother's favorite singer. She had recordings of all his songs, which she played nearly every day; so I pretty much grew up listening to his music. I was wondering... if I were to sing a few of his tunes to you and provide you with the lyrics, would you be able to learn them on your instrument and sing the melodies? I would like to surprise Kala one evening. It would mean very much to me to hear you sing them and to dance to them with Kala."

Kerabac's eyes twinkled. "Tibby, I would be delighted to do it. I'm sure I will be able to reproduce these songs, unless your singing is so bad that I can't identify a note."

"Well, I won't ever win any singing contests, but I can carry a tune. I will certainly never come close to your singing talents."

"Hmm, we'll see. One never knows what one can do until one tries," Kerabac said with his million-dollar smile.

"These – what did you call them...Mugorian shellfish? – they're delicious, Kerabac, truly delicious."

"Close, Tibby. *Magarian* shellfish... and thank you. I'm pleased that you're enjoying them. They have always been a favorite snack food of mine, but until I began working for you, I could not afford them very often."

I decided on a few of my favorite Cole songs; but I found that translating the lyrics into Federation language within the context of the melodies was not as easy as I had anticipated. However, by applying a bit of creative license and some slight modifications, we managed to achieve something close enough to preserve the meaning of the songs. I was amazed at how quickly Kerabac was able to take to the tune and play it on his keyboard instrument, which he said was called a *Judaras Sound Machine*. I was especially surprised that he was able to match the musical sounds of Earth instruments so well when all he had to go by was my simplistic descriptions and the sound of my voice as I mimicked qualities of the instrument sounds.

"How do you know how to duplicate the musical sounds of Earth so well?" I asked.

"I don't know really," he answered. "It just seems like this is how it should sound and anything else would be wrong."

"Well I have to tell you, you nailed it perfectly."

"Thank you for teaching me these wonderful tunes. When do you plan to bring Kala by the lounge for her surprise?"

"Tonight, I think – if nothing comes along to interrupt our plans, that is."

"Great.   I should have these songs well memorized by then."

My wrist com started beeping just as Kerabac finished.   I answered to hear the recorded voice of Captain Stonbersa saying that I should come to the bridge immediately.   No sooner did I end the call than Kerabac's wrist com also beeped with the same message. The two of us headed to the bridge immediately, only to be met en route by the admiral and one of his aides.

"What the hell's going on!?" the admiral asked.

"I have no idea, Admiral.   I just got the call to go to the bridge moments ago."

Just then I saw Kala rounding a corner ahead of us, also heading for the bridge.   We all arrived at the same time and entered to find Stonbersa and another crew member at a vid screen.

"What's going on?" Admiral Regeny demanded.

"We just came into range of the Rabanu communication beacon and picked up a message from the Enpowor System.   Apparently, when the message of the Brotherhood rebellion and seizure of the *DUSTEN* reached the system, the Brotherhood members of the frigate *TECCION* revolted and took over the ship.   They left the ship's loyal crew members at the abandoned relay station on the moon of Nasgoria with enough supplies to last them a month.   Not long after that, word apparently reached the mutineers that the *DUSTEN* had been reclaimed by the Federation, causing them to go into hiding while the star ships *URANGA* and *CACHATORA* searched for them.   Now reports are arriving that the Federation freighter *MOOGAWOE* was intercepted by the *TECCION* and that the crew of the

TECCION believed that the *MOOGAWOE* was carrying the *TRITYTE* and the solbidyum. Of course, they found no ship aboard and no solbidyum; so their next move was to eject the freighter crew in escape pods over the planet Koobs and commandeer the *MOOGAWOE*. The two ships left the system together and are now believed to be hiding in the asteroid cluster near the Zanoid Nebula."

"Where are the *URANGA* and the *CACHATORA* now?" asked the admiral.

"Well, our data is about three days behind; but the last communication stated that the *CACHATORA* was headed to the Nasgorian moon to pick up the abandoned crew members, while the *URANGA* continued on its search for the *TECCION*," advised Stonbersa.

"Damn, damn, damn!" Regeny cursed. "Do we know if the *URANGA* and the *CACHATORA* received orders to test their crews and whether their crews have been confirmed as loyalists; or do we face the risk of a Brotherhood mutiny on those ships as well?" Lieutenant Commander Goncest, the new aide to the admiral rapidly punched commands into his vid pad.

"Ah, sir, when the orders were issued, the *URANGA* and the *CACHATORA* were both closer to us than the *TECCION*; so they should have received the message to test their crews prior to the mutiny incident on the *TECCION*," stammered Goncest.

"Let us hope so. At least it sounds like they did. Damn, though – the *TECCION* – we can't have our fleet divided up and fighting against each other. Tibby, I think we're going to need to implement your plan to get solbidyum to trusted systems using the GW pods first thing tomorrow. I have a list of about 30 outer planets and 30 inner planets that we can target. If we can secure a significant number of deliveries at the core and the perimeter of the Federation territories while we move toward them from the center, we will effectively be able to confine rebel activity somewhere in the middle. If the Brotherhood is flanked by loyal systems that have already successfully implemented their solbidyum power distribution, they will also have a more difficult time enticing others to join them."

"I agree, Admiral. I don't think we really have any other choice. What do you think, A'Lappe?"

Everyone looked around the room, but A'Lappe was nowhere to be seen.

"A'Lappe's not here. Why are you asking for his opinion?" the admiral demanded.

"A'Lappe *is* here," I insisted. "Show yourself A'Lappe."

All of a sudden, A'Lappe appeared by the admiral's right elbow and said, "Boo!" and the admiral actually jumped.

"Damn it, don't do that!" objected the admiral. "Besides the fact that it's unnerving, it also undermines my trust in you which, may I remind you, is already fragile!"

"So, A'Lappe," I said, "what do you think?"

A'Lappe twisted his mouth as he thought a moment, then looked at me and said, "The *TECCION* and the *MOOGAWOE* are *not* in the asteroid belt; but you can be sure they want you to *think* they are. My bet is they are hiding at an old quarry site on the third moon of Ludation."

"Oh, and just why do you think they are there?" the admiral fumed.

"It is in line with the asteroid cluster but it is a much quicker – and safer – destination. Pursuers will naturally anticipate that they will flee into the cluster and not give the moon much scrutiny. Even if they do, the quarry will hide them quite well, since their ships' profiles would be concealed below the surrounding surface terrain.

"There is another reason to consider the moon as the more likely destination – it is where the Brotherhood has an established underground base. When the quarry was still active, the Brotherhood secretly began mining into the walls of the quarry and then tunneling vertically into the moon. After the quarry's resources were tapped out, the site was pretty much forgotten. The site was purchased about fifteen years ago by a member of the Brotherhood; and the organization has been stockpiling arms and equipment there ever since."

"And you're expecting me to believe you?" the admiral said.

"No, not at all, Admiral. I'm expecting you to check it out," A'Lappe said plainly.

"Humph!" the admiral grunted. "Well, you're right about that; we *will* check it out."

I tried to suppress my amusement over the admiral's attempts at intimidation and A'Lappe's complete refusal to be pushed into a defensive posture.

"Well, Admiral, if you are not in need of me anymore, I will leave you and your staff to deal with this issue. I need to get A'Lappe and Cantolla together on several matters that could greatly aid the Federation, in the event that we have to engage the Brotherhood or any other hostile forces in the near future."

"Would you care to share a few of these things now, Tibby?" the admiral asked. "At this point hearing some good news for a change would be most welcome."

"I would prefer to wait just short while, Admiral. I would hate to raise false hopes and then not be able to deliver favorable results."

The admiral gave a heavy sigh. "Alright Tibby, so far your methods and actions have been pretty sound. I'll give you the benefit of the doubt on that. I hope you have something good and that it doesn't take you too long to let me in on it."

A'Lappe, Kala and I left the admiral and his staff and the captain and his crew on the bridge to confer over these latest developments as we headed aft to Cantolla's laboratories. Cantolla had briefly met A'Lappe, when she and Kala conducted his loyalty tests; but since then there hadn't been a real opportunity to get acquainted, nor had I found an opportunity to talk with them together. Cantolla greeted us as we entered her lab.

"I wondered just how long it would be before you brought A'Lappe to see me," Cantolla said. "I suspect he is full of information about the ship and the RMFF system."

"More than that," I said. "Besides being the engineer and architect for this ship, A'Lappe was also the chief architect of the original 10X fusion reactor. Your brother worked with him on Astamagota."

"You knew Kimmie!?" Cantolla exclaimed.

"I knew him very well. He was the brightest physicist on the project. When Galetils asked me to move onto the ship to prepare for the installation of the 10X reactor, it was Kimmie that I left in charge of things. He was a good man."

"Kimmie never mentioned you," Cantolla said. "But then he never mentioned anyone or even discussed his assignment, other than to say that it would revolutionize the power industry."

"How would you feel about finishing the work he was doing?" I asked Cantolla.

"Finish it?   How can I, when I don't know anything about what he was doing?"

"A'Lappe can fill you in on the project details and status at the time of the solar flare. He also has the plans and calculations for the 10X reactor; but before we build one, I want to see if the two of you can maybe find a way to make it smaller. As the design is now, the only Federation ships that can make use of it are star ships and frigates – and for the frigates it means surrendering a lot of space. Oh, one other thing – see if the two of you can resolve the power issue on the personal cloaking device that A'Lappe has invented."

"You have a *personal* cloaking device?" Cantolla said in amazement. A'Lappe shrugged his shoulders and vanished. "Well, I'll be damned," said Cantolla as A'Lappe reappeared about three meters away.

"The goal is to extend operation from the current 20 minutes to at least two hours before the device needs recharging," I said.

Cantolla gave A'Lappe a wide-eyed a look of admiration. "How did you ever come up with a personal cloaking device?"

"I actually stumbled on to it while trying to figure out why and how the RMFF acted as a cloaking device when subject to certain radio frequencies, as Kerabac discovered shortly after Tibby bought the *NEW ORLEANS*. I was monitoring developments from my suite; and when Kerabac inadvertently triggered the cloaking frequencies, I noted all sorts of crazy readings on my monitoring devices. It took me a few weeks to sort out the details, but I was able to come up with a small personal device that is based on a similar mechanism. Unfortunately, the current prototype draws a lot of power and lasts only a few minutes. My latest focus has been to find a more potent energy source to power it."

"Have you tried making it more efficient so it requires less power?" asked Cantolla.

A'Lappe blinked several of those incredibly hypnotic blinks and then said, "No, to be honest, I never gave that aspect any thought."

"Well, in that case I think I can help you," Cantolla answered. Suddenly, the two of them went off into some sort of rapid techno-speak, as they discussed potential improvements to the cloaking device with great excitement. Kala and I looked at each other and shrugged. Kala offered me her arm and the two of us left unnoticed by the two now entirely engrossed scientists.

"How long do you think it will take them to solve the problem?" Kala asked.

"Which one, the cloaking device or the reactor?"

"Either... or both," she said with a grin.

"Well, my guess is about two days for the cloaking device and hopefully no more than a week for the reactor. I'm just hoping this will keep A'Lappe busy enough so that the admiral doesn't feel like he has an invisible intruder lurking over his shoulder every hour of the day and night."

Kala laughed at my comment. "Yeah, A'Lappe sure had the admiral rattled. He's not used to having someone around who possesses more information about what's going on than he does."

The rest of the day went by quickly and it was evening before I realized it. After we ate a light meal, I casually suggested to Kala that we should visit the entertainment lounge. She was most receptive to the idea. I found a light colored pair of trousers in my wardrobe and picked a shirt in a slightly darker shade and of the special cut that I had Piebar create for me. Kala dressed in a very sexy outfit of dark shimmering green. The short skirt displayed her long legs in all their beauty. She was breathtaking; and I could tell she was pleased with my reaction when I saw her. I was almost tempted to forego the lounge when I saw her and instead spend the entire evening making love to her; but I knew dancing would only enhance that pleasure later, so I restrained myself.

We arrived at the lounge to see a small group of musicians made up of crew members playing on stage. I was struck by the similarity of the beat to Earth music from the late 1970s period. When the band began playing a tune similar to one from an entertainment vid story or "movie" on Earth, where the star of the movie performed a stunning solo dance routine, I couldn't resist showing off just a bit for Kala. When the movie first became popular, I was determined to learn every step and nuance of the dance. I practiced relentlessly to get it right. Over the years I made a habit of including the routine as a warm-up for my martial arts drills, so I hadn't forgotten any of the choreography. Since it was the first time anyone had seen me dance solo, it didn't take long before everyone stepped to the perimeter of the dance floor and to watch and clap in rhythm to the music. When the music ended I dropped to my knees and slid across the floor, ending up at Kala's feet in a perfect pose. The onlookers went wild with cheers and applause, while Kala just looked at me with a beaming smile.

The crowd wanted to see another dance, but I declined. The band played another number and people once again filled the dance floor, while I sat with Kala and caught my breath.

"Tibby, that was incredible! I only wish Lunnie had been here to see it. She loved dancing so much and truly admired anyone who could dance well; and what you just did was fantastic."

"Kala, I would cut off both my legs and never dance a step again, if it would bring her back," I said somberly.

"I know, Tibby, but I'm sure that, if there is an afterlife, someplace out there Lunnie was watching and dancing with you."

Kala and I relaxed at our table while we listened to the talented musicians and watched the dancers. Kala ordered an afex for me and, surprisingly, one for herself. I made no comment about it, however. After finishing the last song of their program the band left the stage; and immediately Kerabac stepped up. As before, Kerabac was greeted with cheers and shouts from people requesting songs. Kerabac started out with one of the songs that seemed to be a favorite with the crowd. Kala and I got up and danced through the number. When the song finished, everyone applauded and again started to call out their next requests; but Kerabac interrupted with an announcement. "I have a special request from First Citizen Tibby. This is a song from his home planet of Earth, which he wishes to dedicate to First Citizen Kalana," and with that he began performing one of the Nat King Cole songs that I discussed with him earlier in the day – one of my favorites called *The More I See You.* I took Kala by the hand and led her to the center of the floor, where we danced in a soft spotlight as everyone stood back to watch. Kerabac's rich voice and the magical lyrics of the song had their effect on Kala; I saw tears glisten in the corners of her eyes. Soon her head was on my shoulder as I held her close throughout the rest of the song. It ended all too soon to another round of cheering and applause and Kala kissed me gently on the cheek.

As we walked off the dance floor, Kerabac began another announcement. "And now I have another surprise for you. Most of you have not met our latest crew member, though a few of you have seen him accidently a few times," he added with a chuckle. "You'll be seeing him a lot more in the future, I assure you; and after tonight I think you will be hearing him a lot more often, as well. Ladies and gentlemen, I present to you… A'Lappe."

Both Kala and I stopped in our tracks and turned around to see A'Lappe take the stage with Kerabac as a mixture of murmurs and clapping stirred the room. A'Lappe sat himself down in the middle of a number of musical instruments arranged in a close configuration at the center of the stage. When he was situated and satisfied with his adjustments, he nodded to Kerabac, who had also seated himself at his *Judaras* keyboard. Suddenly, the room was filled with music and both Kerabac and A'Lappe were singing together in perfectly blended and effortlessly harmonized voices. Like his speaking voice, A'Lappe's singing voice was rich and mellow, which belied his diminutive stature. His hands flew over the various instruments to produce exquisite sounds as the two of them sang a popular tune that was apparently composed for a duet. As the melody reached its last note, a deafening applause erupted in the room; and in the span of three minutes A'Lappe had endeared himself to the ship's entire crew.

"You know, Tib, I almost think you and A'Lappe are related," Kala said into my ear over the roar of the crowd.

"Oh? Why do you say that?"

"Because it seems there is nothing the two of you can't do." I couldn't take my eyes off Kala; her skin glistened under the lights of the dance floor and her elation was almost tangible as she gazed up at the stage, clapping enthusiastically along with the rest of the throng. At that moment I couldn't imagine this life without her.

Early the next morning I met with Admiral Regeny and his staff to assemble a list of key planets whose contacts he and the High Command believed to be

secure. Before long, we had loaded a number of GW
pods with reactors and solbidyum and an encrypted
message directed to each contact. Admiral Regeny
chose to include in the initial shipments several
destinations mid-way between the central Federation
sector and the outlying areas, believing a strategy that
included successful deliveries to these highly frequented
planets would facilitate rapid spread of news in both
directions that solbidyum distribution was in progress.

A'Lappe showed up as we were loading the last
of the pods we intended to launch for that day.
"Admiral," he said, "I suggest that once these pods are
away that we postpone the trip to Aburn and your visit
with the crew of the *PURFIRE* and expedite our journey
to Plosaxen so you can quickly test and secure all the
troopers and leadership there. Then I recommend that
you immediately establish a stock of solbidyum on
Plosaxen and notify local planets to dispatch their own
secure contingent to pick up their allotment there, if they
do not wish to wait for the Federation to deliver it.
Without going into the details as to why, let them know
that the Federation simply doesn't have enough ships
and troops to transport and guard every one of a million
deliveries; and if they wish to receive their solbidyum
sooner than the Federation schedule allows, they will
need to respond with their own ships and guards. I
believe most of the Federation planets have their own
home guard and a few ships at their command. This will
place less strain on the Federation and will help to
prevent spreading the fleet over too much territory.
There will no doubt be attempts to intercept and raid
their ships; however, by that time you should have all the
troopers and Federation ships in and around Plosaxen
cleared and equipped with 10X reactors and RMFF
shields, so the military will be able to provide rapid

assistance, should anyone's private contingent be attacked."

"Humph," the admiral snorted, "you want us to split up the solbidyum supply so there is more than one location that can be attacked and that have to be defended? The more places we have involved, the easier it will be for the Brotherhood to find a weak spot and take that supply."

"Yes, that's true in some regards; but weighted against the impossible odds of ever getting the solbidyum distributed, it's one worth taking. Plus, as it is now, the risks posed by having all the solbidyum in *one* location are immense. Should the Brotherhood be able to infiltrate this ship or should this ship be lost by one means or another, the *entire* supply of solbidyum is lost. That scenario, too, is unacceptable, Admiral," A'Lappe asserted, blinking in his spellbinding fashion.

"Damn!" the admiral said running his hand through his hair as he paced the floor. "Why do you have to be right?" the admiral sighed with exasperation. "Okay, I see what you're saying and I agree; however, we need to work out security details and distribution protocols. We can't just have a bunch of ships lining up to get their share and then taking off, only to run into a raider that comes from behind the nearest asteroid to pick them off." The admiral rubbed his forehead as he continued, thinking more out loud to himself than anything. "I just wish we had more ships and more loyal crews to escort the solbidyum to the Federation planets."

"Wishing isn't going to help you, Admiral. You need to work with what you have. Deploying shipments via GW pods and allowing systems to pick up their own shipments from secured and well-defended sector headquarters are what you have as available options."

I had an idea.

"A'Lappe, you told me that the ship in the lower hangar is faster than a patrol ship but equally armed, didn't you?" I asked.

"What ship? What lower hangar?" the admiral blurted.

"It's a smaller, sleeker ship than the patrol ships that is suited for both in and out of atmosphere flight and is fully capable of engaging in combat situations. Before long, it will hopefully also be equipped with a small-scale cloaking device, once the design A'Lappe has been perfecting with Cantolla's help becomes serviceable. The ship is in a hidden hangar that Galetils included for emergency escape purposes," I said.

"Yes, Tibby, the ship is armed as heavily as a patrol ship and can achieve much faster acceleration and sustained speeds. Also, as I'm sure you recall, it is equipped with longer range sensors than those found on the Federation patrol ships," A'Lappe said with a grin.

"How long does it take to build one?" I asked.

"With the right automated fabrication and assembly machines, that craft can be constructed and commissioned in three days, given the required parts are at hand. If this is not the case, then the parts must be pre-fabricated and the total construction time increases to five days. If you mean to have such a craft built by way of *manual* labor on one of the less advanced worlds, you're looking at a construction schedule of almost a year per ship," A'Lappe answered.

"Does Plosaxen have a modern fabrication and assembly facility?" I asked, shifting my gaze from A'Lappe to the admiral.

"Well, yes," the admiral drawled out, "but they are busy building two badly needed frigates at the moment; and those are months from completion."

"There is a well-established personal and commercial airship fabricator located in the city of Yoroa in the southern hemisphere," A'Lappe interjected. "Their facility is most certainly large enough to handle this size ship. If they were able to dedicate most of their assembly lines to the project, they might be able to turn out three ships a day, once the project reaches full production. There's also another assembly plant outside of Gingham in the northern hemisphere that could probably turn out the same results."

I didn't want to share any more of my idea just yet, so I thought silently to myself, working out the math related to producing more of these ships. I figured that, if each star ship were to have a squadron of 180 ships it would take about 30 days to fabricate a full squadron at six ships per day.

Then I asked A'Lappe, "Where is the next closest facility?"

"On Colangee, but there is only one moderately equipped facility located there that I know of; it could turn out a ship a day at best."

"Admiral, if you're up to it I think you, A'Lappe, and I need to take a test flight in my little baby to assess its capabilities."

"As much as I would like to go, I'm afraid I must stay here to attend to Federation matters," replied Regeny. "However, one of my officers could join you and report back to me on the ship's operation. I think Lieutenant Commander Blissop would be a good choice. He was one of the top Federation pilots when he was flying."

"Whatever you think best, Admiral," I replied.

Since Lieutenant Commander Blissop wouldn't be available for the next two days, I sent A'Lappe back to Cantolla's lab to see what the two of them could accomplish by then, while I spent some extra time with Marranalis and the recruits to advance the training programs and with Kala to catch up on some administrative matters. I invited A'Lappe and Cantolla to dine with Kala and me on the second evening; but strangely they both declined by way of separate, somewhat cryptic messages advising that a breakthrough was near and they would be working through the night in an effort to complete some prototypes.

I really wanted to take Kala on the flight with me; but with A'Lappe, Lieutenant Commander Blissop and I onboard the ship was full. As a seasoned pilot and one of the best in the Federation, I felt it best to let Blissop run the little ship through its paces. We launched from the small hangar on the underside of the ship and accelerated to an incredible speed in seconds. Even with the gravitational field dampers engaged, my stomach still had to manage a mild effect from the G forces.

"I guess I'll need to modify and strengthen the gravitational dampers," remarked A'Lappe. "I didn't realize that the ship's added power exceeded the capacity of the existing system."

"This ship is fantastic," Blissop exclaimed like a boy in a toy store. "I'm registering speeds one and a half times that of the fastest ships we have in the fleet at the moment. If you can add a cloaking device, this craft will be incredible!"

"I only wish I could give it RMFF capabilities; but it's not possible at this point to produce a field generator small enough for this ship. The generator would be bigger than the ship itself," A'Lappe said.

"The maneuverability and speed of this ship are unmatched; if you can create an independent cloaking device for it, I don't think the RMFF will be needed. I assume weapon capabilities are intact while cloaked?" Blissop asked.

"Yes, in this case cloaking poses no problem for the weapons. Unlike the constraints created by the combined RMFF/cloaking functions on the *NEW ORLEANS*, cloaking does not need to be deactivated to fire weapons from this craft. In fact, at my first available opportunity, I hope to make some modifications to the *NEW ORLEANS* so the RMFF and cloaking device are not linked. It was an accidental discovery made by Kerabac that revealed the specific conditions required to produce the cloaking effect. I've since discovered that the RMFF is not necessarily required to produce these effects; and the independent version of the cloaking device doesn't require near the energy to operate as the RMFF-dependent version."

"Tibby, the admiral is going to be genuinely excited when I tell him about this ship," Blissop said enthusiastically.   Then in a more disappointed tone he continued, "But I fear we won't be able to get these ships for years.   The military is required to submit a request to the Senate and, after five to eight years of debate and arguments as to the merits of adding this new craft to the fleet, we may be authorized to build a dozen or so, just to try them out."

"I can solve that problem," I said. "I'm under no restrictions by a Senate or anyone else.   I can order the fabrication of as many ships as I want for my own security forces; and if I choose to let the Federation borrow those ships in defense of the Federation, no one will have a legitimate foundation for complaint.   I can build a fleet of thousands without making so much as a scratch in my wealth.

A'Lappe, when we get back to the *NEW ORLEANS*, I want you to contact the shipyards on Plosaxen, Gingham and Colangee – and, of course, speak with Orcpipin at the Nibarian shipyard.   Get quotes as soon as possible; and tell them I want several hundred of these ships on an expedited schedule.   After a price is established, tell them I will pay double for every ship they commission and deliver in perfect operating condition within 30 days.   An incentive program that strong should inspire them to suspend their other projects and make this a priority."

A'Lappe laughed.   "I think they'll drop everything and have crews working around the clock from now until then."

"If we can build this fighter fleet quickly and quietly, we should soon have enough squadrons available to protect the *NEW ORLEANS*, the *CACHATORA*, the *DUSTEN and* the *URANGA* and also serve as escorts for solbidyum transports; and we can have more fighters fabricated for starships at facilities in other sectors as deliveries progress. Agreed?"

"Agreed," replied A'Lappe. "This would be most effective."

"I'm just glad we are not back on Earth," I said. "A job like this would take almost a year to get out the door – just for *one* ship. It's the automated fabrication capabilities that are key to making this solution possible in the first place."

"I hope I can have the design for the cloaking device ready by the time the first ship is ready to come off the assembly line," said A'Lappe.

"If not, that feature will have to be added later," I replied. "Actually, I think it's best if the cloaking device is installed by the Federation military rather than at the factories anyway; so provide the fabricators with a design that includes the required space and infrastructure, but have the ships delivered without the actual device installed even when you do have it ready. We should retain control of our cloaking technology – and other proprietary inventions, for that matter – mainly to minimize the risk of revealing such critical capabilities to the Brotherhood or other enemies. Obviously, they'll sooner or later manage to obtain this or other forms of cloaking capability by other means; but let's not make it too easy for them.

"As soon as these ships are complete, I want pilots waiting for them at the factories. Once each ship passes commissioning and test flight protocols, I want them dispatched immediately to the *CACHATORA*, the *DUSTEN*, the *NEW ORLEANS*, and the URANGA with whatever orders and protocols are defined by Admiral Regeny. Try to work it out so each star ship and the *NEW ORLEANS* are continually protected by squadrons of equal size as we grow the fleet – assuming, of course, that the admiral approves. If he doesn't, then order them all to respond to the *NEW ORLEANS*; we will take in tow what we can't fit in our hangars. We'll need them sooner or later, I'm sure."

"I don't think the admiral will reject your idea – not after I report to him," assured Blissop. "I'd like to see every star ship supported by at least fifty of these flying miracles. We need a name for it, A'Lappe. Did you or Galetils have a name in mind?"

"We jokingly referred to its development as the *Blackhole Project*," said A'Lappe, "but we never managed to settle on a name for the design."

"Hmm. How about we call them the *Mirage Fighters*?" I suggested.

"That works for me!" Blissop said.

"It's as good as anything else, I think." said A'Lappe.

"Good," I said. "From now on this is a *Mirage Fighter*; and I think I will name *this* ship the *ALI*, after a famous pugilist back on Earth."

On the way back to the *NEW ORLEANS* Blissop let me fly the ship. The controls were similar to those of the *TRITYTE* and other patrol ships, which I had never actually flown myself outside of simulations. It was actually quite simple to maneuver manually; and it was equipped with a computer system similar to the *TRITYTE* that would navigate and fly the ship by voice commands, if one elected to do so.   I was a bit apprehensive about landing the ship in the hangar bay, until Blissop reminded me that I didn't need to manually do so.   I simply instructed the *ALI* to dock and the maneuver was performed automatically.   We barely had the hangar door sealed and air pressure restored before the admiral and Kala were there to greet us.   As we stepped out of the *ALI*, the admiral said, "So, how was it?"

Blissop could barely contain his excitement. "Admiral, you won't believe it.   This thing is 50% faster than the fastest ship we have at the moment.   Not only that, it maneuvers like a dream... and even though we haven't tested it in an atmosphere, I think – from what I have seen anyway – it will outperform any in-atmosphere aircraft we or anyone else has."

"Great!   Now all we need to do is convince the Senate that we need some...and by the time they decide to fund a few, when you and I are long dead, our grandchildren might – I say *might* – be able to see one or two of them fly."

"You're going to see them a lot sooner than that, sir," Blissop said with a gleam in his eye.   "Tibby is ordering several hundred as his personal security ships – and he's going to loan them to the Federation until the Senate gets around to funding them."

There was no verbal reaction from Regeny to this announcement.   For the first time since I arrived with the solbidyum and met him at the dinner gala on Megelleon, I saw the admiral shed a tear.

Aside from training FSO operatives, overseeing Marranalis' work with the Special Ops troopers and tending to the daily tasks of shipboard life, the rest of the trip to Plosaxen was relatively uneventful. A'Lappe and Cantolla were able to get the personal cloaking device to work for up to an hour and a half. I felt this duration was acceptable; but A'Lappe was certain that they could improve on that capability. In the meantime, they began producing cloaking units for all the Special Operations troopers, FSO agents and for my security force. A'Lappe didn't have the same luck with the cloaking device for the Mirage Fighters, but both he and Cantolla felt that they were making significant progress and would have it working within a few days.

Component fabrication for the first 10X fusion reactor was quickly completed and the unit was assembled in the compartment that had originally been designed for it. From there it would be transferred to the star ship *URANGA,* which was also scheduled to receive the first 25 Mirage Fighters to come out of the plant at Yoroa. A factory on Plosaxen had been located to build a second 10X fusion reactor and work was underway to have it ready for the *CACHATORA,* which had just left the Enpowor System for Plosaxen after being relieved by the star ship *SHANKUNO.* All three star ships and crews had been tested and certified as being clear of Brotherhood members. Between the three ships a little more than 3,500 Brotherhood members had been discovered and discharged from duty, a number that bothered the admiral greatly.

"By the time we're done purging the ranks," he said, "we stand to lose over a quarter of our forces. I am afraid we may lose a few ships as well."

"By my estimate you will lose nearly a third, Admiral," A'Lappe said with a rather serious look on his face, "but it's inevitable, given all that has transpired and considering how long the Brotherhood has been operating free of detection or opposition."

The admiral looked at A'Lappe a moment and shook his head. "I received word today from Senator Tacfacs of Plosaxen that the Senate is considering provisions for amnesty to any Brotherhood members who wish to disavow themselves of the Brotherhood and swear full allegiance to the Federation. They would still be allowed to remain in the Federation military with their current rank, but they would be transferred to support positions and removed from high-security defensive and combatant duties. Personally, I don't know how I feel about it. I can understand that many may have been drawn into the Brotherhood without knowing the full intentions and purpose of the cult, but part of me wants to hang the lot of them!

"Tacfacs wanted my thoughts and opinions on the matter. I told him that I'm in favor of it, with one uncompromising condition – each individual that accepts the offer of amnesty must provide every detail of knowledge they have on the Brotherhood's membership, operations, base locations, resources...*every shred* of information. I also told him that I didn't want the FOI handling it. He balked on that one, so I told him why. I didn't tell him about the FSO; I said only that the military would set up its own investigative team to obtain and analyze the data gathered from such interrogations. I'm not sure how well that went over, to be honest. I also suggested that individuals who provide key information that leads to the successful shutdown of a significant element of Brotherhood operations should be allowed to re-establish themselves with combat units in their original positions after one year with probationary oversight. He seemed to like that idea. He'll be headed back to the capital tomorrow to resume discussions. He thinks a vote on the issue could come as early as a month from now. That's unbelievably fast for the senate."

"It sounds like a good idea," I said. "If they make it happen quickly and broadcast the decision Federation-wide, it could prevent a lot of mutinies from occurring on other Federation ships. It would also open a whole new set of sources and avenues for gaining insight into Brotherhood's operations and broaden the Federation's means of weakening the Brotherhood's overall structure."

"As always, the time constraints associated with the broadcasts and subsequent communications are the main obstacle for making any of this happen quickly enough to be truly effective," A'Lappe asserted. "It would be almost two months *after* these factions receive news of the revolt on the *DUSTEN* that they would learn about the amnesty deal. In the meantime, they may decide to move forward with their own revolts, thinking that the time has come for the Brotherhood to act."

After we finished our discussion and left the hangar, Kala said to me, "Tibby, I have some good news and some bad news. The good news is that you've wanted to go planetside to do some sightseeing – and now we can. The bad news is that the people of Plosaxen wish to have a huge parade and banquet in our honor."

I moaned, "Not another ceremony! Well, we'll be here for a week. Let's make arrangements for the *TRITYTE* to be flown to the surface as a special exhibit for the citizens.

How soon is this parade and banquet thing taking place?" I asked in frustration.

"The parade is set for tomorrow and the banquet the next evening," Kala said with a sympathetic smile, "and I already made arrangements for the *TRITYTE* to be put on display. It should be on its way to the surface as we speak. I even saw to it that the dummy solbidyum container you used to get aboard the *DUSTEN* was loaded into the cargo hold."

"Kala, you're a dear...and you're brilliant. What would I do without you?" I said.

"Well, as I've said before, Thibodaux James Renwalt, I suggest you never try to find out!" Kala scolded playfully.

Since the parade was planned for the next afternoon, I suggested to Kala that we perhaps do some clandestine sightseeing before the celebration with less chance of being recognized. Kala laughed at this suggestion, insisting that there was no way we would go to the surface without being recognized, unless we were disguised. Even so, it would still be hard for us not to be spotted, since we would be surrounded by fully armed and ready bodyguards. I had forgotten about that provision. I had decided some time earlier that, for the safety of all my personal staff, none of us were allowed to venture away from the estate property or off ship without a contingent of bodyguards. "We can go," she said, "but we are going to have to be accompanied by bodyguards, per your own protocols."

"Well, at this point I don't care," I exclaimed. "I just want to see what the other worlds are like. I'm tired of only seeing the inside of ships or being restricted to my estate. I want to see the people in the towns and explore the shops and learn how they live and work."

Kala looked at me quizzically for a moment and then said, "I have an idea. Let me work on it a bit. Maybe I can arrange something."

Shortly after leaving Kala, I met with the FSO trainees. "I have an assignment for you. You will all be shipped down to Plosaxen's surface. Your assignment is to seek out and gather any information you can about the Brotherhood; their current activities and their plans. No morsel of information is considered too small or insignificant. Also, to try and garner any information you can about the FOI agents and their office here, particularly any information that may indicate Brotherhood connections or involvements within the FOI agents and leadership. Any information you may find indicative of Brotherhood or other subversive activity is to be reported immediately to Commander Wabussie. If you don't have anything to report, simply maintain your cover. You will report back here by noon one week from today – sooner, if you have gleaned something time-sensitive." As I finished this statement my wrist com indicated I had a call.

"Tibby here," I answered into the wrist com.

"Vice Admiral Tibby, this is Lieutenant Commander Goncest. Admiral Regeny requests your presence in the Admiralty conference room."

I was growing to hate being addressed with the honorary military title.

I sighed, "Tell him I am on my way."

The large conference room that I arranged for the Federation High Command as a temporary mobile command center was buzzing with activity when I arrived. As I entered the room, Admiral Regeny pointed to the large view screen. "As if it isn't bad enough that we have to deal with the Brotherhood taking our ships, we now have to put up with this." On the screen a small crowd of protesters gathered outside some government building to carry signs and voice their disgust for the Federation. On the signs were slogans like "Where is the solbidyum?" "The Federation lies!" "Solbidyum is a government lie!" and "Do you know where your solbidyum is?"

"It looks like some things are the same all over the galaxy," I said more to myself than to the admiral.

"This is not good," said the admiral. "I'm almost certain this is the work of the Brotherhood for the purpose of getting the citizens roused and sympathetic to their cause. We need to diffuse this situation quickly, before it gains enough momentum to be effective."

"Just a few more days and the solbidyum reactor will be installed and operating here," I said. "I suggest that, rather than broadcasting that we're here to deliver the solbidyum, we say we've come to make security preparations for its delivery and installation. Announce that the delivery will take place in a few weeks. That way they will be looking for a delivery after everything is already in place. It will also draw attention away from us. If we can convince the Brotherhood and others that we're currently traveling to planets in preparation for *later* delivery of solbidyum, it should make our job easier."

"That sounds like a good idea, Tibby. I'll see to preparing a news release that communicates a statement of that nature. I also want it known that I am touring each sector to meet with their captains and vice admirals. That should put the Brotherhood on alert and make their members nervous. This evening I'm going to the *URANGA* to meet with a number of the officers stationed in this sector; I think we should make some sort of news release about that, as well."

Kala and I were in the lounge that evening to enjoy performances by A'Lappe and Kerabac, when alarms suddenly sounded throughout the ship, alerting everyone to man their stations. Captain Stonbersa's voice came across the public address system. "We have just received reports of an explosion on the *URANGA*. We've been informed that the admiral was injured, though not seriously, and that several casualties and injuries have occurred among the crew. As added security for the *NEW ORLEANS*, the RMFF is has been activated; no one can enter or depart the ship until further notice. Weapon systems are activated – repeat – weapon systems are activated. The *NEW ORLEANS* is moving to provide support to the *URANGA*. Our estimated arrival time is approximately fifteen minutes."

During Stonbersa's broadcast, the alarm on my wrist com went off, indicating an urgent message that the captain was requesting my presence on the bridge. I noted Kerabac and A'Lappe also moving in that direction.

"Do you think it was an attack?" asked Kala as we moved rapidly toward the bridge.

"It's highly probable. If the admiral was injured in the blast, it must have detonated very near to him; and

I don't think he would have had any reason to be near any areas of the ship likely to have an accidental explosion. So yes, it was most likely an attack." Just then we arrived at the bridge. Captain Stonbersa addressed me immediately.

"Tibby, I took the liberty of moving the *NEW OREANS* in the direction of the *URANGA* to provide assistance and protection. I assumed that's what you would have wanted."

"Definitely, Captain. You know you have full authority to run the ship as you see fit. You have my full support. I don't expect you to ask for direction before acting in situations like this. You did the right thing. Have we received any more reports or communication from the *URANGA?*"

"We just heard that one of the admiral's aides was killed in the blast, as well as one senior officer. It is believed that a bomb was smuggled onboard by a Brotherhood crewmember that had been discharged from the service a week earlier. Somehow he still managed to sneak onboard. He was probably not flagged as a threat by anyone who may have seen him, as his face would have been a familiar sight and his discharge from the service may not have been widely known yet. Video surveillance shows him boarding the ship about 10 hours before the arrival of the admiral. There is no evidence of him leaving the ship; so it's believed that he is still aboard, perhaps planning further attacks."

Marranalis stood behind the captain, looking over data as it flowed across the screens of his console.

"Do we have contact with the admiral at the moment?" I asked.

"Yes, sir, we do," responded Marranalis.

"Good, I wish to speak to him immediately." There was a brief pause while Marranalis made some adjustments to control panel before him. Suddenly the admiral's image appeared on the screen. There was a nasty looking bruise on his forehead and his uniform was torn.

"Admiral Regeny," he said.

"Admiral, we received word of the incident and we're en route to provide any assistance we can. I understand that the suspected bomber is believed to still be aboard. I recommend that you allow our Special Ops unit to handle the situation and to pull back the ship's troopers and crew into a supportive backup position. This is the kind of thing we've been training for."

"I agree, Tibby, I'll give an order to the captain to allow your teams to board. How soon will you be here?"

"We're arriving now," I said. I could see the *URANGA* on the screen as Stonbersa assumed a strategic position adjacent to the star ship.

"Tibby, I'm also instructing the captain that you will be taking charge of counteroffensive operations and that he is to follow your recommendations. You seem to have a better head for these situations than we do."

"Well, the first thing I want to see is a defensive ring of patrol ships around the *URANGA*. I don't see any at the moment." I saw the admiral turn his head from the screen and bark an order to someone out of view. While he was doing that I said to Marranalis, "Get your team assembled and moving – full armor and weapons – have them in the hangar and loaded in 20 minutes."

"Yes, sir," he said, issuing orders via his wrist com as he left the bridge.

"A'Lappe," I said turning to him next. "Where do you think this man would most likely plant bombs on the *URANGA?*"

"My guess would be in or near the admiral's shuttle and at the bridge; but without access to the bridge he will most likely try to plant a bomb somewhere adjacent to the bridge. This would be the most logical assumption, since he wants to kill the high ranking officers but not completely disable the ship. The Brotherhood may be planning to carry out a broader attack on the *URANGA*, if they can disable its defenses temporarily."

"Hm, you may be right there. Once Marranalis has his group aboard the *URANGA*, I want the RMFF immediately reactivated. Our presence may keep the *TECCION* from attacking, if they're in the vicinity."

"Admiral, are you still there?" I asked.

"Yes, still here… just listening to your plans. They sound good."

"Yeah, but I just realized something; tomorrow is when we are supposed to attend the parade. If you and I don't show, who knows how the Brotherhood will use that situation to their advantage. On the other hand, if we show up as planned, it will prevent the Brotherhood from putting a negative spin on our absence and perhaps instill a sense of failure and impotence among their ranks in their attempted attack on you. Of course, the parade also presents an opportunity for them to attack again."

"You may have something there, Tibby, but do you think it wise that I leave while the bomber is still onboard?"

"Well, unless you plan to personally track him down while everyone else watches, I see no benefit to your staying there."

"Good point. What do you suggest?"

"First, if you're not too badly injured, I suggest you and your officers get cleaned up and into fresh uniforms as soon as possible. In the event you need to make an appearance on a news broadcast, you'll want to appear relatively unscathed. Any vids or images of you that are seen by the public – or by the Brotherhood, for that matter – should portray a sense of control and security, which is more important now than ever. As soon as you're ready, have someone bring you to the *NEW ORLEANS* in one of the patrol ships. *Don't* use your shuttle or any of the others; they're all likely candidates for a booby trap and will have to undergo a thorough sweep.

Marranalis and his troops successfully secured the main areas of the *URANGA* and ushered the admiral and his surviving staff to a patrol ship that returned them to the *NEW ORLEANS* without incident. After settling back into the command center, the admiral reviewed vids of the incident and read reports that starting pouring in from various debriefings that were underway. When he felt comfortable that he was fully informed as to the known scope of the incident, we resumed our conversation about the following day's events on Plosaxen.

"For security reasons it's obviously best that we wait until morning to shuttle to the surface. Once we're there, I'm primarily concerned about the parade. That sort of venue leaves us pretty vulnerable and I don't want to walk into a situation where we're sitting targets."

"I think I can help you there," offered A'Lappe, "but we'll need to borrow the 10X fusion reactor that's intended for the *URANGA* for a few hours."

"You want us to move the 10X reactor off the ship and back again? You don't think that will be rather obvious?" I said.

"We won't be moving it off the ship; in fact, we won't need to move it at all. What we will do is connect it to the *NEW ORLEANS*' RMFF system in place of the solbidyum reactor, which we can temporarily relocate to one of the surface transports we have here on the ship. The admiral can insist to Senator Tacfacs that we must use our own ground transport for the parade. We can easily install the small prototype RMFF system that I have developed for the Mirage Fighters and power it with the solbidyum reactor to provide a safe shield around the transport at all times. I can install a control switch that will allow us to tailor the field so it is as close as a few millimeters beyond the vehicle's exterior, as it will need to be on the underside during the parade, while it is as far as two meters away at the top and sides. To the crowd everything will appear normal; but if anyone should attempt to fire at you, you'll remain perfectly safe."

"I don't know that I'm too keen on taking the solbidyum reactor off the *NEW ORLEANS*, but it's highly unlikely anyone will even consider the possibility that we've done so, much less find out once we're there," I said. "We can immediately reinstall it when we get back and then deliver the 10X reactor to the *URANGA* as originally planned. We're taking a risk, but I don't see that we have a lot of alternatives that will guarantee our safety. What do you think, Admiral?"

"I don't like the idea of the solbidyum reactor leaving the safety of the *NEW ORLEANS* either, but I agree; it's unlikely anyone will suspect anything, since its existence is pretty much unknown to all but a very few Federation officials."

"Okay then, its settled. Do what you have to, A'Lappe, but limit the number of people who know about it and use only those technical personnel with the highest levels of security."

The next morning Kala and I met with Admiral Regeny for a quick breakfast. Other than for a slight scratch and slight bruise on his forehead, there was little sign of his having been near the explosion on the *URANGA*. The admiral was in the process of telling us about the incident when word came in from Marranalis on the *URANGA*, reporting that the Special Ops team had managed to locate and capture the bomber. They had also located and disarmed a second bomb planted on the opposite side of a bulkhead to the bridge, just as A'Lappe had surmised. The remainder of the ship had been cleared, including the transports and shuttles. The bomber was being questioned by some of Marranalis' investigative detail and the rest of the team was being dispatched to the surface to set up security along the parade route.

I harbored some doubt that A'Lappe would be able to accomplish all that he had suggested, as far as moving the reactors and installing the RMFF on the transport in time for our departure for the planet. However, when Kala, the admiral and I met him in the hangar, A'Lappe advised that the solbidyum reactor and RMFF installation for ground transport was completed and tested and that the transport was already loaded into the small freighter that awaited us in the hangar. Six patrol ships were manned and ready to escort us to the surface. The admiral, Kala, Marranalis and I would ride inside the ground transport with the RMFF shield on while still in the freighter cargo hold, just in case of an attack on the ship. Even if the ship were blown up, the RMFF shield would protect the four of us and we would be safe. Fortunately, the trip to the surface went smoothly and there was no sign of attackers.

The ground transport was a vehicle similar in size to a vehicle we had on Earth called a *stretch limousine*. The sides and a large portion of the top were retractable, so the crowd could see us as we moved along the parade route. A'Lappe assured us that even with the top and sides open, the RMFF shield would remain effective.

The capital city on Plosaxen was similar in features to the major cities back on Earth. The metropolitan areas were defined by tall buildings, endless traffic and crowds of people. The streets were a bit wider than those seen on Earth and there were no traffic lights. Instead, each vehicle was equipped with an electronic device that was synchronized with an automated traffic control system, which slowed and stopped vehicles at intersections and regulated the alternating flow of traffic on perpendicular streets. The system was remarkably simple and traffic accidents at intersections were virtually nonexistent.

I was reminded of my first trip to the capitol on Megelleon as we made our way through the city. The crowds that lined the streets were even denser; and the banners, flags and confetti were as abundant as the ecstatic cheers and waving from the citizens.

We were about half way through the parade route when the assault on the transport took place. One moment all was normal, and in the next the entire transport was suddenly enveloped in what I can only describe as a virtually silent bubble of blinding white light. There were several such bursts before something struck the field with a loud explosion and a ball of fire consumed the space surrounding the transport. Between the bursts of light and fire I could see people fleeing, some falling to the street wounded, and others stumbling in their haste to escape. Kala's first reaction was to want to jump out of the transport to help the fallen and injured. I had to struggle to hold her back and repeatedly remind her that the RMFF shield could harm her if she tried to pass through it.

The field lit up again, as another volley of fire was absorbed. Then, just as suddenly as it began, everything stopped and all was quiet, save for the cries of the injured and fleeing citizens. Troopers appeared from the leading and trailing security vehicles to take up positions around the transport. By means of a headset and the com system inside the transport, Marranalis was able to communicate with the troopers, who directed us to stay in place for the moment. A few seconds later the voice of Major Sokaia came across the com system to report that the attackers were in custody and emergency units were already arriving to triage and transport the injured. The scene was secure and it was now safe for us to move forward.

I gave Marranalis a questioning look and he said, "I sort of anticipated that something like this might happen, so I had most of the Special Ops troops sent planetside several hours early to assume stations along the route."

"Good job," I said and slapped him on the shoulder.

"That's amazing," exclaimed the admiral. "You were able to corner and capture the assailants within just a few minutes of the attack. I never would have believed it possible had I not seen it."

"Just think what it will be like when every star ship in the fleet is carrying about 200 of these Special Ops troopers," I said.

"Yes, indeed... and when all my troopers are trained in martial arts, as well...yes, indeed," the admiral said as he grinned and reclined in his seat.

As a precautionary measure to prevent further threat to the citizens, the parade was cut short; but we maintained our visibility before the citizens from a safe distance as everyone dispersed. This visibility asserted the Federation's unwavering presence in spite of the assault. Marranalis continued to direct his teams and track their deployments on his vid pad maps while we maintained this posture; and I did my best to reassure Kala, who still wanted to help injured citizens, that medical personnel were on their way and would be better able to care for them – that and the fact that our presence could serve to put more people in danger if the Brotherhood tried to attack us again. When I said that,

Kala relented; but I could see the concern on her face for those who were injured. Within an hour we were able to return to the *NEW ORLEANS* to quickly debrief and watch the news broadcasts of the incident.

If the Brotherhood had hoped to advance their cause in the eyes of the people by eliminating the admiral and me with their attack, they failed drastically. While the rest of the parade was canceled the news media was ablaze with vid broadcasts of scenes and comments about the attack. It was quickly noted by the media that some sort of "secret force field" had been employed by the Federation to protect the ground transport and that the attackers were apprehended with unprecedented efficiency and skill by "an equally elite and hitherto undisclosed group of specially trained troopers." The overall message presented by the media was one of powerfully demonstrated Federation superiority, where the Federation was not just on top of the situation at hand but consistently one step ahead of the Brotherhood, an organization that was clearly revealing itself to be nothing more than a band of rebel terrorists.

Admiral Regeny played his role to the hilt when interviewed by the press, hinting that the Federation had advanced knowledge of plans for a potential attack by the Brotherhood and expressing his concern for the citizens who suffered injuries as at the hands of these violent criminals, who clearly had no regard for the welfare of the people of Plosaxen. When asked about the inability of the weapons fired by the Brotherhood to harm those inside the confines of the transport, the admiral simply said, "That information is classified," and moved on to the next question – an approach that put forward an air of strength, control and resolve.

Kala was relieved to also hear in the reports that all injured parties were expected to make a full recovery.

"Well," Kala said as we were watching the vidcasts, "it certainly seems that whole situation worked out to our advantage."

"Yes," I said, "and I think we all owe A'Lappe and Cantolla a measure of gratitude and recognition. Had it not been for A'Lappe's inventions and the combined efforts of the two of them over the last two days, we would most likely all be dead now. As it is, in the minds of the citizens of the Federation – and probably those of many non-aligned planets – the Brotherhood is not a friend of the people; their organization is made up of traitors, liars and violent criminals. Hopefully this incident will lead to desertions from their ranks, at least in this sector of space. In just a few days the solbidyum reactor will be commissioned here and Senator Tacfacs can announce that the delivery has taken place as promised by the Federation. At that point, I suspect the Brotherhood will flee this area to concentrate on another planetary system where they can establish their footing.

"Since numerous Federation vessels arrive here daily, hopefully no one – particularly the press – will assume that the *NEW ORLEANS* was the ship that delivered the solbidyum, though I'm sure there will be at least some speculation of that nature. If we can continue to implement the GW pod deliveries as planned and successfully commission solbidyum power distribution on a few dozen planets in different sectors, especially on planets far removed from anywhere the *NEW ORLEANS* has travelled, I think the idea that we're the ones delivering the solbidyum will vanish. By that time we'll hopefully not be needed for deliveries at all anymore."

The normal calm of the ship was broken suddenly, when alarms again sounded and Captain Stonbersa's voice came over the com links. "All crew members, respond to battle stations. We are under attack - I repeat we are under attack. The RMFF is deflecting fire. There are no reports of damage to the *NEW ORLEANS*. Repeat – there are no reports of damage and the RMFF is deflecting fire from the assailants."

Fortunately, Kala and I were near the bridge when the alarm sounded. I left Kala to communicate with her staff. I entered the bridge by the time the captain finished his announcement.

"Ah, Tibby, you're here. Good. What do you make of all this?" Stonbersa said sweeping his arm toward the view screen. Three patrol ships could be seen speeding toward the *NEW ORLEANS* and attacking with every weapon they had. Flashes of light filled the screen and streaks of energy played around the RMFF field but nothing came even remotely close to penetrating the shields.

"Just three ships?" I asked.

"That's all we've seen so far," replied Stonbersa.

"When they come about on their next sweep, wait until they pass by and then activate the cloaking device just at the point where you think they lose visual contact with us. Then move us in the opposite direction far enough that they don't fly into us but so we are still within sight of them. If I'm right, they will linger a bit and then head for home, wherever that is. Follow them discretely while cloaked and let's see where they lead us," I said.

"Has anyone seen A'Lappe? I need to talk to him." No sooner had I asked the question than A'Lappe appeared by my side, as if by magic. I shook my head, knowing full well that he had been there all the while and that he enjoyed the mischief and theatrics of appearing out of thin air.

"You wish to see me, First Citizen?" he said.

"Yes, A'Lappe, we need to know what communications are taking place between those patrol ships."

"I see. And why would you believe that I would be able to tap into coded channels that the Brotherhood might be using?" A'Lappe said, looking suddenly deflated and pouty.

"I know you have a means of identifying frequencies by way of some combination of sweeps and scans and tapping into coded transmissions between ships. I suspect you've been able to do so for some time and that it's how you've obtained most of the information you have," I said while looking at him like a parent who has just caught a child in a lie.

A'Lappe grinned sheepishly and shrugged his shoulders. "Okay, so you figured it out. But I can't promise that I'll be successful; I am only able to establish a reliable tap about a third of the time. The Brotherhood isn't all that creative with their coding, so let's see what I can uncover," he said as he seated himself at the communication console.

His small hands moved skillfully and quickly across the touch screens and panels as small windows began to display various wave signs and signals. A'Lappe appeared to be trying to capture these transmissions with some kind of combination signal transducer and resonance instrument that he manipulated via the touch screens.

Suddenly a voice came across the speaker on the console. "–one minute as we passed, and then when we came about a second later, they were simply gone. We've searched the area, but there's absolutely no sign of them either visually or on the sensors."

"Very well. Make one more pass through the area. Then head off in the opposite direction from base for the next two hours. After that, split up and return to base using different routes. Keep your eyes open. If you see anything on the sensors, move in a direction away from the base and return only when you're sure you're not being followed."

"Yes, sir."

A'Lappe spun in his seat to look at us. "Will there be anything else?" he asked.

"Yes, A'Lappe. I need the *ALI* fully operational, including the cloaking device, before we get to the Brotherhood's rendezvous point. Do you think that's something you can accomplish in a few hours?"

"It's already done, First Citizen," A'Lappe said with his usual grin. "Installation and testing was completed while you were at the parade. The only constraint is that you won't have an unlimited cloaking time. At the moment the prototype will only provide you with about an hour of cloaking capability; and then you'll have to wait two to three hours before enough energy has built up to support cloaking again."

"That's still enough time to sneak in or to escape from a situation, if necessary," I said, "but I thought you said that energy wasn't a major factor with the independent cloaking system...?"

"Unlike cloaking on the NEW ORLEANS, which doesn't require its own power source, as it is essentially an induced side effect of the RMFF, the *ALI*'s cloaking device must accumulate energy that is slowly discharged under certain conditions to create the field when it's in operation. So, until I'm able to create a smaller and more powerful energy source that is appropriate for the *ALI*, its cloaking capabilities remain limited to one hour. I could probably duplicate the solbidyum reactor arrangement that was used in the transport for the parade; but I don't think it's advisable to do so. The solbidyum reactor serves the *NEW ORLEANS* better than it would the *ALI.*"

"I have to agree with you there, A'Lappe. Frankly I was nervous about using the solbidyum reactor in the transport. Fortunately we did, though, or we wouldn't be here now."

"Captain," I said to Stonbersa, "pick one of those retreating ships and follow it. It's time to find out where the Brotherhood's base is hidden. My guess is that we will find ourselves moving toward the third moon of Ludation, as A'Lappe theorized."

"Why not just head there now, if that's the case?" the admiral asked.

"Because we can't be entirely certain and we don't want to get it wrong. These ships will lead us to their base without a doubt. Aside from that, the base may not be as easy to find as A'Lappe suspects; so again, this is the surest way to locate the underground portal, if there is one. It's also possible that they're returning to an airbase, meaning the *TECCION*. In that case they wouldn't be going to the moon at all, but someplace else in space."

"I see your point, Tibby," said the admiral.

"Tibby," interjected Kala, "what about the banquet tomorrow? After today's incident, it's more important than ever that we don't miss that event."

"I'd forgotten about that," I said, "but this is too important for us to let go. If it looks like we're going to be led too far way to return in time to attend, we'll just have to find a diplomatic excuse for delaying the banquet."

"I can handle that situation," said Admiral Regeny, "I'll contact Senator Tacfacs and tell him that we've heard rumors of a plan to detonate a bomb at the banquet and that we may need to cancel it until we receive more intelligence. That should buy us the time needed to deal with these rebels."

"Good, hopefully this won't take too long to accomplish," I said.

Little did I realize that it would take far less time than even I anticipated. By late afternoon Stonbersa reported that the ship we followed was approaching a much larger craft that was about the size of the *TECCION*.

"It looks like the rebels decided not to hide out on a planet or moon after all; they simply moved out further into the vacuum of space," commented Stonbersa. "What do you want us to do now, Admiral?"

"I'd hate to blow the ship up," said the admiral, "but unless they're willing to surrender, I don't see that we will have a lot of options. We need that ship and *every* ship we have in the fleet to ultimately squash these brigands. We can't afford to go around blowing up every ship the Brotherhood may take."

"Maybe we won't have to blow them up… how about we just shake them up a little?" I said.

The admiral looked at me and grinned, "What's your plan, Tibby? I have a hunch it's going to be a good one."

"First off, we have to back out of sensor range of the *TECCION* just long enough for us to drop shields and launch the *ALI*. Marranalis and two other troopers can take her out cloaked. Then we'll also return cloaked and position ourselves within close distance of the *TECCION*. We'll broadcast our presence to them, giving them the option to surrender peacefully. They won't of course, but they won't be able to see us either.

"In the meantime, the *ALI* will fly around to their other side. When we tell the Brotherhood that they are surrounded and to surrender, we'll then materialize so they can see the *NEW ORLEANS*. They'll most certainly open fire; and when our RMFF shields dissipate the hits, they will again see that their weaponry is ineffective. We'll then return fire aimed to take out some of the GW propulsion systems on the ship, while the *ALI* simultaneously takes out several of the GW drives on the other side the ship while remaining cloaked. The *TECCION* will have to assume that a squadron of invisible ships has surrounded the *TECCION* and that they are outclassed and unable to strike back. I think under those circumstances, and in light of the events of the past few weeks, they will surrender without further resistance. We'll then send over patrol ships carrying Special Ops troopers to round up the rebel crew; confine them securely, and then fly the crippled ship back to Plosaxen for repairs. You can schedule a news conference and broadcast vid clips, like we did at Megelleon, so the citizens can witness the successful operation."

"I like it," said the admiral. "Let's just hope the rebels are as willing to surrender as you think."

According to this plan, Stonbersa moved the *NEW ORLEANS* out of range so the *ALI* could be launched. The captain then moved us back to the *TECCION* in a position adjacent to their main hangar – so close that if we were uncloaked and standing in the open hangar bay those onboard the *TECCION* would have easily been able to see us with the naked eye. In fact, our position would make it extremely difficult for the Brotherhood to deploy any patrol ships out of the hatch of the *TECCION* to retaliate.

A universal communication link was then opened and Admiral Regeny announced, "Attention, rebel insurgents aboard the *TECCION,* this is Admiral Regeny of the Federation Space Force. You are hereby ordered to surrender. You are surrounded."

There was a moment's pause before an image appeared on the screen. It was obvious that these members of the Brotherhood had their own idea of uniforms, as their Federation dress had been replaced with a dark, almost violet blue uniform. This was somewhat surprising, as the Brotherhood troops that had taken over the *DUSTEN* wore black uniforms with contrasting collars. The image on the screen was that of a middle-aged woman.

"This is Captain Ceewurd of the Brotherhood of Light. You seem to be delusional, Admiral, as you have no ships in our vicinity and I hardly believe you are in any position to take action against us."

The admiral signaled to Stonbersa to reveal our position as soon as she stopped speaking. Stonbersa deactivated the cloaking mechanism while maintaining the RMFF defense shields. On the screen we saw Ceewurd's face render surprise as Admiral Regeny said gravely, "We are much closer than you think, Captain. I highly recommend you surrender – now."

Behind Captain Ceewurd one of her officers turned to her in a panic. "They're right on top of us, Captain, what shall we do?"

"Fire, you idiots," Ceewurd screamed. "FIRE!"

For the next several minutes lights and explosions flashed across the RMFF shield as the weapons of the *TECCION* blazed away and Captain Stonbersa and the admiral stood calmly before the vid screen. Eventually the firing stopped; and the shock that consumed Ceewurd's entire posture betrayed her attempt to assert an air of control.

"It's a trick. They're not really there. It's some sort of illusion or hologram," she insisted hysterically.

The admiral replied with grim calm, "I assure you, Captain, this is no illusion. At this moment a squadron of cloaked and shielded Federation ships surround you; and if you do not surrender in the next two minutes, we will open fire."

I was hoping that the *TECCION* would surrender at this point, as time would otherwise run out on the *ALI*'s cloaking device and they would need to withdraw for protection.

"You're bluffing, Admiral," replied Ceewurd with a contemptuous grin. "You have nothing but an illusion of a ship in our vicinity and *that* appears to be a space yacht and not a star ship."

"It is your choice, Captain," said Regeny, "I have no intention of playing games with you."

"Be careful, Captain," I whispered to Stonbersa, as the *NEW ORLEANS* prepared to fire on the *TECCION*'s GW drives. "We don't want a repeat of the underwater base on Megelleon."

"Right," he whispered back. "Kerabac and I have since calibrated for the amplification. We can do this without blowing them to pieces."

We had discovered quite by accident the first time we fired weapons from the *NEW ORLEANS* through the active RMFF shields that the RMFF field amplified the force and energy of any beam or projectile launched from the ship. Consequently, the damage done to the targets was many times over the expected outcome under non-shielded conditions. If we were to fire through the RMFF at normal strength to disable its engines, we would most likely blow the ship into oblivion.

Stonbersa gave the order to the weapons officer, "Fire to take out the starboard GW drives. *ALI*, fire to take out their port GW drives." There were brief flashes of light from the weapons on the *NEW ORLEANS* and small explosion occurred on the GW drive pods on the *TECCION.*

While we could not see what was happening on the other side of the *TECCION,* we could hear Marranalis' voice over the speaker saying, "Port GW drives disabled, sir."

"Thank you, *ALI.* Stand and hold for further orders." Actually the ALI was not standing or holding; Marranalis had moved the craft almost immediately after firing so its location could not be targeted.

"As you can see, Captain Ceewurd, we are not bluffing. Do you care to surrender now?"

"But how!? You have cloaking? How is it we haven't heard?! How many ships?!"

"Do you surrender or not, Captain? Your time is about to expire. I assure you that it is within our power to eliminate you just as we did the *TASSAGORA* in the battle at the *DUSTEN*!" demanded the admiral, now hard-faced and leaning forward in his chair toward the screen.

"No, no, I won't – I can't! This is all a mistake!" said Ceewurd, when suddenly a ray of light pierced her head and she dropped in front of the view screen. A moment later, another uniformed individual appeared, holding a flat gun in his hand.

"This is First Officer Weper," he said. "In the absence of a captain, we surrender."

"Disarm all persons aboard the ship and stow the weapons in the weapons lockers. Open the hangar door and have all your people onboard in the aft cargo hold.

Troopers have already been deployed to take you and the ship into custody," the admiral said, before disconnecting the transmission.

Afterward he turned to me and said, "Not bad. Not bad at all. In just a little over twelve hours we managed to track down and retake the *TECCION*. This should be a real blow to the Brotherhood and should cause some desertion within their ranks.

"I wonder what information the FSO agents have been able to gather on the surface of Plosaxen, he continued. Hopefully some of them have gleaned something new that will help us take our counteroffensive actions to the next level. I need to contact Commander Wabussie when we get back to Plosaxen and find out what he and his teams have uncovered."

"I wouldn't get overly confident, Admiral," said A'Lappe, who was just entering the bridge. "I fear you will soon learn that the Brotherhood has a much stronger hold on some systems than you have encountered so far. The Federation may even want to disassociate themselves with these systems, rather than war with them."

"I hope you're wrong," responded the admiral. "But if you're right, let's hope that the events here will weaken their holds on those systems."

It took about three hours for the Special Ops troops to secure the *TECCION* and to isolate and confine the prisoners. I met Marranalis as he returned the *ALI* to its hangar. He was beaming as he disembarked.

"Tibby that ship is incredible!" he exclaimed. "When we have more of these ships, the Brotherhood –

or any other opponent we come up against – won't have a chance!"

"Let's hope that they never get their hands on one then," I said, smiling at Marranalis' boyish excitement.

His expression became suddenly sober. "I must confess, I hadn't thought of that possibility. It would definitely be a terrible thing if they did. The thought of it alone is frightening as hell."

"That's all the more reason for us to make sure the Mirage Fighter pilots and crews are our own specially trained and cleared people. We can't take any chances on so much as a single incident of a Brotherhood member ever getting aboard one," I replied.

"That shouldn't be a problem," said Marranalis. The ships can easily be programmed to allow access only to the assigned crew in the same way that the *TRITYTE* was when we flew it to Megelleon."

"That's not a bad idea," I said, "but I think it would be better if it were restricted to a squadron rather than just a crew. That way, if there is an emergency situation that requires a change in crew or ship assignment, they wouldn't be hindered by access restrictions. The danger of losing a ship is the same either way, as any squadron member could steal their own ship as well as any other."

It was nearly mid-morning when we arrived back at Plosaxen. The *NEW ORLEANS* had barely reestablished orbit before a message arrived from Commander Wabussie requesting a meeting with Admiral Regeny and me. We flew to the surface on one of the patrol ships accompanied by eight bodyguards. A ground transport flanked by several armored land units that served as escorts was waiting at the landing area to quickly transport us to a headquarters building on the base. Admiral Regeny insisted that I wear my vice admiral uniform, which meant I was saluted and had to return salutes everywhere we went. We were driven to an administrative building on the base, where we then entered a tunnel that led to an underground parking area. The armored escorts remained outside the portal to protect the entrance. Our transport was met by a Federation major, who greeted us and asked that we follow him. We passed by several armed troopers stationed at a large door and that led to a transit terminal building. There we boarded a transit pod that was likewise guarded by several armed troopers.

Admiral Regeny explained to me, "As a result of the incidents that have occurred over the past several days, our personal safety has become a paramount concern of the Federation. You still maintain the position of being the most valuable person to the Federation, Tibby, so several hundred loyal troopers have been specially assigned to protect both you and me at this time. What you witness here is only a small fraction of the troops that are actually here on the site to guard us."

"I assume that information is supposed to make me feel more comfortable, Admiral, but it doesn't. All it means is that my life is still in danger and that I have enemies I cannot see."

The transit pod made several turns and maneuvers before stopping at a station where we changed pods, only to go back in the direction we had just traveled as the first pod continued in the original direction. We only traveled a short distance before stopping again at a station where our small detachment of troopers was redoubled before we were led down several corridors to a passkey protected assembly area.

Once inside this area, most of the troopers took up positions along the perimeter, while a smaller number followed us down another corridor to a conference room where all but our own personal guards and the major left us. From there we entered a modestly appointed but comfortable room where Commander Wabussie stood by a desk. He immediately snapped to attention, saluted the admiral and me, and received salutes and acknowledgements in return.

"Admiral and Vice Admiral, I am glad you were able to make it here so quickly. I received internal reports that you had left orbit in pursuit of the Brotherhood traitors and I feared that it might be days or weeks before you returned. I should have known it would not be anywhere near that long with Tibby involved," he grinned.

"Actually, this time it was more A'Lappe's doing that allowed us to accomplish the task so quickly," I interjected.

"A'Lappe... aye! Do you know I cannot get a single clue as to who he is or where he's from?" Wabussie said with exasperation. "There exists only one vid pic of him prior to your discovery of his presence on the *NEW ORELANS* and that was taken on Astamagota before the solar flare. He was captured in some raw vid footage taken of Galetils at the laboratory where they were working on the 10X fusion reactor for a vid documentary that was never aired. A'Lappe can be seen in the background talking to, of all people, Cantolla's brother."

"A'Lappe said he knew and worked with Cantolla's brother," I said.

"Well, prior to that vid pic we haven't been able to find any records that show he existed before that day. There is virtually no trace of him in the Federation archives – nothing that matches his name or his image.

"But that's not what I called you here to discuss," said Wabussie, as he refocused his thoughts on the issue at hand. "Please have a seat," he said, indicating two chairs by his desk.

"The FSO recruits have uncovered several leads and collected substantial information during their mission that is very disturbing. We've been able to get two agents inside the organization already and have established several other sources and leads in the local communities. In general, the information we have gained from all of these the sources consistently indicates that the Brotherhood is stronger in this sector than they were near Megelleon and that they are resolved to succeed in some major action against the Federation that will bring more attention to their cause and weaken the Federation's organization in the eyes of the citizens. Both of you – and the *NEW ORLEANS* – are the focus of these attacks.

"Prior to the attack at the parade, the Brotherhood had heard rumors and accounts of the failed attacks on the *NEW ORLEANS*, as far as the cloaking and shields; but they had doubts as to the validity of those claims. They believed strongly that they were propaganda tricks circulated by the Federation to make the military appear stronger than it is. Now they're even more resolved to destroy the High Command, Admiral, along with Tibby and the *NEW ORLEANS*. While I do not believe the *NEW ORLEANS* is in any real danger, as long as it keeps the RMFF active and prevents any traitors from boarding, I do not feel so certain about your personal safety when off the ship.

"Vids of the parade continue to be broadcast by the media. The typical newscasts show scenes of the failed attack followed by messages sent to the media from the Brotherhood that denounce the incident as a fake – a fabrication they claim was created by the Federation to vilify the Brotherhood and instill fear among the citizens. The Brotherhood is even going as far as to claim that the defenses used around the parade vehicle were simply special effects.

"So, their goal now is to inflict serious damage. They believe that killing the admiral and the High Command or destroying the *NEW ORLEANS* will prove their claims in the eyes of the public that the Federation is concocting false stories to defame and undermine their organization and retain their hold on the people."

Admiral Regeny sighed, "Well, so far their attempts have proved an embarrassment for them. We recaptured the *TECCION*, so unless the Brotherhood has another of the Federation's warships or have built their own, which I doubt, I don't see where they have much of anything in the way of resources to use in another assault – at least not in this system."

"Maybe not," Wabussie said, "but our FSO operatives indicate that the Brotherhood alludes to having something else that we have not yet been able to uncover; and they seem to feel they can successfully take on the *NEW ORLEANS* with it.

"There's one other thing I think you should know," said Wabussie as he displayed an image of a man on the vid screen behind his desk. "You remember Eulshod Rendoid, the puppet figurehead of the Brotherhood's early movement. Not long after the rebellion occurred at Megelleon, he surrendered himself to the Federation in exchange for information he had on the Brotherhood. We received a communication today from the prison facility where he was being held on Megelleon that he was found dead in his cell shortly after we left. His throat was slit and the guards posted at his cell were also killed. The killer or killers got into the prison wing, killed Rendoid and the guards and fled undetected, apparently within the span of a few minutes. A note was painted in blood on the cell wall above Rendoid's body that read "Silence or Death," which we're sure is intended to be a threatening message directed at Brotherhood members who might defect or get captured. The day that Eulshod Rendoid was killed happened to also be the day the federation leaders made the announcement that Megelleon's solbidyum reactor would be going online. The news of the reactor far outplayed the news of Rendoid's murder. The following day brought news of the commissioning of Nibaria's solbidyum reactor and subsequent broadcasts showing the citizens celebrating and rejoicing on dozens of planets, as word reached them that sector-wide solbidyum distribution is underway. Hence, the impact that the Brotherhood hoped to achieve with the assassination and foreboding message never came to be.

"News of the completed shipments is scheduled to be broadcast here on Plosaxen at noon today, after which Senator Tacfacs will announce that Plosaxen is expecting to receive its solbidyum this week. The fact the solbidyum is already here and the reactor is ready to come online is being withheld at the moment."

"This might be an opportunity to bait the Brotherhood into a trap," I said. "We can find some remote or inactive space port on the planet and beef up security in the area, making it look like something major is going to take place there. Have arrangements made for armed transports to remain on call, as though they will be escorting a valuable shipment from a freighter to another site. Make it look like there is a site in the vicinity of the space port that is being prepared for the reactor installation. Then all we need to do is get some old freighter to land there, one that might fool the Brotherhood into believing it's the solbidyum shipment."

Wabussie turned to look at a vid screen on his desk as his hand played across a keypad, "There's a small port about 350 kilometers from here outside a town called Banur that produces a large portion of the planet's flour and processed food products. The only activity seen at this port are the regular deliveries made by a small freighter that transports grain from Megelleon. As luck would have it, it's scheduled to arrive four days from today."

"Then we luck out twice," Admiral Regeny said. "The star ship *SALNA* is scheduled to arrive tomorrow from the Halpfice System. Its crew has not yet been vetted as loyal, so I can issue orders to the captain to announce that they will be reporting for a top-secret security detail at the Banur space port. We'll test the crew and weed out the Brotherhood members *after* the announcement and, when the dismissed troopers are released, word will quickly spread through their organization's channels about the *SALNA*'s assignment."

"Why is the *SALNA* arriving here at this time with the *URANGA* and the *CACHATORA* are both scheduled to be here this week?" asked Commander Wabussie.

"The *SALNA* is returning with a number of diplomats and dignitaries that were on a mission to the Halpfice. I had neglected to take into account its return when we made the plans to meet with the other two ships but I am now including it in my orders to rendezvous with us here. Once the *SALNA* arrives, I'll meet with all the captains to brief them on our plans for accelerating these deliveries and disseminating news to other systems about the Federation's ability to prevail over the Brotherhood. Before they're redeployed, they should be securely staffed with loyal troops, fitted with 10X fusion reactors and RMFFs, and bolstered with at least a small contingent of fully functional Mirage Fighters. But that part we want to keep secret from the Brotherhood, of course; so the captains will not know any of those details until they and their crews are tested and cleared of Brotherhood members."

"Admiral, I have one question," said Wabussie. "You're clearing the ships' crews of Brotherhood members, but what of the thousands of civilians, ambassadors and dignitaries? Surely there are Brotherhood members among them, as well; and I don't think Federation law permits you to forcefully test them or remove them from the star ships, unless there is strong evidence against them that proves their involvement in subversive activities."

"True, which is why I want you to place at least one or two undercover FSO agents on each star ship to pose as civilians in some capacity or another – positions that facilitate broad interaction with the civilian population and allow them to look for possible

Brotherhood operatives among the passengers and service crews."

"Admiral," I interjected, "that might be a good place for us to insert some of the Nibarian FSO agents. We should place a minimum of one Nibarian and one human agent in civilian roles on each star ship. If the Brotherhood is looking for a spy in their midst, they will most likely assume them to be human, so to blend in with their ranks – which is true to some degree. So we have to expect that the human agent will eventually be identified as a mole. In the meantime, the Nibarian will largely be overlooked, especially after the human mole has been identified. It's very possible that the Brotherhood will retain the human mole as a means of feeding false information through our intelligence channels; but the Nibarian agent is likely to get closer to the more secretive discussions and meetings. The Brotherhood is going to be more suspicious of human service staff, for instance, so they'll probably bring non-human servants into their closer circles. Their members don't think much of non-human races, from what I have been able to discern, beyond finding them useful in what they consider menial service positions; so they would never suspect a Nibarian personal servant to be capable of spying."

"Great idea, Tibby, how many Nibarians do we have in the FSO at the moment?" asked the admiral as he looked from me to Wabussie.

"Ten, Admiral," answered Wabussie.

"Ten! Hmm, well that's a start. We will only need three for now. The more urgent issue is that you need to get some local Plosaxen recruits trained and in place. I expect you to have several agents inserted here as operatives before we move on. You need to establish an office here as well. I'm bothered, though, that these agents are simply too inexperienced. Even with the accelerated learning device and Tibby's tutelage, I'm concerned about the lack of training, which really amounts to only a few weeks."

"You have one thing in your favor though, Admiral," I said. "In the past you haven't had *any* agents trained or operating as these will be. Besides, the headband device has advanced many areas of their training to a level equivalent to a year or more of conventional training – even more so when it comes to martial arts. Your concern is legitimate, Admiral. I agree that the lack of experience is an issue; but the military simply has to act now. In the end, I think the related risks are low compared to not using these recruits at all – especially since the FSO is a secret organization at the moment, known only to those who are employed in it and to your staff and my security team. Oh yes, and Senator Tonclin."

"How long do you think we'll be able to keep the FSO a secret?" the admiral asked.

"I hope for a few years. For the time being, any information we uncover that reaches the general public will be assumed by just about everyone to be intelligence gained through the operations of the FOI. The FOI doesn't even know of the existence of the FSO, so they will assume that we obtained the information by interrogating a prisoner or a Brotherhood traitor. With luck, the FOI won't know about the FSO until that entire FOI is cleared of Brotherhood infiltrators."

"Speaking of the FOI, Commander," I said, "have you located Galetils' brother?"

"Yes I have, Tibby, and I have made arrangements for you to meet him. I talked to his boss here on Plosaxen, a man named Sanuk. I told him that you recently purchased Galetils' ship and that, since you didn't have the pleasure of meeting Galetils directly, you were interested in meeting his brother to learn more about him. I also suggested that the FOI might want to provide one of their agents to join your personal security team and that Admiral Regeny and that I felt Galetils' brother might be a good choice. Sanuk jumped at the opportunity, with the condition that he personally gets to meet you as well. I assured him that he will be seated with you and the admiral at the banquet table tonight. So I've secured verbal authorization to add Galetils' brother to your security team. I think if you were to suggest to Sanuk during dinner that you would like Galetils' brother to accompany you back to the *NEW ORLEANS* to see the ship, he will be more than willing to allow it."

"Excellent. I just have one more question; what's Galetils' brother's name?"

Wabussie and the admiral both laughed.

"I guess *that* would be a good detail for you to know! His name is Halfredies. Here, let me pull up his file for you on the vid screen." The screen lit up with an image of man whose features are hard to describe. I had seen vids of Galetils; and other than for the overall roundness of their faces, the brothers bore little resemblance to each other. Galetils' hair was reddish brown with matching eyelashes and eyebrows and Halfredies' hair was jet black. Galetils' complexion was somewhat ruddy and Halfredies' was more like smooth, white porcelain. Where Galetils' eyes were amber, Halfredies' were startlingly dark, so much so that I couldn't discern the pupil from the iris. He had thin, pale lips, which at first glance made his mouth appeared to be little more than a slit. But even these few odd facial features would not make him stand out in a crowd; to the contrary, he had an overall quality about him that might even cause others to ignore his presence as irrelevant, a quality that was certainly conducive to being a spy.

Commander Wabussie went on to review some facts about Halfredies background and relationship with his brother. "Halfredies and Galetils were quite close; in fact, Galetils purchased and gave him a rather nice estate on the southern continent here on Plosaxen. Galetils also set him up with seed funds, from which he has benefited nicely as a result of some good investments. In fact, he wouldn't have to hold a job, if he so elected.

"Halfredies made an offer to Galetils to help get him back on his feet after the destruction of Astamagota and, although he hadn't accumulated anywhere near the wealth that Galetils once had, that assistance would certainly have helped Galetils to restore his finances and business operations. It's one of the reasons that Halfredies is convinced that his brother's death was not a suicide. Although he's been assigned to other cases, I believe he is secretly trying to track down and find his brother's killers."

"Interesting," I said. "That's the kind of information we can use to swing him to our side as an undercover agent inside the FOI. His search for his brother's killers will coordinate well with our search for the Brotherhood members within the FOI, since there is every reason to believe the two are connected."

"Oh?" Wabussie asked.

"A'Lappe told me the Brotherhood learned that Galetils was developing the 10X fusion reactors and that someone among their ranks had been pressuring him to join their ranks and surrender the plans to them. Galetils immediately went to the FOI to advise them of the situation; and just a few days later he was found dead of an *apparent* suicide."

"I'm curious as to who conducted the investigation and determined the cause of his death," pondered Wabussie, as he typed some commands and looked at another screen on his desk. "This is odd," he said. "The file is sealed and encrypted; and it's labeled for viewing by only those with the highest authorization." He typed a few more commands, "Lucky I have such clearance. Ah, here we are. According to the official file, it was the FOI that conducted the investigation and determined the cause of death."

"Let me guess... Halfredies doesn't have clearance high enough to view the file, does he?" I asked. Wabussie typed a few more commands and looked up again. "No, he doesn't, though it shows here that he has requested access to it several times through different channels but has never been able to see it."

"Admiral, the clearance that was given to me by the Federation granting me access to all top-secret information... it is still in effect?" I inquired.

"Why, yes it is," said the admiral.

"Good. Commander, I would like a copy of that file forwarded to me, if you don't mind. I think I may have an immediate use for it *and* it will serve as a good starting place for tracking down the top Brotherhood infiltrators inside the FOI."

"I don't understand why we can't just pull all the FOI agents and personnel and test them like we do the rank and file of the military," said Commander Wabussie.

"Well, much of the FOI is operating undercover, so it would be difficult to locate all its agents. Depending on how deeply the Brotherhood has infiltrated the organization, the FIO employee files may have been altered or forged, so even their records and databases are unreliable. Of course, we can't let them clean their own house, like they will want to, because the loyalty of the entire organization is dubious at best, aside from Halfredies," I said. "At the moment, they have no knowledge of the FSO. As a ranking officer and member of the High Command, you're able to access information and files in the FOI database without raising suspicion of the FSO's existence. Approaching the corruption in the FOI this way may not be the most satisfactory tactic, but it's definitely the best way to achieve our objectives while maintaining secrecy about the military's secret operatives."

"I see where you're going with this, Tibby, and I agree with you. I trust you'll be able to sway Halfredies to join our operation with the information you find in this folder. He certainly has a personal motive for enlisting in this cause."

The trip back to the *NEW ORLEANS* was equally as guarded as the trip to the underground facility; and we returned without incident. I found Kala in her administrative office surrounded by several of her staff. As soon as she saw me, her face lit up with a beautiful smile that electrified me from the tips of my toes to the top of my head. I felt like I hadn't seen her in ages. She excused herself from her staff to join me.

"How about a good swim?"

I had to agree I needed the exercise and the swim would remove some of the tension that had accumulated over the course of the day. I had pretty much healed from the knife wounds I received at the hands of Lexmal; but the absence of my usual exercise allowed some stiffness to creep back into my limbs.

We arrived at the pool and Kala quickly undressed and dove in. She gave me a grin and I quickly realized that she intended to race me. Kala was very competitive; and most of the time I had to put forth my best effort just to manage a tie when we raced laps in the pool. A few times I managed to beat her, but not by much.

"Come on, Tib, I think I have the advantage today," she said.

"Oh you do, do you? We'll see about that," I replied as I dove in. I stayed under water and raced with all my strength to the far end of the pool. I fully expected to beat Kala to the wall, since I had the speed and momentum from the dive as an advantage; but when I surfaced just a foot short of the wall with my hand out to touch it, I saw Kala at my side with her hand reaching forward as well. We slapped the wall in unison and did a quick flip, speeding toward the opposite end as fast as we could. I could feel the stiffness in my muscles around the site of each knife wound; but I ignored the pain and pushed on. We both hit the wall at the same time and surfaced laughing. Kala threw her arms around my neck and kissed me firmly and passionately on the lips.

"I thought I had you, but it looks like you're back to your old self again."

"Ha," I replied. "Give me a few days more and you won't stand a chance."

"Why, youuuu," threatened Kala playfully, as she laughed and jumped above my shoulders, trying to use her weight to push me under the water. I grabbed her and we both went under, only to pop up sputtering and spitting out water. We held each other and shared one last kiss before Kala pulled away and began slow and steady laps. I joined her and we swam several laps without saying anything. Finally we climbed out of the pool and lay at its edge, slowly regaining our breath and letting our pulses return to normal.

"Tib, do you think this will ever be over – all of these issues with the Brotherhood and the solbidyum and all, or do you think the rest of our lives will be like this?"

"I honestly don't know, but I plan to do everything I can to bring it all to an end so you and I can spend some serious time enjoying life together. Not that I don't enjoy my time with you now, but I would rather it were in a different environment and less stressful circumstances. Since I arrived, it seems that every few days someone is trying to kill us. I suspect they will try again tonight at the banquet. I wonder... do you think they might try to poison us?"

"It's possible, Tib. The food at these events is pretty closely watched; but I have a small scanner that I can bring in my pocket. We can use it to scan the food a second time before we eat."

"Good, bring it along, but we'll give it to one of the security team who will scan our food for us.

Actually, he'll be an agent of the FOI assigned to aid in our security."

"The FOI? You trust the FOI?"

"This FOI agent I do. He's Galetils' brother. I'm quite certain he has the same goals and values we do. He also has a personal reason for wanting to bring down the Brotherhood. We're hoping to recruit him to be a mole agent for the FSO within the FOI."

"You're putting a lot of trust in the idea that he and Galetils were on good terms. Have you ever considered that he may have been jealous of Galetils and wanted him dead?"

"Anything is possible, but I doubt he had any part in his brother's death. He and Galetils were close, from what I understand; and there seems to be evidence within the FOI of an effort to keep Halfredies from accessing key information surrounding Galetils' death."

"Oh," Kala exclaimed suddenly, "I nearly forgot to tell you, Cantolla said she would like to talk to you at your earliest convenience – something about one of the projects you asked her to expedite."

I glanced at my com link time display and saw I had about an hour before I needed prepare for the banquet. "I think I'll head down to her lab and see what she's come up with. You want to come along?"

Kala grinned wickedly and said, "I think I will. I always enjoy watching you squirm when Cantolla eyes me appraisingly."

I laughed and gave her a kiss before gathering up my clothing. A few minutes later we entered the large area of the ship that had been set aside for Cantolla's lab. Several of her assistants were working busily on various projects. We didn't see Cantolla anywhere in the main lab; and before long, one of the staff caught sight of us and directed us into her office.

Cantolla had said when she first joined my staff that she coveted my office, especially the aquarium wall; and I told her that she could have her own office modeled to suit her wishes. So when we were ushered in, I wasn't surprised to see a glass wall behind her desk that looked into an aquarium. Unlike my office, which was walled with rich wood panels, Cantolla's office had bright white walls that seemed emit their own light and a floor of a dark gray polished rock that looked like marble of some sort. Several potted tropical plants were situated around the office and modernistic paintings with bright and dark contrasting patterns adorned the walls.

"Tibby, Kala, come in. I'm so glad you were able to come so quickly. I know you've been terribly busy, Tibby, but I think what I have to show you will interest you. You asked me to find some means of communicating instantly over the vast regions of space. You suggested that some of the ideas in what your planet called *quantum mechanics* might offer the solution. What you called *quantum mechanics* I think is what we call *relative physics*, or at least they sound similar. You talked about the action of sympathetic particles as a possible avenue of investigation, so I looked into it; but everything that I have researched indicates that isolating enough significant particles for a Federation-wide communication system would be much too difficult.

"As I researched this topic, I had another idea churning in the back of my mind. One of the curiosities in the scientific realm are the numerous stories of people within the Federation who have experienced psychic events where they suddenly become aware of some event happening across the galaxy, such as accidents, births, deaths, etcetera. These verifiable events usually have to do with a family member, close friend or acquaintance. Aside from the obvious mystery associated with psychic episodes in general, the scientific aspect of these events that I've always found most intriguing is that the knowledge is practically instantaneous, regardless of the distance between the psychic individual and the event. Somehow the information is transmitted or transferred without having to physically travel in the way, for instance, a radio wave carries a broadcast."

"I've never heard of psychics good enough and reliable enough for a consistent communication network," I said.

"Nor have I," Cantolla continued, "but it got me thinking about what happens, what sort of brainwaves are involved, and how can they be amplified or duplicated. I began sampling the *NEW ORLEANS* crew and found a few individuals who displayed a high level of psychic ability and three that seemed to have some indication of telepathic faculties. At first I tried to isolate various brainwaves to perhaps identify a frequency that might have some unique properties that facilitate instantaneous travel across the galaxy, but I had no success.

"I mulled over these failed approaches and compared the issue to the success of the learning headbands, believing the mechanism in each case was the same or, at least, the fundamentals of each process had to be related closely enough to integrate with each other.

"A question entered my mind. What would happen if we took brainwave readings from persons having successful psychic or telepathic sessions and recorded them into the headband device like we did with the martial arts skills, and then transmitted them in the learning mode to individuals with no abilities? We tried it and, amazingly, those who had no ability before the transmission suddenly demonstrated psychic abilities that were *stronger* than those of the donor. That had me scratching my head for awhile; until I realized that every person has some ability and that the learning device was simply unlocking and/or enhancing their latent skills.

"I began to wonder what would happen if I took readings from each psychic subject and compiled these readings into a single database, which would be transmitted back to all the contributing subjects. I conducted an informational loop experiment to this effect, particularly focusing on telepathic abilities. The result was – well, let me show you."

Cantolla led us out of her office and into the lab, where she called two of her assistants to join us. She placed one in a booth that had a glass wall, much like the booth I remembered from hearing tests that were part of the military's physical exam. The second person was seated near us and behind a screen that prevented him and the individual in the booth from seeing each other.

"This booth is soundproof," explained Cantolla. "At the moment, Fabola can hear us, as indicated by the blue light over the door. Fabola, you hear us, correct?"

He replied over a microphone, "Yes, I can hear you."

Cantolla then flipped a switch, which toggled the light over the door from blue to red. "Now we are isolated, so Fabola cannot hear anything we say. However, the microphone is still on in the booth, so we will be able to hear anything *he* says. Fabola can you hear us?" Cantolla asked. Fabola quietly stared at the wall, showing no sign of having heard anything.

"Now this is the fun part. This is Eludina," said Cantolla, indicating the woman seated behind the screen. Eludina, tell Fabola to scratch his head."

Cantolla barely finished the command before Fabola scratched his head.

"Now tell him to say the name of this ship."

Immediately Fabola said from within the booth, "The *NEW ORLEANS*!"

Both Kala and I looked at each other wide-eyed.

Cantolla continued, "The best part is that we can impart this ability to anyone now, by way of the learning bands.

"However, there is one problem. If we add too many people into the mix, the loop begins to destabilize and the operators start to pick up way too many extraneous thoughts from the people around them. For instance, if someone has bad breath and picks up on a coworker thinking a negative thought about it, he or she may react in different ways. One may simply correct the problem with a breath freshener; whereas another may take extreme offense and perhaps even confront the coworker. In another case, an individual may not especially like their psychic peer for some reason and, when the telepath perceives the other's feelings, they may suddenly feel angry, rejected or even paranoid. So we've learned that, if we carry the psychic enhancement procedure too far, we can't shield the subject from the many extraneous thoughts and trivial feelings that flow from others around them. I've had to send several of my people back to the estate on Megelleon for treatment and exchange them with new people, due to various psychological effects caused by the over-enhancement of their abilities. These operatives are now going through a desensitization program to help them deal with their new ability. I fear some of them may have to be treated with drugs, at least temporarily, in order to dull their telepathic abilities until they're able to cope with the thoughts of others around them and until my team is able to identify and teach them some effective filtering skills that they can 'turn on and off' as needed, so to speak."

"So you're saying you found a way to communicate long distances by way of telepathy; but we can't utilize the method, because it will create a situation for the operatives that is damaging to their psyche?" Kala interjected.

"Essentially, yes, but it gave me some clues as to a direction to take the research. I've been trying to circumvent the problem by developing an external mechanism for amplifying the telepathic frequency via the headband and direct it to a recipient who is operating a similar amplifier, instead of enhancing their innate abilities. With this method the individual would not be picking up on every thought around them and would only be getting messages deliberately sent with the assistance of the machine.

"Eludina, I'm finished with you and Fabola. Tell him he can come out and you can both go back to your other assignments." In an instant Eludina communicated telepathically with Fabola and he exited the booth to leave with Eludina.

"So have you been able to isolate the frequency and amplify it?" I asked.

"Not exactly," replied Cantolla. "I was not able to *isolate* the specific frequency, per se, but I was able to *amplify* it without affecting the operator. We conducted tests between operators here within the lab, as well as between the lab and our telepaths on Megelleon. We first conducted the test with no machines using the enhanced telepaths, and then again using unenhanced operators and brainwave amplifiers of different designs. One particular design seemed to work well – much more reliably than did the communications between enhanced telepaths – at least initially. When we retested the system between individuals here in the lab, it wouldn't work at all; however, when we tested the system using operatives communicating between the lab and Megelleon, we had instant success. Then, for some unidentified reason the amplifier stopped working in the middle of a transmission. I thought the problem was with the machine – a bad circuit or something. It wasn't until this morning when you and the admiral went to the surface of Plosaxen that we discovered why we were getting erratic results. We were in the middle of a test run with Megelleon as you were leaving, when we suddenly lost all contact."

"The RMFF," I said, as is suddenly dawned on me what had happened.

"Right, Tibby, the RMFF. When the RMFF is active the telepathic machine works and produces instantaneous telepathic communications of remarkable accuracy; but when it's turned off, the transmissions stop completely. Only one end of the communicating parties needs to have an RMFF to successfully create a two-way communication; but without an RMFF field activated between the operators, the apparatus does not function."

"Most interesting," I said. "The same thing happens with the cloaking device. There needs to be an RMFF field, or some condition produced by the RMFF, that makes it work. Have you spoken with A'Lappe about this?"

"A'Lappe? Why would I talk to A'Lappe about this?" Cantolla asked.

I noted tenseness in Cantolla's voice and a change in her posture that led me to believe there was some friction developing between the two of them. "He has isolated the aspect of the RMFF that makes the cloaking mechanism work and has duplicated it for smaller applications like the personal cloaking device and the Mirage Fighters. It's possible that these same conditions may apply to your telepathy device," I said. I noted Cantolla chewing on her lip as I was talking; and I was beginning to get the feeling that the idea of A'Lappe being part of her project was not something she was interested in.

"I wasn't aware he had done that," Cantolla said.

"Is there some problem or reason that you and A'Lappe are not working together?" I asked sternly.

"I, well, he… he doesn't work well in a team environment," she blurted out.

"Look, I understand that you want credit for your discoveries and your talent, but I didn't hire you to do everything yourself. You're a brilliant scientist and your intellect is leading us to discoveries that are needed by the Federation and by me; but I also need you to be able to work with others who are equally as brilliant and gifted. What you have discovered here is incredible but it could take you months or years to figure out how to get it working optimally on your own. Likewise, what A'Lappe has discovered is incredible and valuable; and it could very well be the answer you need. If I were to ask A'Lappe to develop a communication system on his own, he might never discover what you have. Ultimately, each of you has something important to offer to toward the development of this technology and your cooperation with each other is needed to achieve the fastest and greatest success with this and other projects. This is not a contest or competition to see who is the smartest or who is in charge. Besides, you're intelligent enough to know that A'Lappe is not looking for credit or glory, or he wouldn't be leading a clandestine existence where the scientific public knows little or nothing about him – and likely never will.

Think about it," I said as I got up and walked out, feeling myself getting a bit agitated. I glanced back to see Cantolla leaning on her hands against the table, staring at the floor with a sullen, contemplative look on her face.

The presence of security at the banquet that evening was obvious and impressive. Fully dressed and armored troopers were seen everywhere along the route to the banquet hall. My own security force maintained positions as bodyguards around our immediate perimeter and snipers positioned themselves out of site on the rooftops and balconies. Hidden in buildings along the route were squadrons of Special Ops troopers who were operating under the direction of Major Sokaia, since Marranalis was part of the banquet party. We arrived at the banquet hall without incident, where we were briefly ushered to a private room adjacent to the main banquet hall.   There we were introduced to the FOI security contingent; and it came as no surprise when I was introduced to Halfredies.

"Ah, Halfredies, I understand that you are the brother of Galetils," I began.   "I never had the opportunity to meet him, as his death occurred before I arrived here in the Federation territories; but I certainly wish I had. He was a great man with grand visions."

"Thank you, Honored First Citizen," he began. "I believe that if my brother were alive today, the two of you would become great friends. If there is an afterlife, I have no doubt that he is very pleased to know that it is you who occupies his estate and flies his yacht."

"I would be greatly honored if you would visit me on the *NEW ORLEANS*.   I understand that you haven't had the opportunity to see the ship your brother built and I would be honored to give you a tour of his creation," I said.

"I would enjoy that greatly.   Galetils had planned to take me on the maiden voyage when it was completed; but, as you know, his death occurred just weeks before construction was completed. I heard, of course, that you had purchased it; but I never dreamed I would have the opportunity to see it for myself."

"Well after this ordeal is over tonight, I would like very much for you to accompany me back to the *NEW ORLEANS*.   Other than for a few compartments that have been converted into laboratories, the ship is pretty much as your brother built it."

"I would enjoy that very much; though I'm not sure I'll be able to get the time off on such short notice."

"I don't think that will be a problem," I grinned. "I have a *little* political pull and I think your superior will be more than happy to allow you a day or so."

Halfredies laughed. "Yes, I would say you have more than just a little political influence. I will be honored to accompany you back, given, of course, that your influence is sufficient to sway my boss."

"Good, then it's settled. Oh, I do have one special request for you. I would like you to personally see to scanning all our foods this evening before we dine. Kala, do you have the scanner?"

"Yes, Tib. Here it is." She handed me the scanner, which I then gave to Halfredies.

"It's not that we don't trust the staff and people here," I said, "but after the events of the past few days, I believe it's better for us to be safe than sorry."

Halfredies paused a moment as he took the scanner. I looked him in the eye and I could see that he gathered there was more behind my request and comments than I was making plain at the moment.

"I'll personally check every item as they are served," he said and I nodded to him as I let go of the scanner.

The banquet was another of those events that I have come to detest – or I should say it was the fanfare and attention that I detested. Prominent leaders got up to speak verbosely, thanking me, Kala, Marranalis, and the admiral; heaping praise on us; and honoring Lunnie,

Reidecor and Captain Maxette in their absence. Vid clips were shown; battle scenes were chronicled; and the death of Lunnie, Maxette, Lexmal and Thimas were recounted in vivid detail. I found myself nearly drifting off to sleep as they talked on.

Our food was served while the dignitaries made their speeches. I noted Halfredies discretely checking each dish delivered to the table and even the utensils and glasses. My eyes played over the thousands of faces that filled the banquet hall and noted their rapt attention to every detail that played out on the vid screens as the speakers continued on and on.

I was so absorbed in watching the audience that I nearly missed hearing Senator Tacfacs say, "After seeing the incredible feats performed by First Citizen Kalana in the vid chronicles, I'm certain that you would all enjoy a demonstration of the martial arts skills that First Citizen Tibby has brought to the Federation and its military forces. We were able to get Lieutenant Marranalis to provide us with two trained fighters to demonstrate some of these techniques."

I looked at Marranalis questioningly. He shrugged his shoulders and said, "I didn't have time to mention it to you. I thought you would approve."

"It's all right by me," I said. "It just came as a surprise."

Two troopers from the Special Ops unit came out and performed a number of routines in a central area of the banquet hall that had been left clear of tables. Gasps, oohs and ahhs filled the room from those in attendance as the troopers demonstrated some hand-to-hand combat techniques. They finished to the expected round of applause and cheering.

Then, as things settled down and I was about to get back to dining, Admiral Regeny got to his feet. I felt my stomach sink, as I could see by the grin on his face that he was about to do something I wasn't going to like.

"As impressive at that was, it is nothing compared to the skills of First Citizen and Vice Admiral Tibby. When I first met him, I scoffed at the rumors of his skill and abilities. I asked him to demonstrate his techniques against a fully armored trooper with only his bare hands, making some joking comment about getting his clothing wrinkled. Not only did he defeat one of our best troopers in seconds, but he finished without producing a single wrinkle in is uniform. I would like to ask both him and Lieutenant Commander Kalana to show you what two well-trained combatants can do when going up against our best conventionally trained troopers."

Applause and cheering broke out in the hall and I knew that this was a matter in which we had no choice. The crowd expected it; and even though we had just eaten, we were still expected to go through with this demonstration on full stomachs. As Kala and I walked toward the central area where two of the largest troopers I had seen to date stood waiting, I turned to the admiral and said, "Last time I did this I got something in return. This time you owe me."

The admiral grinned.

Instead of Kala and I each sparring off with one trooper at a time, we were asked to fight them simultaneously. They attacked with bare knives –

quickly and without warning. I was glad that I had gone swimming earlier to loosen up my muscles; otherwise, my reflexes may have actually been too slow and I might have gotten injured. As it was, I quickly sent my opponent flying over me as I disarmed him of his knife in the process, holding it to his throat as he landed on his back with a heavy thud. Even though Kala's opponent was nearly twice her size, she too had her opponent disarmed and on the floor with his knife at his throat.

Cheers and applause echoed through the banquet hall as people chanted, "Tibby" and "Kalana." Kala and I simultaneously helped our opponents to their feet and handed them their knives. As we turned to walk back to our seats, I suddenly saw Kala's opponent lunge forward and sink his knife deeply into Kala's back. At the same moment, I sensed my opponent moving behind me and I turned just in time to deflect his blade with my arm, but not quickly enough to prevent him from slashing me with it.

I heard one of men scream out, *"For the Brotherhood!"* as multiple flashes of light filled my vision when the security forces opened fire on the two attackers. Seconds later, both lay dead as I rushed to Kala. She was alive but bleeding profusely. I put pressure over the wound to stop the bleeding.

"It's okay, Kala, you'll be ok," I said, hoping and praying that I was right.

She looked at me with a weak but loving smile; and then her eyes closed as her head lolled to the side.

It seemed like hours before anything else happened, though in reality it was only seconds before security troopers surrounded the scene and ushered in

Special Ops medics to assess and treat Kala, who had slipped into unconsciousness. I was faintly aware of someone pulling on me and looked to see a medic trying to apply bandages to my bleeding forearm. I started feeling dizzy and my surroundings began to spin around me as sounds echoed in my head. The last thing I recall is a blur of screams and scrambling images fading away from me, as if retreating into a distant tunnel.

Then all went black.

I found myself sitting in a field of long grass. There was a sweet fragrance in the air and a sense of familiarity about the place. I felt compelled to remain very still as I tried to remember what happened and figure out where I was.

I looked up to see a figure approaching me. It was Lunnie... but Lunnie was dead. I wondered, was I dead too?

Lunnie stopped some distance away and greeted me with her familiar vibrant smile. "Hello, Tibby. You really *must* stop coming here before it's your time. You have a hard battle to fight if you're going to save Kala. You *can* save her, Tibby. She's counting on you and so am I."

I looked past Lunnie to see Kala lying on the ground behind her. I tried to get up from the grass and go to her, but I couldn't move.

"It's not her time yet either, Tibby, so you must save her," said Lunnie in a very insistent but loving tone.

Things began to swirl again and my head was filled with a relentless buzz. Then I suddenly found myself lying in a bed with a medic hovering over me.

A'Lappe, Marranalis and two Special Ops troopers stood by.

"He's coming around now, sir," the medic said to Marranalis.

"Kala?" I said, no doubt with a great deal of fear and desperation in my weak voice.

"She's stable for now," said Marranalis immediately, sensing my need for immediate reassurance.

"Stable *for now*? What does that mean?"

I saw Marranalis look at A'Lappe questioningly and A'Lappe nodded.

"Tibby, the knives that were used to injure you and Kalana were laced with a lethal poison. For some reason, you seem to be largely immune to it – or at least it's not killing you and you seem to be recovering so far. On the other hand, the toxin has infected Kalana's entire body. Immediately after being stabbed, her organs began to rapidly show signs of shutting down. The medics responded quickly by placing her in stasis until an antidote can be found."

Marranalis' words hit me like a hammer. For a few minutes I felt like I was going to black out again.

"The two troopers you fought in the demonstration were both Brotherhood members. They killed and took the place of the two loyal troopers who were originally selected to oppose you. Their sole purpose was to kill both you and Kalana. Somehow they knew or found out that Admiral Regeny was going to have you and Kala participate in a demonstration. As soon as we saw what was happening, security shot and killed both attackers; but we were a split second too late to prevent them from wounding you and stabbing Kala. The medics believe there is something unique to your genetic makeup that is responsible for your resistance to the poison."

"Will Kala be okay?" I asked, closing my eyes tightly.

"Honestly, Tibby, I don't know. The medics say that as long as she remains in stasis, she is stable; but unless an antidote can be found, she will only live a few hours if they bring her out of stasis."

Anger filled my mind... then anguish... then rage. This was insane. All of this happened because Admiral Regeny wanted once again to turn the dinner event into an exhibition and military extravaganza. As ill as I was, I still felt a growing, seething fury building inside me as I thought about how the admiral had been using Kala and me politically to strengthen the position and image of the Federation – and his own image – with little consideration for either of us, other than how we could serve as his tools. As a result of his flagrant and pompous disregard, Kala and I walked right into a trap – and now only an induced stasis stood between Kala and death.

"Where are we now," I asked, "on Plosaxen or on the *NEW ORLEANS*?"

"We're all back on the *NEW ORLEANS*," Marranalis replied. As soon as the medics stopped both of you from bleeding, we loaded you on a patrol ship and got you out of there as quickly as possible. This is the safest place for you... and the medical units here on the ship are the best in the galaxy, Tibby. Kala is in good hands."

"Where is the admiral?" I asked without making even the slightest effort to mask my bitterness.

"He's still on Plosaxen in a meeting with fleet captains and senior officers."

"As soon as he gets back onboard, I want to see him. Before he goes *anywhere else*, he comes to me. Is that clear?

"I need to get out of this bed," I said while trying to swing my legs over the side.

"Sir," the medic began, "you need more rest. Perhaps tomorrow you can get up and move about, but for now you need to stay still and rest."

"Right now," I responded, "what I need is to get out of this bed and find whoever it is that knows the most about Kala's condition! We need to concentrate on finding her the antidote to the poison!"

I turned to A'Lappe as I began to deliver orders in a focused panic. "A'Lappe, I need you to find out all you can about the poisons used against Kala... and what we need for the antidote... and what we need to do to get it."

A'Lappe nodded. "I'll get right on it, Tibby, you have my word on it," and he headed for the door.

"Tibby, you really should lie down and rest, "said Marranalis.

"You *do* know I can fire you and get someone else to help me, don't you?" I said.

"Okay, okay, I'll help you; but I do so with protest. This is not in your best interest to be up and moving about just yet." Marranalis managed to locate a wheelchair-like conveyance and he helped me into it.

"Where to now, Tibby?" he asked in a defeated tone as he sat down in front of me.

"I want to see Kala. *Don't* say I can't; just take me to her."

Marranalis looked at me and sighed deeply. The pain showed in his eyes. "Okay," he said quietly.

Since Kala and I were both being treated by the toxicology specialists, we were located in the same hospital wing. Marranalis pushed my chair out of the room and into a semi-circle of treatment rooms arranged opposite a medic's station and then stepped away to speak to the medic seated at the desk. It wasn't long before the same medic escorted us to the far end of a corridor extending behind the station to a single door where a trooper stood guard, an extra safeguard that Marranalis knew I would appreciate. The trooper recognized us immediately; but he waited for orders before standing aside to let us pass.

There are some things that are better left unknown, the workings of the device keeping Kala alive in stasis was one such thing in my mind. That she was still alive was all I needed to know. I entered the room where she lay in stasis, entombed in a horizontal cylindrical capsule, split along its long axis with a transparent top half. Though I understood that during stasis all molecular motion ceased in her body she was technically still alive and could be revived at any time; but that as soon as she was, the deadly poisons in her body would continue their assault, which would ultimately lead to her death.

The lighting in the room was dimmed, but within her capsule was additional lighting that bathed her in a natural glow. She looked beautiful; and immediately my mind flashed to the story of Sleeping Beauty, a story on Earth of a young princess who falls under the curse of eternal sleep after pricking her finger on a spinning wheel spindle. The princess falls into a deep sleep, perfectly preserved, until many years later when she is released from the spell by the kiss of her true love.

In my grief and bitterness I wished I could raise the lid and kiss Kala to awaken her from her sleep; but her salvation rested on an antidote and not on a kiss.

Never in my life had I felt such despair and loneliness as I did at that moment. When my parents died, my grandparents were there for me; and though I felt great grief at the loss of my father and mother, I still had love. Later on I faced the deaths of my grandparents, but this time I was more emotionally prepared. The knowledge that they would one day die and the changes I saw in them as they aged prepared me; and while I mourned the loss intensely, it was nothing like this. Kala had become my life; all that I knew or cared about was in her. Without her there was no meaning to my existence, no reason to live this crazy life that sometimes seemed to drown me in chaos; and I resolved myself to do whatever it took to see her made whole. I was the richest and most powerful person in the universe and I would move every star in it, if it meant finding the cure and see her well again.

"Kala, I'll get you the cure, I promise. I won't stop until you are well again. I swear it," I sobbed as I threw myself across the encasement and wept. "I love you Kala... I need you here with me."

"Damn Regeny and his shows!" I thought, "It's his fault that Kala is here dying! If Kala survives this, I swear I'll never let any this happen again."

Suddenly I felt the presence of someone else in the room and I looked up to see Piesew standing near the door.

"Is there anything I can do, First Citizen?" he asked with tenderness and genuine concern in his voice.

"Yes, Piesew, there is. I want some live plants in this room with Kala; and I want some of her personal mementos brought and placed around her. Also, if there are any recordings of Kerabac and A'Lappe's singing available, I would like them played here while she's in stasis. One thing more – I don't want her left alone in here. See to it that someone is always here with her when I'm away. I don't want her left alone."

"I'll see to it personally," Piesew said solemnly.

"Marranalis!" I called.

I turned once more to look at Kala laying there in her capsule. "I need to go for now," I whispered to her. "I'll find the cure. Nothing in the universe will stop me. I swear."

I turned to see Marranalis at my side. "Just tell me where and I'll take you there, Tibby."

"To my office. I need to do some thinking."

While Marranalis navigated through the corridors toward my office, I asked him questions as things began to fall into place in my mind. "How many of our own trained personal security people do we have on the *NEW ORLEANS* – not including any of the Special Ops people?"

"Two hundred fifty," replied Marranalis.

"How many of those are fully trained at a level equal to or greater than the Special Ops teams?"

"Two hundred," he said.

"Do you know how many Mirage Fighters have been produced so far on Plosaxen that are ready for delivery?"

"As of yesterday they were finishing up number 20, I believe. They have been expediting component fabrication and have been able to advance a little ahead of their production schedule."

"If we reduce the number of patrol ships we personally have and remove all the Federation ships that are currently aboard the *NEW ORLEANS*, how many Mirage Fighters do you think we can hold on the *NEW ORLEANS*?"

"Hm, I'm not sure but I would estimate we could hold maybe a total of a hundred. There aren't that many Federation ships on the *NEW ORLEANS* at the moment." Marranalis answered just as we arrived at my office. He helped me from the conveyance into my desk chair; and I motioned weakly for him to take a seat.

"Do you know what the status is of the 10X fusion reactor installation on the Federation star ships?" I asked.

"Installation is underway on the *URANGA*, I believe, and there are two other reactors ready and waiting to be installed on other star ships."

"How long will it take for the reactors and RMFF systems to be installed and commissioned for service?"

"That's really not my area of expertise. A'Lappe could give you a much better estimate. I can only tell you that I heard a conversation between him and Admiral Regeny about it earlier today; he indicated that it would take about a week for all three ship installations to be complete and operational."

While I was talking to Marranalis, I saw the one of the secret panels open to the ship's substructure, through which A'Lappe had taken me on a tour. I knew he had arrived and was in the room; cloaked as usual.

"What do you have to report, A'Lappe?" I asked.

Marranalis turned to scan the room just as A'Lappe materialized in the chair next to him.

"By subjecting a sample of Kala's blood to spectral analysis and comparing it to the ship's database of known toxins, I was able to quickly identify the poison. It is a rare toxin, one that can only be extracted from a *ruguian*, a small amphibious creature found on the planet Alle Bamma. There is one antidote; but none is available in stock here on Plosaxen or anywhere within the Federation alliance, as Alle Bamma is one of the more isolated non-aligned worlds. It is a rather primitive world, characterized mostly pervading jungles. Except for the people on the planet who might encounter a ruguian, the toxin has presented little threat; so there has never been a need for storing the anti-toxin off world. There aren't even any ruguians in laboratories or zoos that I can find in available records.

"Preparation of the antidote requires the eggs of these same creatures, which are not easy to find. Ruguians do not make a nest; rather they lay their eggs randomly. Even though they are amphibious, they do not lay their eggs in water. The planet of Alle Bamma is a very wet place that maintains a level of humidity at or near 100% year around; so eggs laid on land are rarely in danger of drying out. Ruguians are not prolific breeders, either, which further complicates the matter."

"How far is it to this planet, Alle Bamma?"

"Five weeks with the *NEW ORLEANS* traveling at max GW speed," advised A'Lappe with a sad tone in his voice.

"Five weeks!" I exclaimed with frustration. "What about traveling with a Mirage Fighter at top speed?"

"Just under four weeks," said A'Lappe.

I was fighting a sense of desperation as I asked, "I was infected with the same poison as Kala, wasn't I? I'm getting better. Can't you make an antidote from my blood?"

"It's highly unlikely, from what I can see, though we can try. Your body has a natural immunity to the toxin for genetic reasons. It's not that your body is producing anti-toxin to combat the poison; it's that the toxin's chemical or molecular mechanism cannot operate against your body's cells in the same way that is against Kala's. While humans or humanoids have evolved on many planets throughout the galaxy, there are minor deviations in DNA and cellular structures on each world. I fear the only way we will be able to produce an antidote for Kala is to obtain some ruguian eggs."

Suddenly I felt very tired and was having difficulty sitting up in my chair. Marranalis saw that I was struggling and came to my aid. "Tibby, please, you need to rest. You lost a fair amount of blood and even with your immunity you may still suffer some effects from the toxin until it's entirely metabolized or evacuated from your system."

"I think you're right, Marranalis," I said, as I stubbornly tried to get up from the chair. In that instant the room began to spin and I felt myself falling toward the floor, as I descended into blackness once again.

It seemed I was surrounded by a dense fog, but I sensed someone's presence. As I looked about, I noted a form moving toward me; and as the figure drew nearer, I realized it was Lunnie.

"Tibby," she began, "Kala will be alright. It's not her time yet. But you will need to perform several feats before you can save her. Follow what you know in your heart is right and you will succeed."

Then the fog thickened around her and I was alone. I awoke to find myself in my own bed. Piesew was seated in a chair beside me; and when he saw my eyes open, he immediately got to his feet and approached me.

"How are you feeling, Honored First Citizen?" he inquired in is typical formal fashion, though there was a great deal of concern in his voice and on his face. "Is there something I can get for you?"

"Piesew, thank you. I'm feeling much better," I replied. As I slowly got my bearings and assessed my strength, I added, "I could use something to drink – some fruit juice perhaps. And I'm rather hungry."

"Excellent, sir. I shall arrange for your beverage and something for you to eat, as well."

As he turned to leave the room I asked, "How long have I been asleep?"

"A little over a day, sir."

I was momentarily stunned at his reply.

"Is there anything else, sir?"

"Ah, no, not for now. Thank you, Piesew."

After Piesew left, I got out of bed and stood still for a moment. Remarkably, I felt like my normal self again, aside from the thirst and hunger. While I showered, I took a closer look at the cut on my arm. I could see through the clear plasta-bandage that the wound was already healing. It was a surprisingly small slash and it didn't seem to be all that deep. As I left the shower, I saw that Piesew had returned and placed a glass of some kind of juice on the vanity. The flavor was reminiscent of tomato juice, which I drank nearly every day on Earth. This juice seemed to invigorate me almost immediately.

I returned to my bedroom to find that Piesew had laid out one of my honorary vice admiral uniforms. It angered me to look at it, as it was a tangible reminder of how Kala and I had been placed in danger by the admiral's wish to show us off for his agenda. Instead of putting on the uniform, I went to the wardrobe and selected a pair of slacks and one of my casual shirts that were rapidly becoming a fad on the ship. As I dressed, Piesew returned with a tray of food and advised me that he had placed it on the table in the dining area. Without asking any questions he removed the vice admiral uniform from the bed and returned it to the wardrobe.

"Honored First Citizen, the admiral requests a meeting with you and your senior staff in an hour in the High Command main conference room."

"He does, does he? Okay, thank you Piesew."

Inside I was fuming. On one hand, I liked the admiral and pretty much agreed with what it was he was trying to accomplish. On the other hand, I was more angry with him than I had been with anyone in my life – angry for putting Kala in harm's way; angry for the way in which he put us on display like a circus side show; and angry about his lack of respect for our needs, our personal feelings, and most certainly our lives.

I finished eating and went to my office. I stared into the aquarium, hoping that watching the fish would calm my fury so I could think clearly. I had not really paid close attention to them in the past, as I had always been rather busy on most occasions that I managed to be in the office. I found their unique colors and flowing fins rather mesmerizing, as I pondered what made some of them swim in schools, while other swam about individually. I studied the fish in this way for nearly half an hour, but it seemed as though only a few moments had passed before my desk com notified me that was time to meet with the admiral and his staff. I was still angry; but I felt amazingly clear-headed and ready to confront the admiral.

When I arrived at the conference room, everyone was already there and seated.

"Ah, Tibby, good to see you up and about. You're looking much better," said the admiral.

I nodded and took my seat at the opposite end of the table from the admiral. The High Command staff was seated on one side the table and all of my senior staff were seated on the other side. The juxtaposition seemed especially significant, I suppose because of my frame of mind at the time.

"Well, once again the Brotherhood's plans have been spoiled and the Federation has come out the victor," the admiral grinned. "Commander Wabussie tells me that our FSO agents have reported hearing that the Brotherhood is falling for our plot to lure them to a fake solbidyum delivery site. I've ordered Stonbersa to move the *NEW ORLEANS* to an orbit over the location and to remain cloaked. We will be joined by the *URANGA,* which will also be cloaked, thanks to its newly installed 10X reactor and RMFF system. They will be joined by the Mirage Fighters. We anticipate having twenty by that time. I think the Brotherhood will be in for a huge shock."

"I'm sorry to correct you, Admiral," I said. "The *NEW ORLEANS* will *NOT* be participating in the Banur mission."

"What?!" said the admiral with shock in his voice.

"I said the *NEW ORLEANS* will *not* be joining in the trap operation! In fact, the *NEW ORLEANS* won't even be in this system when the battle occurs. Oh, and you won't have twenty Mirage Fighters either; you will have ten."

"What do you mean the *NEW ORLEANS* won't be here? The High Command needs to be here to oversee the battle!" challenged the admiral, as he pounded his knuckles into the tabletop.

"The High Command will be there, Admiral, but you will be on your new flag ship, the *URANGA* and not on the *NEW ORLEANS*."

"What?!" the admiral exclaimed red faced, "This is our mobile headquarters, our base of operation. Where do you think you're going with the *NEW ORLEANS?*"

"Alle Bamma," I said. "And for the record, the *NEW ORLEANS* is no longer your headquarters or your base of operation. It was never intended to be your long-term base; rather I offered it as a safe *temporary* location until a secure space could be prepared on a Federation ship. You have one now with the *URANGA*. You don't need the *NEW ORLEANS* anymore."

"But I do. I have no intention of moving the High Command anywhere. Its staying here with the solbidyum until even last grain of it has been delivered," the admiral barked. I could see the veins beginning to protrude in his neck.

"I'm glad you mentioned the solbidyum; you're taking it with you to the *URANGA*. The *NEW ORLEANS* is not a delivery vessel, nor is any part of my crew your delivery service. This is *my* yacht. It is not a Federation ship, nor will it ever be a Federation ship. Captain Stonbersa and the crews answer to *my* orders and it goes where *I* chose; and right now it's going to Alle Bamma."

"Oh, you think so?" the admiral said smugly as he leaned over the conference table. "Well I am commandeering the *NEW ORLEANS* to serve the needs of the Federation military in a time of war!" he said tersely, as if quoting a long unused code of martial law would abruptly end the argument in his favor.

"No, I don't think so, Admiral," I replied, noting the mounting reactions to our exchange on both sides of the table.

"And why not?!" Regeny exploded.

"For many reasons, not the least of which is that I do not believe anyone on this ship will cooperate with you in that decision. Secondly, it would destroy the image you are trying to create within the Federation of solidarity and control. Thirdly, until I came along your military capabilities had become static and had not evolved in centuries. You have made more leaps forward in the past three months than you have in three centuries and you know it. You have the core for the beginnings of a new and improved military and you no longer need me to keep its momentum. To take the action you propose, that of seizing the *NEW ORLEANS* for your purposes, would weaken you in the eyes of the Special Ops troopers, in the eyes of FSO, the eyes of the citizens of the Federation and in the eyes of your own High Command staff."

Regeny looked at the faces around the table. On the side where my staff sat he saw defiant grins; on the side of the High Command Regeny stared into disapproving and severe expressions of each of his staff.

"Hmmpf! Very well. However, I seem to recall that you have several of my officers assigned to the *NEW ORLEANS* as a part of your staff. As of this moment I am recalling them to duty. Marranalis and Lieutenant Commander Kalana will be transferred to the *URANGA* to serve there.

"Begging the admiral's pardon," Marranalis interjected, "I resign."

"What? You can't!"

"Sir, I don't think the Senate or citizens will allow even an admiral to take actions against a widely acclaimed Federation hero without responding with some significant resistance," said Marranalis, "and I don't think any of your Special Ops troopers will feel too kindly toward the Admiralty if you take the action you plan," Marranalis said plainly.

"And you won't be taking Kala anywhere," I said. "We're taking her to Alle Bamma. It's the only place where we can find what we need to create an antidote for the toxin in her system; and I don't plan to let her spend years in stasis while some admiral plays warlord."

I looked at Regeny with resolve. Suddenly his face began to soften and his eyes fill with tears. He turned his back to us for a moment and stared at the wall. When he turned around again, there was a different man looking back at me.

"You're right, Tibby. I apologize. "You and Kalana and your crew have served the Federation far greater than anyone has and I guess, well, I got carried away with riding on your reputations and successes. You're also right to take Kala to Alle Bamma, if that's where the anti-toxin is to be found. And you are also correct that we can handle the situation here without the *NEW ORLEANS*.

"I'm curious about one thing. You said we will have only ten Mirage Fighters. There are already more built than that, so why only ten?"

"I'm taking ten with me. May I remind you that the fighters I take with me are paid for out of *my* funds; and the ten that will join your Banur operation are *also* able to do so at the courtesy of *my* coffers; so I think I am entitled to take as many as I want."

"I see. And do you have a reason for taking ten for yourself, other than for personal vanity?" Regeny asked with a bit of arrogance returning to his voice.

"Yes," I said, "because I have every reason to believe that if the poison that was used against Kala came from Alle Bamma, we are going to find a nest of the Brotherhood when we get there. If that's the case, things could get messy."

"Do you have information that I've not seen or heard?" Regeny asked.

"Nothing concrete, but the poison used on the knives of the Brotherhood assassins is specific to Alle Bamma; the source of the poison is found nowhere else. Alle Bamma is a non-aligned world populated by a primitive society; it's not part of any of the established trade routes, nor is it visited frequently by outsiders. It's the perfect place for the Brotherhood to establish a base and hide out. I don't think the Brotherhood went out of their way to make a trip to Alle Bamma to find a poison to try and kill us. I think they used it because it was convenient for them and because it was at hand."

"It's an interesting conjecture. You seem to be better informed about Alle Bamma than I am, but I would like to know more."

I looked at A'Lappe. He nodded to me and turned to the admiral.

"As Tibby has explained, Alle Bamma is one of the non-aligned worlds. It was not brought into the Federation because the indigenous inhabitants of the planet live in a non-technical society whose tribal culture is arboreal and nomadic. They live off the land and do not function within the constructs of any political system, engage in industry for trade, or even utilize currency. They have only minimal metalworking skills, which they apply only to minerals and ores they find on the planet's surface. They produce nothing; they desire nothing from the Federation; and except for exotic woods and possibly plants that would be useful in pharmaceuticals, there is little the planet has to offer for trade.

"Alle Bamma has no space port, so only small ships or ones capable of landing on or in the water have a place to set down. The planet's predominant features amount to jungle swamps and shallow oceans and seas. Only a fraction of the life forms on the planet have ever been cataloged. The inhabitants speak several languages and tend to be superstitious, territorial and extremely difficult for outsiders to approach. Early attempts to establish relationships with them for the purpose of advancing their education and level of technology met with total failure. It was deemed by the Federation that Alle Bamma, which is somewhat removed from the normal trade routes, would be best left alone and allowed to develop at its own pace. The planet's information was archived with the understanding that, if they ever their peoples evolved a high enough culture and wished to join the galactic community, the Federation would be willing to consider their application at that time."

"So why is the Brotherhood interested in it?" Regeny asked.

"The planet is close enough to the Federation for them to come and go with relative ease and without being noticed. Also, since there is an abundance of natural food sources across most of the planet, they can sustain themselves indefinitely without having to rely on synthesizers. We don't know a great deal about how many or what types of ships are used by the Brotherhood, but I think it's safe to assume that they do not have a very large fleet or we would know about it. Likewise, I suspect that most of their ships are small and most likely old. But on a planet like Alle Bamma that has no commercial space port and very a limited number of places that are appropriate for landing ships, smaller vessels are better suited for the environment and, of course, easier to hide. They could be anywhere on the planet – above or below water. Anyone setting out to locate them would have a difficult time."

"If you run into a nest of the Brotherhood out there you're on your own, Tibby. I'm sure you'll be okay in the *NEW ORLEANS*; but if you're going to be planetside in the jungle, looking for whatever it is you need to cure Kalana, you're vulnerable," the admiral said.

"If everything goes as it should, it's unlikely the Brotherhood will even know we're there. If the *NEW ORLEANS* is cloaked and we fly to the surface in a cloaked Mirage Fighter, we can simply be dropped off to search for the ruguian eggs, after which we'll signal for it to retrieve us. Under those circumstances it's unlikely we will be discovered, even if the Brotherhood occupies most of the planet. Regardless, we're going, Admiral, and we'll do what it takes to get our hands on the ruguian eggs and get the antidote produced."

"I think I can improve your odds, Tibby," said Kerabac. "I've been on Alle Bamma. I spent several months there as part of a flight crew that escorted a team of scientists to the surface about 15 years ago. Once we landed and set up camp, there wasn't much for the ship's crew to do; so I volunteered to accompany the science team into the jungle on several of their expeditions. There weren't any Brotherhood outposts established there at that time that I know of; but then we weren't aware of the existence of Brotherhood either. If they were there, they remained well hidden and we never saw any sign of them. The indigenous peoples, though, are another matter. They can pop up at any time; and you never know what to expect with regards to their behavior. They were mostly curious about our presence; however, on a few occasions they became rather aggressive and damaged our camp sites and any equipment that was left unguarded. They never really attacked us physically, though. I managed to pick up the basics of some of the tribal languages; but it's been a long time and I'm not sure how much I'll be able to remember clearly."

"Good, I'll need to take two people with me. Marranalis will need to stay on the ship to run security and assist Captain Stonbersa in a combat situation, if needed; but I think you're a perfect choice as one of the team, Kerabac."

"I have a candidate I would like to recommend," Cantolla chimed in. "There is a xenobiologist on my staff that I think could be of real assistance to you, in terms of dealing with Alle Bamma's particular environment and finding the ruguian eggs, which sounds like it may be challenging. His name is Hotyona. He would jump at the chance to set foot on Alle Bamma."

"Excellent," I said.

"I don't like it, Tibby," Regeny interjected. "I understand your reason for going; but if you run into a large contingent of Brotherhood on the planet, it will be five weeks before you can get word to us about it. Before we could assemble a force to respond, they would have a chance to move someplace else. It would be a full ten weeks from the time you sent the message until we'd be able to get to Alle Bamma."

"It's a risk I'm willing to take, Admiral. I'm not leaving Kala in stasis indefinitely or until circumstances best serve the Federation before taking action to acquire the cure she needs."

"I think I can help with that one, Tibby," Cantolla said. "Errm, actually, I should say A'Lappe and I can help you. At your coaxing I consulted with A'Lappe about the communication device you wanted us to develop. You were correct about A'Lappe's technological discovery possibly being the answer to overcoming the obstacles I've encountered when trying to achieve a means of instantaneous communication across the vast distances of space. The problem is that we haven't been able to design a proper receiver yet.

We're close, but it will most likely be another week before we have two functioning units; and by then we will be well on our way to Alle Bamma."

"Maybe not," A'Lappe said. "Both of us know pretty much what is needed and how to build it. There's no need for us to be together to complete the project. If you would be willing to stay here at Plosaxen with part of your team working on one device while I stay with the *NEW ORLEANS* to work on the other, we might be able to get a complete system operational before Tibby goes to Alle Bamma's surface. If it turns out that we detect the Brotherhood *is* in fact there, we can communicate our findings instantly to you and the fleet at Plosaxen. By that time, the Federation should have sprung the trap at the fake receiving site and have those rebels under control."

"Why should I be the one to stay behind?" asked Cantolla. "Why not you? After all, most of my staff is on the *NEW ORLEANS,* as is my lab."

Before A'Lappe could answer I spoke up. "Normally I would agree with you, Cantolla; but in this instance there are special circumstances that make it necessary for A'Lappe to stay with the ship. If I leave a Mirage Fighter and crew at your disposal to rush you back to the *NEW ORLEANS* when you get the communicator working, will that be acceptable?"

"Okay, but you'll owe me a special favor for this one, Tibby," she said.

As the meeting adjourned and everyone began to disperse, I pulled Admiral Regeny aside to tie up a few loose ends.

"Admiral, there are a few more things I need to make clear to you. First and foremost, the life threatening injuries to Lieutenant Commander Kalana are *not* to be treated as some kind of collateral damage in your war with the Brotherhood. She is *dying* because of *your* insistence on showmanship and glorification of the Federation military under your command. I am quite familiar with the belligerence and reflex for arrogance that is often associated with high-ranking military leaders such as yourself, so I do not generally feel a need to respond to your personal attacks on me or my motives. But the next time your arrogance blinds you to the dangers you bring to others – particularly my crew – you will see a new side of me, Admiral – one that will not handle a confrontation with the diplomacy I granted you today.

"I respect the tremendous challenges you've faced since my arrival and I will continue to value your professional opinion; however, the events of the last two days have marred my trust in your judgment for the time being. Hopefully we won't have to revisit this issue when I return; but if you decide you wish to discuss the matter further, I will make time to do so after Kala is well.

I turned to leave and paused to add one last thought. "Oh, and as far as your comment about my *personal vanity*, Admiral, I suggest you look to yourself on that point. You've damaged your standing among your staff today and you may want to find a way to repair that situation before you execute your trap operation on Banur."

I left the admiral alone in the conference room, looking out a small window into the depths of space.

Just outside the conference room door I was stopped by Commander Wabussie. "Tibby, I am truly sorry for all that has happened and I understand and respect your decision; but there is one matter left hanging and... well, I was sort of hoping that you might still talk to Halfredies before you leave."

"Halfredies – I'd completely forgotten about him. I'm afraid I won't have time to make a trip to the surface to meet him and we won't be around long enough to arrange for a trip up here before we leave."

"You won't have to. He's here on the *NEW ORLEANS*. He was a part of the security contingent that brought you and Lieutenant Commander Kalana back to the ship. I told his superior that he was needed here for debriefing. I've stalled them as long as I can; his superiors have been pressing for him to return. He's scheduled to leave in about three hours."

"I see. Can you bring him to my office in a few minutes?"

"I think so. Thank you, Tibby. I truly appreciate this and all you have done. I wish I could go with you to find those ruguian eggs. It's time the Federation returns the support you have provided to the alliance and its military forces. Besides that, you and Lieutenant Commander Kalana – well, I've grown rather fond of both of you."

"I appreciate that; really I do, Commander. Having you accompany me and my team would have been an honor and a much welcome addition to my team's skills; but you are needed here as the leader of the FSO and that's very important right now," I said.

"One more thing, Tibby. Don't be too angry with the admiral. He truly respects and admires you and, if you ask me, I think he thinks of you as a son. I don't think he realized just how much he was asking of you. For so many years the military sat in the shadows with little to engage them beyond very small and occasional police actions. There was even a motion brought before the Senate during the months before your arrival that proposed a cut in funding for the military and implementation of a large reduction in forces. Then you showed up with the *TRITYTE* and solbidyum and everything changed. Suddenly we've learned we have an enemy among us that we didn't know about. Who knows if they were already ramping up their activities and preparing to strike after the proposed reduction in military forces was announced – or they may even have been the ones to suggest the cuts to begin with. Besides the threat posed by the Brotherhood, there are other nefarious elements who want to seize the solbidyum. So now the need for the military is greater than it's been in centuries. You illustrated that need and made the Federation look strong and prepared in the face of global and alliance-wide acts of violence; and you set stage for the Senate to instead increase funding for the military. It was only natural, I suppose, that the admiral got carried away – not that it makes any of it right."

"I understand and, honestly. I'm fond of the admiral; but right now I'm not as enamored with him as I was. He put Kala in danger needlessly, with no warning and without asking us if we would be willing to participate in his side show. He repeatedly assumes that we will get up and put on a demonstration every time he snaps his fingers –with no concern for our feelings or safety. Kala is the most important person to me in the universe; I do not and will never take kindly to anyone placing her in harm's way, nor do I appreciate her welfare being put on hold for *any* reason."

It was only a few minutes later that Wabussie brought Halfredies to my study.

"Please come in and have a seat," I said. "I'm sorry I wasn't available to personally give you a tour of the ship. I hope you were able to see it. I know you depart in a few hours."

"Yes I was. A'Lappe personally gave me a guided tour. I was surprised to learn that he was here working for you. Although I had never met him, my brother spoke very highly of him. I'm truly amazed by the ship. It's even more magnificent than my brother told me it would be."

"I'm glad you had an opportunity to see it. It is indeed a grand ship. Your brother was quite a visionary and he had impeccable taste. I wish I were able to make his acquaintance."

"In many ways the two of you are alike, actually – not in physical appearance, but in manner and character. I'm sure the two of you would have been good friends. Like you, my brother had a strong dislike for the Brotherhood."

"Actually, Halfredies, that's sort of what I wanted to talk to you about. You didn't just happen to get assigned to my security detail by accident; we more or less arranged it. I have something you've been trying to gain authorization to see."

I activated a vid screen on the wall and inserted a small silicon recording cube into a receptacle on my computer.   Instantly the file on Galetils and his death came up on the screen.

"How did you get that?   I've been trying for months to get permission to see this file and have been denied access to it on every attempt."

"You're welcome to read it.   I regret I can't let you take it with you, but you can view it here.   All I ask in return that you listen to what I have to say and that you not reveal to anyone what we are about to discuss. Is it a deal?"

"As long as it's nothing illegal, you have a deal."

"I assure you it's not illegal, but it will mean withholding some information from your superiors and fellow FOI agents."

"I'm not so sure I can do that," Halfredies said, squirming slightly in his chair.

"I think after I share what I have to say, you will agree; but I'll let you decide on that.   We know that your brother had been approached by the Brotherhood, who was trying to *persuade* him, shall we say, to turn over the designs for the 10X reactor designs.   We also know that he refused and was found dead a few days later; and we believe that he was killed by the Brotherhood."

I carefully watched Halfredies for his reactions while I spoke, but he displayed no physical reaction to anything I was saying.   He obviously had a tremendously stoic control over his emotions and reactions.

"We also believe that there is a strong infiltration of Brotherhood members within the FOI that stretches all the way into the higher ranks, which is why the Federation military forces never received warning about the growing threat of their presence. It's also the reason I believe his file and case information have been withheld from you. My guess is that they have kept you away from a lot of stuff recently."

"I must confess that what you're telling me is nothing I haven't surmised on my own; but I don't think you have gone to all the trouble of getting Galetils' file for me just to tell me this."

"You're right – and now we come to the part that I must ask you to *not* reveal to anyone. A great deal is at stake for the Federation's security and your secrecy is required."

"I've sworn my allegiance to the Federation; it was required when I joined the FOI," Halfredies said a bit stiffly.

"Yes, and so did a lot of Federation troops and many of your associates in the FOI who have been working for the Brotherhood. I want your personal word, on the honor of your brother, that you will keep secret what I am about to say."

Halfredies again adjusted himself in his chair and looked me in the eye. "I'll swear on my brother's honor, so long as there is nothing illegal in what you say."

"Good enough for me," I said. "As I stated earlier, we believe there are a number of Brotherhood operatives within the FOI, so many and so strategically placed as to make any intelligence reports coming to the Senate or the military's High Command highly questionable and nearly worthless. The military would like to clean up the FOI – test and weed out the

Brotherhood, I guess is the plainest way to say it. Admiral Regeny's teams can't get at them because of the structure within the FOI organization. For this reason a new covert group has been set up independently of the FOI to collect intelligence and ferret out Brotherhood operatives in all branches of government, *without* those branches and the Brotherhood knowing about the agency's existence or its activities."

I could see Halfredies reacting to this news with interest. I continued, "In light of everything I've just told you, I believe that once you see the information in your brother's file, you will see that we share a common interest."

"So what is it you want?" Halfredies asked. "Do you expect me to resign my position with the FOI and go to work for this new organization you're forming? Don't you think the FOI will find my actions suspicious and realize that I've left to work for some new agency? For that matter, why not just dismantle the FOI completely and recruit and test into the new one?"

"For one thing, we want to find out who the Brotherhood agents are in the FOI without them realizing we are on to them. With that approach the infiltrators are sure to lead us to their higher-ups. Secondly, we want to find leads into their organization to get operatives inside the Brotherhood. Ultimately, we hope to clear out the Brotherhood presence from the FOI, while still keeping the second agency operational and secret as long as possible."

"Oh, I get it now. You want me to spy for you within the FOI, to be an undercover agent for your new agency."

"Something like that, yes," I said. "We're not asking you to do anything illegal or to divulge any classified information, because all the people you would report to already have the highest clearance granted by the Federation. Any information being withheld from them would be in violation of Federation laws; so if you find that agents within the FOI are violating that law, your clandestine actions to make the High Command of the Federation aware of such matters would be within your duties and moral code. All we're doing is asking you bypass the regular chain of command where Brotherhood members might intercept and divert your reports. Of course, you would still report things to your superior at the FOI on your regular assignments as expected; but you would also be looking for anything that might indicate Brotherhood cover-ups or activities within the FOI.

"Why don't you look over the file I gave you? You still have two and a half hours before your return to the surface. You should be able to review the file in its entirety by then. Just be sure to leave the file with Commander Wabussie before you leave – and we would also like your answer before you leave. You can provide that to Wabussie as well. Regardless of your decision, we ask you to keep the information we have shared with you a secret."

Halfredies took the file cube I offered him, "I'll consider what you ask and I will keep your secret."

"It was a real pleasure meeting you, Halfredies. Regardless of your decision to join us or not, I hope that, when things are less tense, I can get back this way and entertain you in a more polite and proper fashion here on the *NEW ORLEANS*."

"Thank you, First Citizen. I would consider it a great honor. It was a great pleasure meeting you; and thank you for allowing me to see this file."

After Halfredies left with the file in hand, I reviewed the status of our first delivery of fighter ships. It appeared that the *NEW ORLEANS* could plan to be underway to Alle Bamma about 20 hours later. I was delightfully surprised when Admiral Regeny suggested that Cantolla and some of her team take up residence on the *URANGA* where they would be safely protected by the RMFF field. The admiral's gesture also meant it would be unlikely that she would need a Mirage Fighter to bring her back to the *NEW ORLEANS* or that we would need to retrieve her at all; as I anticipated that, as soon as the Federation finished with their encounter with the Brotherhood at Banur, the admiral would immediately direct the *URANGA* on a heading for Alle Bamma in anticipation of my team finding a Brotherhood presence on the planet at some point during our excursion.

I found it impossible to go to bed without Kala by my side, so I made a fire in the fireplace and reclined in one of the oversized chairs to rest and wait for news from the bridge that we could prepare for departure. The heat and fragrance of warm cinnamon that radiated from the flames lulled me into a few hours of much needed sleep, which was broken by a status message from the bridge.

The arrival and stowing of ten Mirage Fighters on the *NEW ORLEANS* signaled the moment of our departure.

Kerabac, Hotyona and I boarded the *ALI* and we were quickly underway with the *NEW ORLEANS* following behind. We would arrive a week before the *NEW OREANS* and would hopefully have located the ruguian eggs by the time they arrived.

I hadn't had the opportunity to meet Hotyona before our departure on the *ALI*. He stood almost two meters tall and had an athletic swimmer's build, blue eyes and nearly straw blond hair. There was an air of intelligence about him that was slightly intimidating but not threatening; and he had a broad smile and good sense of humor.

"First Citizen, it is a true honor to be going to Alle Bamma with you," he said.

"Just Tibby, please. I prefer not to have all the honorifics, especially with my team members."

"Very well, Tibby. I hope you don't mind; but I met with Kerabac to discuss the best possible place for us to search for ruguian eggs. Although they're found all over the planet, they are concentrated in some areas more than others. Kerabac seems to recall an area he visited when he was there 15 years ago that seemed to have a fairly significant concentration of them, though they may not be as heavily concentrated now as they were at that time. The ruguian population levels seems to be based on food availability; and when the population density gets too high the food levels fall and the population of ruguians decreases correspondingly. I suspect we will be pretty much relying on luck to find a good spot to secure eggs," Hotyona informed me.

"The weather is an issue, too," added Kerabac. "The planet has a strange wobble to it that affects the weather patterns. Technically you can say they have seasons, but those are mostly described as *wet* and *wetter* and not really characterized by any substantial change in temperature. During the wettest seasons, rain storms pass through the same locales several times a day. There a day is 28 hours long; so you can expect to experience at least five to eight storms in that period, which last from a few minutes to several hours. During the less stormy season, rains that are less severe in nature occur on average about three to four times a day. The humidity stays pretty close to 100%. It's not the most comfortable place in the galaxy; I can tell you that for a fact."

"Wow, with weather like that I can understand why the people there are so primitive, they probably have never developed fire because everything is too wet," I said.

"They have fire and use it in their camps and homes," said Kerabac. "There are a number of plants dispersed throughout the planet's vegetation that produce flammable oils in relatively large quantities. The natives harvest these plants and extract the oil to burn in lamps and small cooking pits. Throughout the jungles grows a large nut-like fruit with a hard fireproof and waterproof shell. The meat of the fruit is removed and eaten and the large shells become fire pit liners – to act as a barrier, of sorts, from the moist earth. The smaller shells are utilized as cooking pots. They also burn the oil in these smaller shells for light."

"This place is sounding more and more complex all the time. I can see where I've got a lot to learn before we arrive. I need both of you to tell me everything you can about the planet and the ruguians. It sounds as though Alle Bamma is a dangerous place and I don't want to get eaten or poisoned by something while we're there," I said.

"About the only creature you need to worry about in that regard is a large reptilian creature called a drodoceal, which grows to about six meters in length," Kerabac said. "It spends a great deal of its time submerged just below the surface of the water, where it looks like a saturated log. Whenever prey comes near, it snatches the unwary victim in its large and powerful jaws with lightning speed, drags it underwater, and holds the pray there until it drowns. Once the prey is dead, the drodoceal makes a meal of it. A drodoceal is large enough to eat a whole human and it has been known to do so."

"That sounds amazingly like creatures we have on Earth called alligators and crocodiles. Alligators were indigenous to the swamps where I grew up. We used to hunt and kill them for both their skins and the meat in their tails."

"It's quite possible that they are close in nature," said Hotyona. "On planets of similar atmospheres and environments evolution of life has been demonstrated to be very similar. As far as poisonous life forms, they're easy to identify on Alle Bamma, as every poisonous species has bright, nearly fluorescent blue color on them – plants and animals alike. Anything that doesn't have blue on it is safe to eat or touch, unless, like the drodoceal, it has teeth with a bite that can injure or kill. It might help you to review the flora and fauna of Alle Bamma that I brought along on my vid pad. I can download it into the ship's computer if you like."

"I think that's a very good idea. I also think it would be a great idea if the main topic of conversation from now until we arrive at Alle Bamma is about the planet and its life forms and tribal customs. I want us to be as prepared as possible when we arrive."

Since my arrival in the Federation territories, there had been only a few instances where I had been away from Kala for more than a few hours. Even then I felt her absence and found myself eager to be with her as soon as possible. When I first saw Kala in the stasis chamber, the short space between her and the casement window felt like a million galaxies between us; and I didn't think the longing to touch her and hear her voice could get any greater. But now I couldn't even see her or be near her, and as soon as Kerabac, Hotyona and I left in the *ALI*, the separation from Kala redoubled the depths of my anguish. She would remain on the *NEW ORLEANS* while I sloshed about in the jungle on Alle Bamma, looking for the cure that would release her from the poison that was killing her.

To keep the pain at bay and stay focused I spent as much of my time as possible talking to Kerabac and Hotyona about life on Alle Bamma and looking at the vids of the flora and fauna of the planet. I was indeed surprised to see the similarity between Earth alligators and the drodoceal. I was also surprised to see how much the ruguians looked like the giant mudpuppies of Earth. The ruguian grew slightly larger than its Earth cousin, often reaching a length of half a meter. Its tail and belly were bright blue; and it was not a venomous bite that posed the threat, but a chemical secreted from their skin that was poisonous. Even their eggs were blue in color and looked like a bunch of blueberries stuck in a slimy clear gelatin blob. Usually the eggs were laid under leaves or fallen logs, but they could just as easily be found lying anywhere. It was advisable not to allow the eggs to come in contact with the skin on a person's hands – not because touching them was harmful, but because the toxin on the eggs could contaminate any food one touched; and just the smallest trace of ingested poison was almost always fatal. Those who survived generally went blind or became partially paralyzed from the toxin.

Life on the *ALI* didn't differ a lot from life aboard a patrol ship. It was smaller and more compact but like any deployed patrol ship, at least one person was always expected to be at the control console. Though the computer did most of the flying, a discerning pair of eyes was needed to monitor the screens and make sure all was going well.

We were about a week's travel from Plosaxen and I was taking my turn monitoring the instruments. Kerabac and Hotyona were taking a break in the small dining area, when I felt the call of nature and a need to visit the facilities. It was neither uncommon nor forbidden for one on duty in the control room of a small ship that was navigating on autopilot to take a 'quick bio break'; so I left the control room and proceeded to the small toilet near the galley. As I passed by the dining area, I glanced in and saw Kerabac and Hotyona playing a game on a vid screen that looked remarkably like chess. I took a closer look and found that, while the pieces were differed in shape, it was obvious from their configuration and movements that the game was not *like* chess, it *was* chess, just as I knew it back on Earth.

"Excuse me, but… that game you're playing… where did you get it?" I asked, somewhat shaken by the unmistakable fact that what they were playing was the very same game.

"From the computer," Kerabac said, "there are lots of games in the computer."

"That's not exactly what I meant to ask. I mean where did the game originate?"

Both Kerabac and Hotyona shrugged. Kerabac punched something into the computer and it brought up a page of information and rules of the game. There was a brief paragraph in the description that stated the game was found on most planets and cultures throughout the galaxy and that it was in existence before recorded history; but its origin had never been found. It was said that, even on planets that seemingly never had any outside contact with other worlds, the first explorers often found the locals playing the game. For this reason, it was often used to promote positive cultural relations with the natives, as it was a tangible representation of the commonality of their peoples. The game and play pieces have gone by as many names as there are planets, but the moves of the pieces are the same and follow the same rankings on every world where it has been discovered.

"This is amazing," I said. "This exact game also exists on Earth. Its origin there is a mystery too, though it was believed by some to have originated on one continent anywhere from 2,000 to 6,000 years ago, from which point it spread around the planet. Today it's played universally on Earth, where it's called *chess*."

"It says here that it appeared on the planet Reyes roughly 8,000 years ago and on Pakaras nearly 10,000 years ago," stated Kerabac, as he delved further into his research on the vid screen. "There doesn't seem to be any pattern as to where it first appeared or when. There are about ten worlds where the game seems to have originated at the same time. The interesting thing about all of them is that the game was known and played long before the people achieved space flight or contact with outside worlds; and all of them were in about the same stage of development and technology when the game appeared on their planets."

I had nearly forgotten my need for the toilet until Kerabac said, "Is that what you came back here to ask us?"

"Ahh, actually I need to use the toilet, but I was distracted by your game." I said and quickly made my way into the facilities. When I came out, Kerabac and Hotyona had resumed their game. I watched them a few seconds and then, shaking my head at how this game remarkably emerged independently on so many worlds, I returned to the bridge to ponder the mystery.

Hotyona turned out to be an encyclopedia of information. Whether he was an expert on the peoples and wildlife of Alle Bamma before he joined this mission or if he was constantly studying during our journey and regurgitating the information didn't matter; it just gushed forth from him like a giant waterfall.

"You'll be interested to know that there are no insects on Alle Bamma like those known on other planets. They are replaced in the ecology by new family of creatures we call rubloids. Like insects, they have no internal skeleton; but unlike insects, they have no exoskeleton either," he said. "Instead they have a network of microstructures in their skin that allow the various segments of their anatomy to harden and soften as required, at times serving as a skeletal frame and other times becoming soft and pliable. In their flexible state, rubloids are capable of moving through very small holes; hence, using screens as a barrier from them is completely useless."

"That sounds like a serious problem. How do you get around that issue?" I asked.

"There are several ways. For instance, the use of a kind of ultrasonic device seems to scramble their insides if they get too close. Applying the saps of certain plants to your skin will also repel the rubloids."

"We tried double-weave electric-net screen on the expedition when I was here," said Kerabac, "but it didn't work well, as the rain and moisture kept shorting out the circuits. In the end we just gave up and bathed our skin with foccee before we went out, which was rather effective. It seems the little buggers don't like foccee very much either."

"Hmmm, I'll have to try that and make a note of it for my reports if it works. Foccee hasn't been reported as a remedy in any documentation I've seen thus far," remarked Hotyona.

So it went, every few minutes some new fact on the flora and fauna would emerge. I had asked for it and I was getting it. Kerabac, on the other hand, tended to present more information on the natives and their customs and lifestyles that he gleaned from his past excursions to the surface.

"This culture has strange mating habits," he said. "Women play the primary role in the mating rituals. They woo and select their mates instead of men taking the lead in romance. Men may flirt with women, but it is the woman who makes the selection and asks the man to be her mate. When a woman is looking for a mate, she and a chosen male go off to her sleeping and living area, where she fixes him a meal. If he eats it, they might then have sex. If she finds him satisfactory, she invites him back again, until she is sure she wants him. Once she has made her decision, an announcement is made before the tribe that he is her man, which means he is no longer available to any women in the tribe. Should he stray and have a sexual relationship with another woman while he is claimed, he is castrated and banished from the tribe and the woman who seduced him is put to death. However, should his partner decide she no longer desires him as a mate, she makes an announcement to the tribe that he is not wanted, in which case he must then leave the tribe and find a new one to join."

"So the women run the tribes," I said.

"No, not at all. Rule is by tribal council under an elected leader. There are both males and females on the council, all of whom are chosen by the members of the tribe. Once elected to their posts, they serve for life or until voted off the council by the tribal members. The council elects one person among them to serve as the leader; but his or her power is limited by the council and it is not absolute. The leader can make decisions for the tribe in daily matters; however, if the council doesn't agree with a decision or if they are displeased with the outcome, they have the collective power to revoke the decision in favor of another solution. Too many repealed decisions and the leader is removed from their role and replaced by another member of the council."

"What are the people and their villages like?"

"Well, as far as anyone knows, there is one race of people who are mostly about A'Lappe's height but much thinner. Their eyes and irises are pointed at both the medial and lateral ends, more sharply than with most humanoids, and the iris is oval and not round. You won't see any overweight Allebammians; they're mostly arboreal, though they do come down to the ground in their search for some food items. They're also good swimmers and don't hesitate to go into the water to spear fish. It's a good practice to watch where they swim, as they will not enter water where a drodoceal is present. How they know exactly when a drodoceal is present is a question I would like to have answered; but if you ask, all they will say is *Drodoceal is not where drodoceal is not*.

While Hotyona was providing this background, Kerabac retrieved a vid pic of an Allebammian native male. The first thing that struck me were the patterns on his skin that looked much like patterns used on camouflage fabrics back on Earth. Kerabac said that these were natural pigmentations and that no two natives had the same patterns. When standing against a jungle background, they were nearly invisible. They had no eyebrows or facial hair and, except for the dark brown hair that hung roughly to the shoulders, they appeared to be devoid of hair anywhere else on their bodies.

My thoughts shifted back to the alligator-like drodoceal, which seemed like it would be a rather formidable opponent for these rather small people. "Are drodoceals herding animals?" I asked as I laughed to myself. I knew that a group of lizards was called a *lounge*, but I always found that term awkward. Besides, I didn't know how to ask precisely in Federation language whether drodoceals were "lounging" animals. The right term seemed to be absent from the vocabulary.

"Hardly, said Hotyona. "They can't seem to stand each other and will fight off or kill any drodoceal that enters their territory. They are notorious for eating their own young, as well, which accounts for their relatively low numbers. And unlike amphibians or reptiles on most planets, they give live birth to their young. The young are born while the female sleeps, after which they quickly scurry off into the jungle before she awakens. The only time they are receptive to company is during breeding season, during which the female will travel miles to find a male. Males put out a very pungent odor that females seem to be able to detect at great distances, despite the persistent wet and rainy environment. Only when fertile do females emit an odor, though it is less pungent and more comparable to a spice-like scent. Again, that's only when they're fertile; the males stink all the time."

"So if I smell something spicy, I should run; and if I smell something really pungent, I should run?" I said jokingly.

Hotyona grinned and continued, "I would suggest you climb a tree. Drodoceals are surprisingly fast runners and can easily catch you, but they cannot climb. You're safe once you get about two meters off the ground."

"They can be killed, I assume?" I asked.

"Yes, a good shot between the eyes usually does the trick. Body shots don't seem to stop them however. The natives use a spear to stab them between the eyes. They carefully sneak up on them while they're asleep and kill them with a quick and hard thrust. They use the hides and eat the meat of the legs, tongue and tails. The meat in the rest of the body is too gristly to eat.

"But back to the natives... the tribes all seem to believe universally in the same deity, a god they call *Thumumba*, a word which also means *thunder* in their language. They believe that Thumumba is in everything, including themselves, like a *life force* that they believe also has intelligence and control over all things. Thumumba is not a personal god that responds to the prayers or voices of individuals; rather, many must join together to implore the favor of this god in hope their prayers will be answered.

"In their belief system Thumumba is neither a just god nor an unjust god; Thumumba cares only about the survival of the world in general; and the needs of a single individual are insignificant in that regard. Thumumba is neither male nor female. The natives believe that all things are part of Thumumba, who created all things out of Thumumba's own being. They do not give sacrifices to Thumumba, but they do celebrate their god in dances and rituals meant to show respect and reverence."

And so it went daily as we traveled to Alle Bamma. I learned that the natives seldom wore clothing other than a belt or a shoulder bag to carry items for daily use, both of which were made from drodoceal hide or woven plant fibers. I found that the natives were in many ways similar to tribal jungle-dwelling tribes on Earth, such as those in the rainforests of New Guinea and the Amazon. Like the Earth tribes, the Allebammians hunted their food using bow and arrow, spears, and short blow guns.

We had been traveling approximately three and a half weeks when Kerabac woke me to say that Alle Bamma was in sight and that he had turned on our cloaking device. Kerabac thought it best that we try landing at the location where he had been years earlier. He entered the coordinates into the computer but didn't activate them immediately. We decided we would circle the planet a few times to see whether we could identify any sign of the Brotherhood, but we didn't see anything out of the ordinary. Nevertheless, we decided to remain cloaked and hide the ship once we had landed. Landing was not as easy as we thought it would be. In the years since Kerabac's visit the jungle had advanced to claim the landing site that had been cleared for the ship at that time. Instead we were forced to move on to a nearby lake that had a wide, gravel-covered shore that was relatively flat and free of vegetation. I was impressed with the size of the trees in the surrounding jungle, many of them reaching heights in the hundreds of meters and diameters of up to 75 meters. Where the jungle met the gravel bed was a grove of very large trees spaced many meters apart. The broad space between trees at the ground level and the extremely dense canopy overhead provided ideal cover, at least to conceal the *ALI* from aerial view. Hotyona explained these were *I'aban trees*, a species that leached large amounts of minerals from the rich soil and deposited these metallic compounds in the leaves. Hence, a canopy of such trees not only concealed the ground visually, it also shielded anything beneath it from aerial scanners or space detection instrumentation. So unless a craft flew down to the surface level and over the lake where they could peer under this canopy, it was unlikely the ALI would be detected.

With the *ALI* safely hidden we were ready to venture forth into the jungle and begin our search for ruguian eggs. As soon as we opened the hatch we were hit by a wave of hot moist air. Our sensor reading showed CO_2 levels that were somewhat higher than inside the ship and a humidity level of 98%. Almost instantly we began to perspire and our clothing stuck to our skin. The air was filled with the familiar rich scent associated with a damp forest or greenhouse full of plants. Numerous squeaks, chirps, whistles and buzzes could be heard coming from the jungle around us as various creatures called for mates, heralded our presence, or communicated whatever other message their noises may have represented. We wore standard body armor at Kerabac's suggestion "for protection from the jungle itself," as he put it. He explained that there were several species of large plants with long sharp thorns that could be launched up to five meters like an arrow or projectile for the purpose of killing any creature in its path. The plants then derived nourishment from the decaying carcasses as the nutrients seeped into the ground. Other thorned plants didn't release their thorns but instead had rows of them attached to long spring-like branches that tripped on contact, whipping outward and impaling anything in their range. The armored leggings would protect us from such plants, as well as smaller animals that might try to bite us, though Hotyona insisted that it was very unlikely anything smaller than a drodoceal was likely to attack.

A'Lappe had told us before we left the *NEW ORLEANS* that he would require nearly 500 grams of ruguian eggs to produce the anti-toxin; but it would be unlikely we would find more than a few grams at a time; so we were both surprised and elated when we discovered a small 50-gram gelatinous blue mass under the fronds of a giant fern shortly after leaving the ship. Hotyona confirmed that they were indeed ruguian eggs and placed them in a small stasis container and began searching the surrounding area for more.   However, several hours of searching proved futile. Other than the ruguian tracks in the mud that led away from the site, there was no sign of more ruguians or eggs.

One problem we encountered was that our navigational tools failed to work properly, most likely because of the I'aban trees. It was only when we were out from under this grove into an area where the canopy was not laced with minerals and metals that we were able to obtain a clear signal and get our bearings. I asked

Kerabac about the devices and how they were able to triangulate without satellites. He explained that the instruments were designed to read the radio signatures of various stars and compute the exact location of anything on the surface from a combination of these signatures, much like the navigation systems on the *ALI*, the *NEW ORLEANS* and other ships, only on a smaller scale.

It was mid-afternoon when we landed and began our search; and before we knew it, evening was upon us. Darkness descended quickly under the canopy and the sounds of life in the jungle around us grew louder as we made our way back to the ship. I didn't realize just how comfortable the ship's interior could be, until the door was sealed and the environment filters adjusted the CO_2, humidity and temperature levels to simulate the atmosphere that we were accustomed to inhabiting. Kerabac and I fared much better than Hotyona. The sweltering conditions on Alle Bamma were quite similar to those of the swamps where I grew up; and Kerabac had been to Alle Bamma before and knew what to expect. Hotyona, on the other hand, had not bothered to drink much water, so he was quite dehydrated and feeling poorly by the end of the day. However, after slowly drinking a liter and a half of water and eating a delicious bowl of some kind of stew that Kerabac brought from the synthesizer, he seemed to recover and feel normal once more.

Originally we planned to drop off two of the team and return the *ALI* to an orbit above the meet point until the *NEW ORLEANS* arrived; but the fact that we could not keep the ship cloaked for more than a few hours at a time convinced us that it would be better to keep the ship on the surface and hidden in the jungle.

On our second day out we didn't find any ruguian eggs, but we did come across a ruguian. It was slow and sluggish in its movements and it was very obvious that it had no fear of being bothered or eaten by a predator. We tried back-tracking along its trail in hopes of finding some eggs, but to no avail. As we traced our own tracks back to the ship, Kerabac said, "Keep moving and don't act suspicious, but glance down at our tracks on the trail." I did as he said and noticed the imprints of small, bare human-like feet overlaid on the tracks we had previously made.

"Do you think they're still around?" I asked.

"I'm sure of it," said Kerabac. "I suggest we act as though we are unaware of their presence and let them be the ones to make contact."

As we moved further down the trail, I tried to look about the jungle casually without appearing to be looking for anything in particular, but I failed to see anyone or note anything out of the norm. I asked Kerabac, "Do you think they will attack us?"

"I doubt it. They prefer to avoid contact with outsiders; but one never knows." It took us nearly an hour to reach the ship, during which time we didn't see even a single native. We made doubly sure the hatch was sealed for the night before going to bed. The next day when we exited the ship to begin our search, we were shocked to find the head of a drodoceal mounted on a pole near our hatch.

"Please tell me this is a welcome and not what I think it means," I said.

"I wish I could," said Kerabac, "but I fear it means precisely what you fear it does. We obviously are not welcome here."

"Perhaps we should relocate. There don't seem to be a lot of ruguians in this area anyway."

Hotyona spoke up and said, "According to my research, ruguians are constantly on the move; and though they don't appear to deliberately congregate, they are most likely to be found in greater numbers near their typical food sources."

"What do they eat?" I asked.

"Reports indicate they are herbivorous; but I have no real data on specific food preference."

"When I was here before, I noted several of them eating blossoms from a bush," said Kerabac, "but I don't know if that was a preference or coincidence."

"It well could be a preference, as there are many animal species that prefer to eat blossoms."

"There doesn't seem to be much in the way of flowers here," I said. "Everything is green or gray. Again, maybe we should relocate. On the other hand, if we could make contact with the natives, perhaps we could find a way to recruit them to help us locate the eggs."

"At this point I don't think recruiting them is a good idea," replied Kerabac. "My vote is we move."

"I would agree with Kerabac," said Hotyona. "According to what I've been able to find in the plant catalog, there should be numerous plants in bloom year around that would attract ruguians, if they do, in fact, prefer flowers."

I wasn't sure how much of what I was hearing was prompted by true concern over finding ruguian eggs and how much of it was because of the drodoceal head mounted on the pole that morning; but I was willing to look elsewhere, if it meant finding more eggs.

Kerabac carefully navigated the ship out of the cluster of I'aban trees and over the gravel beach. Fortunately, he had turned on the cloaking device before leaving the cover of the canopy, because we were barely out in the open when the sensors alarms were triggered, indicating the presence of another ship. We had been on Alle Bamma for only two days and we knew it would still be several days before the *NEW ORLEANS* arrived; so we were immediately on the alert. Kerabac checked the screens and announced that it was a small armed fighter, similar to those used by several of the non-aligned worlds. These ships were manufactured on planets that were known for specialized production of all kinds of arms and military equipment. Kerabac said the ship could belong to a mercenary, a pirate or the Brotherhood; there was simply no way of telling. I wished that we had A'Lappe with us to attempt to intercept any communication to and from the ship; but he wasn't, so we simply retreated some distance away and watched as it circled about the lake and then slowly headed off.

"Do you think they're aware that we're here?" I asked.

"I doubt it," said Kerabac. "But someone is obviously patrolling the area to look for something or someone. It may simply be a routine patrol; but I think we need to be careful. There shouldn't be anyone here at all, let alone a fighter. If it were a prospector or drug company looking for new plants to research for medicinal purposes, they would have been in a small research ship or transport and certainly not a fighter. I recommend we find a new place to hide quickly, before our cloaking time is used up."

"I agree, Kerabac. Were you able to monitor where the ship went?"

"I was able to track it until it dropped below the horizon west of here," replied Kerabac. "It seemed to be heading pretty much in a straight line, stopping periodically to circle lakes in the region before continuing on."

"Well, I would recommend we move about 50 kilometers south of here and see what we can find," I said.

The flight lasted only a few minutes and brought us to the shore of one of the larger lakes on the planet. It, too, seemed to have gravel beaches around its edge and I'aban trees growing in groves along its perimeter. Once again, Kerabac was able to find us a place to slip in among the trees. We were able to get deeper into the tree line than before, as there was a natural corridor formed by the trees that gently curved away and inland from the lake, allowing us to retreat to a location where we were not directly visible from the shore.

Once the *ALI* set down, we wasted no time in getting out of the ship to begin hunting for ruguian eggs. Hotyona suggested that we would have a better chance of finding flower-bearing plants near the edge of the I'aban groves, where there was more light passing through the canopy; so we headed off in that direction. As we came nearer to the edge of the grove, we began to see flowering bushes and other plants scattered about the jungle floor.   We hadn't traveled far before we encountered the first ruguian and another about 10 meters away, this time chomping on some blossoms. However, we didn't see any eggs, so we spread out, trying to keep in sight of each other while we searched. We came upon a few more ruguians; but as it neared time for sunset, we knew we had to stop searching and head back to the *ALI*, knowing that it was important to be inside before the rapidly approaching darkness left us vulnerable.   We were nearing the point where the flowers ended at the thick of the I'aban canopy, when Hotyona found our second cluster of eggs – this one weighing in at 70 grams. It was obvious that finding the eggs was not going to be an easy or fast project.

We no sooner collected the eggs than one of the rainfalls so common on the planet broke loose in a torrent. At first, the large leaves of the canopy above us deflected most of the rain; but as leaves began to sag under the weight of the water, we found ourselves quickly soaked as large drops and streams of water descended on us from the heights of the canopy. We arrived back at the ship totally soaked and uncomfortable in our protective gear just as it was becoming almost too dark to see. I was rather glad to see the ship, as I didn't like the idea of trying to find the *ALI* in the dark, especially in the heavy rain. Hotyona placed the eggs in the stasis container with the other eggs; and then we took turns showering and getting into dry outfits before gathering in the small crew area for a meal.

"Kerabac, you said you picked up a bit of the language used by the many of the tribes here. Is any of that available through the learning headbands?"

"I don't know, Tibby, that's a good question. Fifteen years ago is wasn't in the computers, but it may have been added since then.   There are hundreds of different languages among the natives here from what I can tell.   What I mainly learned is a sort of broken language that is universal to most of the tribes from what I understood; but whether it's been cataloged and added into the computer system I don't really know."

"Is it possible for you to check?" I asked.

"I can check the ship's computer; but ships the size of the *ALI* generally have only an abbreviated database that is nowhere near as comprehensive as, for instance, the one on the *NEW ORLEANS* or on a star ship.   It is possible, though, because great efforts are made to have as many languages available as possible, in case of a crash or a situation that leaves travelers stranded on a planet for an indefinite period."

"The *ALI* isn't just any ship; it was designed to serve as Galetils' personal ship and I can't imagine him putting anything less than the most advanced and sophisticated computer in his personal craft."

"You have a point there, Tibby. Let me check." Kerabac got up from the table and headed into the control room.

I turned to Hotyona and asked, "What do you think our chances are of finding all the eggs we need in the next four days? We need five times what we have now to make the anti-toxin."

"Honestly, Tibby, I have no idea; but if the numbers of ruguians we've encountered at this site are any indication, I would think our odds have increased substantially. As long as we keep the eggs in stasis, they will remain viable; and as long as Kalana is in stasis, she will be alright."

"I know, but I don't like it. What if something should go wrong and the stasis containment should fail?" I could hear myself choking on my words and I began to feel ill.

"Tibby, that's not going to happen. Even if the ship's power failed for some inexplicable reason, there is a built in backup power system in the stasis container that would maintain the stasis conditions for up to five years." Everything he was telling me was something I had been told before. A'Lappe had thoroughly explained the functions and backup systems on Kala's stasis chamber before we left, but I still wasn't comfortable with it.

"There's got to be some way we can expedite things."

"Tibby, I'm sorry, but you're just going to have to bear with the situation until we find the eggs, no matter how long it takes. We *will* find them."

"Tibby," said Kerabac as he came back from the control room, "I have good news. You were right. Galetils did indeed have an advanced and enhanced memory cube installed in the ship's computer. Practically every tidbit of knowledge in the galaxy is stored in that cube, including a learning module for *Bammaspeak*, which is what the scientists dubbed the universal language used by the various tribes when they encounter each other. It's not a complete language, but most of the tribes apparently share certain words and word roots; so with Bammaspeak we will be able to understand them and get our intentions across to most of the natives."

"Great. Before we go out there tomorrow, I want each of us to complete a session with the learning device so we're able to communicate with the locals, if we encounter them."

"There's even more than the planet's language in the learning database, Tibby," continued Kerabac. "There are also catalogs of Alle Bamma's plants and animals, at least those that have been studied. Even though the information is incomplete, it should certainly prove useful or at least help us to know what to avoid out there. The database also includes a comprehensive module on the geography of the planet."

"Well, what are we waiting for?" I said. "Let's get this over with. I'll go first."

Hotyona hooked me up to the learning band and Kerabac loaded the modules into the computer. I had been introduced to the learning headbands when I discovered the *TRITYTE* back on Earth, though not until after I was already in space. I discovered then that it gave me a bad headache when in the teaching mode – an effect it didn't seem to have on most others in the Federation. This time was no different than any other, except that the headache seemed to be worse, more like a severe migraine – nausea included. While Kerabac and Hotyona assisted each other, I excused myself and went to my bunk, where I promptly fell into a deep sleep.

I had never been one to believe in psychic abilities, ghosts or the paranormal; but the dream I had that night and the events over the next several days were to change my mind about such things. During the night I dreamed that I was tied to a tree next to Kerabac and Hotyona. Near us on a platform sat several bowls that held burning oil, the flames of which provided light to the immediate surroundings. Around us on the platform stood the small figures of native Allebammian natives, who carried spears and small daggers that appeared to be made from giant thorns. One small native woman in a headdress made out of woven grasses and leaves approached me with a ruguian in one hand and a long thorn in the other. She stuck the thorn into the skin on the side of the ruguian, which squirmed in her hand as she slid the thorn along the body just under the surface of the skin. Then she withdrew the thorn and stuck it into my arm. As she did so, a tall figure suddenly appeared who looked similar to the natives despite the fact that this individual was at least a full head taller than I am. This figure also wore a headdress; but this one appeared to be a live and growing organism, rather than one fashioned by human hands, as live plants began to bloom within the headdress as the eyes beneath it gazed at me. When the figure appeared, all of the natives dropped to their knees and pressed their heads to the wooden platform, chanting "Thumumba, Thumumba, Thumumba," as thunder rumbled in the background. The tall figure I assumed to be Thumumba walked up to me, looked me up and down, and then leaned forward to whisper in my ear, "*Aye ucombey nortelia Thumumba. Telalle aye eugoray seballe.*" Then I woke up trembling and drenched in sweat. I got out of bed feeling ill and stumbled to the shower. Afterwards I felt better, but I was still rather shaky.

"Are you okay?" Kerabac's voice came from the direction of the doorway and I turned to see him standing there.

"I'm not sure," I said. "I just had the strangest dream."

"About Thumumba?" he asked.

"Yes! How did you know?"

"When I was here before it happened to some of the people on our team," he said.

"Did you all have the same dream?"

"No, everyone who had the experience reported different dreams and most of the team didn't have any. In some dreams Thumumba was angry and in others kind. What happened in your dream?" he asked.

I related my dream to him; and when I got to the part where Thumumba said *Aye ucombey nortelia Thumumba. Telalle aye eugoray seballe* (which, oddly, I remembered verbatim), Kerabac raised an eyebrow and said "*I speak for Thumumba. See I do not die*"... interesting. Was there anything else?"

"No, that was it," I decided to reply. "What dream did you have when you were here last?"

"On the last day of the excursion I dreamed that Thumumba came to me and said, "*When come next to Sweet Home you will help to save my people.*"

As he told me this, I realized he was translating the native language and that "Alle Bamma" means "Sweet Home." I began to laugh.

Kerabac gave me a puzzled look and asked, "What's funny about that?"

"Back on Earth there is a popular song called *Sweet Home Alabama*; and here I am now on a planet named *Alle Bamma* which, in the native language, means *Sweet Home*."

As I was talking, Kerabac moved over to the synthesizer and prepared a cup of foccee and handed it to me. "Here, drink this. It's nearly dawn and I know you will want to get an early start today. Tibby, I'm not a superstitious man; but I will tell you that things here on Alle Bamma can get a bit strange at times."

"Thanks," I said as I took the cup from him. "Is it this way for everyone that comes here?"

"I don't think so. Only a few of us on the team had dreams that I know of.

"What's the weather like outside?" I asked, changing the subject.

Kerabac laughed. "It's raining so hard that you can't see two meters; but it will most likely be over in a few minutes. Rains here are frequent, but not usually long."

It was still raining when we left the *ALI*, but it was no longer pouring. Even so, it was only a few minutes until the slow, steady rain left us soaked to the skin. We went directly to the region where we had been the evening before; and we were rewarded with another mass of ruguian eggs, which Hotyona placed in the container and stored in his back pack. We had barely resumed our search when we heard numerous voices and scurrying sounds in the jungle. Kerabac motioned us to crouch down to avoid being seen by whomever or whatever was coming; but the effort was hardly necessary, because what we saw next was not on the ground but in the air. We stood again, gazing in amazement at dozens of natives swinging and leaping high up in the canopy of the trees about 150 meters away from us as they hurried deeper into the jungle away from the direction of the *ALI*.

"What the–!" I started to say, when this strange sight was followed by the sounds of heavy machinery coming through the jungle in the direction that the Allebammians were fleeing. We immediately crouched back down in time to see several armed all-terrain vehicles crashing along behind the fleeing natives. Not far behind the vehicles came about thirty armed troopers on foot, some dragging natives on leashes attached to collars fastened around their necks. Captives who resisted or didn't move quickly enough were disciplined with electrical shocks that seemed to be transmitted through the collars in an effort to control them and prod them forward. We ducked even farther into the dense tangle of the jungle and watched as the nearest trooper passed within 10 meters of us. Fortunately, we were not seen and they were moving in a direction away from the *ALI*. We remained hidden and quiet until the noise receded into the distance several minutes later.

"What do you think that was all about?" I asked.

"I'm not sure," said Kerabac, "but I noted Brotherhood emblems on the uniforms of the troopers."

"Why do you think they were after the natives? Why were they restraining them with those collars and leashes?"

"I'm just guessing, but I think the Brotherhood is taking them as slaves. When I was still in the military, we were deployed to a police action on Gorvan. The planet had recently been accepted into the Federation, under the condition that they give up slavery. In spite of the agreement with the Federation and the actions taken by the planetary government, there were entire colonies on the planet that refused to give up their slaves. Hence, the Federation was called upon to provide troops and enforce abolition in all colonies and settlements. I saw those same collars on the Gorvan slaves.

"There are still many non-aligned worlds where slavery is practiced. Since this is a non-aligned world, it's not too likely that anyone will come to the aid of the Allebammians."

"Well, if that's what the Brotherhood thinks, they're totally wrong," I said, rising to my feet.

"What are you thinking, Tibby?" asked Kerabac.

"I'm thinking that I'm going to try to save those natives," I said.

"Tibby, if you go out there and up against those troops, you're not going to be able to get your eggs as soon as you want!"

"I know, but I can't sit by and watch these natives being killed and enslaved by the Brotherhood either. I don't believe Kala would be pleased with me if I didn't do *something*."

Kerabac smiled, "That's what I like about you, Tibby! You have an unwavering sense of justice and you're not afraid to examine your priorities. I'm with you!"

"I'm not sure what I can do to help," said Hotyona. "I'm not a trooper or trained for combat, but I will do what I can."

"Well, the first thing I think we need to do is to find their base. I would suggest we follow their rather obvious trail and see where it leads. Then, once we size things up, we can decide on our next course of action. The *NEW ORLEANS* should be arriving in three to four days. With our own security forces and the Mirage Fighters, I think we can handle pretty much anything the Brotherhood has for defense resources here. Let's just hope that A'Lappe and Cantolla have managed to get that new communication system up and operating, so we can contact the fleet once the *NEW ORLEANS* arrives."

Before we began to follow the trail of the Brotherhood, we returned to the *ALI* to put the ruguian eggs into the stasis capsule and to get into full body armor. We also needed to arm ourselves with more weapons, as we carried only the small flat guns while collecting eggs. The flat gun was a small hand weapon that looked much like the television remote controls used on Earth. While it served as a convenient and easily concealed personal protection weapon, it was not easy to aim and certainly not designed to use in a combat situation. I also made sure that each of us was equipped with one of the personal cloaking units that A'Lappe was so fond of using as he moved about the ship. Even though this latest revision only had a useful time limit of about an hour and a half, it was still something that could prove to be useful. We had not worn them earlier, because we believed that we were not likely to encounter anyone while we hunted for eggs; but now it was clear that our safety may depend on it.

Before leaving the *ALI* we activated the ship's cloaking device. Even though we knew it would only cloak the ship for a short time and that the ship would be visible again by the time we returned, it was still better than nothing at all. The door locks were sealed and keyed to only open only to the handprints of the three of us; so even if the ship were discovered, no one other than the three of us were going to get in.

The Brotherhood's trail was easy to follow, as the large wheels on the vehicles had left deep impressions in the loam of the jungle floor and the smaller plants and bushes also lay crushed and broken in their paths. In a few places we found the corpses of Allebammians that appeared to have fallen from the high canopy of trees after being shot.

"I don't understand it," said Hotyona. "If they want slaves, why are they killing them?"

"My guess is they're trying to intimidate them into surrendering. By killing those that flee and showing that the captured remain alive, they're sending a clear message to surrender or die," explained Kerabac.

"What do you think they want the Allebammians for?" Hotyona asked.

"Like any slaveholder, they want the natives to do some sort of work that they don't want to do themselves," Kerabac answered with a great deal of disdain in his voice. Earlier generations of Kerabac's people practiced slavery; and though his planet had since joined the Federation and abolished the practice, many still held the old views and prejudices. Some even continued to keep slaves, though they had to do so away from their home planet. Kerabac's personal experience made him very knowledgeable about the topic, including the motives behind the slaveholders' actions; but he never spoke of it without showing visible discomfort, repugnance, and perhaps a bit of shame on behalf of his people.

We had been following the trail for about an hour when we noticed the jungle foliage seemed to be thinning. We assumed we were arriving at another of the many lakes that dotted the planet; so we were somewhat surprised when we reached the edge of a large clearing. Several tall structures were spaced at intervals around the clearing; over which a tent of camouflaged netting was draped. Approximately 50 troopers could be seen moving about the area where about a dozen patrol ships and another dozen or so armored ground transports were parked. There was also one much larger ship that was about the size of a corvette but of a different configuration – the likes of which I had not seen before.

"What kind of ship is that?" I whispered to Kerabac.

"I'm not sure, to be honest, Tibby. It looks to be well armed, from what I can see of the torpedo tubes and gun hubs. It appears to be a new ship; so I would say it's a new design by one of the non-aligned planets that specialize in arms manufacturing. It looks deadly, that's for sure. It's nothing that would be able to harm the *NEW ORLEANS*, but it could do serious damage to the *ALI* in a firefight."

"What do you think we should do?" asked Hotyona.

"Well, for right now I suggest we move around the edge of this clearing and over to the other side to see what's there," I said.

"I agree," said Kerabac. "I think we need to see as much as we can before we make any decisions as to what we will do next."

We slowly began to work our way around the edge of the clearing, staying very mindful of the presence of Brotherhood troopers and guards. As we moved around the perimeter of the encampment, we saw groups of natives restrained by the electrified collars who were being forced to perform different tasks – carrying boxes, clearing brush and felling trees, and digging in the ground to prepare for enough foundation installations to support several structures, the functions of which we only could guess at. We reached the halfway point around the clearing when we noted a large building within the compound into which the enslaved natives carried bales of some sort of vegetation and then exited empty-handed. We also noted members of the Brotherhood in white lab clothing who came and went from this same building.

"What do you think they're doing in there?" I asked.

"I don't know," said Kerabac. "It appears they're processing that plant material for something."

As Kerabac replied, several armed Brotherhood guards directed a single-file line of natives out of the building who were burdened with sealed shipping boxes, which they carried across the compound and into a small freighter.

"I think we need to find out what's going on in there," I said.

"If I knew what plant it is they're processing, I might be able to tell you what they're up to," said Hotyona.

"You two stay here," I said. "I'm going to cloak and sneak into the building for a look. I'll try to get a sample of the plant for you, Hotyona. If I'm not back in two hours, you two head back to the *ALI* and seal yourself inside until the *NEW ORLEANS* arrives. Don't let them blow this base up with the natives inside."

Kerabac and Hotyona concealed themselves in the dense foliage along the clearing edge as I activated the personal cloaking device and jogged across the clearing to the far side of the building. As I moved along the side of the building, I passed some exhaust pipes that emitted strong chemical odors. The smell was overwhelming and left me feeling a bit light-headed until I was able to get past the last of them and pause to breathe in some clean air. I noted several locked doors as I made my way around the structure; but the one into which the natives were carrying the bales of leaves was standing wide open. There was a period of about two minutes between lines of natives where there was no one in the doorway and I used that as an opportunity to slip inside.

Immediately inside the door I stepped to the side to let my eyes adjust to the darkness, after which I noticed the glow of artificial lighting coming from a corridor a few meters ahead. I followed the corridor a short distance to a larger room where the bales were stacked. A guard watched over four naked natives who dropped the bales into a shredding machine that emptied to a conveyor, which then moved the shredded material to another machine. Here the material was dumped into a large hopper that apparently squeezed all the sap out of the plants. The sap was collected in vats arranged on yet another conveyor that moved in a circuit to the adjoining room through a hole in the wall. I carefully snuck past the guard and opened the door into the next room.

Inside the room I could see the vats moving along the circuit until they emptied into a larger vat. Two of the men in lab coats stood at a nearby banister, apparently making adjustments to some instruments. Under the watchful eyes of a guard, a small native carrying a container poured some powder into the vat. As the guard and native left, I quickly slipped through the door behind them and into yet another room.

Here I could see more technicians in lab coats, this time taking samples from a tap on a line that came through the wall from the vat and subjecting the liquid product to various chemical tests.

I heard one of them say, "Excellent. We should get top money for this batch," as he examined the changing colors inside a test tube. "Those poor suckers on Sepra are so addicted to this juice that we'll soon have all the wealth of that planet in our pocket. They'll be so broke and addicted that they will do anything we ask for a fix. We'll be able to use them for cannon fodder against the Federation while saving our troopers for mop up operations."

All the lab workers laughed.

By this point I estimated I had been cloaked for about twenty minutes, so I needed to start making my way back to Kerabac and Hotyona before the cloak expired. Getting out of the building was not as easy as getting in. Just as I arrived at the exit, a large group of natives and their guards arrived with bales of plants. I had to retreat back into the bale storage room and squeeze myself into a corner where I would not be bumped by anyone as the natives filed in and out of the room. To make matters worse, the natives stacked several bales in front of me, virtually trapping me in the corner. Realizing my cloaking device might fail before I could get out, I turned it off. I was concealed behind the bales, so I wasn't concerned about being seen. Fortunately I didn't have to wait too long before I saw the top bale begin to move away from the stack and I quickly reactivated the cloaking device. It took another few minutes before all the bales were cleared away and I was able to make my way to the exit. Even then it was a close call, as another group of natives bearing bales were almost ready to enter the building. Once outside, I stopped briefly to wait for the last native to approach the entrance before plucking a leaf from the bale he was carrying. The guard stood at the opposite side of the native, so there was no risk of him seeing a leaf suddenly leave the bale and vanish into thin air.

As I approached Kerabac and Hotyona, I spotted several troopers sneaking up on them. It was obvious that the troopers planned to capture the pair; otherwise they could have shot them from where they stood. Kerabac must have heard a noise or noticed something that clued him in to their presence, as he suddenly turned to see three Brotherhood troopers with guns trained on him and Hotyona. Both Kerabac and Hotyona raised their arms in surrender, while I quickly moved up behind them. With a swift series of martial arts blows I took out two of the troopers. The other was distracted stunned long enough at the sight of his partners dropping to the ground to allow Kerabac to lunge forward and knock him to the ground.   Unfortunately the sound attracted attention of other troopers in the clearing, who turned all at once to see the scuffle.   Kerabac rendered his opponent unconscious with a solid blow to the jaw as I uncloaked and told both Kerabac and Hotyona to follow me.

We sprinted into the jungle in a direction away from our ship.   Behind us we could hear yells as an alarm was issued and more troopers joined in the chase. When we reached a large I'aban tree that had roots sloping up to the trunk like a set of stairs, I quickly led the others to the top and then instructed them to cloak and remain still.   Just as we cloaked the first of the troopers in the pursuit appeared below us.   We were standing on a branch just a little above the troopers head height; and had we not been cloaked, we would have been in plain sight.   As it was, we were able to remain in this obvious location, invisible and ignored, as the troopers scoured the dense vines and brush beneath the surrounding trees.   Eventually they all moved off deeper into the jungle, reporting to the other pursuers that the area was clear.

I was beginning to worry, as I had no idea how much time I had left on my cloaking device.   We uncloaked and descended to the jungle floor to head back toward the compound in the direction of the *ALI*, all the while keeping an eye out for Brotherhood troopers.   As we approached the clearing we had to cloak twice, as we spotted small bands of troopers heading in the general direction of the first group of pursuers.

Just as the last of the troopers receded from view, my cloak failed.

"I sure hope we don't encounter anymore of the Brotherhood before we make it to the *ALI*," I said. "My cloak has used up all its power."

"Once we get around the compound area we should be free of them, unless they sent out troopers in all directions," said Kerabac.

Just as we made it past the clearing, one of the daily showers broke loose with a vengeance. The rain was pouring down so heavily that our visibility was restricted to only a few feet. There was simply no way to clearly discern our heading and we soon faced a greater chance of getting lost than finding the ship. The hammering of raindrops against the jungle canopy was so loud that we couldn't even communicate with each other. As we passed by the base of an I'aban tree, Kerabac grabbed both Hotyona and me by the arm and nearly dragged us into a space between the large roots at the base of the tree. Suddenly we found ourselves standing in a large and surprisingly quiet room-like space inside the tree.

"I think it might be wise for us to wait out the rain here," said Kerabac. "If we try to continue traveling in this storm, I'm afraid we will get turned around and end up wandering right back into the Brotherhood camp."

"Thanks, Kerabac," I said, truly grateful to be out of the torrent. "I have to agree with you. I think if I'd have stayed out there much longer, I'd have started to grow gills."

We stood quietly for a moment, each of us appreciating the relative dryness of our refuge as we shook the sogginess from our clothes and hair.

"Oh, before I forget, Hotyona, I believe you want to look at this." I reached into my vest pocket and pulled out the leaf I had taken from the bale and handed it to him.

Hotyona showed great curiosity as he took the leaf and walked over near the entrance to our root shelter where there was a bit more light. He looked at it briefly, first one side and then the other, then he sniffed it before tearing off the tiniest bit and putting it in his mouth. He only held it there a brief moment before spitting it out.

"It's very alkaline," he said.

That was the last intelligible utterance that came from him for several hours, as his head suddenly began to bob and sway. His eyes expanded and pupils dilated and his jaw hung open loosely as he began to drool.

"Um, Hotyona, are you okay?" I asked. Hotyona turned his head toward us and grinned. Then his gaze drifted off as though he were watching something floating by.

"Oh, shit," said Kerabac. "I don't know what the scientific name is for this plant, but I know what the street name is. I remember the scientists on the expedition team discussing it when I was here years ago. The natives use it in their religious practices. Its sap is highly hallucinogenic. The natives will only use it under the supervision of their shaman – and then only once or twice a year because of its additive properties. Persons who become addicted will literally starve themselves, taking more and more of the drug without eating, until they finally die."

"That would explain what I saw and heard in the lab," I said. I related to Kerabac the comments I had overheard and what I saw inside the processing plant at the compound.

"I've heard in recent years that there was a new drug sweeping some of the outer worlds and that it was becoming a real scourge that caused its users to spend or surrender all their assets just to get more of it. The name of this drug on the streets is *God's Sweat*. If that's what this is," Kerabac said as he gestured toward Hotyona, who was now reaching and gesturing in slow motion toward something visible only to him, "no one has ever figured out where it comes from, until now. God's Sweat is illegal on all Federation planets; however, on some of the non-aligned worlds it can be purchased anywhere legally. Even with the laws against it and a very stiff penalty for peddling it, the demand for it in the Federation by drug users is high."

At this point Hotyona's head had dropped to his chest and he was swaying from side to side mumbling and humming.

"How long before it wears off?" I asked.

"I don't know," said Kerabac. "Aside from what I just told you, I know very little about the drug. I would say, based on his appearance now, that it will be hours at best."

I looked outside. The rain had not let up and I could see it was beginning to get darker; the sun was setting and it would only be minutes before it would be too dark to travel.

"It looks like we will be here for the night," I said. "Is there anything we need to know or prepare for?"

"I saw a few reeds just before we entered the tree that I believe have a high oil sap content. The natives burn them like candles. If we can collect some and get them lit, it will at least provide us with some light, and the smoke may keep most of the rubloids out, or at least prevent them from biting us. I think it's safe to go out to gather some reeds. I don't believe the Brotherhood will have anyone out looking for us in the dark. The smoke won't travel far in the humid air; and the opening to this tree is narrow, so unless someone is standing in just the right location, I don't think the light can be seen either."

Just then I felt something bite my neck and I swatted it. The small, dead creature on my hand was about the size of my little fingernail. It was sort of soft and had an iridescent pinkish green color.

"There, that's what I'm talking about," said Kerabac. "Once the sun sets, there will be swarms of those little vermin all over the place. They are repelled both by light and the scent of the oil sticks."

The bite was still stinging and burning when I replied, "Well, what are we waiting for? Let's get ourselves enough to last us through the night."

Collecting the plants was not difficult as they seemed to grow abundantly in the area around the tree roots. We tried not to take too many from one spot, electing instead to pick one here and there, so as not to make it obvious that they had been harvested and give away our location. Fortunately, the rainfall had slowed somewhat, enough to make it a bit easier to see and complete the task. By the time we ran out of daylight we had a large stockpile of the plant piled up in the back of the cavity under the tree. Kerabac stuck five of the reeds

in the ground across the entrance and, using a device he
pulled from a pocket in is uniform vest, he lit the ends.
At first the stems didn't seem to want to burn. Then,
slowly, a flame began to grow on the end of each reed
and before long there was a row of beautiful yellow
flames casting light into the space. Black oily smoke
curled from the flames, spiraling upward and spreading
out like a small cloud throughout the tree cavity. The
accumulating smoke had a rather pungent smell that was
not unpleasant to breathe; but it was a bit uncomfortable
on the eyes, as it stung and made it difficult to see. Once
Kerabac was certain that the reeds were burning well, he
stripped off his shirt and twisted it to wring out the
water.

"I would suggest you wring as much moisture
out of your clothing as possible," he said. "While you
won't be able to get completely dry, you'll be a bit more
comfortable." In the light of the reeds Kerabac's white
teeth seemed to be accented by his black flesh as he
smiled broadly."

"Thanks for the suggestion. I couldn't get any
wetter if I jumped into the lake."

As we stripped and wrung our clothing out as
best we could, I commented with praise for the scientists
who developed the textile used to make our uniforms.
The fabric didn't hold much moisture and, under normal
circumstances, probably had wicking properties that I
had not appreciated until that moment. After dressing
again, we both looked at Hotyona in his soaked clothing.
He was still humming and rocking gently, oblivious to
our presence.

Kerabac said, "I don't think it will make any difference to him. He's off in another world someplace and not feeling anything here."

It had been our intent that we would take turns sleeping during the night so one of us was always on watch. As we settled in, we found ourselves caught up in conversation. I told him how much joy it brought me to hear him sing at the lounge; and then I taught him another Nat King Cole tune. He later shared more of his adventures on some of the worlds he visited as a trooper, stories that I found enlightening and intriguing.

We replaced the burning reeds with new ones only once during the night. It was obvious that we had picked way more than we actually needed. The smoke from the reeds seemed to hang within our space and add to the fatigue we felt from the eventful day. Without realizing that it was happening, we both fell asleep.

Once again I dreamt of Thumumba. In my dream this figure stood beside me with one hand on my shoulder. We seemed to be standing on a large branch at the top of an I'aban tree looking at the ground. The trees in the area around us seemed to have their leaves removed, allowing us to see the ground clearly. Thumumba pointed out certain features with the free hand while keeping the other hand on my shoulder. My vision seemed to zoom to a magnified view of whatever I was directed to observe. As we surveyed the jungle floor from our lookout, Thumumba directed my attention to a nearby clearing. It was then that I recognized we were looking out over the Brotherhood's compound. Thumumba pointed out a large, low building.

"There is where my children are held as slaves. You must free them."

Then it seemed that the tree was shaking; and I heard Kerabac's voice.

"Wake up, Tibby. Hotyona is gone."

I opened my eyes to the daylight streaming in through the narrow opening in the tree trunk. The last set of reeds we lit in the night before falling asleep were burnt to the ground and barely smoldering.

"What happened?" I asked groggily.

"We fell asleep and now Hotyona is gone. I just woke up and he's nowhere to be seen. I looked outside in the immediate area; but I don't think we dare call out his name or the troopers might hear us. I don't know if he's wandering aimlessly, still under the effect of the drug, but there's no doubt that he's nowhere nearby."

"Is it still raining?"

"No, it stopped sometime before I woke up and the remaining clouds are thin. By the looks of the shadows, it's been daylight for hours."

"Can you see Hotyona's tracks? Maybe we can we follow them," I asked.

"Wait here. Let me look," Kerabac slipped outside and soon returned. "Yes, I can see his tracks."

As Kerabac and I began to trace Hotyona's steps, it was obvious that he was still not fully functional, as his tracks weaved back and forth, periodically looping in small circles. We traveled about a half kilometer from the tree, when suddenly the tracks stopped in the middle of a broad patch of mud, as though he had vanished into thin air. Kerabac and I stood dumbfounded as we tried to sort out the mystery, when suddenly I saw a small feathered dart sticking from Kerabac's neck. Within a couple of seconds he began to drop to the ground; and as I reached to grab him, I felt the sting of a needle in my own neck.

The next thing I recall was hearing chants inside my head; and for a moment I thought I was dreaming again. Everything was so dark that I couldn't discern what was around me. Slowly the world came into focus and I found myself looking at a band of natives dancing about, singing and chanting. Most of them were naked, save for headbands woven from plant fibers, strips of bark or leather. The faces of the natives were devoid of eyebrows and the lenticular shaped eyes that gazed at me as they danced were a bit unnerving, to say the least. I also noted that they had a pair of catlike fangs in their upper jaw and a complementary pair of smaller ones in the lower jaw; but their other teeth appeared to be flat and more like the molars of a human. This was a feature neither Kerabac nor Hotyona had mentioned. As I came out of my stupor, I realized that I was tied to the branch of an I'aban tree. I looked to my right to see both Kerabac and Hotyona likewise tied to tree branches. We appeared to be high in the air on a platform of about 30 square meters built into the fork of the tree trunk. Kerabac appeared to be unconscious and Hotyona was most certainly still under the influence of the hallucinogenic plant from the day before, as he was still mumbling and gazing into space. He seemed to be a bit more alert than yesterday, but he was no doubt unaware of what was taking place.

A small elderly woman wearing a woven headdress separated herself from the congregation of dancing natives to approach me. She had an air of

authority about her that hinted at her status as a tribal
leader.

"Why you come to Sweet Home?" she said.
"Why you make children of Thumumba harvest sacred
plant, make them do wrong things, make them work with
binding around neck?   Why you destroy trees of
Thumumba, make big ugly place and hurt and kill
children of Thumumba?"

I was immediately able to reply in the broken
universal Bammaspeak that I learned via the headband
device.

"We not do wrong things. Other men – bad men
–make ugly places and bind children of Thumumba.
Bad men our enemies. They not men like us and we not
bad like them," I answered.

"You lie! You look like them. You smell like
them." She gestured toward Hotyona, "See your brother
take sacred plant and dream the dreams of Thumumba
without guidance. Forbidden by Thumumba to take
without guidance of elder."

"He take sacred plant as accident. He not know
your sacred plant. He make mistake. He taste only drop
on tongue. He not know."

"Why he do such thing if he not know? You lie!
You come to Sweet Home from sky like others. Take
and destroy, hurt and kill children!"

"No," I protested. "We seek eggs of Slow
Mover to make cure (I used Slow Mover, realizing as I
spoke the word that it was the name the natives used for
the ruguian). Must save friend who is poisoned."

"Where is friend? We watch you three days now. We see no friend. You lie."

"Friend not here. She lay sick in house in the sky."

In spite of my efforts, the elder clearly found my answers to be incredulous. She came close to my face and squinted her angular eyes at me. "How friend get poison on house in sky?"

"From bad men who bind children of Thumumba, who cut sacred plant and destroy Sweet Home. They try kill her and me, stab with poison from Slow Mover. Now she sick and face death if we not gather Slow Mover eggs and mix medicine cure."

"You lie. You say you poisoned by Slow Mover poison. Why you not dead or sick?"

"I no tell lie. I poisoned too. See scar on arm? Slow Mover poison stabbed into skin from bad men blade, but I not die."

"Only children protected by Thumumba not die. You lie, man. You not child of Thumumba. Thumumba not save you. You lie!"

She then turned to one of the natives standing nearby and said, "Bring Slow Mover."

The native quickly ran off and the woman turned back to me. "We see if you lie or not lie. If you lie, you die and friends die, too."

The native that she sent off reappeared carrying a woven basket covered with a lid that had a long thorn protruding from the center of it. She pulled the thorn free, reached into the basket, and extracted a ruguian. Holding it firmly in one hand, she stuck the thorn into the ruguian, sliding it up the creature's back just under the skin. The ruguian squirmed in an effort to free himself, but it could not escape her grasp. Then she extracted the thorn.

"Now we see, man, if you lie!" She stabbed me with the thorn, first into one arm and then the other.

The chanting suddenly stopped and everyone on the platform stood still and dead silent. I looked at Kerabac and saw that he had also regained consciousness, but I had no idea how long he had been awake or how much he had heard.

"What do you think is going to happen?" I said to Kerabac.

"I don't know," he said. "If you live like before, it will be a huge shock for them, I assure you; but what they do after that is beyond my ability to guess."

I looked at the woman before me who stood in silence with the rest of the tribe, watching and waiting. After a few minutes I felt the familiar wave of illness that overcame me when Kala and I were poisoned on Plosaxen. For a moment I felt like I might black out like I did the first time. I looked at the old woman to see a smile on her face as though she had proven me a liar and that she and her people were witnessing my death. I knew that ruguian poison did not kill quickly. From what I learned from A'Lappe and the medics, the poison acted by rendering one unconscious relatively quickly, after which the victim would fall into a coma for several days before dying.

The natives continued to watch me in silence; and after a few minutes I began to improve.

Kerabac asked, "How you holding up, Tibby?"

"Okay," I answered. "I felt a bit ill for a few minutes and thought I might black out, but now I'm starting to feel better again."

I could see that some of the natives were starting to get nervous and were commenting and whispering to each other in a hushed panic. "He not die! He not fall into death sleep!" they murmured.

A look of amazement replaced the smug smile on the elder's face as I quickly rebounded from the ill effects of the toxin. For a brief moment I felt dizzy again and thought I was about to pass out. I looked up to see the tall figure of what I believed to be Thumumba walking toward me through the gathered crowd of natives. It was clear that the elderly woman and natives did not see this figure among them. When Thumumba reached my side, I heard the familiar whisper in my ear, "*Aye ucombey nortelia Thumumba. Telalle aye eugoray seballe!*"

Intuitively I knew what to do next. I looked at the old woman and repeated, "Aye ucombey nortelia Thumumba. Telalle aye eugoray seballe!" which I now understood to mean, *I speak for Thumumba. See I do not die!* As I said the words, three loud peals of thunder filled the air in succession. The natives collectively fell to their knees and pressed their heads to the wooden platform, shaking and trembling in fear of retribution for doubting the one who spoke on behalf of their god.

All was silent for nearly a minute before heads raised to look around and gaze into the sky. The old woman rose to her feet and came forward. She cut me free of my restraints using an odd-shaped knife that appeared to be made of bone.

"You speak truth, man from house in sky. You speak for Thumumba. Children of Thumumba listen."

I heard Kerabac exclaim, "Well I'll be damned, just like your dream. You're going to convert me to be a follower of Thumumba, if you keep this up."

As he spoke, two natives came forward to cut him free, while another two cut Hotyona free – though Hotyona was still looking about aimlessly and didn't seem to know what was happening. The old woman spoke quietly to one of the two who freed Hotyona and the native nodded and ran off. She then turned to me.

"Tell us, man who speak for Thumumba, what is Thumumba wish?"

"Thumumba wish children set free from bad men who bind them. Thumumba wish all bad men be gone from Sweet Home," I said.

"Children of Thumumba wish same, but bad men strike with lightning and fire sticks and ride metal animals that kill children of Thumumba. Bad men also wear hard skins. Arrows and darts not pierce, so children fight but not win, only flee."

All hopes I had that the natives could join us in the battle against the Brotherhood vanished, as she related with sadness and desperation the reality of their situation. I realized that what she said was true; and if anything was going to be done to get the Brotherhood off the planet, it was going to be up to me and the crew of the *NEW ORLEANS* to accomplish it – or at least hold them at bay until the Federation could arrive. I wasn't sure just when the *NEW ORLEANS* would arrive. They could be here already or it could be another day. In any case, we needed to get back to the *ALI* to contact them. The natives had unfortunately taken our guns and our cloaking devices and smashed them after we were captured, believing we were enemies. We had no idea where we were in the jungle; and if we were going to get back to the ship, we would need the natives to guide us.

"Your name?" I asked the old woman.

"My name Jnanara," she said. "I speak for children of Thumumba."

"My name Tibby. I speak for Thumumba." I hoped that I was saying things properly and using the proper protocol. One wrong response and we might have ended up tied back onto the tree.

"Friends and I need guide. Take us to sky boat to gather fire sticks. We fight men who bind children of Thumumba."

"No! No return to sky boat! Bad men wait in bushes and shadows... wait for Tibby and friends return."

This was getting worse all the time. Apparently the Brotherhood had found our ship after the cloaking device expired. They would not have been able to get in; and since none of them had ever seen or heard of a Mirage Fighter, they wouldn't have the first clue as to its origin. They had no doubt decided to wait for the owners to return with the intent to capture them and gain access to the ship to find out who we were and what threat we posed to them.

Kerabac overheard the conversation. "What are we going to do now?" he said.

"I don't know," I said. "I need to think this over."

"How many men hide in bushes and shadows?" I asked Jnanara. She turned to one of tribesmen nearby. Using his fingers he counted out twenty-five.

"Well," I said, "I don't think we'll be going back there unarmed to try and overpower them. If we still had the cloaking devices, we might've had a chance, but not this way."

"Maybe we can build a large fire and signal the *NEW ORLEANS*," offered Kerabac.

"I don't think that's a very safe idea. First they may not realize it's us and just assume it's a forest fire; and second, the Brotherhood would also see the signal and know where we are. I think we stand a better chance if we go back to the compound. We should be able to stealthily taking out a few troopers, arm ourselves with their gear and, if we have the chance, disguise ourselves in their uniforms. Maybe we can create a diversion while we're there, as well – do some damage to the facility that distracts their forces long enough to set the natives free. If we do it right, they won't know how many of us there are and they'll pull back the troops staged at the *ALI* to help defend the base. If we can find a good place to hide after we release the natives and hold there until the guards at the *ALI* pass us, we may be able to move quickly enough to get back to the ship and escape before they return."

While Kerabac and I made plans and communicated with Jnanara, two natives returned with a nutshell bowl containing some grayish liquid. Using a large, pliable leaf that they folded to make a cup, they scooped the liquid and coaxed Hotyona into drinking it.

Jnanara noticed my look of concern at what was happening and she said, "Children give friend *naga juice*. Naga make friend see this world Sweet Home again – no more see world of Thumumba."

"How much time before friend no see world of Thumumba?" I asked.

"Soon!" She said. Before long it became obvious that *time*, as perceived by the children of Thumumba, was divided into only a handful of categories – *many days*, *days*, *not soon*, *soon* and *now*. In this case, *soon* turned out to be about ten minutes, at which time I could see Hotyona returning to normal rather rapidly. His confusion as to where he was and what had happened to him was apparent. At first he talked nonstop about Thumumba and heaven. He believed he had been gone for years. He had difficulty reorienting to his surroundings and the actual timeline of events; but slowly, more and more details of what had actually taken place returned to him as though he were recalling a dream.

I asked Jnanara if she could provide us with a guide to get us back to the Brotherhood camp. I could see the concern on her face at my request, so I explained that we wanted to set Thumumba's children free and destroy the place where they took the stolen sacred plant. Jnanara looked at me silently, her unique and sad eyes filling with tears, as I did my best to communicate in the rudimentary language that we wanted as much as she and the children of Thumumba to free the bound ones, restore control of the sacred plant to the elders and remove all signs of the Brotherhood from Sweet Home. She called another native and instructed him to guide us to the Brotherhood compound.

As we descended from the I'aban tree, I was surprised to find that we were nearly a hundred meters off the ground. At first we descended by moving down branches while holding onto vines for support. Our guide moved swiftly and gracefully, stopping often to wait for us, as we were not nearly as sure-footed or at ease with the decent. We had to finish the last 25 meters using the vines alone, lowering ourselves hand over hand until we reached the ground. Kerabac and I were able to do it without much trouble; but Hotyona had some difficulties, possibly because he was still groggy from the drug in his system, but more likely because he was not accustomed to such endeavors and exercise.

Once on the ground we moved at a more rapid pace. Our guide was constantly looking about and scanning the trees, to which he would direct an occasional whistle or chirp that sounded like one of the local jungle creatures. This signal always received an answer; but only on two occasions did we get a glimpse of the native who supported the search from above. As we progressed, he stopped once to point out one particular I'aban tree. It took a few moments for me to recognize it as the tree where we had spent the night. In the light of day the dark shadow of the narrow opening that led into its interior didn't seem like an opening at all.

Another time he stopped us and sniffed the air, then diverted us on a route around the path we were taking. "Beaguna," he said, and I knew that the word meant *female drodoceal* in the universal Bammaspeak language. It took a few minutes before I saw it lying along the edge of the path. An unwary traveler walking by would probably not have noticed it until right on top of it, which is precisely too late. As we passed by at a safe distance, I caught the strong spicy scent that the guide had picked up on much sooner. I was surprised at the size of this drodoceal. It was much larger than I anticipated – easily large enough to eat a man. I expected it to have a hide like an alligator or crocodile, but it appeared to have smooth skin, not scaled or rough at all.

A little later he stopped and pointed to some small, hairless, simian-like creatures in the trees that seemed to be excited about something. He motioned us off the trail once more and into a thicket of the oil-producing reeds we had used the night before. He gestured to us to crouch down; and as we did so, I saw in the distance six Brotherhood troopers moving through the trees along the trail. They didn't seem too alert to their surroundings, as they were talking and laughing while they passed by.

I heard one of them say, "Major Undoth thinks they'll head back to their ship, but I say they got lost in this jungle and probably got eaten or poisoned by something. The ship isn't a federation design, so I think it's either a drug runner that followed one of our ships back here, looking to score some God's Sweat, or a pirate hoping to steal something. One thing for sure, they aren't going anywhere now... and when we catch them...." At that point they were so far past us that I couldn't hear the rest of the conversation.

They were heading straight toward the drodoceal. I motioned to Kerabac and whispered, "This could be our chance. If the drodoceal attacks them, we may be able to take them out in the confusion." Kerabac nodded and said something to our guide, who nodded in return and crouched down in the reeds. Kerabac, Hotyona and I began to follow after the troopers while trying to remain concealed in the thick reeds that flanked the path.

As we started out, I asked Kerabac, "What did you tell our guide?"

"I told him to wait there and that if we got killed to go home."

I chuckled, "Yeah, I'm sure he will have a great tale to tell either way. Hotyona, I suggest you turn back and stay with our guide. This shouldn't take long."

It was about then that we heard a scream and saw flashes of shots fired. Kerabac and I took off running toward the scene and saw four of the troopers firing away at the creature on the ground, who had a firm hold on one of their brethren in its mouth. Another lay on the trail, motionless and bleeding. The drodoceal thrashed about and swung its large thick tail, catching a third trooper across the legs. Even from our distant location in the reeds we could hear the crack of his bones as both of his legs broke. Finally, one of the troopers got a good beam on the monster's head and managed a kill shot that brought the battle to an end. By this time we had moved to a position nearly on top of them; and before they saw us coming, Kerabac took out one and I took out the second. The third started to bring his gun up to fire, but I kicked it from his hand and dispatched him with a few quick blows. The trooper with the broken legs tried to raise his weapon, but Kerabac had already armed himself with the weapon of the first opponent and fired, killing the trooper before he got the gun into position.

While searching the bodies of the troopers, we discovered that each carried one of the restraint collars like they used on the natives. Kerabac quickly put a collar on each unconscious trooper. We then stripped them of their uniforms and weapons and donned their outfits. By now our guide had risen from the reeds and he and Hotyona stood by watching and grinning. It was only a short distance back to the tree where we had camped the night before; so we carried the prisoners there and deposited them inside. Kerabac made some adjustments on the collars and I saw the unconscious bodies of our prisoners stiffen.

"What did you do to them?" I asked.

"There's a setting that paralyzes the wearer," explained Kerabac. "They'll stay like that until someone turns it off or until the power on the collar runs out, which is normally two full days, if the units are fully charged."

"Very handy," I said. I noted the grin on the face of our guide, as he watched the troopers get a taste of their own brutality. "This should hold them long enough for us to wreak havoc on the camp."

Kerabac and I walked back to the carnage site and collected the last of the weapons that belonged to the troopers. We now had six rifles and six side arms, as well as a few grenades, three restraining collars, six knives and a few backup power packs for the guns – enough to arm Kerabac, Hotyona and me.

It was starting to rain again. Kerabac was about to remove the bodies from the trail, when I said, "Leave the bodies. It won't be long before someone misses these guys and comes looking for them. When they do they'll find these three bodies. On one hand, it will be apparent that they encountered a drodoceal, but it will create a mystery as to what happened to the other three and where the weapons went. In fact, leave the communicators on these three, it will confuse things more. Leave the other communicators from the three back in the tree, as well. I suspect they have some sort of tracking system built in that allows them to locate lost or downed troopers, which means they could also track us if we keep them."

"You're right, Tibby. I forgot about the possibility of trackers."

Just then a voice came over one of the communicators. "Noden, where the hell are you guys? You were supposed to relieve us 15 minutes ago!" There was a pause and then "Noden! I'm going to bust your ass if you don't show up here in a few minutes! So help me, if you guys are using God's Sweat, I will personally shoot you all!"

About that time, the same voice barked over the wrist band communicator that belonged to one of the other troopers. "Locline, where are you? Is Noden with you?" There was a pause, then *"Damn* you guys! Locline, so help me, if you and Noden are together and the bunch of you are high, you're *done*! You hear me? I will personally drag your bodies to the captain's office and dump your sorry asses on the floor in front of him. That's *after* I've beaten the shit out of you! You know he has no reservations about shooting anyone on the base that's using God's Sweat."

When there was still no answer, one last message came across both communicators at once. "All right you asses, we're heading in. If we meet you on the trail, you better have one hell of an excuse as to why you haven't responded to our calls."

"Should we wait for them and take them out?" Kerabac asked.

"No," I said, "I think now is a good opportunity for us to get into the camp. If we hurry, we will be there before these guys find the bodies on the trail and call in a report. In the meantime, the camp will be expecting troopers to come in from the field and we can probably get in with little notice in these uniforms. When these bodies are found, the first conclusion will be that this bunch encountered the drodoceal and that, in trying to free one of their group members, they accidentally shot one of their own; and rather than try to explain what happened, they decided to run off. The responding party will find three dead troopers, two obviously killed by a drodoceal and a third injured by the drodoceal, but shot. Meanwhile, three other troopers will be unaccounted for, along with all the weapons, but their communicators will be left behind with the dead. I think it will create a mystery and a potential story that will divert attention from us. You heard them discussing that we are believed to be dead in the swamp someplace and they don't believe our ship to be a Federation ship, so they're clearly not expecting any Federation reinforcements."

"It's too bad we can't use their communicators to contact the *NEW ORLEANS*," said Hotyona.

"Unfortunately we can't. These are short range field communicators used for combat situations and all of them are encrypted on select frequencies," Kerabac said. "Our best bet is to use the equipment in the *ALI* or to find a transmitter in the Brotherhood compound."

"Of the two options I think our best bet is going to be the compound," I said. "They're expecting us to return to our ship. I seriously doubt they will be expecting us to return to the encampment under any circumstances. If we can set the native prisoners free, the confusion of them escaping will allow us to get to a transmitter.

"I wonder… how many men do you think are on that strange-looking corvette they have parked in the clearing?"

"I would think maybe a half dozen at best, if they're stationed here full time and not preparing for a flight; but if they're just here temporarily and their using the ship's quarters as their accommodations, there could be a hundred or more onboard."

"Damn, I wish there was some way we could find out," I said.

"Maybe there is," said Hotyona. "We have three prisoners. Maybe we can encourage them to talk."

"Encourage them how?" I asked.

"Those slave collars have pain inducing elements included in the settings that deliver intense pain like the worst headache you can imagine. The pain is almost explosive; at least that's what I've heard. Perhaps a little pain therapy will induce them to give us the information we seek."

"I don't know," I said, "even though they're the enemy, I'm not in favor of torture."

"Tibby, it's not like these guys don't have it coming," Kerabac said. "They've been enslaving and torturing the natives for who knows how long."

"I agree, but I still don't like it!" I said. "Well let's get this over with. Those other goons these guys were supposed to replace will arrive at the drodoceal site shortly; and when they do its going to get crazy out here."

Kerabac nodded and quickly went to the prisoners and selected the one who showed the most fear in his eyes. Using a small remote control like device he had taken from one of them earlier, he changed a setting on the collar that allowed the man to relax and speak.

Kerabac pulled the man to a sitting position and asked "How many men are on the large ship in your compound?"

The Brotherhood trooper spat at Kerabac but missed. "I'll never tell you, you scum."

Kerabac pressed a button on the control and the prisoner dropped to the ground howling. I was glad we were inside the I'aban tree and hoped the roots would muffle his cries.

"You realize, of course, that was the lowest pain setting on the collar you're wearing. There are four higher settings here...so, shall we try again? How many men are aboard the ship?"

It was necessary for Kerabac to ask twice more before our prisoner broke down sobbing on the dirt and told us he wasn't sure, but he believed it to be less than ten. The ship had been stationed there for months, waiting for a replacement for the food synthesizer, which was currently not functioning. The delivery was to come on the next Brotherhood transport, which was scheduled to arrive in three days. The ship was to drop off supplies and pick up the drug contraband for delivery to other worlds. In the meantime, all the crew, except for the captain, his first officer and a few other essential personal, had been placed in barracks and were serving as ground troops. He and the others we captured were part of that crew.

Once we had gotten the information, Kerabac reactivated the collar so that it once again kept the prisoner in a ridged state and unable to call for help. Then the three of us hastily headed toward the compound. We were glad for the rain that was falling as we knew it would wash away the tracks at the drodoceal site, making it difficult and unlikely for the troopers to find clues that might lead them to their brethren hidden under the I'aban tree. I doubted that they would even try to look for their comrades; as self-interested as these low-life hoodlums were, I was sure they'd want to get back to the compound and out of the rain as quickly as they could.

Fortunately, we didn't meet any other troopers on the trail; and by the time we reached the compound it was pouring rain and no one was out and about. Even if there had been, it was unlikely that anyone would have looked up at our faces in the downpour to take notice that we didn't belong there. I turned to tell our guide to stay back in the trees, but he had already vanished. I guess he felt that he had done what was asked of him and he had no desire to stick around.

We made our way to the large ship in the compound and found the hatch open. Kerabac took the lead, moving us in a direction he hoped would be the

way to the bridge. We moved quite far into the body of
the ship without seeing anyone. Eventually we arrived at
a lift that Kerabac thought would take us to the bridge.

As we waited for the lift to arrive, a voice behind
us said, "You three, what are you doing here?" We kept
looking forward and made no movements. I could hear
the man walking closer to us.

"I said what are you three doing here? You have
no business here."

By this point I knew he was directly behind me.
I spun quickly; and before he knew what had happened, I
had knocked him out. Just then the lift arrived and the
door opened. A female officer stepped out before she
realized what was going on. Her eyes first caught sight
of the trooper on the floor and then the gun in her face,
as she looked up in shock at Kerabac.

"Don't make any sudden moves or try to trigger
any alarm," he said. "I would hate to have to kill you."

Hotyona and I dragged the body of the
unconscious officer into the lift, after which Kerabac
motioned with his gun for the female officer to follow.
While in the lift, Kerabac kept his gun firmly trained on
her as he demanded information.

"How many personnel are at the bridge?"
Kerabac asked the woman. She was clearly shaken and
had no intentions of becoming a hero.

"Just two," she said, "the captain and the
communications officer."

Just as she finished her statement the lift door
opened to the bridge. Both the captain and the

communications officer were lounging in the observation chairs away from their stations.

"Just stay where you are, gentlemen, and don't try anything stupid," I said.

Kerabac moved across the bridge to a small access panel, which he opened to reveal an arms locker. He withdrew several pairs of restraints and placed them on the hands of the captain and the two officers, as well as those of the unconscious officer we carried in with us from the lift. He then patted them down, finding a weapon only on the unconscious officer.

"How many people are aboard the ship?" I asked.

The captain sat stoned-faced staring at the far wall.

Kerabac lifted his gun and placed it at the female officer's head and asked her, "How many people are on the ship?"

The woman was shaking and sweating as she replied, "Please don't kill me. Nine, maybe ten. I'm not sure if Necox is aboard or if he went to the barracks."

"A corvette this size should have nearly one hundred people on board. Where are the rest?"

"The ship's food synthesizer is down and they have all moved into the barracks temporarily."

"Kerabac, close and seal the hatch," I said, as Hotyona and I kept our weapons trained on the four officers. The one I had knocked out earlier began to regain consciousness and was first confused, then

angered to find himself a captive. Kerabac went to the
console and activated some controls. Soon a change in a
console light indicated that the hatch was closed and
sealed. He touched a few more controls and another
light came on which indicated that a coded lockout was
in place and that only by entering the proper code could
the hatch be opened.

"Okay, we have four here, so there are five,
maybe six more out there in the ship someplace. Our
best bet is to get them to come to us instead of us hunting
them down."

I turned to the woman and said, "What position
do you have on this ship?"

"I'm acting first officer; the first officer has gone
to Flerarox on a temporary assignment while we wait for
a new food synthesizer."

"Shut up, you stupid doesee," the captain spat
bitterly. "You're giving them way too much
information."

"I don't care," the woman sobbed. "I never
wanted to be part of this drug business and only joined
the Brotherhood because of Harral. Then he dumped me
and I was stuck here. I'm not going to die for this stupid
cause."

"Is there a conference room nearby?" I asked.

"Yes," she answered, "right next to the bridge.
It's used for staff meetings."

"Good. Now I want you to go to the
communication console and open a link that will
broadcast throughout the ship. You're going to say

exactly what I tell you. You will order everyone to report to that conference room immediately for an important situation update. You will then repeat the message and disconnect." I then turned to Kerabac and Hotyona. Before transmitting we need to place restraint collars on all these officers. We can't risk one of them trying to be a hero and shouting out while the microphone is open."

We still had three restraint collars with us. Once the collars were in place and activated, Kerabac set them to paralysis mode. He then led the female officer to the console at gunpoint so she could make the announcement.

"What's your name, if you don't mind telling me?" I asked.

"Felenna," she said. "What's your name?

"Tibby."

"TIBBY! Oh my god, you're the guy that brought the solbidyum and the *TRITYTE* back and recaptured the *DUSTEN* at Megelleon. Your ship blew up our base on Megelleon. This isn't possible! You're supposed to be dead – our agents on Plosaxen said they killed you!"

"Yeah, yet here I am," I said with a grin on my face.

Felenna was visibly shaken and confused. Her hand was trembling as she reached to activate the controls required to make the broadcast.

"Just take a deep breath and relax," I said. "We have no desire to kill anyone, unless we have to. Now just make the announcement exactly as I told you."

Felenna toggled the controls to broadcast mode and said, "All personnel, the Captain orders all persons to report to the staff conference room immediately for an important situation update. All personnel report to the staff conference room *immediately* for an important situation update."

She then closed the link and asked. "What are you going to do with them?"

"That depends a lot on their reactions. If they surrender without a fight, we'll simply lock you all in a hold until after the conflict is over; but if there's opposition, it's difficult to say what will happen. Is there a camera in the conference room?"

"Yes," she answered and indicated where to activate it on the control panel.

"Can we turn it on without them seeing us in here?"

"Yes."

"Good. Hotyona will you see if you can do that? Not that I don't trust you, Felenna, but I'm not alive because I am overly trusting."

Felenna stepped aside and Hotyona activated the controls on the console. The view on the vid screen displayed an empty conference room.

"I want to wait until everyone is in the room and seated before we enter," I said. "Hopefully none of them are armed so we can make this relatively easy. I'd just as soon get it done without anyone getting injured."

As I spoke the first two people arrived, a young woman and a man. Both appeared to be officers and neither were armed, at least not obviously so. They each took a seat at the large conference table and began to talk just as a third person arrived. From his uniform it was obvious that he was an engineer stationed onboard to maintain the ship's equipment. He was followed by a trooper and another officer.

After waiting a few minutes Kerabac and I moved to the conference room door, while leaving Hotyona to guard the others on the bridge. When we opened the door to the conference room, everyone inside just stared silently at us for a moment, not immediately realizing that we weren't Brotherhood members.

"Who are you? Where's the captain?" the trooper finally asked, reaching for his side arm.

"I suggest you not go for your gun, trooper," I said. "Remove it slowly with two fingers and slide it across the table to me."

The trooper slowly withdrew his gun and placed it on the table; but instead of sliding it to me like he was told, he suddenly grabbed for it and tried to aim and fire. Kerabac and I fired at the same time and he dropped to the table dead.

"I'm sorry he did that," I said. "We truly don't wish to kill any of you, if we can help it. Now, if the rest of you are willing to cooperate, perhaps you'll live to tell stories about this one day."

It took us about 15 minutes to move them all into a small empty cargo hold. One by one, we made them strip down and dress in simple jumpsuits. Once locked away inside, we left Hotyona to guard the hold from outside the door.

In all it had been less than 50 minutes since we entered the ship. If the dead men had since been discovered on the trail, it hadn't been reported to the base yet. If they had been was more likely that no one had bothered to venture out into the rain to search for what they probably believed were deserters.

"How long do you think this rain will last?" I asked Kerabac.

He checked some instruments on the control console and said, "By the looks of the weather radar, I'd say a few hours. This is a pretty large storm."

"Listen, I'm going out there. This is our opportunity to free the slaves. If my latest dream about Thumumba is accurate, they're in that large building behind this ship. If I can disable the guards and let the natives out through the back, it'll create a large diversion. We can use this ship to disable the other Brotherhood ships here at the base; and once the natives are clear of the area, we'll destroy the lab. By the way, this is probably a good time to contact the *NEW ORLEANS*. It should be in orbit by now."

Kerabac had already activated the communication system and set it to a coded frequency that the *NEW ORLEANS* would expect for our transmission. When he opened a communication link, Stonbersa's image appeared on the screen. "Tibby, it looks like you've joined the Brotherhood."

"Not exactly," I said. "Not everything is at it appears. Things are a mess down here. We ran into a base where the rebels are manufacturing God's Sweat, the illegal drug that's been plaguing dozens of planets in the galaxy. The Brotherhood has been forcing the natives into slavery to harvest and process the plants used in its concoction. Right now we're in their base camp, or at least one of their bases. I suspect there are many more to be found elsewhere on the planet.

"We're about to steal one of their ships and create total havoc at this site. For the moment, I would appreciate if you could keep the *NEW ORLEANS* cloaked and shielded. Have Marranalis get two squads geared up. The *ALI* is at a hidden location in the jungle; I'm going to have Kerabac give you the coordinates. The *ALI* is currently surrounded by Brotherhood troopers that are hoping to capture us when we return to the ship; but that number may soon be reduced, once the fireworks begin here. I want Marranalis and his men to retrieve the *ALI* and fly her back to the *NEW ORLEANS*. Marranalis is the only one who can access the *ALI*, as we sealed the hatch. His prints are still registered with the ship, so he'll be able to open her. Once we've done what damage we can here, we'll join you in orbit. Have the fleet of Mirage Fighters ready to go; we may have a real battle on our hands in a short while.

"What's the status of A'Lappe and Cantolla's efforts with the instant communicator?"

"You won't believe it, Tibby, but their contraption works. It still needs some refining but the damn thing works."

"That's great news. Listen, I need to speak quickly. I need you to get a message back to Admiral

Regeny apprising him of the situation here. Tell him that the Brotherhood has been financing their expansion at least in part with the drugs they're manufacturing on this planet. The ship we're in at the moment is like nothing we've ever seen. It's armed like a star ship but it's the size of a corvette. Right now I wish it had an RMFF on it, but I would settle for a cloaking device. See if A'Lappe can get a cloaking device built that we can put in this ship as soon as we get back to the *NEW ORLEANS*. I think we're going to need it.

"One more thing – how is Kala doing in stasis? Is everything alright?"

"Yes, Kala is fine and the stasis system is functioning well. How did your hunt go for the ruguian eggs?"

"We were able to collect some, but not enough yet to make the anti-toxin. We ran into the Brotherhood before we could finish.

"I need to cut this transmission short. I have some natives to free before it stops raining. Kerabac can give you more details."

I turned to Kerabac and said. "I'm headed out. If I'm not back in 40 minutes, I want you to take this ship and the prisoners and head for the *NEW ORLEANS*. On your way out, use the torpedoes to take out the processing plant and as many other buildings and ships on the ground as you can. Then move out fast, in case someone on the ground gets a message to other bases to pursue you."

"Understood," said Kerabac. "Good luck."

I descended to the hatch level and exited the ship using the code Kerabac entered to secure the door. It was still pouring rain and no one was in sight. I resealed the door and quickly headed to the large building Thumumba had shown me in the dream. I found a door and walked in quietly, only to find myself face to face with a trooper standing guard just inside the entrance. Since I was in a Brotherhood uniform he didn't realize that I wasn't one of them.

"They must have sent you here on something really important for you to come in this storm," he said. "I'll be glad when they get the underground connecting tunnels completed."

"Yeah," I said… and then I hit him square in the face, knocking him out cold. On the wall behind him were storage racks filled with slave control collars. I placed one on his neck and activated the full restraint setting. His body immediately went rigid.

I opened a nearby door to a large area of holding cells loaded with natives from wall to wall. A long corridor separated the cells, at the end of which I could see a small room behind an open door, where four guards sat around a makeshift table, playing some sort of gambling game. I went back into the room I had just left and gathered about a half dozen collars and a controller unit and then walked confidently down the corridor as if I belonged there. At first the sight of the restraining collars the natives flinched; then they appeared somewhat confused when I passed right by them and headed straight for the end of the corridor.

As I walked boldly into the room, one glanced up briefly from his cards and said, "I take it that it stopped raining and you need some of the ants to do some work?" It was obvious from his tone that the "ants" were the natives.

"Not exactly," I replied, as I lifted my gun and aimed it at them. I tossed the collars on the table. "Put one of these on... all of you... NOW!"

One guard's eyes shift toward the wall beside me. I glanced quickly to see all their arms propped up against the wall. The guard moved quickly in that direction, but I shot him before he moved very far, almost instantly recovering my aim on the other three.

"Anyone one else want to join him or are you going to follow orders?" Slowly, they each put on a collar, after which I used the remote device to activate the restraint setting, leaving them rigid on the floor. I took their weapons, just in case they were somehow able to free themselves before I finished my task.

I looked about the room and noted toggle switches on a wall panel that appeared to be used for opening and closing the cell doors. I opened all the doors and then went back to the cell corridor. None of the natives tried to flee; instead they just stood there looking scared and confused.

Using their universal language I said to them, "My name Tibby, friend of Jnanara. I speak for Thumumba. Thumumba send me to free children of Thumumba. Go quickly into jungle. Return to your people."

They began murmuring and repeating "Thumumba" among themselves as they slowly began to emerge from their cells and move tentatively past me. I told them to move quickly and gestured toward the large roll-up door at the back of the building that faced the trees, away from the rest of the compound. Unless there were troopers standing back there in the rain, which was unlikely, the natives would be able to make a clear break for the jungle. I found the control to open the door and then, holding my gun at the ready, I pressed the button. I held up my hand to quietly hold the natives back, until I was able to glance past the slow-moving door into the rain.

Seeing no one in the area, I said to the natives, "Go! Go quickly! Thumumba wish you free."

I didn't have to repeat the command. They all moved forward and out the door with remarkable speed and silence, disappearing quickly into the shadows under the jungle canopy.

I noted several cans of fuel sitting near a piece of equipment by the large roll-up door, which I used to soak the building walls, before dragging the bodies of the guards outside to the jungle's edge where the rain and trees would protect them from the flames. It was not an easy task, as they were quite large men. I searched the pockets of my combat vest that I had taken earlier from the trooper as I made my way back inside. As I anticipated, I found a lighter device like the one Kerabac had used to light the oil reeds. I tossed the lit device into the fuel that pooled on the floor and instantly the building was ablaze. I then quickly ran to the corvette and punched in my code at the hatch – and none too soon, as alarms started to sound within a minute or so and men came running out of buildings toward the burning prison just as the hatch opened. Once inside, I quickly resealed the hatch again and took the lift to the control room.

"Get us out of here," I said to Kerabac, "and blow up as many buildings and ships on the way out as you can."

"Right!" said Kerabac. "How about you do the shooting and I'll fly us out. We're going to be taking the netting over the compound with us, I fear."

I laughed as I dropped into the chair at the weapons console. "I don't think they'll be needing their camouflage any longer."

When I originally found the *TRITYTE* back on Earth, I spent weeks aboard with nothing else to do while the ship navigated through the galaxy on autopilot; so I let the ship teach me how to use most of the ship's flight and navigation controls. Though the ship didn't actually allow me to take control, due to its prime directive, I was permitted to simulated flight and navigation as much as I wanted. I was, however, restricted from learning any of the weapons systems during my passage through space; so I made sure to have Marranalis and Reidecor teach me some fundamentals of locking aim and firing the basic armaments during our long clandestine trip to Megelleon from the *DUSTEN*. It seemed that the technology for these control systems was pretty much consistent in all ships designed in the area of the Federation territories; so by learning one, I could pretty much understand and successfully execute the same commands in any ship. The only problem was – the bigger the ship, the more screens and controls there were to manipulate. I was a bit slower to get oriented than I would have liked, but eventually I found the appropriate controls.

Kerabac raised the ship about 50 meters above the compound, which allowed me to take aim with a clear view of everything on the ground. The first thing I took out was the drug laboratory. Then I started taking out the smaller patrol ships parked about the compound. In just a few minutes the entire compound was ablaze.

"Okay, get us out of here, Kerabac. Take us to the *NEW ORLEANS.*"

"Your wish is my command," Kerabac said with a grin. "Just before you got back from the prison building I received a message from Marranalis that he and his men were on their way to retrieve the *ALI*. They should be arriving planetside about now."

"Great!" I said. "Let's hope that the Brotherhood called all their troops in to help here at the camp and that there are relatively few, if any, left to guard the *ALI.*"

"If they use Federation procedure, which is how most of them have been trained, they'll leave only a half dozen or so to watch the *ALI* and the rest will be called back with orders to stay on the lookout for us, in case we are fleeing back to the ship. But by now I suspect they know we're the ones in control of this ship, so they may just pull them all back from the *ALI*. Considering that we just destroyed all the ships at this compound, they're grounded until they can get reinforcements from another base. I just wonder how many bases and processing plants they have here."

"I'm getting readings on the weapons screen of dozens of ships taking off from various locations on the surface. It looks like we have our hands full. Send word to Stonbersa that we're on our way and to get the Mirage Fighters out of the hangar and ready for a fight. Once the enemy is in range, have them cloak and wait until the rebels begin to attack the *NEW ORLEANS* before they open fire.

"This ship should fit in the hangar of the *NEW ORLEANS*. I want it docked safely inside until we can at least get a cloaking device on it. We should arrive long before the enemy gets mobilized sufficiently to figure out where we're headed.

"Oh, be sure to let Stonbersa know what we look like, so he doesn't blow us out of the sky as we arrive."

Kerabac grinned, "I agree with you there, Tibby, and I promise you I will make every attempt to make sure the *NEW ORLEANS* knows who we are."

The approach and berthing with the *NEW ORLEANS* went smoothly. I could see the Mirage Fighters holding a broad formation some distance from the ship as we approached. We were no sooner aboard and opening the hatch than we were greeted by a dozen of my security forces who were ready to retrieve the prisoners.

As they escorted the captives from the ship, I overheard their captain muttering to Felenna, "You're *dead*. I promise you, you filthy doesee, they won't be watching us all the time; and the first chance we get, you *will* die!"

I could see that Felenna was shaken by his comment as tears of despair filled her eyes. I stopped the guards escorting her and said, "I don't want this prisoner going with the rest. Find her a small, modestly furnished cabin and post a guard at her door. She is not to have contact with any of the other prisoners. Is that clear?"

"Yes, sir," they answered together.

I told Kerabac to accompany me and we headed to the bridge to see Captain Stonbersa. When we arrived, Kerabac went directly to the captain to brief him as to the nature of the unique ship we took from the compound and that more of them would likely be among the pursuing ships.

In the meantime, I noted A'Lappe sitting in the chair normally occupied by the communication officer; rather, I was able to see his short legs dangling inches above the floor until he spun the chair around to greet me.

"Tibby, so good to see you back," he said. "Were you able to acquire the ruguian eggs?"

"I fear we only managed to find a portion of what is needed before we ran into the Brotherhood. We're going to need to clear them off the planet before we can continue our search."

"I noticed that you brought back a prize ship; I was monitoring it as you approached. She's a beauty. Markazian, from the looks of her."

"Markazian? Is that a planet or a style?" I asked.

A'Lappe chuckled, "Markazia is a planet – a nonaligned world noted for making some of the best armed ships in the galaxy. They'll sell to anyone for any purpose. They really don't care how the ships are used, as long as the buyer pays for it. Do you mind if I look it over?"

"Not at all. In fact, I'm hoping you can work you magic and get a cloaking system installed on it in short order. We're going to have a battle on our hands soon and we'll need every ship we can get. We may not have the luxury of giving her an RMFF shield before the action starts, but we can give her cloaking ability and that's almost as good."

"I'll get right on it, Tibby. I think I have a cloaking unit already built that should be able to cloak a ship of this size. What's the ships name?"

"Damn if I know. We were so busy I never looked to see. Kerabac, do you know?"

"It's the *RUNANA*," answered Kerabac as he scanned the captain's console and discussed a deployment plan for the Mirage Fighters.

"Tibby, I'm glad you made it back okay," said Captain Stonbersa. We're tracking fifty ships coming in pursuit from the surface. They should be here in about ten minutes. I've ordered the Mirage Fighters to cloak and wait for orders."

"Good," I said. "This should be interesting, keep the RMFF up but leave us uncloaked. I want to crush the morale of the Brotherhood. If we can consistently instill a sense of despair and impotence in these conflicts, it will soften their confidence and create dissention within their ranks. The more battles they lose, the more conflict it will create within.

"By the way, were you able to get the message off to Admiral Regeny about the situation here on Alle Bamma?"

"Yes," said Stonbersa, "but he was already on his way here. He and his forces are about two weeks away. The Brotherhood fell into the trap at Plosaxen when they tried to overtake the fake solbidyum reactor site. After that, the admiral immediately loaded every Mirage Fighter onto the *URANGA* that was completed at that point and issued orders for the ship to head this way at top speed. He's aboard the ship. He's itching to be in the fight… and I also think he wants to be redeemed in your sight, Tibby."

"I'm glad the trap on Plosaxen worked," I said. I didn't respond to his last comment.

"Oh, it worked alright. It worked much better than anyone expected. The Brotherhood came with three corvettes and close to a hundred patrol ships. They thought they were prepared for any scenario to unfold, including a trap; but they weren't expecting cloaked and shielded star ships in addition to the patrol ships… and a dozen Mirage Fighters – also cloaked. When the trap was sprung and they saw what they were up against, they bolted. The Federation patrol ships and the Mirage Fighters took off after them and destroyed the better part of their armada. Two of the corvettes escaped and a hand full of patrol ships; and according to Admiral Regeny, they're heading this direction."

"By any chance did you happen to note the departure points of the ships here from the surface so we can deploy ships to their bases?" I asked.

"It's all recorded in the bridge records. We can easily backtrack to retrieve their points of origin," said Stonbersa.

"Good. As soon as we finish reducing their fleet to rubble we need to go back to the surface and free the natives that they're holding as slaves before we can blow up their bases."

We watched calmly as the first of the Brotherhood ships arrived and fired at the *NEW ORLEANS*. Due to the RMFF, their shots were absorbed as the familiar bursts of energy. We watched the lightning patterns play on the surface of the field of the ship, waiting for the rebels to realize the futility of their assault. Meanwhile, I hoped that the cloaked Mirage Fighters were far enough from the line of fire to keep from getting hit by an errant shot.

More of the Brotherhood's ships arrived and joined the assault. Though we were safe, it was becoming difficult to see beyond the shield that was constantly distributing the energy flashes from the barrage of gunfire.

"Well, Captain, would you like to give them the option to surrender before we swat them like a bunch of flies?"

Stonbersa grinned and moved over in view of the bridge's vid screen, then nodded to Kerabac, who had resumed his normal station on the bridge. Kerabac opened a universal communication channel and the captain spoke.

"This is Captain Stonbersa of the space yacht *NEW ORLEANS*. Do you wish to surrender now or would you prefer we destroy your fleet?"

A moment later a rather rugged individual wearing a Brotherhood captain's uniform appeared on the screen. "This is Captain Ruraldo of the corvette *MIZBAGONA*. You must be high on God's Sweat if you think your space yacht is any match for our ships. However, if *you* wish to surrender, we'll be most happy to take that fancy play toy away from you."

Laughter could be heard in the background on the *MIZBAGONA*.

Stonbersa said, "I see. Would you like us to pick you off one at a time or a bunch of you at once?"

On the screen we could see Ruraldo laugh arrogantly. "Why don't you pick us off in a bunch? I'll enjoy the laugh."

Captain Stonbersa glanced at me and smiled and then he said to Kerabac, "Tell the Mirage Fighters to open fire and knock out their bigger ships."

"Yes, Sir," replied Kerabac.

A few seconds later the skies over Alle Bamma were lit up with an inferno of explosions in every direction. The shots from the *NEW ORLEANS* totally vaporized every ship under their fire. The collective rapid fire coming from the cloaked Mirage Fighters quickly decommissioned Brotherhood ships across the broad expanse between the *NEW ORLEANS* and the planet; and in less than a minute there were thirty ships either gone or out of commission, prompting the rest to flee back to the surface.

One by one, the Mirage Fighters decloaked and pursued the retreating enemy ships, which didn't get very far. Rising from the planet were three patrol ships and another Mirage Fighter – the *ALI.* Guns blazed as they intercepted the scattering rebels and more Brotherhood ships ceased to operate. Captain Ruraldo and his crew, however, were still actively transmitting; and the look on Ruraldo's face was priceless.

"Would you like to reconsider your decision?" Stonbersa asked calmly; but before he could finish,

Ruraldo terminated the vid transmission and turned his ship to flee like the others.

"I wonder how many more ship they have on the surface," I said. A'Lappe had not left the bridge yet so I instructed him to send word to Admiral Regeny to apprise him of the situation. As he transmitted by way of the instant communicator, the standard communication system activated and Marranalis appeared on the screen.

"We have more ships heading our way – and real fast," he said. "Do you want us to re-cloak or to take them out?"

Stonbersa looked at me. I ordered, "Take them out! We don't have time to play games; they've made their choices."

We watched silently. A few seconds later the sky danced with flashes of light. Explosions filled the vid screen, as our returning ships wreaked yet more havoc on the Brotherhood. Even so, three ships managed to elude the Mirage Fighters and return to the planet where they disappeared into the jungle. Before they vanished, Stonbersa broadcasted one last message to them.

"You still have a chance to surrender before the Federation ships get here. If you think this little 'fancy play toy' damaged to your ships, wait until the Federation get here with their big play toys – and they're a lot closer than you think."

"May your ass roast in the sun!" Ruraldo spat. "This fight isn't over yet!" and he terminated transmissions.

"I suspect that morale in the rebel camp is going to be very low tonight," I said.

"Tibby," said A'Lappe, "the admiral says to tell you that his fleet is still in pursuit of the Brotherhood ships that escaped after the battle at Plosaxen. He wants to know if you want him to launch the Mirage Fighters to catch up with them and take them out there before they get to Alle Bamma."

"Tell him that I think it may be more enjoyable for him to nail them here, but it's up to him. In the meantime, I'm taking some of my security forces to the surface to free as many native slaves as I can and blow up a few of the Brotherhood drug labs while we're at it."

"The admiral says he understands and he appreciates what you're doing."

After A'Lappe sent the message he announced he was going to look over the *RUNANA* and turned over his seat at the communication console to a cute blond female officer that I had never noticed before. It wasn't surprising that I didn't recognize her, as my ship was very large and staffed with so many people that I had so far become acquainted with only a few of the key personnel. Most had been hired by Kala, Stonbersa, Piesew or Marranalis, all of whom I trusted implicitly. As A'Lappe left, she positioned the headband on her head that facilitated the thought amplification required for successful and instantaneous communication across vast distances.

"Excuse me," I said, "is that thing difficult to operate?"

"No, not really," she said with a smile.

"How does it work? How do you direct your message where you want it to go? I mean, if all you know is the name of the ship and not the operator at the other end, what happens to the message?"

She laughed at my confused question. "I asked A'Lappe that same question and his answer was, *Don't try to figure it out. You will never be able to understand it.* He said even he and Cantolla don't fully understand it. Basically, all you have to do is to think about the destination of the message. For instance, I think of the particular ship where the message is to go; and somehow it hooks up to whoever is wearing the headband on the other end. A'Lappe thinks it has something to do with what he refers to as *universal consciousness.* He says everything is made of the same energy; therefore, all things are connected. Cantolla thinks that his idea is rubbish, but she is at a loss to explain exactly how it works herself. All that we know for sure it that it works."

"Ah, I see. Thanks. By the way, I'm Tibby. And you are…?"

She giggled and said, "Yes, I know you're Tibby, everyone knows who you are. I'm Verona. I began working for you just shortly before the *NEW ORLEANS* left Megelleon."

"Well, nice to meet you, Verona, and thanks for the explanation… I think."

I left the bridge and went directly to see Kala again. Even though she was still in stasis, I needed to see her and I went to the room where she lay in the chamber. When I last saw her, the room was stark and barren, except for the stasis capsule. I had instructed

Piesew to bring plants and some of her personal possessions into the room with her. Even though I expected to see a change, I was surprised to find it tastefully decorated with flowering plants from the many atrium areas of the ship and several comfortable chairs positioned around the room, two of which were occupied by crew members. As I approached the stasis chamber, I saw Piesew gazing at several picture cubes of Kala's family and friends. The pictures were arranged on shelves that stood between vid frames mounted on the walls to display pictures of her favorite places. As I entered, the two crew members rose and left quietly, but Piesew remained.

"First Citizen Tibby, I am glad to see you have returned. I trust you were successful in acquiring the materials necessary for Kalana's recovery."

"I'm afraid not, Piesew; but we will have them soon, I hope. I just needed to check in on Kala and see her before I continue the effort," I said as I walked over and looked into Kala's stasis capsule.

She looked exactly as I had last seen her. I felt like she would open her eyes and smile at me at any moment and everything would be as it was before. I sighed as I realized that was not about to happen; and tears filled my eyes. I lifted my head and looked about the room. Arranged throughout the space around Kala's chamber were several tables, on which I saw what appeared to be thousands of coins. I walked over to one of the tables and picked up one of the coins to examine it. On one side was a circle that surrounded an oval with a smaller circle inside it, within which a rust-colored stain was visible. On the opposite side of the coin was a circle inscribed in a triangle. I looked at the other coins to find that they were all inscribed with the same symbols and that each had the same rust-colored stain in the small circular marking.

"What are these?" I asked Piesew.

"They are life tokens."

"Life tokens? I've never heard of them before. Can you explain them to me?"

"Life tokens are used commonly throughout the Federation as an expression of concern and wishes of wellbeing for a person in a critical health situation. It is believed that the practice of offering these tokens originated on the first capital planet before it was destroyed in the war that was waged when the solbidyum disappeared."

"What is the stain?"

"What you see on each of those tokens a drop of blood from the well-wisher," said Piesew. "Originally it is believed that small pebbles were used instead of the tokens. Back then a person would prick their finger and place a drop of blood on a pebble before leaving it with the person in critical condition. It symbolized the concern of the well-wisher and also acted as a pledge on the part of the well-wisher to do whatever they could – even at the cost of their own life – to see to the recovery of the individual. The brown stain you see on each token here is a drop of blood from each crew member on the *NEW ORLEANS* who has pledged their life to see to First Citizen Kalana's recovery."

As Piesew explained what I it was I had in my hand, I broke out in tears and fell to the floor on my knees.

As I sobbed, Piesew approached me and placed a hand on my shoulder. "She will be alright, Tibby. She is safe in stasis; and I know you will find the ruguian eggs for the cure."

It took me a few moments to recover my composure; and when I got back to my feet I asked Piesew to tell me more about the symbols on the token, as I looked through the capsule at Kala.

"The oval inscribed with the circle is the recognized symbol of life throughout most of the Federation. It was not always so; but slowly it became accepted universally by most worlds as such. The outer circle represents the universe. The triangle on the back of the token represents the three aspects of a person's life – body, soul, and spirit."

I was shocked when I heard him say this, as many religions on Earth believed in the same concept of a triune nature of life in a person. *Body* and *soul* I thought I understood; but as to the validity of the *spirit* part, I was unsure. In any case, I was at this point hoping and praying that they existed and all were well in Kala.

"How many tokens are in here?" I asked Piesew, as I scanned the collection of tables covered with the symbolic coins.

"How many members do you have in your crew?" came Piesew's answer in the form of a question. "There is one token there for every member of the crew."

I choked up again for a few moments; and when I regained my composure I said. "Thank you, Piesew, and please find a way to express my thanks to all the crew for their efforts and concerns."

"I'll leave you alone with First Citizen Kalana for a few moments. I'll be waiting outside when you leave," He said as he departed the room. It was not until after he left that I realized when he was trying to comfort me, Piesew had dropped all honorific formality and called me Tibby; and I knew him at that moment for the true friend that he always was and continues to be.

I stayed a few moments longer with Kala; but I soon realized that if I was going to get her the cure, I needed to rid Alle Bamma of the Brotherhood and I needed to do it quickly; so I said goodbye to Kala and left. I needed a shower and a shave, as it had been several days since I had either.

When I came out of the shower, I noticed Piesew had returned to my suite. He paused in the doorway, holding the soiled Brotherhood uniform in front of him and away from his own clothing.

"Excuse me, Honored First Citizen, what do you wish me to do with these articles? Do you wish them cleaned and preserved or shall I dispose of them?"

"Hm, good question, Piesew. For now I think it might be best for us to clean and preserve them. They might come in handy for future covert operations."

"As you wish, sir. Would you care for a meal, sir? You look as though you have not eaten in the past few days."

Up until then I must confess that I had not thought about food; but now that Piesew mentioned it, I found I was quite hungry. "Yes, Piesew, I would like to eat, but I think it would be best to make arrangements to dine with Captain Stonbersa, Marranalis, Kerabac and

A'Lappe. Could you see if they are all available to meet in about an hour here in my personal dining room?"

"I will see to it, sir. Will there be anything else?"

"Yes, Piesew, I want to thank you for all you are doing for Kala. Have the medics said anything at all about her? Are there any changes since she was placed in stasis?"

"Nothing has changed, sir, and as long as she is in stasis, nothing will change. Will that be all?"

"Yes, Piesew. Thank you."

My wrist com sounded the reminder for dinner and I once again gathered my thoughts around planning the next phase of operations on Alle Bamma. I realized that I would need to find Jnanara as soon as possible and find out if she knew where and how many other Brotherhood bases were spread across the planet. We knew where some were by tracking their liftoff points during the day's earlier conflict; but there could be others as well.

As I emerged from my room, I heard the low voices of Piesew and two other attendants in the dining area where they finished preparing for the arrival of my team. One wall had been moved to expand the space and the table was enlarged, all done with the touch of a button on a control panel. Piesew's staff finished arranging the linen and place settings and took their stations at the perimeter of the dining room. Shortly after, Piesew opened the door to Captain Stonbersa, Marranalis, Kerabac and A'Lappe, who arrived together. I greeted each guest individually and motioned for them to be seated.

"Things are going to be very busy around here the next few days. I don't have time to meet with you separately for updates and orders; so I thought we might accomplish it while we dined. I hope you don't mind."

"Not at all, Tibby. You are the busiest man I've ever seen; and to be able to spend just a few minutes with you is always a delight," said the captain.

"Ha," said Kerabac. "You haven't had the pleasure of spending a night with him inside a hollow I'aban tree after hunting for ruguian eggs in a storming rain."

"No I haven't, Kerabac, and I think I will pass on that, even as adventurous at it sounds."

Everyone laughed and Piesew and his staff began serving the food.

"We were unable to get more than a few ruguian eggs before we ran into the Brotherhood. We need to collect more; but before we can, we need to make sure there are no rebel forces running about or operating on the planet. We also need to free the natives from the slavery they are suffering at the hands of the Brotherhood."

"Kerabac told me about that after you left the bridge," said Captain Stonbersa. "They sound primitive and barbaric.

"The natives are certainly primitive, but it is the Brotherhood that is barbaric. I suspect we don't know the depth of horrors that has gone on there; but we don't need to in order to put an end to it. Here's what I think we need to do – and if any of you see problems or have any better ideas or suggestions, please don't hesitate to bring them up. As I see it, we need to deploy several of our security tactical units to the surface – fully armed and equipped with personal cloaking devices – to free the natives and take out the Brotherhood bases. We need to either destroy or capture as many of their ships on the ground as we can. I'm hoping they have more ships like the *RUNANA* that we can perhaps capture rather than destroy. Once things here are cleaned up and the Brotherhood is ousted, there needs to be a force left behind as a deterrent to the Brotherhood or any other unscrupulous group that might try to return with the intent of restoring drug operations, enslaving the natives again, or profiting from their frailties in any way. The Federation won't protect them from such threats, because it's not a Federation planet or even a candidate for membership; but I can do it – and I would like *nothing better* than to do it using ships that once belonged to the Brotherhood."

"I think we have a good chance of taking the ships at one base," Marranalis interjected, "but I doubt we will be able to pull it off again at a second base. I don't think the Brotherhood yet realizes that we have the ability to cloak our troopers; so we can enter the first compound and seize their ships with relative ease. But if the word gets out that we can cloak individuals, we won't have this advantage again. Communication here between bases is instantaneous, unlike their communications between solar systems. It only takes one broadcast advising other operations that we have personal cloaking capabilities for every base on this planet to be alerted to that fact. At that moment every rebel ship will be sealed."

"I agree, Marranalis, so we need put forth our best efforts to find the base that holds the most and best ships. The canopy of the I'aban trees creates a natural screen against electronic surveillance and the Brotherhood is using camouflaged netting enmeshed with electronic filters that also block electronic surveillance penetration. I wonder if our computer can filter and enhance visual images that will help us pinpoint their bases. On Earth our military used a similar technique for detecting camouflage and it worked quite well. I think if we use color and light filtering and maybe thermal imaging we'll be able to spot the camouflage netting from space. This won't help us with any units hidden under the I'aban trees; but I'm hoping the natives we free will be willing to assist us in identifying the rest of the bases.

"A'Lappe, I know you have your hands full while you're outfitting the *RUNANA with* a cloaking device, but as soon as you get to a point where others can finish the installation, I'd like you to turn your attention to coming up with a system for detecting the camouflaged bases. In the meantime, I don't want any ships leaving the surface. Maintain patrol ships around the entire planet to make sure none of them try to slip away at a blind spot. Until we can get down there and clean things up, anything leaving the surface that isn't ours is to be shot down. Captain Stonbersa, I would like you to take charge of these matters and oversee the entire operation."

"Why aren't you going to be in charge, Tibby? These are your plans and you understand the situation on the planet better than I do."

"I need to be on the surface," I said. "The natives aren't going to speak to anyone else; they'll only hide. But I've established a relationship with them. They will speak to me and listen to me, so there's no way around it – it has to be me down there. You have the experience and the ability to oversee and run things from here. Hopefully I will be able to stay in touch and keep you informed as to what is unfolding on the ground."

"If you're going back down there, I'm coming with you," said Marranalis.

"You're right about that, Marranalis. We're, going to see how well you trained your men for ground action this time. We already know how well they do in the air. To make it more interesting, your team will have to meet with Hotyona for an introduction to ruguian egg hunting before we go. While we're down there I want anyone coming across the eggs to know precisely how to collect and save them. I want Kala out of stasis as quickly as possible."

During the rest of the meal I was briefed on the events that occurred at Plosaxen after we left for Alle Bamma, when the Brotherhood walked into the trap at the fake solbidyum reactor site near Banur. The Brotherhood expected the site to be heavily guarded and came with a small armada of ships. Some were Federation ships seized by mutinous Brotherhood crews and some were ships that the Brotherhood had acquired through other nefarious means. The presence of a Federation star ship at the location didn't surprise them at all; they had expected it. What they didn't expect was a second cloaked star ship, three cloaked frigates, scores of cloaked patrol ships and, lastly, a dozen Mirage Fighters – also able to cloak and move with more speed and maneuverability than anything they had ever seen.

The Brotherhood attacked without warning, but to no avail. The RMFF shield on the *URANGA* prevented any of their firepower from doing even the slightest harm. Even so, the Brotherhood managed to get troopers on the ground and into the fake facility only to discover empty buildings. Admiral Regeny offered the Brotherhood a chance to surrender; but with typical Brotherhood arrogance they refused. Even after the star ship *CACHATORA* decloaked behind them, they refused to surrender and the fight was on. Cloaked patrol ships opened fire on the ships that tried to escape, while the *URANGA* and the *CACHATORA* literally demolished all traces of the larger Brotherhood ships. Within just a few minutes two-thirds of the Brotherhood ships were destroyed while the other third fled.

News of the event quickly spread across Plosaxen and was broadcast to other star systems in the Federation. It was a glorious day for the Federation when newscasters announced not only the victory over the Brotherhood, but also the installation and commissioning of the solbidyum reactor on Plosaxen. At the same time it was announced that five other planets had received their solbidyum and that their reactors were also up and running. It was not released to the media that these deliveries were made by GW message pods; the illusion that the solbidyum and reactors were delivered by conventional means was maintained.

After the meeting was over, I instructed Marranalis to bring our prisoners to the conference room. They arrived with two specially trained security personnel guarding each prisoner. The last to arrive was Felenna. She had used the wardrobe in her room to change out of her Brotherhood uniform and into a modest, yet attractive civilian-style dress common on most of the Federation planets. She also had availed herself of the bath facilities and restyled her hair. As she entered the conference room, her Captain said, "Well if it isn't our little traitor. Didn't take you long to get out of your uniform, did it?" She didn't respond or look at him as she took a seat on the opposite side of the table from the other prisoners.

"I'm sure by now you're all aware that you're on the *NEW ORLEANS* and that I am Tibby. You are also aware that this ship is the one responsible for liberating the *DUSTEN* at Megelleon and for destroying the Brotherhood base located there. For your information, this ship has also liberated the *TECCION* from Brotherhood control, destroyed numerous Brotherhood patrol ships and currently holds your ship, the *RUNANA* – or should I say *my* ship, the *RUNANA*, as I'm claiming it as a spoil of war."

At that comment the captain flinched and clenched his jaw.

"Rather than continue the litany of accomplishments of this ship, I'll let you watch a short vid of events that have unfolded since you were brought aboard."

I activate the large vid screen on the wall and watched the expressions on their faces as recordings of the recent battle, as seen from the bridge of the *NEW ORLEANS*, were played before them. The battle had lasted only a short period of time and the evidence of carnage had its impact on the captured crew. Most of them sat in their chairs wearing expressions of shock.

The Brotherhood captain lost all color from his face and stared blankly at the screen. "But how??? How can this be? You've got both shields and cloaking!"

"Not just on this ship, but also on the fleet in pursuit of the few Brotherhood ships that managed to escape after the *failed* mission at Plosaxen. Those ships, by the way, are currently headed here."

"How would you know that? Even with a GW pod the news of what's happened at Plosaxen would not have reached here yet!" the captain said defiantly.

"True," I said, "if we're using the *old and slow* GW pods."

"You can't have instant communications through this distance of space," he responded in complete denial.

"Another of the Brotherhood's arrogant conclusions," I said. "Whether you believe me or not, I can assure you that what I am telling you is true. Two thirds of your ships that participated in the attack on Plosaxen were destroyed; and unless they surrender, those headed in this direction will suffer the same fate in a few days. So, in the end, I'm giving you a choice. Cooperate and it will go easier for you. Resist and you'll be in prison for a very long time. Those of you who cooperate will be separated from the rest in a nicely appointed cabin like Felenna has been given. You'll still be guarded and under arrest, but your conditions will be better."

None of the officers budged, but a few hung their heads. Their captain, however, sat stiffly in his chair and said, "You think you're winning? We're stronger than you realize. A few fancy ships aren't going to eliminate the Brotherhood or our cause."

"Well, so far the statistics on the matter don't seem to favor that opinion; but it's your choice. Take them back to their cells – except for Felenna. I wish to talk to her."

After all the Brotherhood prisoners were taken out of the conference room under heavy guard, I sat down with Felenna. Captain Stonbersa and Marranalis were also present.

"Felenna, I want to thank you for your help in the capture of the *RUNANA* and in our escape. I know it must have been difficult for you and I realize that the Brotherhood may have a price on your head now."

Felenna's eyes looked tired and swollen, as though she had been crying. "It wasn't so hard, really. I hated being in the Brotherhood. It was the dumbest thing I ever did. I was young and crazy and in love with this jerk named Harral, a Federation officer. When he joined the Brotherhood and told me about it, I thought it sounded great. This was before you arrived with the solbidyum. When we got word of your arrival and the return of the lost solbidyum, I started to see a different side to the Brotherhood and I didn't like it. I had quit my job as a shuttle pilot and was enmeshed in the Brotherhood by then and I didn't know how to get out. It was when I was assigned here on Alle Bamma that I discovered we were the ones supplying God's Sweat throughout the galaxy – and then I wanted out badly, but didn't know how to do it. Harral had dumped me for some big-breasted bimbo stationed off-world and he transferred to be with her... and I was left here."

"You were a shuttle pilot? Then you weren't in the Federation military forces?" I asked.

"No. I had applied to join before I hooked up with Harral; but after he recruited me for the Brotherhood, telling me how the Brotherhood was going to replace the Federation and make things better, I never followed up on my application."

"That's good information," I said. "The fact that you weren't in the Federation military will make things a lot easier on you, I think. I'm going to make you an offer and I want you to think it over carefully. I can't make you any promises; but if you accept my offer, there is a good possibility you will never be charged or tried for your involvement with the Brotherhood."

"Right now I'm willing to listen to anything you have to say; but none of it matters much. Even if I do go to prison the Brotherhood will find me and kill me. No one who becomes an officer leaves the Brotherhood and lives."

"Don't be so sure of that. I think I have a solution to that problem that will put you out of reach of the Brotherhood. First, how many years were you a Brotherhood member?" I asked.

"Four."

"You obviously were pretty good at your job to have reached the position you did in that short a time. I would surmise that you've gained a good deal of knowledge about their operations throughout the galaxy, like base locations, their overall fleet size, and details as to their immediate and future plans. If you're willing to cooperate with us and tell us everything you know and if you can pass our computerized loyalty and truth test, I'll go to bat for you when it's time for you to face the Federation courts. I have a strong influence within the Federation; my word carries a good bit of weight, not only with the Admiralty, but with the Senate as well.

"As for your safety, you will have two choices. One is that you go to work for the Admiralty and remain stationed on the admiral's flagship, which is protected with shielding technology like the *NEW ORLEANS*. The other is that you go to work for me here on the *NEW ORLEANS*. You would be as safe here as you can possibly be anywhere."

"I could use another competent officer on my staff," added Captain Stonbersa. "Kerabac is an excellent first officer; but I need someone to stand in for him when he's off duty or on assignment with Tibby. If you're any good I would be willing to give you a chance – again, providing you pass all our security and loyalty checks."

As I spoke, Felenna eyes filled with tears and she broke down sobbing. We allowed her a few minutes to regain her composure.

"I thought my life was ruined when I discovered the truth about the Brotherhood and what a mess I had gotten myself into. I can't believe you're giving me a chance to redeem myself. You have no idea what this means to me. That you would be willing to take a chance with me here on the *NEW ORLEANS* is beyond belief. I promise I won't let you down."

"Just so you understand; you will remain under arrest until A'Lappe has administered the loyalty tests and other security checks. Thereafter you will remain on a probationary status and will continue to be monitored and tested periodically, so that we can be absolutely certain of you allegiance. So if you're willing to undergo the intense and ongoing scrutiny, I'm willing to take a chance on you," I said.

"I think I would like that very much," she said.

"Good. Now, the fact that you were never in the Federation military means you are not under military judgment for court martial. On top of that, the Senate is considering amnesty for Brotherhood members who defect. So I think these factors put you in a pretty good position," I informed her. "Right now the only Brotherhood members who know you have helped us and that you're no longer part of their program are the ones in our holding cell. None of the other Brotherhood members know about this development; so as far as they're concerned, you're still with them.

"You mentioned that you were only *acting* first officer on the *RUNANA*. How long did you serve on her?"

"Only a few weeks. I was on temporary assignment while the regular first officer was away on another assignment."

"How many bases does the Brotherhood have on Alle Bamma?"

"Fourteen that I know of; but there could be more"

"Do you know how many Brotherhood ships are here on the planet at the moment?"

"I know they had 31 corvettes like the *RUNANA* and over a hundred patrol ships before today's conflict. They also have freighters coming and going and a few other miscellaneous ships. What the status of ships is after today I don't know."

"If we can get you to the planet near a base with another corvette like the *RUNANA*, what are your chances of getting aboard unchallenged?"

"Unless they changed things in the past few hours, I should have little or no problem doing so. I'm one of but a few personnel that is experienced in flying all their ship types. I've also served at a number of bases here, so I will be immediately recognized as an officer of the Brotherhood. Since my rotation through the major bases was frequent, my coming and going was a routine thing. If I were to suddenly show up on any base, I don't think anyone would really notice. Plus, the destruction of the base where I was stationed creates a situation where the camp's survivors will have to be displaced to other bases. So, all things considered, I'm pretty sure I won't be seen as a suspicious presence anywhere. Why would you want me to go back?"

"I want you to help us steal another corvette," I said.

"That's going to be difficult. Normally there is a crew of about 50 on each corvette. They can hold double that; but the Brotherhood has been spreading crews pretty thin, operating ships and bases with fewer staff and two long shifts instead of three shorter ones. The *RUNANA* was an exception, since the food synthesizer was out of order and all but a few core officers were displaced to barracks. Any other corvette you may find will be more heavily manned."

"Is there any way – *easy* way – to disable one for a short period of time without destroying it?" I asked.

"There may be, but I'm not an engineer. If there is I don't know what it would be," she said.

"I believe there is a way, Tibby," said A'Lappe. In his typical fashion he had suddenly appeared in the meeting. Felenna looked startled.

"You'll have to excuse A'Lappe. He likes to make sudden and dramatic appearances. You'll get used to it."

"I'm still trying to get used to it," said Stonbersa offhandedly.

"Okay, A'Lappe, how can it be done?" I asked.

"The ship is definitely Markazian-built. Markazian engineers are notorious for using a Dietyte fusion reactor. Though it is sufficient for powering the ship, this reactor is cheaply designed and poorly built. Well-built reactors include a safety mechanism that facilitates necessary shutdowns without killing the reaction potential or the reactor itself, thus making it possible to restart the reactor and associated power distribution without excessive effort. The Markazians, on the other hand, use a cost-cutting method to lower the price of the reactor, as well as the required construction effort. Their design employs a simple kill system that successfully stops the reaction; but at the same time it kills the reaction potential and the reactor. Once the reactor kill switch is activated, that reactor is terminated. Only by installing a new one will the ship be operational again."

"Yes, there is such a kill switch on the bridge," confirmed Felenna, "but I never knew that the reactor couldn't be restarted once the switch was activated. Only the officer in charge on the bridge has the key, which generally means the captain or the first officer."

"Another thing you should know," A'Lappe interjected, "the weapons system on the ship is powered solely by the reactor. If the reactor is down, the weapons are completely disabled."

"That is good and valuable news, A'Lappe, but why are you here and not working on the cloaking of the *RUNANA*?"

"Ha, like I'm needed to install that thing. After confirming some simple dimensional parameters, I turned over the installation to the maintenance crew. While you were away, I had several spare cloaking devices constructed, which are now stored in the hangar; so after I completed the necessary calculations, all I had to do was tell them where and how to install the system. I assumed I would be of more value to you here," he said with a grin.

"Oh, before I forget," he continued, "I was also able to repair the food synthesizer on the ship. It really wasn't anything that difficult. The Brotherhood engineers must be a joke."

"That's probably a fair assessment, A'Lappe," I said with a grin.

"Okay, so now all we need to do is to figure out how to get you on the bridge, get the kill switch key in your hands and deactivate the reactor without getting you killed in the process," I said.

"There may be another way," A'Lappe said. "While that is the only *manual* switch to kill the reactor, the actual kill mechanism on the reactor is sensitive to electromagnetic pulses. If it's hit with a strong enough pulse, the mechanism will trigger. The ship itself is shielded from EMPs, but there is no additional shielding that specifically protects the reactor room. If you were to place an EMP device of the right strength in the reactor room, it would disable the reactor within seconds, leaving the corvette completely dead. The crew would have no choice but to abandon ship, as everything in it would stop working – life support, lights, weapons, lifts, everything. The Markazians cut a lot of corners when they designed and built these ships. They're strong enough, but there are no backup systems, reserves or redundancies anywhere. If you planning to keep or use any of their ships, Tibby, I advise that we modify them rather extensively to include these backup systems."

"Duly noted, A'Lappe. Thank you.

"Okay, so if you can provide Felenna with a device that emits an EMP burst close to the reactor with a timed detonator, we'll have a chance at disabling and gaining a ship. If we time an attack at a base to coincide with detonation of the EMP device, the crew should recognize that they have to abandon the ship immediately, especially if we hit the base aggressively with a full-on attack."

"If you really want to undermine them, then I think I know the ship you should go for – and I think I know how to gain access to its reactor room," said Felenna. "What you want is the *MIZBAGONA*, Captain Ruraldo's ship. He's in charge of all defenses for the planet's surface, as well as all the ships stationed here. If you can seize his ship, it will seriously demoralize the rest of the Brotherhood on these bases. The chief engineer on the *MIZBAGONA* has been trying to get my...*personal attention*... for some time, but I've had no interest in him. If I were to stop by the *MIZBAGONA* to visit him, I'm sure he would end up showing me around the engine and reactor rooms, as those are his pride and glory. He brags about them constantly." Felenna rolled her eyes, clearly unimpressed by anything this man had to offer. "I could carry the EMP device in my duffle and, if it's is small enough, place it in the reactor room when he's distracted. Once it's planted, I can make an excuse that I need to be someplace else and leave the ship. Unless I get caught with the device, which is unlikely, I should be able to pull it off with no problems."

"How small a device can you make that will do the trick, A'Lappe?" I asked.

"The entire device and timed activator would be the size of a flat gun," he said. "In fact, I can house it in the flat gun casing. You carry arms on the ship anyway, so it would be perfectly normal for you to have one."

"Yes, that would be perfect," said Felenna.

"Before you go, let's look over the reactor compartment on the *RUNANA*. I would imagine the reactor rooms on both ships are much the same, if not identical. Let's see if we can plan an optimal place for you to leave the detonator," said A'Lappe.

The rest of the meeting was spent planning an extensive assault on the bases of Alle Bamma. On a vid map Felenna identified the general location of the Brotherhood base where we would most likely find the *MIZBAGONA*. Marranalis said he would send some of our security team in a cloaked ship to scout the area and verify its location. We were pretty sure the Brotherhood had bolstered their defenses by that point, but it was highly unlikely that they would realize we had personal cloaking capabilities, as well as the cloaking for the ships, which they had already witnessed. At the moment, we were relatively sure they weren't going to make an attempt to flee without knowing how many cloaked ships were surrounding the planet. They would choose to wait for reinforcements to arrive and help them out of their quandary.

Marranalis' plan consisted of putting cloaked men on the ground some distance from the base to scout out the layout, manpower and location of the *MIZBAGONA* and other parked ships, as well as the prison and other infrastructure, after which they would return with the information. It would be a week or more before the Brotherhood ships fleeing Plosaxen would arrive with the Federation in pursuit; and I doubted the rebels had any other ships anywhere near Alle Bamma, perhaps with the exception of a freighter. This situation gave us some time to deal with things on Alle Bamma at our own pace.

One thing that I felt was necessary was to return to the surface and talk to Jnanara. For this journey I would be taking Marranalis and Hotyona. While I didn't know exactly where their village was located, I had a good idea how to find her. We would take some of our security forces along to assess the condition of the base we had destroyed earlier and scour the area for any clues or information that the Brotherhood might have left behind.

Each man deployed to the surface would also carry a small container for collection of any ruguian eggs they might find in the course of their operation. With these plans in mind we adjourned for the evening. I asked Marranalis to provide a security escort and to give Felenna an abbreviated tour of the ship; and then to see to it that she was provided a meal. Marranalis suggested that it might be a good idea for her to dine with the some of his security team in their dining room. I got the impression from the way he said it that he had a specific reason for wanting to do so. I decided to let things play out and see what he was up to.

Instead of returning to my suite after the meeting I headed to the gym for some martial arts exercises and a swim. I had hoped the exertion would erase some of the thoughts in my mind, but all it served to do was remind me of Kala and how we swam and practiced martial arts together. Eating dinner alone that evening just intensified the loneliness; the food seemed tasteless without Kala sitting across the table from me.

Before retiring for the night I went to the ships hospital and stared into the stasis chamber, taking what solace I could from being near her. I'm not sure that it helped, as I happened to arrive when the fog-like gas that stopped all cellular aging and suspended the spread of the poison in her body was refreshing itself within the chamber, creating a dense mist that glowed with the chamber lights and obscured the view of her face.

I must have been much more tired than I realized, because I had no memory of going to bed and I seemed to sleep without dreams. When I awoke, I felt rather disoriented and unsure of where I was. It took a few moments for my head to clear and for everything to fall back into place. Just as I was getting my senses back, Piesew arrived and asked me if I cared for some breakfast. I was never quite sure just how Piesew always knew exactly when to make an entrance and I never bothered to ask. To my surprise, I was actually hungry. I found myself craving Endarin sausages with Yendera flat cakes and gravy, a dish Kala had introduced me to one morning after I described a meal on Earth called buckwheat cakes and sausage. In his usual efficient manner, Piesew had the meal ready and on the table by the time I finished my shower. There were times when I wished for a shower like those back on Earth, where I could lounge in a massaging stream of hot water for as long as I wanted, rather than just clean myself in the strange three-minute mist and ultrasonic treatment.

After I finished eating, I headed to the bridge and was surprised to see A'Lappe sitting once more in the communication officer's chair.

"Ah, good morning, Tibby," said Stonbersa. "I hope you rested well."

"Yes, I did.   Thank you," I replied.   "I'm surprised to see you here this morning, A'Lappe."

A'Lappe turned toward me in the chair and said, "I sleep very little compared to you humans; I've been here for several hours intercepting Brotherhood communications. There's lots of buzz going on about their losses. You have them really shaken, Tibby. They're preparing for an all-out assault. From what I can gather, we've wiped out two-thirds of their local fleet. Right now they're praying you don't attack them before reinforcements show up. If they only knew that a mere one-third of their fleet is coming back – if that."

"You know, if it weren't for Kala lying in stasis, I would say let's just wait two weeks and let them see what a mess they're in when their crippled fleet comes home and the planet is surrounded by Federation warships; but I'm not prepared to wait that long. I think there's a good chance that we can pull this off without losing any men or ships on our side. Frankly, I don't give a damn what happens to the Brotherhood.

"Is there any new word from the admiral?"

"The admiral is sending out the Mirage Fighters every day. Their additional speed over the Brotherhood's fleet and their cloaking capabilities have allowed them to come up behind the Brotherhood ships and pick off one or two every day. There might not be any that make it here before the admiral is done; he's really in his glory with this new-found success."

"Well, if he's going to pick off the Brotherhood fleet before they get here, the least we can do is to take out all their bases in the meantime," I said. "We'll spend the day today on reconnaissance missions. I want to set down on the planet with Marranalis and see if I can contact Jnanara and possibly find some ruguian eggs. Tomorrow we may be well positioned to wreak some more havoc on the Brotherhood."

It was about two hours later that I met Marranalis and Hotyona in the hangar, along with twenty of my security forces that crowded into the cargo hold of one of the patrol ships with us. We flew to the surface and landed at the location where we had the parked the *ALI* when we first arrived. Two men were left aboard the patrol ship as the rest of us set forth. Marranalis and his men headed off to do recon at the Brotherhood base and Hotyona and I headed to the location where we were ambushed by the natives only days ago.

We searched only a short time before recognized the spot where Hotyona's tracks had ended just prior to that first ambush. I stood in that very spot, lifted my gaze toward the canopy, and called out, "I speak for Thumumba. I wish to speak with Jnanara."

We waited a few minutes, but nothing seemed to happen. I was about to give up and try another location, when suddenly, as if by magic, we were surrounded by about a dozen of the small multi-colored natives. One stepped forward who I believed to be the same individual who had led us to the Brotherhood camp. He motioned for us to follow him and then he set off down a small path I had not noticed before.

We traveled for about half a kilometer to the base of a large I'aban tree, where he started to scale the tree, followed by half of the other natives.

"I hope he's not expecting us to follow him," said Hotyona. "How did they get us up there before?" He barely finished his statement before we saw vines attached to a basket just large enough for one as it dropped down from the canopy overhead.

"There's your answer, I think." I said.

"Oh no, I'm not getting into that thing. What if it breaks?"

"They got us up there before without it breaking. I think they can do it again," I said.

The basket was on the ground quickly and two of the natives soon pulled on my arms to get me into it.

"You come.   Ride in basket.   Thumumba's children not let you fall," said one of the natives.

I must confess that sitting in the basket as I was being hoisted about 40 meters into the air was not an enjoyable experience. There was no doubt that I was being pulled up hand-over-hand by a team of natives. I could imagine them straining to lift my weight, as I clearly weighed as much as three of them. Once the natives had both Hotyona and I hoisted to a broad branch, our guide once more began leading us along the

boughs and cross several small rope vine bridges.   I
could see Hotyona's pale and sweaty face as we passed
through alternating patches of shadow and light and I
knew he was terrified; but, to his credit, he never
complained or waivered and kept up with the pace.

Traveling in the trees was very deceptive. It's
difficult to ascertain just how far we travelled; but my
best guess is it was close to a kilometer before we
arrived at the platform where Hotyona, Kerabac and I
had been before and where Jnanara now stood, waiting
for our arrival. She bowed her head to me when I set
foot onto the platform and I repeated the gesture to her,
hoping it was the right thing to do.

"Children of Thumumba welcome you, man who
speak for Thumumba.   Children grateful for freedom
from binding."

"Binding of children of Thumumba not over.
Many more bound ones from other tribes still in evil men
traps," I said. "Thumumba wish free children to help
man who speak for Thumumba – together find where
evil men make all ugly villages and trap bound ones.
Then man who speak for Thumumba and friends of man
who speak for Thumumba free *all* bound ones, restore
sacred plant to elders, destroy all ugly villages, remove
all bad men from Sweet Home."

Jnanara went on to tell me that what I asked of
her people was difficult; that the tribes of Sweet Home
live and move across many places. She also confirmed
what I already knew, which was that she and her people
didn't know where every Brotherhood base was located.
In the end, she committed her people to making every
effort to spread the word through the jungle as fast and

far as possible to notify all tribes of our presence and our efforts to free their captive brethren.

How children send message to man who speak for Thumumba when children find bad men villages?" Jnanara asked.

Fortunately, I had thought this out ahead of time. Taking four nuts from a basket on the platform I said, "When children find village of evil men," as I placed the first nut on the platform, "children must go out from bad men village in three directions. Go same distance from bad men village as this tree is to lifting basket. There children make three very big fires, place in flames many plants that make much smoke," I said placing the three other nuts equally spaced about the center nut. "I see big smoke from house in sky and know evil men village here in center."

Jnanara nodded and said, "This is wise thing you say. Jnanara and children tell all tribes how to make fire message.

"Man who speak for Thumumba, when all evil men leave Sweet Home and children of Thumumba all free, come back to this place. See Jnanara."

"I will," I said.

We were returned to the ground in the same basket used to take us up into the trees and the same native who led us before now escorted us back to the ship. On the way back I had to stop twice when I spotted ruguian eggs. Hotyona collected and stored them in a container. If our guide thought anything strange about our behavior, he made no indication of it and waited patiently until we had the eggs safely stored away before leading us on again. Once back at the ship, our guide quickly vanished into the foliage.

We checked in with the two guards on the ship who reported that the reconnaissance party had not returned, so Hotyona and I spent our waiting time searching for more eggs in the immediate area around the ship. We had no luck, however, nor did we see any other sign of ruguians.

It was about an hour later that our recon team returned and reported that the base had been totally deserted. Damaged ships still littered the site but every one of them had been stripped of whatever valuable parts were easy to remove and transport. The same held true for the buildings, most of which had been destroyed. All armaments had been taken, as well as all power modules. Every scrap of viable lab equipment and all salvageable drug packages and bales of plants had been removed.

"How well are we equipped with incendiary devices on this ship?" I asked Marranalis.

"We have a good supply, if needed; but if you're thinking of torching every Brotherhood base on the planet after we oust them, we won't have enough. I'd suggest you use the lasers on the *NEW ORLEANS*. Target the bases with the RMFF turned on and the amplification of the energy will probably fuse everything into a molten blob of metal and glass."

"Not a bad idea; but if we do that, we need to make sure there are no natives in the area. I would hate to toast any of them."

After all our recon men were onboard and we were headed back to the *NEW ORLEANS*, Hotyona approached me. "Tibby, what you were saying back there about torching the Brotherhood facilities – is there any way that can be avoided?"

"Possibly, but why? Don't you want to see their bases destroyed so they can't reestablish themselves here?"

"Oh, I definitely want them and their facilities gone, but destroying the bases with fire or laser is going to have an impact on the environment. Damage has already been done simply by their presence here and their operations; but anything that can be done to reverse and erase the damage rather than add to it is most important at this point."

"Hm, I hadn't given that any thought, but you're right. Plus I don't think the natives would appreciate having traces of the Brotherhood left behind. I've actually been thinking of leaving the *RUNANA* and possibly a few other ships behind, if we're able to capture more, and staff them with my own people to protect Alle Bamma from the Brotherhood and any other persons or groups that might want to exploit the planet or the natives.

"It would also be nice if researchers were able to come here to conduct pharmaceutical studies. I'll bet there are dozens of plants here that could be cultivated for medicinal purposes. Let me give it some thought," I said.

When we arrived back at the ship, A'Lappe was there to greet us, hoping we had found sufficient ruguian eggs to make the anti-toxin for Kala.

"I'm sorry, A'Lappe, but we're not even halfway to the quantity we need. I'm afraid we will have poor pickings until we get this issue with the Brotherhood resolved."

"All the more reason for us to get rid of them as quickly as possible," A'Lappe said. "You might be interested to know the communications between bases down on the planet seem to indicate that some of them may be considering an escape attempt. At least a few of them are convinced that we don't have that large a force out here, otherwise we would be attacking. They believe that, if they can locate our approximate location, they can fly from the opposite side of the planet and slip out of our range by flying on a vector that keeps the planet between us and them."

"Maybe we need to shake them up a little. Tomorrow I think we'll destroy several of their surface bases. We'll have to make the targets as far removed from each other as possible to let them know that we're aware of their locations and able to attack any point that we wish."

"Also, Tibby, Admiral Regeny has sent a message that two of the fleeing Brotherhood ships have veered off from the others and are making a run for a nearby asteroid field. He's sending two Mirage Fighters after them and he's pretty sure they'll outrun the enemy ships before they even get close to the asteroids."

"You would think by now the Brotherhood would be getting the message that it is futile for them to run."

"Tibby, the problem is distance and communication. By the time news of events gets to anyone here, it is old news. The events of the *DUSTEN* and the revolt are just now getting here; and much of what they are hearing is doubted as being anything more than rumor."

"Well you and Cantolla are changing that," I said with a grin.

"Only to a small degree. We are only able to convey verbal news or communication, which then has to be repeated by the receiving person on the other end. Messages can be changed in the telling; and the person receiving a message can totally misinterpret or change the meaning of the message by adding or deleting a single word, either intentionally or accidently. It's not like anyone else can monitor the transmission to make sure every detail is exact. We can't send any visual data by this means, or show you scenes of carnage. Everything is subject to the two people sitting in the transmission and receiving chairs."

"I hadn't thought about that until now. We'll have to think about developing confirmation protocols. Will you eventually be able to modify the system to accept visual images or to broadcast to more than one receiver at a time?"

"I don't think so – at least not if this is working the way I think it does. I'm not sure I want to go into the theories behind my opinion, lest I sound crazy or unscientific; but let's just say that this works by way of universal consciousness – and I try not to think about that aspect too much."

I laughed, "A'Lappe, I would prefer not to think about it at all."

Just then, A'Lappe's and my wrist communicators activated. Captain Stonbersa's voice said, "Tibby, A'Lappe and Marranalis please report to the bridge. It looks like the Brotherhood is about to attempt something."

A'Lappe and I headed to the bridge at a fast pace and arrived to find Marranalis already there.

"We just intercepted some communication from the surface using the codes Felenna provided us. From the chatter we're intercepting it looks like the Brotherhood is planning to make a run for it. They hope to join up with their ships that are en route from Plosaxen and launch a two-front attack on us. They believe we will pursue and that once we see the size of their combined fleet – rather, the fleet they *believe* is responding to assist – we will not engage them. They have no idea that most of their fleet has been decimated.

Their true intent is to leave several ships behind while we pursue, ships that will then flee with their cargo holds loaded with drugs. They're saying that once we're out of range, those transports will take off toward another hidden base somewhere in the Blandaran System. They intend to blow up all their bases when they leave, killing all the native slaves in the process. They're planning to make their move in about seven hours."

"It looks like we'll have to act quickly if we're going to stop them and save the natives. Get someone to bring Felenna to the conference room and get all our top security people in there as well," I said.

Fifteen minutes later we were all assembled in one of the larger conference rooms in the ship.

"I'm afraid we're going to have to take action a lot quicker than anticipated," I began. "The Brotherhood is preparing to make a run for it. They intend to draw us away from the planet in a pursuit, during which time they plan to take their drugs and flee in the other direction. They also intent to destroy each base as they leave without first releasing the slaves. We need to stop them before they get their ships in the air. I want all our Mirage Fighters to make repeated passes over the bases to knock out all the ships they can. For the time being, don't target any buildings; I don't want any structures hit that might have natives inside.

"Felenna, do you have any idea where the *MIZBAGONA* might be hiding?"

"I'm pretty sure I do. Captain Ruraldo is the number two man. He and all the top Brotherhood people hang out at the main base. It's located in the southern hemisphere along a river that flows from a lake created by a meteor impact."

"If you can direct one of my ships to the area, they will fly in cloaked. You won't have much time – maybe an hour – to get aboard the *MIZBAGONA* and plant the EMP device. My suggestion to you is to stay aboard and hide. Once the device goes off, everyone will abandon the ship. Shortly thereafter I'm hoping we will have the base sufficiently under control for some more of my people to fly in cloaked with a new core for the reactor and have it operational again within an hour. After that I want you to take charge of the ship and fly it back here with the crew that replaced the core. You'll be provided with security codes to clear you so you won't be shot down by friendly fire."

I could see the shocked look on Felenna's face. "You want me to take charge of the *MIZBAGONA?* I'm not a captain. I'm not even one of your crew."

"You're the best and most qualified person for the job. As acting first officer on a sister ship, you know the ship better than any of my men do – and we don't have time to train anyone."

"Kerabac has flown the *RUNANA*. He could do it," she said nervously.

"Yes, and Kerabac will be busy flying the *RUNANA* again. We're manning the ship and he's taking her out cloaked to assist in destroying as many Brotherhood ships that leave the planet as he can. He'll have the firepower to take out the larger ships on the Brotherhood bases; and with the cloaking device A'Lappe has installed, his risk of coming under fire is greatly reduced."

"Why don't you simply put an RMFF shield on it... like you have on the *NEW ORLEANS*?" she asked.

"There is a matter of space limitations. The components of the RMFF system are too large to install on anything smaller than a frigate, I'm afraid."

"Oh, I never thought about that. Even so, the Brotherhood doesn't know that, so their ignorance gives you an added advantage, doesn't it?"

"Exactly!" I replied.

"Marranalis, I want all your troops to understand that every effort is to be made to locate and free all slaves. At the same time, all care must be taken to protect them and not put them in harm's way. If it's a question of allowing the Brotherhood to escape in order to free or protect the natives, so be it; but they are to be freed and protected at all costs.

"If it's possible to capture a ship, do so; but don't make it a priority. My guess is they're pretty low on ships right now and they're going to protect them as best they can.

One more thing – I suggest that the men assigned to ground operations each carry two cloaking devices; so when the power on one runs out, they have a back-up. I've no idea how long this operation will take."

Marranalis nodded; and if he had any questions in his mind about my orders, he didn't show it. I must credit Marranalis and his team; they were assembled and underway within the hour.

Before we left the *NEW ORLEANS* I went to see Kala again. I felt helpless standing there with a million things I wanted to say to her; but nothing seemed right. At the moment all wanted was to end things with the Brotherhood as quickly as possible so we could find the ruguian eggs needed to wake her from the nightmare that was in her veins.

"I'm trying my very best, Kala. I'm doing everything I can to get you out of there. Just a little longer," I said. "I love you, Kala."

I felt anger as I left her, anger toward the Brotherhood who poisoned her and anger at them for standing in the way of us getting the eggs that could provide her salvation. I was still angry at Regeny, too; but my focus now was on the Brotherhood, as they were ultimately the ones that had caused all this and I wanted it to be over.

Against everyone's wishes, I went with the team that took Felenna to the camp where she believed that Ruraldo and the *MIZBAGONA* were located. The base itself was hidden in the jungle and covered with camouflage netting similar to the other bases; but this base was stretched out along a river in a long, narrow configuration rather than the circular encampment that I saw at the other base. Our pilot deposited us at a wide place along the shore where there was a large sand bar. He disengaged the cloaking device just long enough for us to disembark and then re-cloaked and departed with instructions to return in about two hours to begin firing on buildings in the camp. We hoped to free the slaves and damage the netting before his return, as well as capture the *MIZBAGONA*. Onboard our patrol ship were the replacement reactor components that would be installed after we had control of her. We would need to get her back in the air as soon as possible.

Felenna, the ground troops and I had only gone a short distance into the jungle, when a native suddenly dropped from a tree in front of us and said in his native tongue, "You man who speak for Thumumba?"

I was taken aback. We were hundreds of miles removed from Jnanara's village. It was impossible for word of my presence and my plans to have spread this far to the south so quickly.

"I am man who speak for Thumumba," I replied, unsure what would happen next.

"Come," the native replied. "Thumumba wish you to come this way," and he set off on a route perpendicular to the river and parallel to the camp.

"Do you think it's wise to follow this native instead of going to the camp?" Felenna asked?

Not in our logic it wasn't; but I had a feeling it was the right thing to do. Suddenly the small native stopped and indicated with his finger for us to be quiet. Then he turned and slowly started leading us in the direction of the camp while constantly looking to his right and sniffing the air. Several times he stopped and motioned with some urgency and agitation to be quiet, when one of my men would inadvertently snap a twig or produce some sound. At one point our guide stopped us beside a very large fallen I'aban tree, which created a barrier nearly 50 meters high and 350 meters in length between us and the river. He motioned for the others to remain quiet and perfectly still. Then he motioned for me to follow him, as he began climbing the branches on the side of the fallen tree.

As we neared the top, he again motioned for me to be quiet and then slowly raised his head to peer over the top of the tree. He looked left and right, then brought his head down and indicated I should do the same. When I looked past the tree trunk, I was stunned to see about a hundred natives harvesting the plants that were used by the Brotherhood to produce God's Sweat. Approximately 20 Brotherhood troopers guarded the slaves that were restrained by electronic collars. I ducked my head back down and nodded to my guide, who then led me back down to the others.

Back on the ground my men looked at me with silent anticipation as I stared back at them. We had 25 troopers with us, not counting Felenna and myself. I tried to think quickly; I needed to figure out how to revise my plans.

Very quietly I whispered what I had just seen. "There are about a hundred slaves guarded by about 20 troopers on the other side of this tree. If we had taken the route along the river, we would have walked right into them and they would have alerted the base before we could take any action.

"The troopers are stationed around the natives at equal intervals. We're going to cloak and file out in a line – everyone follow behind me. I am going to walk around the tree and to the farthest guard. I want each of you to stop one guard short of the person in front of you. You won't be able to see each other, so you'll have to pay attention and count to figure out your exact position. All the guards will be visible from our point of approach; so you should be able to figure out which one is yours. This is going to be tricky. Since I will be farthest away, you will have to watch for signs that I've initiated my attack. When you see that guard fall, you will all take out the guard before you. Is that understood?"

Every one nodded.

"You two," I said, indicating two of my men not needed for this task. "You go with Felenna to the Brotherhood compound. She knows what to do from there. Wait to see which ship she enters and then one of you come back to lead the rest of us back to the camp. We'll free these slaves and then join you."

I turned to the native guide. "We now free children of Thumumba. You take woman and two men in hard skins to bad men village, protect from drodoceal and keep hidden in jungle?"

He nodded and then motioned for Felenna and the pair of security officers to follow him.

Once Felenna, the officers and their guide were out of sight, the remainder of us switched on our cloaking devices and set out around the trunk of the tree. I hoped we wouldn't run into each other, since we basically were invisible not only to the Brotherhood goons but to each other as well. Instead of moving around the outside of the semicircle of guards, I moved along the opposite side of the tree trunk which would be the shortest route to the far end where I would approach my target. Once I came within three meters of him, I moved very cautiously, so as not to make any noise or disturb the leaves in a way that would seem unnatural. I maneuvered around until I was positioned behind him; then I waited several minutes, hopefully enough to allow all my men ample time to get situated by their respective targets. Then, using a quick martial arts technique, I broke the neck of the guard in front of me. As I released his body, I looked about the semicircle to see guards struggling and falling to the jungle floor. When I could see no more guards, I turned off my cloaking device and heard the gasp of the natives as they dropped their harvesting tools and fell to their knees. One by one my men began decloaking and appearing around the circle. I could only imagine what must have been going on in the minds of the natives.

"I speak for Thumumba," I said. "Children of Thumumba now free. Return quickly to trees and to your people. Tell children stay away from places of evil men until ugly villages and evil men gone." Slowly they got to their feet and looked about at each other. Then they quickly departed in a direction away from the Brotherhood camp. In a matter of only seconds they were all out of sight.

"What now?" asked one of my men.

"Now we head for the Brotherhood base. Hopefully we can find and follow the trail used by the guide who took Felenna and the guards. We should meet up with the guard who's coming back to guide us in. If not, we can only pray we don't get lost."

"It didn't look much like the Brotherhood was planning to leave, if they had slaves out here gathering these weeds just hours before they were supposed to flee the planet," said another one of the men.

"On the contrary, it makes perfect sense; they want all the drugs they can carry. From what I've seen, just the smallest drop of this sap will have a person high for days. I imagine they extract the sap and dilute it down before it's sold, which will double or triple the street value of each harvest. Heaven only knows how much of this stuff they must be making. Certainly they're producing enough to buy and support the ships and manpower they have here," I said.

We had only gone a short distance down the path when we spotted someone coming toward us. We took up locations in hiding until we were certain that it was one of the two men that had accompanied Felenna. We then stood in view; and when he came near he said quietly, "The village isn't far. There are a lot of troopers posted around the base, so we'll have to be quiet and careful. Felenna made it to the ship she wanted and got inside after talking to a guard posted there. She hasn't come back out. Wilnod is cloaked and keeping watch. That native fellow you sent with us disappeared shortly after we got to the camp. He never said a word – one minute he was there, the next he was gone."

Just then my communicator began vibrating on my wrist. I lifted it to my face and said quietly, "Tibby here."

"Tibby, this is Stonbersa. I'm not sure how the natives across the entire planet knew we were coming; but all over the surface are clusters of three pillars of smoke rising from the jungle. Right now I can identify about a dozen locations where the Brotherhood camps have been marked. We're setting down as many men as close to the bases as possible; but we don't have enough men to tackle all these bases at once. We do have Mirage Fighters in the air, though; and if the Brotherhood doesn't have too many ships coming up at one time, we should be able to pick off any that try to leave."

"That's good news, Captain," I said. "Be sure to feed the location data into the computer on all the bases. Those we can't get to today we can save for the next assault."

Then I turned to my men and ordered, "Okay, let's get going. We have a lot of work to do."

As part of our plan we had given Felenna an hour from the time she boarded the *MIZBAGONA* to plant the EMP device. It was set to detonate 15 minutes later. We reached the base about 20 minutes after the trooper met us on the path, meaning we had 35 minutes before the device would disable and ground the *MIZBAGONA*. We needed to synchronize our attack so everything would be set in motion just after the EPM device crippled the ship.

My men were instructed to spread out about the camp and plant bombs in key locations so to inflict maximum damage. We knew the natives were not on the base, so we didn't need to spare any structures or other items in the camp, save the *MIZBAGONA*, which we hoped to capture intact.

I was a bit anxious, hoping that our timing would be right. We had no way of knowing from outside the *MIZBAGONA* if and when the EMP device would detonate, as there would be no explosion or anything visible to indicate that the ship had lost power.

When the time arrived for the bombs to detonate, chaos erupted. Buildings and ground conveyances began exploding one by one. The laboratory building went up like it was sitting on a volcano. Buildings burst into flames and troopers and men in white lab clothing began running manically in all directions. Many of the troopers and technicians instinctively ran toward ships, but most of the ships were in flames as well.

Suddenly, men and women were running out of the *MIZBAGONA* to another smaller craft that that appeared to be something other than a military ship – something more like a very small personal yacht. Within seconds it lifted into the air and took off, hugging the treetops as it fled.

Seconds later more men fled from the *MIZBAGONA* to look for refuge and, finding none, took off running into the jungle. They didn't make it very far, as my men picked them off one by one. Within a few minutes the base appeared empty of people, with the exception of the few wounded and dead laying here or there. All the buildings were in flames, as were three transports and two patrol ships.

I got another buzz on my communicator and answered, "Tibby here."

"This is Captain Stonbersa. We spotted four ships that left your location. They all seem to be heading to the same location in the far north of the planet. Ships are also escaping from other bases we've hit and they're heading to that same location. Do you want us to pursue and eradicate them?"

"No, just mark where they land for now. You can also tell the patrol ship that brought my team here that it's safe to land at the base with the new reactor core. We need to move quickly and get the *MIZBAGONA* out of here."

"Right, Tibby. He should be there in less than three minutes."

By now most of my team had returned to the rendezvous point. "I need five of you to come with me. The rest of you take up positions where you have broad visibility; and if any Brotherhood men approach the *MIZBAGONA*, shoot to kill."

I led the five men into the *MIZBAGONA*. Amber emergency beacons lit up the main corridors and spaces within the ship, but everything else appeared to be nonfunctional. We managed to find our way to the bridge. The door was standing open and inside I could see a figure sitting slumped in the captain's chair. It was Felenna; she was badly wounded. Blood covered her left shoulder and arm but she was still conscious.

"Felenna, are you okay?! Medic!" Almost immediately one of my men appeared and quickly began assessing Felenna's injuries.

"Nasty shot," he said, "but it will heal. We need to get her back to the *NEW ORLEANS* and into the infirmary."

Felenna looked at me and said somewhat weakly, "Sorry, Tibby, but I don't think I'll be captaining the *MIZBAGONA* out of here after all."

"Nonsense," I said. "You can still talk and give commands. My men can do the flying. You're not getting out of this for a little flesh wound. What happened anyway?"

"Everything went as planned until the EMP device went off. The chief engineer must have deduced that I was the one who planted the device, since I was the last one to come aboard and I'm not a part of the ship's regular crew. While everyone else fled the ship when the explosions started erupting across the compound, he came looking for me. I thought everyone was gone, so I came out of hiding to find that he had lingered behind. He spotted me just as I stepped into view. He shouted and called me a traitor, and then he shot me before I could take cover. He managed to hit me in the arm. I had a flat gun in my other hand and got a shot off as I fell that struck him in the head. He's dead, back there in one of the corridors."

Just then one of my men came into the bridge with a status report. "Our patrol ship just arrived with the spare reactor core. They're bringing it in right now and we should be ready to fly in 20 minutes. The patrol ship is going to cloak and scout around until we're airborne; then he'll escort us back to the *NEW ORLEANS*. By the way, there's a guy in a Brotherhood captain's uniform lying dead back there in the corridor…looks like a head wound… but other than that the ship's clear."

I chuckled, "Okay, carry on. Good work."

By then the medic was finished patching up Felenna and she was looking better, though still quite shaken.

"How are you feeling now?" I asked.

"Better," she said.   "The medic sprayed something on the wound and it doesn't hurt as much, but I'm still trembling. I've never killed anyone before."

"It's never fun or pleasant," I said.   "Listen, what I said a minute ago about you giving orders to fly this ship back – If you're not able to do so, I understand. You've done plenty already, just helping us capture this ship."

"No, no, it's alright; and if you're still willing to let me, I would be deeply honored to command the ship on its return to the *NEW ORLEANS*."

"Good, then that's settled."

While we talked, some of my security troops came in to take up stations at various positions on the bridge.   They had all been briefed on the ship's operations and had familiarized themselves with their respective equipment and consoles using the *RUNANA* as a training model.

With a series of whirls and pings the lights and instruments suddenly came to life and a message came over the com link. "Reactor is operational, we're ready to go."

I turned to Felenna and said, "Well, Captain, the ship is yours to command. Take us home."

Immediately upon our return to the *NEW ORLEANS* I went to see Kala once more. Nothing had changed, but I needed to see that for myself. My time with her was cut short as we were still in the middle of a hostile situation and there were many details for me to address. I needed to meet with the assault teams and get reconnaissance reports. I needed to meet with Stonbersa and A'Lappe. I needed to do a million things if I wanted to see this all brought to an end and see Kala out of this stasis. Sitting there with her, as much as I wanted to stay, was not going to get her out of there. Taking action would.

The rest of the day was jammed with meetings and decisions. After the day's triumphs everyone on the *NEW ORLEANS* was in a celebratory mood. The operation was a success, though we did have a few injured troopers and two damaged patrol ships that suffered some mild damage from glancing blows as they collided while cloaked. Fortunately, everyone was expected to recover fully and nothing on the patrol ships was too seriously damaged; both ships were still operational. We weren't able to get both of the captured corvettes into the hangar on the *NEW ORLEANS*; so the *RUNANA* took up an orbit position near the *NEW ORLEANS* and the *MIZBAGONA* was brought inside to be looked over and fitted with a cloaking device.

A'Lappe was like a small child with a new toy as he crawled about the *MIZBAGONA*, examining every mechanism and support system.

"These really aren't bad ships," he said. "They're remarkably well built, except for the lack of redundancy. They're armed with just about everything you can think of. Not much good for anything else than fighting; but a real war platform, nonetheless, for a planet or mercenary who needs affordable performance. I'm surprised the Brotherhood didn't start using these ships sooner."

"I don't think they've had them more than a few months," I said. "They seemed to be ramping up drug production on the surface; and I think the drugs have been their main source of revenue, at least for these big purchases. I'm sure the arms merchant that sold them to the Brotherhood operates on a cash-only basis; so they've likely developed a pay-as-they-go agreement for their orders and transactions. Their drug operations on Alle Bamma are so new that they wouldn't have had time to bring very many of these ships into service. I don't suppose there's any way you can make a smaller energy source for the RMFF that will fit into the *RUNANA* and the *MIZBAGONA*?"

"I'm afraid not, Tibby, not unless you can obtain some more solbidyum and convince the Federation to let you have it."

"I wouldn't even want to ask," I said. "Since you mention it, though, I have been thinking about the solbidyum. When I first arrived in the Federation territories, Captain Maxette explained solbidyum as a rare element produced in the collapse of a black hole. I know from what he told me that this event occurred on the outer edge of the galaxy; and it has me thinking. If it happened once, it most likely has happened in more than one place. There must be other black holes out there that collapsed for one reason or another. If so, there must be a way to detect them. Do you think you can do that?"

"Hmmm, that's an interesting thought. These anomalies would most likely not be in a galaxy itself, but in between galaxies. The black hole that produced the solbidyum was most likely a competing black hole or possibly a small one that was caught up in the spiral arms of our galaxy as the two objects passed one another. It would have to have been very small – that is, it would have absorbed relatively little matter, at least not enough to sustain itself.

"But you're right; if there was one, there must be another someplace. It could take centuries to find it; and even then there's no guarantee that the collapse would have also produced solbidyum."

"Well, play around with the idea, A'Lappe. If you come up with a good theory as to where to find another or how to detect one, I would be willing to fund an investigative expedition.

"I do have one other question that has been bugging me. My understanding of a black hole is that it compresses material tighter together by way of gravity, causing the incredibly dense singularity. According to my understanding, a grain of solbidyum should be so dense and heavy that we would be unable to lift it; yet in reality, the whole lot of it isn't at all heavy, not to mention a single grain."

"I can understand your confusion," said A'Lappe. "It was nearly overlooked by the scientists that discovered it for that very reason. You're right. Its weight should be astronomical but for one thing; solbidyum has an anti-gravity property to it – not enough to totally repel normal gravity as we find on worlds suitable for humanoids, but enough to make it very lightweight, so to speak, while still being very dense. It's quite intriguing stuff actually."

After leaving A'Lappe, I located Piesew and asked him to make arrangements for a staff dinner that evening to celebrate our victory and to make additional plans for resolution to the situation on Alle Bamma. I advised Piesew that I expected everyone to be in formal attire; and I gave him one other instruction that caused his eyes to widen a bit; but he said nothing and simply replied, "As you wish, sir."

After I finished dressing for dinner I slipped off for a few minutes to be with Kala again. As with previous visits there were several crew members present in the room where she lay in stasis. I walked over to the stasis chamber, thinking it looked all too much like a casket for my liking.

"Only a few more hours Kala," I thought. "Just a few more hours and well have the planet under control and we'll get you the cure... and you'll be alright again." I placed my hand on the capsule over her heart for a moment and then turned and headed for the dining room.

The usual staff members were there that evening as we gathered in the dining room – Captain Stonbersa, A'Lappe, Kerabac and Marranalis. As we sat down, it was obvious that there was an extra setting at the table where Kala would normally be seated. "Gentlemen, we have a new staff member joining us this evening. I'm pleased to present Captain Felenna, the newly appointed captain of the recently acquired *MIZBAGONA*."

As I made the announcement, Piesew opened a side door to the dining room, through which Felenna entered. Her injured arm was immobilized, but the sling did little to detract from the formal white uniform she was wearing. There was a brief look of shock on everyone's faces, which then gave way to applause and congratulations.

After she was seated at the table, I continued, "I have a few other announcements to make. As of today Kerabac is advanced to the level of captain in my services. Likewise, Captain Stonbersa is advanced to commodore. In this role he oversees and commands my entire fleet of ships, now and in the future.

"Unfortunately, I cannot advance Marranalis, as his rank is still determined by the Federation military, since he didn't formally resign after verbally announcing to the admiral in a recent meeting that he was doing so." Everyone at the table laughed, except Felenna, who wasn't present at the meeting to understand the joke.

"I'm sure some of you are wondering what I plan to do with the *MIZBAGONA* and the *RUNANA*, though I've mentioned bits of my idea to a couple of you. Once all signs of the Brotherhood have been removed from Alle Bamma, I want this planet and its natives protected, so the Brotherhood and any other group that might try to repeat what has happened here are prevented from reaching the surface or interfering with the planet in any way. We know now that Alle Bamma was the source of the drug God's Sweat. No doubt the Brotherhood has already taken seeds or cuttings of the plants and has begun growing crops elsewhere; so this will not be the last we have seen of this drug scourge. There will be others who will want to manufacture and peddle God's Sweat; and if they find out its source, you can be sure they will be coming here for it. It is my intention to maintain both the *MIZBAGONA* and the *RUNANA* on guard here, each equipped with a squadron of Mirage Fighters and several patrol ships, which is about all that they can carry. In addition, I plan to have two other ships stationed here. As to what those will be only time will tell.

"Ultimately, my hope is to develop a space station, complete with quarters and laboratories, which will house scientific teams focused on pharmaceutical research. These teams will have to seek approval from me to conduct such research. After we have removed the Brotherhood's equipment and infrastructure and restored Alle Bamma to her natural state, no one will set foot on the planet without my approval."

I noted some stunned looks at the last statement. "Yes, I said *removed*. Soon the *NEW ORLEANS* will head back to Megelleon, where I will hire a team to respond to Alle Bamma and stay only as long as it takes to perform a thorough reclamation of every Brotherhood field and encampment area. Hotyona, who is not here with us and has not yet been told, will be overseeing that operation. I hope to not ruffle too many feathers by circumventing Cantolla's authority and appointing him to this temporary assignment.

"As far as the Brotherhood presence that is still here, I plan to make a final offer to them tomorrow regarding terms of surrender. If they refuse, we will move forward with a final cleanup assault. So far we've been lucky; we haven't suffered any casualties or lost any ships in our operation thus far, though two ships were damaged slightly in a collision that occurred while cloaked. Let's hope our luck continues.

"At this point, our best weapons are our cloaked ground forces, which are instrumental in preparing each site for aerial assault. Their stealth will allow us to enter each camp with little risk of confrontation, free the slaves from the holding cells and secure their safety before we commence any organized aggressive attacks. Our ships will stand at the ready and will attack any base that does not surrender tomorrow, but not until every last native is clear from the strike zone.

"Brotherhood ships coming from the raid on Plosaxen will be arriving in a few days, providing the admiral hasn't destroyed them all by then. I don't want any Brotherhood bases or ships still in action here if they do show up, so we'll be moving quickly and decisively against each encampment.

"I cannot begin to express to you all how pleased I am with your performances. I'm proud of each of you individually and proud of what we stand for together. More than anything, I will be immensely happy when this is all over with so we can locate the ruguian eggs we need to get Kala out of stasis and cure her of the poison that threatens her life.

"And now I'm done with my little speech, so let's eat."

The food served by Piesew and his staff was impeccable, as always.   Most of the conversation centered on the battle of the day. Felenna received most of the attention, since her role had involved the greatest danger. I was pleased to see the others opening up to her and welcoming her into the group. Shortly before we launched the mission to seize the *MIZBAGONA*, A'Lappe administered the computerized tests to Felenna that indicated her true feelings about the Brotherhood and the offer I had given her. At the time, A'Lappe simply told me that her test results showed she was loyal without a doubt and was clear to move forward with her crucial role in the operation. Now at dinner, while the captain and commodore talked with Felenna about the mission, A'Lappe quietly told me that the tests had verified that she did indeed loathe her involvement with the Brotherhood and had wanted to get out ever since she discovered their true intents. A'Lappe also said that her tests indicated a high degree of skill and strong leadership abilities, which I believed would become evident in her new position as captain of the *MIZBAGONA*.

After dinner we continued our conversation while sipping some wine from the collection I acquired as part of my purchase of the Galetils estate. Toward the end of the evening I said, "I have one request before we adjourn for the evening. I would like very much for A'Lappe and Kerabac to sing us a song."

The two of them looked at each other and A'Lappe said with a wicked grin, "On one condition; we sing a Bandarian drinking song and at the end of each verse everyone must drink a shot of Bandarian brandy!"

Kerabac laughed and the rest of us just looked at each other, unsure of what this meant.

Kerabac said, "Come on, don't be chicken. Bandarian brandy won't give you a hangover. This brandy is known for that particular benefit.

"I'm in!" said Marranalis slapping his hand on the table.

"Oh, what the hell," said Stonbersa. "Let's give it a go."

"Okay," I said.   "Piesew, find us some Bandarian brandy, please."

True to Kerabac's claim, I didn't have a hangover the next morning; but I also didn't remember any of the singing, drinking, or even going to bed that night – though I did have a strange tune running through my head as I showered and dressed. I wondered if I had gone to see Kala before going to bed, but I honestly could not recall anything after my first sip of brandy.

When I arrived on the bridge, everyone from the night before was present and looking well rested. I was glad to see that, as I feared maybe one or two might have some measure of hangover in spite of Kerabac's assurance that we wouldn't.

"Marranalis, what's the status of your men?" I asked.

"They're in full gear and standing by in the hangar. We can have them onboard and deployed in the patrol ships in less than two minutes, if needed."

"Go ahead and get them aboard ground transports. Have the rest of our ships deploy to staging areas over their targets; but they are not to take any action until we give word. If the Brotherhood turns down this chance to surrender, I want the attack to begin almost the instance they say NO. We will alert you from here. Get your ground troops to the surface and stage at your respective targets. You have about an hour and a half before we make contact.

"Commodore," I said turning to Stonbersa, "What's the status of the Mirage Fighters?"

"I sent them out on patrol earlier. Just before we contact the Brotherhood I will issue orders to cloak and report to their attack positions."

"Good. Captain Kerabac and Captain Felenna, we have crews assembled and aboard the corvettes. Kerabac, you will captain the *RUNANA*, and Felenna, you will captain your own ship, the *MIZBAGONA*. The *RUNANA* will cover the southern polar region and the *MIZBAGONA* will cover the northern polar region. Your orders are to destroy any Brotherhood ships that try to leave the surface. You will remain cloaked during your operations. Remember, your ships do not have RMFF shields, so you are vulnerable to enemy fire. If you don't have any questions, I suggest you get underway."

After the crews departed, the *NEW ORLEANS* grew strangely quiet. This large, private space yacht was capable of housing several thousand people. However, the absence of my security forces, all of which were deployed for the anticipated final conflict at Alle Bamma, meant only a few hundred service staff and skeleton crewmen were left onboard; and on a craft as large as the *NEW ORLEANS*, a staff of 300 made this enormous yacht feel like a derelict ghost ship. But even with the entire security contingent deployed, the ship was quite safe. The RMFF shields and the cloaking system made the *NEW ORLEANS* impervious.

As the hour and a half mark approached, Stonbersa turned to me and said, "Tibby, I think you should be the one to announce terms of surrender to the Brotherhood. It's through your plans and actions that we have them contained as we do; and it's only right that you be the one to make contact."

I nodded; but before I could respond, he added, "…and I think you should be wearing your vice admiral uniform when you do."

It was and electrifying sensation when he said it; and I didn't realize until that moment just how much hostility and anger I still felt toward the admiral. I knew that Regeny had never really done anything where he believed we were in harm's way, but I was still harboring anger at him for Kala's demise. Sure, it was at his request that we went into a martial arts demonstration that led to her injury. If we hadn't done the demonstration, they could just as easily have administered the same fatal toxin by way of a blow gun and dart or a waiter with a piece of broken glass at the banquet table or any one of a number of different means. It was not the admiral's fault, nor the Federation's, nor the military's. It was the fault of evil traitors with greedy, self-serving ambitions to enslave and dominate the galaxy who were to blame; and I needed to let go of my anger toward the admiral and set things right.

I looked at Stonbersa, who stared at me with sadness in his face; and I knew he understood the struggle I was going through. I saw tears in his eyes and I realized how others near me must also have been secretly feeling my pain through this ordeal.

I nodded to Stonbersa again and said, "I'll be right back."

I thought I would never wear the vice admiral uniform again. I never wanted it to begin with and I think I had been feeling growing resentment about it all along, even if it was only honorary. When Kala was struck down, that resentment grew into a tidal wave of fury; but now, as I donned the uniform and prepared to deliver the final blow to the rebels on Alle Bamma, all that anger and resentment melted away. It was the Brotherhood that was causing the pain and suffering; the Brotherhood who was rising up in violent attempts to destroy the Federation and steal the solbidyum for selfish purposes; and it was the Brotherhood that struck down Kala.

I felt a sense of strength and purpose as I adjusted the uniform and looked at myself in the mirror. I looked at the image and saw a man who held in his hands thousands of lives – the lives of his crew; the lives of hundreds, maybe thousands of Brotherhood members; and the lives of the gentle natives of Sweet Home, the *children of Thumumba*. I smiled a crooked smile, saluted myself using the old Earth style salute and said, "It's time to kick some ass."

Then I made an *about face* and headed to the bridge.

When I entered the bridge, all eyes turned toward me. Stonbersa stood there with a beaming smile on his face. Verona, who sat at the communication station, and A'Lappe, who acted as navigator and pilot in Kerabac's absence, and two other officers on the bridge all applauded.

"All right, let's gets this show on the road. Open a communication link on all channels." I saw Verona make some adjustments on the console in front of her as the communication vid screen activated.

"Attention, members of the Brotherhood on planet Alle Bamma, this is First Citizen and acting Vice Admiral Thibodaux James Renwalt of the Federation. I offer you one last chance to surrender. All bases that wish to surrender must lay down arms and shut down all ships and power sources. Remove your camouflage netting, immediately release all slaves that you may be holding, and assemble in the center of your compound to await troopers who will accept your surrender. I repeat, all bases that wish to surrender must lay down arms and shut down all ships and power sources. Remove your camouflage netting, release all slaves, and assemble in the center of your compound to await troopers who will accept your surrender. Failure to so will result in the destruction of your ships and bases and, ultimately, in the deaths of many of your members. Those who surrender, depending on circumstances, may be eligible for amnesty from the Federation. Those who do not surrender, but are captured and found to be soldiers and officers of the Federation military will be prosecuted to the fullest extent of Federation law."

I had barely finished the message when the vid screen lit up and a gray-haired man of about 60 years appeared on the screen. "You want us? Come and get us, if you think you can. Just because you caught us off guard the first time doesn't mean you will be so lucky this time," and then the screen went blank.

"Tibby," said A'Lappe, "I'm getting readings from the surface of three compounds withdrawing their netting. It looks like they're following your instructions for surrender, but I don't see indications from any of the others."

"I'm now getting readings of three ships taking off from the polar region where many of the escaping ships headed after our raid. It looks like two patrol ships and one corvette similar to the *RUNANA*. What do you want us to do?"

"Nothing," I said. "Felenna is there in a cloaked ship. She'll handle it."

"Tibby," Stonbersa said, "these are people Felenna lived and worked with for the past several years. You don't really think she will fire on them, do you?"

Just then from a point in space where nothing appeared to be, several laser weapons and torpedoes flashed across the blackness. The two patrol ships vanished in nearly simultaneous explosions, leaving only the corvette. Captain Felenna's image then appeared on our vid screen as she broadcasted on all channels, "This is Captain Felenna of the *MIZBAGONA*, now in service to First Citizen and acting Vice Admiral Thibodaux James Renwalt of the Federation. I advise all ships fleeing Alle Bamma to stop now and comply with Vice Admiral Renwalt's terms. Surrender or be destroyed. You have ten seconds to comply."

I needed only to look at Stonbersa; there was our answer.

At the nine second mark the fleeing ship suddenly came to a halt and the face of the gray-haired man appeared once more on the screen. "We surrender."

The screen split to show both Captain Felenna and the gray-haired man. "Vice Admiral Tibby, I turn the prisoners over to you."

"What is your name," I asked the gray-haired man.

"Captain Theberas," he said.

"Captain Theberas, I want you to land your ship back at the base from which you just fled. You and all your crew will then disembark and gather in a group about 50 meters away from the ship. Anyone found on the ship once we take possession of it will be shot and killed. Is that understood?"

"Yes," he replied.

"Leave *ALL* your weapons on the ship. Take nothing with you. Wait at the gathering point until my troopers come to you. Do not attempt to escape or you will be killed."

"Tibby," said Verona, "I'm getting reports from all our patrol ships of surrenders that are underway at the Brotherhood bases. We're going to be crowded if we bring them all here."

"You have a point. Have each team evaluate the size of the prison cells on each base and see if we can get all the prisoners collected and imprisoned in one place.

"On second thought, I want all the officers brought to the *NEW ORLEANS* and the troops secured on the planet in the slave pens. Any functioning ships are to be flown off world and held in an adjacent orbit. Should the Brotherhood members change their minds and attempt a breakout, they will have nowhere to go.

"Have one of our cargo holds prepared as a prison for the officers. It is to remain heavily guarded and under constant visual and audible observation via vid monitors until we can transfer them to the *URANGA*, when it arrives. Also, contact Admiral Regeny and let him know that we have taken control of Alle Bamma and have secured several hundred prisoners so he can make similar preparations. Find out when they will be arriving."

"Yes, sir," said Verona.

"And now if no one has anything else for me, I'm going to get out of this outfit and see Kala."

When I got to the room where Kala lay in stasis, I found Piesew sitting there alone with her, unaware that I had entered. He was gaily chatting away with her as he sat casually in a rather comfortable easy chair with his legs crossed, sipping on a cup of tea.

I was struck by the informality of his demeanor – something totally out of form for him normally; yet in this situation, it seemed somehow perfect. When he finally saw me, he rose immediately from his chair and said, "First Citizen Tibby, I will leave you and First Citizen Kalana alone. I will be outside when you leave."

"It's alright, Piesew. I'll only be staying a moment. I just wanted to tell Kala that we have defeated the Brotherhood; and first thing in the morning we will return to the surface to finish gathering the eggs necessary for her treatment. We should have them in just a few days," I said as I gazed at Kala through the encasement.

"That is indeed great news, Tibby. I'm sure First Citizen Kalana is most pleased."

After a short visit I took a quick swim in the pool to undo some of the tension that had built up in my body over the past few days; but it was not the same as swimming with Kala and I ended my swim sooner than I normally would have.

The patrol ships started arriving about an hour later to transfer officers of the Brotherhood into the vaulted cargo hold that was prepared as their confinement. The hold was equipped with a large hatch that accessed space and a double airlock within the ship that served as a guard station for the hold area and allowed another set of guards to remain posted outside the airlock in the connecting corridor. The cargo hatch also represented a significant and ever-present threat to the prisoners that told them any attempts to escape and take control of the *NEW ORLEANS* would be resolved by simply opening the cargo hatch and allowing them to float off into space. As it was, most of them had simply given up. They were a pretty broken bunch by the time they were herded into the hold. They seemed to be expecting conditions equivalent to their own treatment of prisoners; and the relief was visible on their faces when they saw the bunks, toilet and food synthesizer that were set up within the space.

Reports from the planet indicated that it took two camps to hold all the non-officer prisoners. They, too, were a pretty docile bunch that put up no resistance, especially after it was explained that their stay on the planet would be at most a few days. All in all, we had taken over a thousand prisoners. We had also gained five fully functional corvettes, 17 patrol ships and two small cargo ships that were loaded to the hilt with processed and packaged God's Sweat. We decided to dispose of the drugs by ejecting the packaged cargo into the local star. The freighters would be sent back to my estate for repurposing. Four of the corvettes, all under the command of Captain Felenna, would remain at Alle Bamma to protect the planet and its people. The other ships would be filled from the crew of the *NEW ORLEANS*. One of the corvettes was to return to Megelleon with us where it would receive a new crew. On a five-week rotation one of Alle Bamma's contingent of ships would return to Megelleon for crew leave and ship maintenance as the fifth corvette returned to service at Alle Bamma.

As all of these arrangements unfolded, we received word from Admiral Regeny that the *URANGA* was two days out from Alle Bamma and only two Brotherhood ships remaining in the pursuit. The admiral decided to give them one last chance to surrender, which they did. One of the two ships also was a corvette; and the admiral was surprised to see the level of armament it contained.

On the day following the surrender of the Brotherhood troops, Kerabac, Hotyona and I returned to the surface. I had promised Jnanara I would return once the Brotherhood was defeated. I looked forward to telling her that we had succeeded in freeing the children of Thumumba and capturing the evil ones and that we were proceeding with the restoration of their jungles as promised. I also wanted to formally ask for permission to continue my search for ruguian eggs and hoped that she would allow me to return after unloading all the prisoners to the *URANGA*, which would free up my security teams to assist in the egg hunt and minimize the duration of our stay to a day or two.

We set the ship down in our original landing place and exited the ship with the intent of finding Jnanara and her tribe again; so we were surprised when we opened the hatch to find that hundreds of natives had suddenly appeared from the jungle. Not one of them were visible when we landed; but seconds later the ship was surrounded by them. As we stepped out, they began waving their arms and making a sort of cheering noise that emanated from their throats. The sound of their collective voices reminded me of the call made by creatures on Earth we call *howler monkeys*. From the rear of their ranks I could see a small entourage of natives preceding Jnanara's arrival. This time she wore a lei made of red flowers. As she moved through the crowd, the natives around her bowed their heads in her direction. When she reached the place where we stood, she stopped and the cheering ceased all at once. She smiled; and I sensed she was waiting for a formal greeting.

"Greetings, woman who speak for children of Thumumba," I said as I bowed in her direction.

"Greetings, man who speak for Thumumba," she said and bowed her head momentarily.

"I return as you ask. Children of Thumumba again free. In days all evil men gone from Sweet Home. After many days all ugly villages gone and Thumumba's jungle again clean and new, like evil men never here. I bring many friends in days to take away all possessions and signs of evil men."

As I finished saying this, three peals of thunder filled the air and all the natives bowed down in a low murmur of prayer.

"Man who speak for Thumumba speak true," said Jnanara.

I proceeded to explain to Jnanara that there will be periodic short visits from small groups who would be allowed to come only with my permission and that these groups would study the plants and animals of Sweet Home and search for medicine to help other good men.

"I now keep houses in sky where friends live and watch over Sweet Home, so evil men not come again to take sacred plant and bind children of Thumumba. Friends stay in sky houses and watch from above, not come down or walk on Sweet Home unless evil men come."

Again came three peals of thunder and again Jnanara said, "Man who speak for Thumumba speak true. Children of Thumumba will welcome friends who seek medicine and will protect from Slow Mover and other dangers on Sweet Home."

Then she turned around and nodded to the four men waiting behind her. Each approached me carrying nutshell bowls covered with large I'aban leaves, which they set on the ground before me. I felt compelled to kneel in front of the bowls; and when they removed the leaves, my eyes filled with tears of joy. Each bowl was filled with ruguian eggs, more than enough to supply the anti-toxin needed for Kala's recovery. I was speechless and in complete awe of the natives' kindness and hard work. Tears ran down my face uncontrollably as I looked up and smiled at Jnanara. I would be forever grateful for the natives' gift.

"Man who speak for Thumumba, this gift from Thumumba. Children of Thumumba hear call and gather eggs as Thumumba say. Take to strange little medicine man in sky house. Make medicine to fix woman who sleeps. When she again whole, come back, you and woman. No go away from Sweet Home until you come back, you and woman. Thumumba say you must come back together."

Then she kissed all three of us on the cheek and said, "You three now children of Thumumba. You now in our hearts and welcome here always."

Then the cheering renewed and we were suddenly besieged by hundreds of natives, these mysterious children of Thumumba, who streamed toward us with outstretched arms. Once they touched all three of us, they vanished, one by one, quickly and quietly into the jungle, leaving us alone and in silence with four bowls filled with ruguian eggs.

"Tibby, I don't know if I believe what just happened," Hotyona said. "How did they know we were coming? How did they know Kala was the one who was sick? You never told them it was a woman. And how did they know of A'Lappe and that he would make the anti-toxin? I mean, they could have figured out that we needed more ruguian eggs; they had been watching us collect them; but beyond that, I don't understand how they knew any of this. Up until now I thought that the dreams of Thumumba were the result of hallucinations caused by the plant that God's Sweat is made from, but that would not account for this. I'm at a loss to figure it out."

"Well don't worry," I said, "you're going to have plenty of time to figure it out. I'm putting you in charge of planetary flora and fauna studies here. Any scientific teams coming to Alle Bamma will have to get your approval and I expect you to participate in their expeditions."

"Wow, I don't know what to say... I mean, I want the job... but what about Cantolla? I'm part of her staff!"

"Let me worry about Cantolla. She works for me," I said. "It may cost me a fortune, but I'm sure I can come up with something that will make her happy."

When we returned to the *NEW ORLEANS*, A'Lappe was waiting at the hangar.

"We've been able to extract some information from the computers recovered from the Brotherhood's bases and from the prisoners. The entire operation on

Alle Bamma was run by a man called Lendera. Unfortunately for us, he left the planet just days before we arrived to set up another drug production operation somewhere a few light years from here. He's not expected to return here for several years, if ever."

"Lendera," Kerabac exclaimed with disgust. "It figures it would be him.

"You know him?" I asked.

"Hell yes, I know him. He was one of the botanists on the team when I was here 15 years ago. He's a real asshole, but a very intelligent man. He had only total disrespect for everyone and everything; and he acted like he was in charge of the expedition. The bastard actually suggested one day that we should shoot the natives for sport, as he didn't consider them to be anything more than just dumb animals."

"Do you know anything about him that would help us find or capture him?"

"Unfortunately, no. I felt like I knew way more about him than I wanted to as it was."

"I want round-the-clock research conducted on the man until we find every shred of information there is to be found about his origins, his associates and his history. This information is to be provided to the FSO as we find it; and they are to assemble a task force to uncover more information in the field. It may take years to find him, but that isn't a reason to not begin searching now."

"A'Lappe, here. Please get these to the lab immediately." I handed him the stasis container that held the ruguian eggs."

"You've got them already? But how? You were gone only a little over an hour."

"That, my friend, is something we will discuss over dinner. It's a fantastic tale; and it will be easier to tell everyone once at a staff dinner. Now get to it. Kala's been in stasis far longer than I like already.

The production of the anti-toxin took several hours; but at last, A'Lappe was satisfied that it had been properly produced and that its potency would be effective in halting the progression of the toxin as soon as Kala was brought out of stasis.

I reluctantly followed A'Lappe's request and waited outside the recovery room where Kala was taken to bring her out of stasis. Once the stasis fluids were removed from her lungs and she was breathing again, I was allowed to be by her side. She was still unconscious and the anti-toxin had not yet been administered; so it was all I could do to contain my anxiety. The moment I entered the room, I was struck again by her beauty, as I was every time I saw her. The month and a half of suspended animation had not altered one atom of her precious being; she looked exactly as she did when they placed her in stasis. A'Lappe and a medic moved quickly to insert the IV and attach electrodes to her head and body at various locations. As each electrode was attached, readings began to appear on the vid screen by her bed.

"We're just in time," said A'Lappe. "And it's good they got her into stasis so quickly after the attack. There is no indication of permanent damage to any organs; and once the anti-toxin goes to work, she should make a full recovery...maybe in a few days."

"How long will it be before she regains consciousness?" I asked.

"I'm not sure. I think it depends on how long the poisons have been in her system and how much damage has been done. In Kalana's case, only a few hours elapsed before the medics induced stasis. The reports I've read indicate that patients have been successfully revived up to two days after being poisoned; but there is no documentation as to how long it was before subjects regained consciousness."

A'Lappe and I watched the vid screen in silence. Only seconds passed before I noticed measurable changes in Kala's vital signs.

"This is good. The anti-toxin is working," said A'Lappe. "See here? You can see her pulse is picking up and there is a slight increase in her blood pressure and blood oxygen level. I will venture a guess and say that she'll be awake in a few hours, if she continues to improve at this rate."

A tremendous wave of relief swept over me. Up until this moment I had been harboring the fear that I might lose Kala; and the thought of it had become nearly unbearable. In a way, I was glad for all the troubles created by the Brotherhood over the past several days because it detracted from these fears.

I stayed at her bedside and held her hand as I thought of our time together so far – like the first time I saw her in the hangar on the *DUSTEN* and how she walked with an air of grace and authority; and how that same day she stripped down and stepped into the shower beside me and how I stumbled over my own confusion from her actions at the time, because I was unaware that nudity taboos didn't exist in most of the Federation. I thought of our swims together, our dinner conversations, falling asleep in front of the fireplace, and the sweet love she gave me at the end of every day.

I thought, too, about Kala's sister, Lunnie. Lunnie brought Kala and me together, breaking down our walls with her constant teasing and joking. I thought about the day I kissed Kala for the first time and made love to her for hours. I thought about our journey on the *TRITYTE*, and about receiving honors before the Senate and the Military High Command. My heart ached as I recalled the battle to free the *DUSTEN* and Lunnie's tragic death at the hands of the maniacal traitor, Lexmal. It was Kala who saved me. Really, it was Kala who saved the entire Federation by her heroic actions. I thought of the death of Captain Maxette, Reidecor, and the thousands of others who fell in the battles that ensued; but every memory came full circle to Kala, our life together, and our future together.

At some point I must have drifted off to sleep, because I found myself standing in the jungle on the I'aban tree platform where I first met Jnanara. Kala stood at my side and held my hand. We were nude, except for red floral leis around our necks. Before us stood Thumumba, who smiled upon us as he placed his hands on our heads and said, "My children."

Then Kala squeezed my hand. As she squeezed my hand in the dream, I woke to find that she really was squeezing my hand! I gazed into her face and whispered her name; and my heart quickened when I saw those beautiful eyes open slowly to look at me. She tried to speak, but only a dry rattled sound came from her throat. She tried again; I could just barely make out "water." Quickly I reached for the container of water by her bed and held it to her lips. She slowly drank from the nub-like attachment and then laid her head back on the pillow. I waited silently as she gathered the strength to speak; and I did my best to control my tears as we stared into each other's eyes.

Finally she smiled and said, "You need a haircut and a shave. How long have I been asleep?"

"About six weeks," I said.

Shock and confusion spread across her face. "Six weeks?!" she exclaimed in a weak voice. "The last thing I remember was putting on a demonstration for the admiral. What happened?"

"The two men we fought in the demonstration were Brotherhood members who had killed and replaced the troopers originally assigned to the demonstration. After we defeated them and turned our backs to return to the banquet table, they attacked with knifes that were laced with a rare toxin that first renders the victim unconscious and then slowly shuts down all body functions. For some reason my Earth DNA makes me immune to this toxin; but you slipped into a coma almost immediately. A'Lappe was able to identify the poison quickly; but we had to travel several weeks to obtain the material to produce the anti-toxin. In the meantime, you were placed in stasis so no further damage would occur to your body."

"So I take it you were able to make the anti-toxin," said Kala, as she slowly reached for the water again. I picked it up and handed it to her.

"Yes," I said.

"I hope it wasn't too difficult. How has everything else been going?"

"Nothing unusual… just typical daily events," I said, still trying to keep the tears of joy from welling in my eyes.

Kala nearly choked on her water and said with a grin, "That bad, huh? How many battles have you fought and won? That reminds me – what happened with the trap at Banur? Did the Brotherhood fall for it?"

"Brotherhood showed up in force with a small fleet of ships; but the Federation was ready and waiting. The admiral destroyed most of them right then and there," I said.

"The Federation destroyed them? Do I detect by your comment that you weren't there?"

"She always was a smart lady," said a voice coming from the doorway. I turned to see Admiral Regeny standing just inside the entry with Commodore Stonbersa.

"Admiral, so good to see you; but where was Tibby, if not at the battle?"

"Tibby was on his way here to conduct an egg hunt," replied the admiral with a grin.

"Egg hunt? Here? Where is here? Where are we?"

"You're at the planet Alle Bamma," said the admiral. "The poison that infected you comes from this a non-aligned world; and as soon as Tibby found out that the source of the anti-toxin could also be found here and *only* here, he left Plosaxen as fast as he could to get you the cure."

"What about the Brotherhood and the trap at Banur? If the *NEW ORLEANS* came straight here, you couldn't have been there to deploy the trap."

The admiral laughed, "Oh, we were there. Tibby threw us off the ship when I threatened to take it away from him for use as our command post during the Banur operation. He wasn't about to let anything delay his mission to get the ingredients for the anti-toxin you needed. I have to tell you, there were some tense moments; but Tibby didn't relent and I'm glad he didn't. He made me see the truth and put my actions into perspective – and I'm grateful for that."

"Wait a minute," Kala said while trying to prop herself up on her elbows, "you're telling me that you tried to commandeer the *NEW ORLEANS* and that Tibby threw you off the ship and came here instead of staying to help you trap the Brotherhood at Banur? Then you executed the trap anyway, while Tibby was on his way here?"

"That's right," replied the admiral.

Kala opened her mouth to say something else, when Kerabac walked in and said to Commodore Stonbersa, "Excuse me, Commodore, but there's a call coming in for you from the *MIZBAGONA*." Before leaving, Kerabac threw a smile in Kala's direction and said "Welcome back, Kalana."

"Thank you, Captain," said Stonbersa. He then quickly took leave of Kala and headed off toward the bridge.

"*Commodore* Stonbersa?   *Captain* Kerabac?" asked Kala wide-eyed? "What have I missed?"

"Not much, really," I said.

"Ha," blurted the admiral. "Not much? He has only expanded his personal fleet by five corvettes, ten Mirage Fighters, two freighters and who knows how may patrol ships. He's managed to capture a planet full of Brotherhood rebels, destroy their bases and put a huge dent in the God's Sweat drug trade in the process of freeing thousands of native slaves on Alle Bamma. While he did all of this, he managed to find the ruguian eggs necessary to produce the anti-toxin that saved your life. In the end, it seems he needed to promote some officers to handle all these ships he kept acquiring from the Brotherhood."

Kala started to laugh. "I knew it! Tib's typical day is finding the enemy in the morning, defeating him in the afternoon and going dancing in the evening."

All the while that Kala conversed with her visitors about the events of the past several weeks, I watched her life signs on the vid monitor and was pleased to see them continuing to climb closer and closer to the normal range.

A'Lappe entered the room and greeted Kala. He looked over the monitor readings and said, "It would seem the antidote is working properly, Kalana. All body functions are returning to normal. I think by tomorrow you will be able to return to your suite and continue your recovery in more comfortable surroundings; and perhaps soon after you can begin moving about the ship."

To everyone's delight, Kala's recovery was much faster than predicted and by the end of the next day she appeared to be fully recovered. That evening we had a quiet dinner alone in our suite and I filled her in on all the details of the events that had occurred while she was in stasis.   It was when I began to tell her about Thumumba that she stopped me.

"Tib, I had dreams of Thumumba. I don't know when, exactly. I know it was after I was poisoned, but I don't know if the dreams occurred before or after I was placed in stasis. I remember the two of us standing before him in the trees. He called us his children."

I was shocked when she said this, as I had not yet related to her my own dream of this event. When I told her that I had dreamt the same dream, she asked, "What do you think it means?"

"I think it means that it's time to make one more trip to the surface before we leave," I said.

We were still discussing the events that had unfolded during Kala's long sleep, when Kala's communicator signaled that someone was trying to reach her.

"Kala here," she said.

The call was from one of her personal staff who first inquired about her condition and then said that an invitation was sent from the *URANGA* by Admiral Regeny that requested our presence at a victory dinner celebration the next evening.   The *URANGA* was scheduled for departure the following day. The admiral and his crew now had the arduous task of interrogating each prisoner while transporting them to a proper prison facility, where several weeks of tribunal and court proceedings would take place.

Kala said she felt up to attending; so we accepted the invitation, but only on the condition that neither of us would be required to put on a martial arts demonstration. Kala's assistant also informed her that the admiral and a team of legal experts had arranged a meeting earlier that same day to discuss some issues that had to be resolved in terms of disposition of the prisoners. Since Kala and I were scheduled to be at the celebration on the *URANGA* that evening, we agreed to go to the *URANGA* early for the meeting.

The *NEW ORLEANS* was a large ship – the largest privately owned yacht in the galaxy – but compared to a star ship it was like a baby. The *NEW ORLEANS* could easily accommodate a few thousand people, though I had so far staffed it with a considerably smaller crew, leaving many cabins and suites unused. By comparison, more than 10,000 people could easily be accommodated in a star ship; and every one of them would be surrounded with luxury and style. Star ships were so large and their journeys so vast that, in addition to serving as military platforms, they also served as mobile government offices that hosted diplomats, ambassadors, senators and other government officials during transit between planets. Scores of civilians served aboard as support personnel; and various stores, shops, restaurants and clubs were found in the common areas throughout the ship.

It was on one such star ship that I lived when I first arrived in the Federation territories – the magnificent *DUSTEN*. Boarding the *URANGA* brought back all the awe and wonder of that first experience on the *DUSTEN*. We were transported to the hangar of the *URANGA* on a luxurious transport craft, where we were greeted by the Federation's Color Guard and armed troopers who lined the pathway from the transport to the

ship's interior. Kala and I were both dressed formally –
Kala in her lieutenant commander uniform and me in
my honorary vice admiral uniform. Commander
Stonbersa, Captain Kerabac and Captain Felenna were
present in their respective non-military uniforms of the
style and cut of my staff. Lieutenant Marranalis rounded
out the party and was dressed in his formal Federation
military attire. Even though we would only be on the
ship a few hours, we were still assigned a large suite
with rooms enough for all of us and a full staff to see to
our needs as long as we were aboard the *URANGA*.

Since Kala and Felenna didn't have an
opportunity to meet prior to departing for the *URANGA*,
I left them to become acquainted while we were on the
transport. Kala had heard of Felenna's participation in
the battle with the Brotherhood and was eager to talk to
her. Likewise, Felenna was excited to meet Kala and
was in total awe of her, as both Kala and I were rapidly
become legend throughout the galaxy. Their
conversation continued even after our arrival; and I
watched in amusement throughout the day as Felenna
was mesmerized by Kala's every word.

The time arrived for the meeting with the
admiral, the High Command, and the Federation legal
team. I was under impression that only Kala and I were
to be involved in the discussion from my side of the
issue, so I was a bit taken aback when Kala and I entered
the large conference room and saw a number of people
already seated on our side the table.

"Who are these people?" I asked Kala.

"This is our legal team," she said.

"We have a legal team?"

"Of course we do, silly. With all your wealth, property and vast number of employees you don't think a legal team is necessary?"

"To be honest, I hadn't given it any thought; but now that you mention it, I guess it is."

"Let us begin," said Admiral Regeny.

After making the necessary introductions, the admiral came directly to the purpose of the meeting. "Disposition of the prisoners is not going to be easy or straightforward. The undisputed actions relate first to prisoners who were serving in the Federation military during their membership with the Brotherhood. Their membership and rebellious actions on behalf of the Brotherhood, up to and including the armed conflicts against the Federation, constitute treason, for which they will be tried in a military tribunal. It is also generally agreed that the civilian Brotherhood prisoners who participated in the attempt to steal the solbidyum at Banur on Plosaxen should be treated as enemy combatants and tried accordingly in a Federation court.

"The difficulties emerge when determining the course of action against civilian Brotherhood members not involved in the Banur conflict or any other conflict against the Federation. This category of prisoners is comprised of those involved in the drug production and transport operations at Alle Bamma. Since Alle Bamma is a non-aligned world which, by definition, means actions here do not fall under Federation jurisdiction, neither the military or civilian courts have recourse against these individuals. According to treaties with most of the planets throughout the galaxy, such individuals can only be charged with crimes committed on the planet that are defined by its laws. In this case, the problem hinges on the fact that Alle Bamma has no known formal set of laws. There are tribal edicts and decrees that are understood in their verbal traditions and laws; but no one is sure what they are or whether they apply globally to all tribes.

"Do we turn over those prisoners who don't fall under Federation jurisdiction to the natives of Alle Bamma, or should they simply be released? This seems to be the real issue."

This debate began in earnest and it wasn't long before everyone in the meeting recognized that the solution was not going to come about that day. In late afternoon it was decided that the *URANGA*'s departure would be delayed until the legal team had an opportunity to visit the planet and speak with tribal leaders. Kala and I were asked to go with them the next day to seek out Jnanara and resolve the issue.

As the meeting broke up for the day and we prepared to leave, Kala asked me, "What will happen to Felenna after all this, since was a Brotherhood member?"

"I don't think a lot *can* happen to her," I said. "She was not a member of the allied forces, so the military has no jurisdiction over her. She was not a part of the battle at Banur, so she cannot be tried in a civilian Federation court as an enemy combatant. Beyond that, she fought against the Brotherhood here and played a major role in their defeat. Unless the natives of Alle Bamma feel she needs to be punished – and I don't see that happening – she will be free."

The victory celebration that night was larger than I anticipated. The event took place in the largest social hall on the *URANGA* and thousands were in attendance. Giant vid screens were located throughout the hall to afford every guest a close-up view of the central tables that were prepared for the guests of honor. Admiral Regeny, Captain Xantaee of the *URANGA* and several other officers who played significant roles in the battle at Banur were all seated at the host's table. Nearby at the main table sat Commodore Stonbersa, Captain Kerabac, Captain Felenna, Lieutenant Commander Kalana, Lieutenant Marranalis and I. Surrounding the main table were additional tables that seated officers of the ships that had served in the battle of Banur and officers of my own security force, and another where A'Lappe, Cantolla and Hotyona sat with other members of the science team. Beyond that were tables filled with senators, ambassadors and diplomats; and beyond them the other crew members and passengers of the *URANGA*. Captain Xantaee acted as host of the event.

"Good evening, everyone, and welcome to all. This evening we are gathered to celebrate the stunning victory over the Brotherhood that has unfolded in the past few days. The confrontation at Banur was the largest attack by the Brotherhood to date. The Federation's superior strength and intelligence were demonstrated when the Brotherhood walked into a trap designed to draw in the local Brotherhood forces; and though they came with a sizeable fleet, they lost almost all of their ships in the conflict, the remainder of which retreated here to Alle Bamma. Under the orders of Admiral Regeny the *URANGA* pursued. Using the newly designed Mirage Fighters, loaned to the Federation by Vice Admiral and First Citizen Thibodaux James Renwalt, the Federation military forces were able to make daily raids on these fleeing Brotherhood ships, picking them off one at a time, until the last of their ships surrendered just two days ago. Little did we know during this pursuit what was waiting for us here at Alle Bamma. I will leave the rest of the story to Admiral Regeny."

Captain Xantaee took his seat and Admiral Regeny stood to speak.

"Forgive me, if I go back a bit further than the battle at Banur; but in order for the true story to be told, it is necessary. As many of you may know, the High Command operated for a period of time from First Citizen Vice Admiral Thibodaux James Renwalt's yacht, the *NEW ORLEANS* – by his invitation, I might add. The truth of the matter is that, had we not been there under his protection, we most likely would have perished.

"By now many of you know that the Federation military has recently begun installing new 10X fusion reactors, Reverse Magnetic Force Fields and cloaking devices on our star ships and frigates. The cloaking devices are also being installed on all our other ships that are not large enough to house the 10X reactors that are needed for the RMFF shields. The credit for the development and availability of these devices belongs to two individuals; one is First Citizen and Vice Admiral Thibodaux James Renwalt and the other in an enigmatic individual we know as A'Lappe." The admiral nodded toward A'Lappe. Vice Admiral Tibby's ship, the *NEW ORLEANS,* was the first ship to utilize this new technology, which played a large part in the successful recovery of the *DUSTEN* and the destruction of the Brotherhood base on Megelleon, not to mention the delivery of solbidyum to some of the first worlds to commission their solbidyum reactors. Vice Admiral Tibby's plans, advice and assistance have played a huge role in the successes achieved by the Federation when

battling the threat of the Brotherhood. In all fairness to
First Citizen Tibby and his crew, we may very well have
fallen to the Brotherhood by now, had it not been for
him. I'm sorry to say that although the Federation has
bestowed on First Citizen Tibby the greatest wealth and
highest honors possible, we have not treated him as
respectfully in other regards – at least I haven't, and for
that I wish to apologize.

When First Citizen Tibby first appeared here in
the Federation, I was wowed by his hand-to-hand combat
skills and his keen sense of knowledge for military
tactics. I envisioned a military made up of such
warriors; and soon, through a bit of trickery, I got him to
promise training for my troopers...and *train* he did! Not
only did he train my troopers, but he trained his own as
well, quickly and efficiently enough so that when the
Brotherhood attacked a few weeks later, Tibby and the
recruits *that were still in the middle of training* were able
to take the *DUSTEN* back from the rebels.

"By that point the High Command had moved
aboard Tibby's ship, the *NEW ORLEANS*; but instead of
treating Tibby's offer to set up a safe temporary mobile
command center with the graciousness of a guest, I let
arrogance get the best of me and instead saw the *NEW
ORLEANS* as a war vessel of the Federation military
with myself as its commanding officer. Oh, I was
willing to let Tibby call the shots; after all, he was
making me and the Federation military look quite good.
Tibby has a way of making the exceedingly difficult look
easy. To my shame, I paraded Tibby and his team
around, showing them off as though they were a triumph
for the Federation. I was wrong to do so. I never took
into account the wishes or wellbeing of Tibby and his
compatriots. That foolishness nearly cost the lives of
both First Citizen Tibby and First Citizen Kalana. I

deeply regret my thoughtless actions now, but even then I didn't fully accept responsibility for my self-serving decisions. I continued my foolishness even after First Citizen Kala was wounded and clinging to life in stasis. It was when I insisted that I was going to take the *NEW ORLEANS* from Tibby to use as my command ship for the battle at Banur, instead of supporting Tibby in his decision to come here to Alle Bamma to get the materials necessary to make the anti-toxin for Kalana, that Tibby set me straight on the matter. I'm glad he did. Even today I am horribly ashamed of my actions and my behavior. Never has anyone performed as great a service to the Federation as Tibby and his team; and I was wrong to take advantage of him and his team as I did."

The admiral's heartfelt and candid speech roused the crowd into a roar of applause and cheers that I thought would never end. He waited patiently until the din subsided before he continued.

"It was First Citizen Tibby's idea to set the trap at Banur for the Brotherhood, a trap that worked remarkably well. By our count the Brotherhood arrived at Banur with five corvettes, one frigate and 29 patrol ships. We met them with two cloaked star ships, three cloaked frigates, hundreds of cloaked patrol ships independent of the many hundreds already on the star ships, and ten cloaked Mirage Fighters. We took nearly a hundred prisoners and killed most of the other enemy contingent in battle. We out gunned them by at least 100 to one.

"Tibby, on the other hand, arrived at Alle Bamma with his yacht, the *NEW ORLEANS*, a few patrol ships, ten Mirage Fighters and a few hundred of his security forces. He arrived to find that Alle Bamma had been occupied by 15 Brotherhood bases, nearly a dozen heavily armed corvettes, over a hundred patrol ships, and thousands of ground defenses and troops. Tibby and his crew captured the entire planet; set free thousands of natives held in slavery; and managed to capture – not destroy – but *capture* many of the enemy ships, which he is now using to guard the planet. He also managed to capture over a thousand enemy Brotherhood troops and officers. With one small ship and a fraction of the forces we had at Banur Tibby accomplished ten times over what we did."

Once again there was a roar of applause and cheers.

"There is one thing more that needs to be mentioned. Part of the Brotherhood's plan was to intercept and/or delay solbidyum deliveries throughout the Federation and use these disturbances as a political tool to claim that the Federation is demonstrating partiality to specific planets and systems and to breed propaganda in an effort to convince the citizens of the Federation territories that we are liars who are using the solbidyum covertly for our own power-hungry purposes. It was Tibby who devised a plan to expedite the delivery of the solbidyum; and though I cannot tell you the details of that plan, I *can* tell you that, as of this moment, over 30 worlds have received their solbidyum deliveries and commissioned their global power distribution systems; and nearly 400 additional deliveries are underway as I speak."

Again came the roar of applause and nearly deafening cheers of surprise and excitement. Then the admiral continued, addressing me directly.

"Tibby, you and your crew deserve a rest; so, barring an all-out war where every federation planet is under attack, I promise you, I will not be calling on you every day for your amazing support and assistance."

There was another round of applause and I decided to use the moment for a speech of my own. I rose from the table during the applause and addressed the admiral.

"Do you mind if I say a few words?"

"No, no, not at all. Please do," he said as he sat down.

"There is a lot of talk about me and what I have done," I began, "and though my team is mentioned when relating events such as those that have recently unfolded, they do not receive the full recognition they deserve.

"The wonders of the RMFF shields that now are begin installed on the Federation star ships and frigates, as well as the unique power sources that are required to maintain them are the direct result of A'Lappe's works and discoveries," I said as I walked to his table and placed my hands on his shoulders. "What has not yet been mentioned about A'Lappe is that he also is the architect of my ship, the *NEW ORLEANS,* which was not designed or built for me, but for Galetils, a man who may in fact have been murdered by the Brotherhood in their attempt to seize the plans for the 10X reactor, the *only* reactor capable of generating enough power to operate an RMFF shielding system. It was also A'Lappe who designed the Mirage Fighters, ships that can fly with more speed and maneuverability than any other ship known in the Federation. While it was Commodore Stonbersa and Captain Kerabac that discovered the cloaking technology we use on the ships, it was also A'Lappe who figured out how to develop versions that could be used on smaller Federation ships and by Federation troopers. I did *not* do these things; many of his inventions had already been developed long before I ever came here.

"The learning headbands that have enabled Federation troopers to develop their martial arts skills lifetimes faster than they would with conventional methods were developed by Cantolla and her team of scientists," I said, as I walked behind her chair and placed my hands on her shoulders. "Without her accomplishments we would never have been able to save the *DUSTEN*, nor would these troopers have survived many of the combat situations we have faced thus far.

"Working together, Cantolla and A'Lappe have also overcome the barriers associated with long distance communication. It will now be possible for star ships and the High Command to communicate instantly, even when light years apart; and while this technology is still in its infancy, it is a giant leap forward in communication and in response times for crisis situations." There was a collective gasp and some applause from the audience at this announcement.

It's because of Lieutenant Marranalis," I said, placing my hands on his shoulders, "that so many Federation troopers have been so finely trained; and if it were mine to give, he would have a rank much higher than Lieutenant. He has led the raids on the Brotherhood camps and trained innumerable Federation troopers and officers, many of whom outranked him. Without his skills, keen military intuition and dedication to the citizens of the Federation, I would not be standing here today."

Cheers of patriotism filled the room before I continued to Kerabac and Stonbersa. "Without Captain Kerabac and Commodore Stonbersa and their extraordinary skills as leaders, pilots, and technical experts, none of this would have happened either. It is because of their exceptional and precise execution that these remarkable ships and inventions we speak of so casually have protected lives, defeated our enemies, and expedited the distribution of solbidyum to the citizens of the Federation. Their work is seldom mentioned and far too often taken for granted."

I gathered my thoughts while the applause again filled the room. My next introduction would require a bit of finesse.

"The battles at Alle Bamma were indeed a great triumph, not only because of the dismantling of an entire planetary Brotherhood base and the deliverance of thousands of natives from slavery, but also because the victory here has put a huge dent in the Brotherhood's production and distribution of the harmful and addictive drug God's Sweat. But the victories at Alle Bamma could not and *would* not have happened – without Captain Felenna," I said as I walked to the chair where she sat, her arm still in a sling from the wound she had received. I paused behind her chair and placed my hand on her good shoulder. "Up until a few days ago Captain Felenna was a member of the Brotherhood."

There were gasps all around the room and a buzz of conversation, but I continued without faltering. "Captain Felenna was never in the Federation military. She was never a traitor to the Federation. She became involved in the Brotherhood without really knowing what they were about; and when she discovered the true despicable nature of this organization, she was trapped

here at Alle Bamma with nowhere to go.   When we
arrived, she immediately took the opportunity to show
where her true allegiance lies. She put herself at great
risk to assist us in stealing two corvettes, the
MIZBAGONA and the *RUNANA*, one of which was the
flagship for the Brotherhood fleet that was stationed
here. Captain Felenna was wounded during that mission;
but even after being injured, she was able to kill the
captain of the *MIZBAGONA* and command a crew of
loyal security forces, who successfully seized the ship
and delivered it to the *NEW ORLEANS*. For her bravery
and actions on behalf of the natives of Alle Bamma, the
members of my crew, and the citizens of the Federation,
I made her captain of the *MIZBAGONA* in my fleet. I
tell you with all honesty and truth of heart that none of
what has been accomplished here at Alle Bamma would
have been possible without her bravery."

I heard the beginning of some nearby applause
and I looked to see Admiral Regeny, who was clapping
as he rose from his chair. Beside him Captain Xantaee
did the same; and suddenly everyone in the hall was on
their feet applauding and cheering for Felenna. Her eyes
welled with tears of joy and pride as I leaned down and
whispered in her ear, "See, I told you that you didn't
have anything to worry about. The Federation is not
about to try or charge a hero of your stature."

"Thank you, Tibby," said Felenna.

When the applause calmed down I continued my
speech. "All of you make me out to be a hero and an
icon of the Federation; but I too have my shortcomings.
I would have left before the battle at Banur, even if I had
known it would have meant the Brotherhood getting
away. There was nothing at Banur to begin with; it was
all a ruse, a trap to pull in the Brotherhood.   If the

Brotherhood had arrived and the Federation ships not been there, the Brotherhood would have gone home empty-handed. If I had stayed the outcome of the battle would not have been different. What *would* have been different was that Kalana, the woman I love, would have been left much longer in stasis, where her life hung in the balance until an antidote to the deadly poison in her body could be found. Kalana was and always will be my top priority, ALWAYS!

"Yes, I fought for the future of the Federation so this alliance can continue to succeed and thrive, safe from the contemptible and violent influences of the Brotherhood and other threats. But I also fought for Kala – for her very life. On the world that I come from there is an old saying; *A man cannot serve two masters.* There has to be one that stands above the rest. I highly prize and value my citizenship in the Federation; but make no mistake about this – I prize and value Kalana more; and given a situation where I must choose, it is Kalana that I will protect and serve first.

"So don't make me out to be more than I am; do not expect more of me than I can do. *These* are your *true* heroes," I said as I swept my arm toward my crew. "Give them their credit and their due." Then I went to my seat and sat down beside Kala, who looked at me with teary eyes and kissed me on the cheek.

There was a moment of silence and then Admiral Regeny got to his feet and said, "We salute you all, true heroes of the Federation." He was joined by Captain Xantaee and followed by everyone in the hall as they rose to their feet. All the military personnel in the room saluted, while the civilians and dignitaries filled the room with reverberating cheers and applause.

The rest of the evening went by quickly. We ate and chatted; and numerous dignitaries came by our table to express their gratitude for our deeds. I looked over at the table where A'Lappe was seated. Several people crowded around him to ask questions about the RMFF shields and cloaking devices. He caught my gaze from the next table, looked at me with a mischievous grin, and blinked his eyes in his odd fashion. Then, true to form, he disappeared from his chair to the amazement of those who had congregated around him.

A few seconds later I heard him whisper, "I'll see you all back at the *NEW ORLEANS*. These events sort of bore me."

I laughed heartily, as I knew without a doubt that he was having the time of his life.

That night when we got back to the *NEW ORLEANS*, we had barely entered the bedroom before Kala pushed me on the bed and pounced on me, kissing me passionately. "You made me so hot when you made that speech tonight that I wanted to tear your clothing off and make love to you right there," she said.

"Well, I'm glad to see none of that ardor has worn off," I grinned, and we began undressing each other and tossing clothing about the room.

I woke up in the morning feeling better than I had in months. I lay there staring at Kala, who appeared to still be asleep; and I tried to grasp fully just how lucky I was to have her – not just her, but everything else. I was the richest man in the universe. I had ships in the sky, estates on the planet, teams of scientists and experts surrounding me, some of the most accomplished and influential people in the Federation as my friends and colleagues, and a galaxy of worlds to explore and help along in their development with the endless wealth at my disposal. But even as I thought of all these wondrous things in my life, I knew none of them held the same meaning for me without Kala in the picture. I got a taste of that fact while Kala was in stasis; and I never wanted to find myself that close to losing her again.

As I lay there on my side, watching her breathe and admiring the way the sheet draped over her body's curves, she spoke with her eyes still closed. "Why are you staring at me?"

"How do you know I'm staring at you?" I said somewhat amazed.

"Ha," she said as she opened her eyes and hit me with her pillow, "I can feel your eyes on me," and she whacked me again with the pillow. I was about to grab her, when suddenly my communicator buzzed. It was Commodore Stonbersa.

"Tibby, I hate to bother you, but the Federation legal team is here and waiting for you to go to Alle Bamma."

"Oh crap, I completely forgot about it. Tell them we'll be there in, five – no – make it ten minutes."

"*We'll* be there?" Kala said.

"Yes, dear. You're coming with me. After all, you *are* a military attaché trained in such diplomatic matters."

"Oh, is that why you keep me around?" she said playfully as we both made our way to the shower.

"That, and so I can stare at your lovely bottom," I replied.

Since the hostilities on the planet were over, I opted for attire that was less military in appearance. I donned a simple pair of slacks made of a durable looking fabric and a short sleeved shirt. The back of the shirt was designed with a thin pocket that covered the entire back area. In the event of rainy weather, which was always likely on Alle Bamma, there was a rain hood and windbreaker that could be pulled from the pouch. Kala took note of my attire and dressed similarly. When we arrived at the transport in the hangar, I sighed, as I saw two dozen troopers and the legal team dressed like they were going to war.

"You're not going to need all that fire power and attire," I said.

"Standard attire for a primitive, non-aligned planet," one of the men said flatly.

I laughed and said, "Okay, let's do this."

We boarded the craft and descended to the planet, landing at the same location where I had landed previously. I was not too surprised when dozens of natives appeared around the ship shortly after setting foot on land. The troopers started to react and I said, "At ease, men. These natives are friendly."

Then I turned and spoke to one of the natives nearest us, "We come to speak to Jnanara."

"We know, man who speak for Thumumba, Jnanara come. See." He pointed toward a narrow clearing in the foliage.

Up until this visit I had always seen Jnanara standing or walking on her own; but today she was being carried in a sedan-like chair. In typical native fashion she was naked, save for a woven headband made of some kind of leather with plant fronds stuck into it; and once again, she wore a lei of red flowers about her neck.

When the sedan chair stopped before us, I bowed my head to her and said, "Greetings, Jnanara, woman who speak for children of Thumumba."

"Greetings, man who speak for Thumumba. Thumumba say you will come this day with men from sky."

"Excuse me, sir," said one of the legal team, who had used the learning headband the night before to learn the language in preparation for the meeting, as had everyone else in our party. "What does she mean, *Man who speak for Thumumba*?

"It's a long story; I don't have time to relate it now," I answered.

"Men from sky come to ask Jnanara, woman who speak for children of Thumumba, names of all crimes committed by evil ones who take sacred plants and bind children. Men from sky also ask punishment for each crime under law of tribes of Sweet Home," I said.

"Only Thumumba say," replied Jnanara.

"Thumumba speak for all people of Sweet Home?" asked the legal representative.

"Yes, will of Thumumba for all people. All children listen to word of Thumumba."

"Well, that makes it simple. All we need to do is talk to this Thumumba person," the aide said in Federation language.

"Thumumba no speak to you," continued Jnanara, somehow gathering from the aide's tone what he had said.

"No? How then we learn wishes and laws of Thumumba?" the aide asked, reverting back to Bammaspeak once more.

"Must speak to man who speak for Thumumba. Thumumba tell him, tell you. Only man who speak for Thumumba speak to Thumumba."

"Well I guess that will work," he said in Federation language; then, correcting himself he asked in Bammaspeak, "Where we find man who speak for Thumumba?"

In unison the natives pointed at me as Jnanara said, "He man who speak for Thumumba. He child of Thumumba. She child of Thumumba, too," she said pointing to Kalana. "Speak to them, hear Thumumba's will. You go now back to house in sky. Come back tomorrow. Man who speak for Thumumba and mate must come now. Thumumba wait."

"But wait – you can't just – First Citizen, what shall we do?"

"Go back to the ship like Jnanara told you and return in the morning. Kala and I will be quite alright, I said laughing.

Suddenly, from out of the foliage the natives produced two more sedan chairs and both Kala and I were instructed to get in. Moments later, we were in a parade procession along a jungle path lined with natives who tossed flowers at us and muttered blessings mingled with Thumumba's name. Finally, we arrived in a large area blanketed by low grasses and surrounded by I'aban trees. The dense foliage high above in the canopy that covered this area almost created a sense that we had walked into nightfall. Vines hanging from the heights were attached to our chairs and we were pulled up into the trees.

"I hope you're not afraid of heights," I said to Kala.

"Not at all," she said. "This is all rather fun and interesting."

When we arrived in the canopy, we were led along a large bough and across several rope bridges to a platform in an area open to the sky above. In the center of the platform was a large nutshell that contained a steadily burning oil flame. Framing the edge of the platform were several smaller bowls also burning oil flames. Jnanara stood in the glow of the central fire, smiling one of the kindest smiles I had ever seen.

As she gazed at us with her unique eyes, she said, "You must take off sky men skins."

"I'm hoping she means our clothing," said Kala, as she began to undress. "I'm rather attached to my skin."

Moments later, we both stood naked before Jnanara. Several native women came to the platform carrying shell bowls filled with various colors of paste-like pigments, with which they began to paint patterns on our bodies.

"Do you know what's going on?" Kala asked me in Federation language.

"I haven't got a clue, but I'll bet it's related to our dreams."

When the women were finished applying the pigments to our skin, Jnanara approached us with yet another nutshell bowl. In it she placed a small piece of leaf, after which she slowly poured in water from another shell.

Silently she stirred the mixture with a stick and finally said, "Stick out tongue, man who speak for Thumumba."

I did so; and very carefully Jnanara placed a drop of the water onto my tongue.

Then she went to Kala and said, "Stick out tongue, child of Thumumba, mate of man who speak for Thumumba."

Once more Jnanara carefully placed a single drop of the water onto Kala's tongue.

Then she moved away and said, "Wait here at fire, children of Thumumba. Thumumba come here, speak to you."

As she spoke, lights and shapes about me began to blur and swirl. I felt Kala take hold of my hand and her fingers interlace with mine. Suddenly, in the midst of the flames I saw Thumumba. He seemed bigger and more powerful than he had in my dreams. He looked at Kala and me and spoke; and it was like the sound of thunder.

"My children," he said.   At the sound of his voice I was flooded with a feeling of love and I felt blessed to be called his child.

"You must protect my children here and protect my world, this place called Sweet Home. Keep it safe from those outside who would come and cause my children harm. It is right that you share the medicines of my world with others who have need for them; but you must not allow the use of the sacred plant for anyone other than my children.   This is forbidden.   You understand, man who speaks for Thumumba?"

"Yes, I understand," I answered.

"You understand, woman, child of Thumumba, mate to man who speaks for Thumumba?"

"Yes, I understand," I heard Kala answer.

"It is good," said Thumumba, as he held his arms out toward both of us. "Thumumba blesses you. You stay together for always. It is Thumumba's will. Now you enjoy."

And with that it seemed like we were transported to another world – a world of bright colors and beautiful sounds, a world in which we could talk to trees and plants, to animals, and to all living things. It was a world in which we were a part of everything and everything was a part of us; and all the while I could feel Kala's hand in mine and my love for her grow and grow beyond all measure.

At one point we came upon a mossy place surrounded by all sorts of animals. We lay together on the moss, as the animals moved about, telling us of their lives and purposes in Thumumba's world. Eventually I began to tire. Soon I felt Kala's head on my shoulder and I realized she had fallen asleep; and then I, too, drifted off into sleep.

When I awoke, it was morning, and I found that Kala and I were lying on a bed of moss in a space beneath the I'aban trees, our clothing laid out neatly beside us, and all traces of the pigments washed from our skins. I nudged Kala who still held my hand.

"Hmmm... What? How did we get here?" she asked.

I laughed and said, "You'll have to ask Thumumba."

"But Jnanara said that we can only ask questions of man who speak for Thumumba; and you are man who speak for Thumumba," she said teasingly. "So how did we get here?"

"Magic," I said, and she poked me in the arm.

"We'd best get dressed. I think I hear the shuttle descending."

We had barely gotten our clothes on when the shuttle appeared. I was still pulling my shirt over my head as the craft slowly navigated under the I'aban trees to the site where we had been the day before. The hatch opened and Kerabac appeared around the side. "Anyone need a ride up to the *NEW ORLEANS*?" he asked with a smile, as Kala and I walked hand-in-hand up to the ship.

It was shortly after midday when we met with the admiral, the High Command and the legal staff. As we entered the conference room, I could hear Admiral Regeny say to one of the legal aides, "So you're saying that, by law and according to what the natives of Alle Bamma say, Tibby is their spokesman and what he says is law, as far as they are concerned?"

"Yes, sir, that pretty much sums it up. We flew to several locations on the planet and spoke with several native tribes; and everyone we asked said that Thumumba's wishes are expressed through an individual they refer to as *man who speak for Thumumba*; and everything they have told us indicates that First Citizen Tibby IS *man who speak for Thumumba*."

"Well, I'll be damned," said the admiral. "So, in other words he has all legal rights to guard the planet with his ships; and he has all legal rights to control who comes and goes to the planet's surface; and he has all legal rights to pass judgment on anyone who violates it laws?"

"That's correct, sir," replied the aide.

Just then the admiral looked up to see Kala and me standing there. He shook his head and said as he laughed, "Without out a doubt, Thibodaux James Renwalt, you are *the luckiest* man I have ever known."

And that, my children, is how your mother and I became the guardians of the planet Sweet Home, *Alle Bamma*.

THE END

of

BOOK 2 – SWEET HOME ALLE BAMMA

COMING IN SUMMER OF 2014

SOLBIDYUM WARS SAGA – BOOK 3
THE PIRATES OF GOO'WADDLE CANALS

A year has passed since the events at Alle Bamma, where Tibby encountered the Brotherhood while attempting to acquire the ruguain eggs needed to concoct the cure needed for Kala's recovery from an injury inflicted by a Brotherhood conspirator with a poisoned knife. Tibby and Kala are enjoying life together at their estate on Megelleon, when they receive word that one of the Mirage Fighters Tibby commissioned for construction and loaned to the Federation has been taken in a raid by the Brotherhood rebels. The Admiralty has asked Tibby's assistance in reclaiming the ship, as it has been taken to a non-Federation planet to be reverse engineered. Because the ship has been taken out of Federation space and Tibby is technically the owner, the Federation cannot go after it, lest it be deemed as an act of war against the planet. Tibby, on the other hand will not be viewed in a harsh a light, whatever his efforts may be to recover or destroy the ship.

Tibby has barely begun his mission to retrieve the stolen Mirage Fighter when word arrives that a solbidyum shipment has been intercepted and taken. It, too, has been removed from of Federation territories and its exact location is unknown; so Tibby and his crew must go undercover on a clandestine mission to find and retrieve the solbidyum. During this mission Kerabac must take on the disguise of a Ruwallie Rasson trader, while Tibby and several of his crew disguise themselves as slaves, in order to move about alien worlds in their attempt to find the solbidyum. But their search is hampered by the Brotherhood, who also seeks the individual who has taken the solbidyum. Matters get worse when it turns out there are more Ruwallie Rasson traders operating in the space around the planet Goo'Waddle, who consider Kerabac to be in violation of their guild rules. The Ruwallie Rasson try to commandeer Kerabac's ship, slaves and cargo as a penalty for his not having joined their cartel. Rumors are also heard of a new enemy force that has aligned itself with the Brotherhood. The rumors imply that this ally possesses a powerful weapon said to be capable of penetrating the RMFF shields of the Federation ships.

About the Author

Dale Musser was born in 1944 in a small rural community of Pennsylvania. From 1967 until 2012 he was employed as a structural and piping designer in the industries of marine and offshore resources, cogeneration power and hard rock mining. His work at three shipyards and assignments with several engineering and naval architectural firms during his careers in Virginia, Texas, and Maine, took him to such places as London, U.K., Abu Dhabi, U.A.E., Scotland and Mexico. During this time, he was responsible for the design of reactor compartments for nuclear aircraft carriers and submarines for the U.S. Navy and the structural designs of numerous offshore semi-submersible oil rigs, tanker ships, supply boats, and other vessels and equipment used in the offshore industry. After the death of his wife in 1999, Mr. Musser changed careers and went to work in Arizona and Utah in the hard rock mining industry. He retired in Fall of 2012 and currently resides in Mesa, Arizona; however, his plans for the near future involve a move to New Mexico.

Dale enjoys rock hunting and lapidary work, gourmet cooking, writing, poetry, art, music, religions and philosophy in small doses, astronomy and the sciences in general, hiking, camping, the outdoors and the gifts that nature provides. Mr. Musser is a member of Mensa and remains an avid reader, having lost count of all the books he has read after 3,000.

The greatest joy in his life is his daughter, Heather. Affectionately they call each other "BUBBY."

Contact Information:

Those wishing to write to Mr. Musser may do so at
dalemusser1944@yahoo.com. Although he attempts to
answer all correspondence, heavy emails may prevent
him from responding to everyone.